The Fire and the Ore

ALSO BY OLIVIA HAWKER

The Ragged Edge of Night
One for the Blackbird, One for the Crow
The Rise of Light

The Fire and the Ore

A Novel

OLIVIA HAWKER

LAKE UNION
PUBLISHING

Text copyright © 2022 by Olivia Hawker
All rights reserved.

Published by Lake Union Publishing, Seattle

www.apub.com

Amazon, the Amazon logo, and Lake Union Publishing are trademarks of Amazon.com, Inc., or its affiliates.

ISBN-13: 9781662504198 (hardcover)
ISBN-10: 1662504195 (hardcover)

ISBN-13: 9781542037075 (paperback)
ISBN-10: 1542037077 (paperback)

Cover design by Ploy Siripant

Printed in the United States of America

First edition

The Fire and the Ore

Prologue

Tamar

Centerville, Utah Territory
March 1857

The day was gray and cold, with a blustering wind that blew the rain in sheets up the empty road. Tamar sat primly on the carriage seat, just close enough to Thomas that she could hold the Hanway over both their heads, not close enough to touch him. Thomas was not her husband yet.

She could hear her own heart over the rain beating down on the umbrella and the hiss of the carriage wheels rolling through mud. This was the day she had waited for. The day she had suffered for, the reward she had left her home in England to claim—the promise for which she had walked more than a thousand miles, through the merciless heat of the summer prairie, through the fatal cold of the Rocky Mountains, through death itself to the land of Zion, the kingdom of Heaven on Earth.

I could have wished for a fair day, she thought, glancing down at her pale-blue skirt. Rain had run off the edge of the Hanway to darken the hem of her fine new wool.

Tamar did her best to tuck the skirt closer to her ankles, under the shelter of the umbrella, and scolded herself for the disloyal wish. If the Lord had chosen rain for her wedding day, then so be it. The designs of the Almighty were often inscrutable to women and men. And Tamar had already made up her mind to trust in God, to go wherever He directed without question or complaint.

The carriage left the road and pulled onto the muddy lane of the Centerville meetinghouse. Thomas reined in his cart horse and climbed down, his age-worn boots splashing in a puddle. He tied the horse to a hitching post and offered his hand, helping Tamar descend from the seat. At the feel of his fingers clasped with her own, Tamar's cheeks heated.

When she stood on solid ground—such as it was—she tried to withdraw her hand, but Thomas held it tightly, and with a small, secretive smile, she relaxed and allowed him to go on holding her. Why not, after all? Soon enough, they would be husband and wife. There was no shame in this act, no scandal. She repeated those words insistently in her mind as they made their way to the meetinghouse door, pressed close together under the Hanway.

Thomas opened the door for Tamar and took the umbrella, shaking it well before folding it closed. All the while, his eyes never left hers. She couldn't seem to stop gazing at his rough, broad face in wonder and in love. She felt like a foolish girl, smitten and staring. She *was* foolish, and well did she know it.

"You look beautiful," Thomas said, leading her down the meetinghouse aisle.

Tamar smoothed her free hand down the front of her skirt. She had made her wedding dress herself, of course. She'd bought the fine blue fabric with money Thomas had given her, and though she'd been obliged to make the garment in secrecy, sewing in her secluded bedroom by candlelight after the rest of the household had gone to sleep, she had treasured every moment of its making. Each tuck and stitch seemed to bind her love into tangible form. Someday she would pass the dress along to her own child—to a daughter with Thomas's dark hair and proud stature, his American accent, his unwavering faith.

So clearly could Tamar see that future—the children she would bear, the many years of happiness to come—that she scarcely noticed the emptiness of the meetinghouse. She could have wished for a congregation of friends and family to witness her marriage, as fervently as she'd wished for a sunny day. Tamar allowed one pang of regret—what she wouldn't have given to share this joy with her mother and her sisters! Despite her earnest efforts toward perfect faith and obedience, she couldn't quite reconcile herself to the loneliness of this ceremony. She hadn't been able to invite her mother or her two sisters to the blessed event. She wasn't permitted even to tell them of her great happiness.

Resolutely, she cast that desire away, too. The Lord required a sacred silence from all who were called to walk this path. There would come a day—Thomas had told her—when nothing would be hidden, when all the world knew that the old religion had been restored to the Earth. On that blessed day, the silence would be broken, and all the world would know Tamar as Thomas's wife.

I will fix my heart to that day, she told herself, pacing down the aisle at his side, *as I once fixed my eyes to the horizon of the sea.*

That gray, hostile, unchanging sea. On the voyage from London, there had been days—there had been weeks—when Tamar doubted. Yet faith had always found her again, and she knew that somewhere across the treacherous Atlantic, a new world was waiting, a new religion, a new life full of the love and joy that God promised.

And it had been true. She had suffered much—more than most women or men could bear. But she had believed in the Lord's promise and found it at last in the valley called Deseret. She found Thomas Ricks—her love, her future, and in only a few moments more, her husband.

God will not make me suffer for long under the yoke of this secret. Until He tells me and Thomas both that we may reveal the truth, we shall bear this burden with joyful hearts, knowing we do the work of Heaven.

Brother Joseph Young, Centerville's bishop, was waiting for them at the simple pinewood altar.

"Sister Loader," the bishop said, smiling with all the warmth of a cloudless day. "You blessed woman, coming to this sacred calling with a righteous and loving heart."

Tamar didn't know how to answer. Her cheeks heated at the praise, and she lowered her face shyly.

Brother Young invited the bride and groom to join hands. They turned to face one another, and Tamar glanced up at Thomas. He was beaming at her with such love that for one dizzy, ecstatic moment, she felt as if the very substance of herself was coming apart, dissolving in the honey-sweet warmth of his adoration.

I would melt into you, she said silently to Thomas, *and gratefully.*

Let her very soul assimilate his. What else was a marriage for—even one as unusual as this?

Just as Brother Young opened his mouth to begin reciting the ceremony, the door to the meetinghouse groaned. Tamar glanced down the aisle in surprise. Two young girls entered the building, both wet through.

They must be Thomas's relations, Tamar thought. *Nieces or cousins, come to witness the ceremony.*

She felt a surge of gratitude. Now that there would be a few more souls to celebrate with, perhaps this would feel like a proper wedding after all.

The elder of the two girls stopped in her tracks, staring at the altar. A chill of caution ran through Tamar. There was something strange about the girl's face—something unusual about her eyes—but there was no mistaking her expression of dismay. And anger. She told the younger girl to sit in one of the pews, then looked at Tamar and Thomas again, red-faced, her features pinched with rage.

Thomas cleared his throat, a small and awkward sound. "Here she is, Brother Young," he said hesitantly. "The other girl I told you about."

"Other girl, indeed," the stranger said. "I'd like to know exactly what's going on here, Mr. Ricks. I turn up for my own wedding only to find the groom making his vows to another bride!"

The breath left Tamar's body. Her hands loosened in Thomas's grip, but he was still holding on to her. He wouldn't let her go.

"I—I don't understand," Tamar finally stammered.

The girl came storming up the aisle, snarling like a dog with its hackles raised. Tamar could smell the wetness of her hair and dress, a feral, animal stench.

The girl raged at them both. "This man—this cad—told me to come to the church on this very day and he would make me his wife. Did you forget which girl you'd promised yourself to, Tom Ricks?"

At once, Thomas released one of Tamar's hands and reached out for the stranger. She stepped back, scornful of his touch. Tamar wanted to jerk her own hand from his grip, but she was numb—weak and numb, disconnected from this dreadful scene as if she were watching herself on a stage. As if this were all some terrible pantomime.

"I should have realized," Thomas said. "Of course, you don't under-stand the custom, Jane. You've never been to church, as far as I've seen—and even most who count themselves among the fold have yet to learn of the Blessing of Jacob."

The girl barked out some disbelieving reply. Tamar never heard it. Her head was spinning.

"This is our custom." Thomas's voice came to Tamar as if from the far end of an alley, distant and thin. "It has become so ordinary to us—to the men, at any rate—I never thought to ask myself whether you'd already heard. Whether you'd be unpleasantly surprised . . ."

Brother Young spoke up. "If the lady doesn't like the thought of being involved in such an arrangement, then I can't proceed, Brother Ricks. Not with her, anyhow. Sister Loader has already given her consent."

Tamar shook herself out of her daze. Whatever this meant—whatever new trial the Lord had devised—she was determined to go forward, unwavering. Her faith had brought her this far. She wouldn't fail God's test now, at the very threshold of happiness.

"Yes," Tamar said. "I will marry you, Thomas. I've made up my mind. No force on Earth or in Heaven can dissuade me."

Thomas looked sheepishly at the rain-soaked girl. "I'm sorry, Jane. I should have prepared you for what you would see—what it would mean to marry me. Of course, if you'd rather not, I understand. As Brother Young said, no one will compel you. You may still have my charity, if you wish. But you must keep this a secret. It's a sacred covenant, you see. We don't discuss the practice with those who aren't already called to the work. Do you understand?"

Jane said nothing for a long moment. Her breath was coming hard and fast. Her eyes seemed to have lost their focus—especially the right, which, as Tamar now saw, wandered and tipped in toward the girl's nose. It gave her a helpless air, so much in contrast to her obvious anger that for a moment Tamar pitied her. Then the girl spun suddenly and ran from the meetinghouse. The younger—the child who'd been watching silently from the pews—scrambled out on Jane's heels.

When the girls had vanished and the meetinghouse door slammed shut, Tamar finally found the strength to pull her hand from Thomas's grip.

"I'm sorry," he said rather weakly.

She struggled to keep her voice neutral and calm. She wanted to wail with pain. "Who is she, exactly?"

"An outsider," Thomas said. "No Mormon. She'd been living with her stepfather in the foothills, but he's gone now, and the poor girl is alone—both of them. They're orphans, Tamar. I offered my help, but

Jane would have none of it. She's too proud for charity. The only way she would allow me to help her was if I agreed to marry her. And I thought, since I'd already been called to the Principle—"

Tamar realized her jaw was aching. Deliberately, she unclenched it. "Why did you never mention this girl to me? Why did you hide her when you knew I'd agreed—"

"You must believe me," Thomas pleaded. "I never intended to hide Jane. I would never hide anything from you."

He put out a trembling hand as if to touch her face. Tamar stepped back, out of his reach.

"I've been so busy with the Legion," Thomas said, "training the men, preparing for what's to come. Jane meant nothing to me—nothing except Christian charity. That's why I never thought to speak of her. I'll care for the girl, as God directs me, but I don't love her, Tamar. Not the way I love you."

She swallowed her tears. A sudden realization crowded into her mind, stifling every other thought, even the sting of Thomas's crass, unthinking humiliation. Quietly, she said, "You haven't told Tabitha. About us. About this marriage."

Thomas sighed in surrender. He shook his head, unable to meet her eye.

"You promised! You said you would prepare Tabitha for what was to come."

"I said I would tell Tabitha that I intended to take you as my second wife when the Lord decreed the time was right."

Tamar waited. Silence stretched between them, broken only by the pounding of rain on the roof.

Thomas added weakly, "The Lord never decreed it."

Tamar pressed a fist to her mouth, biting her knuckle. She squeezed her eyes shut. She couldn't look at Thomas any longer, nor the bishop, nor the empty, expectant meetinghouse. She liked Tabitha Ricks. Perhaps she even *loved* Thomas's first wife. Tabitha had been a friend to Tamar since she'd first come to Salt Lake Valley.

I might learn to hide this marriage from my mother and sisters, she thought, *but how can I keep this secret from Tabitha?*

It was too much to ask. Tamar wasn't strong enough to bear the weight, the shame, the danger.

And yet she wouldn't abandon Thomas at the altar, no matter how richly he deserved it. God had brought her from England to Deseret, promising with every painful step that a great reward waited in the valley. Here she was to find a love beyond all reckoning, beyond any she'd dreamed of in her comfortable life in London.

I was brave enough to walk the handcart trail, she told herself. *Now God requires only a little courage more, only a few more steps, and I'll have what I've long sought.*

The door crashed open once more. Tamar jumped, clutching at the collar of her dress, but it was only the bedraggled girls.

She watched as Jane made her sister sit in the pew again. Then she marched back up the aisle, her face pale and resolute. She stepped up beside Tamar and faced Thomas, unflinching, across the altar.

"I won't let you go back on our deal," Jane said. "You *will* marry me, Tom Ricks. You'll keep your word to me and my sister. And I'll see to it that I get what's due to a wife—every scrap and crumb of my due."

Jane turned her piercing eyes on Tamar. The girl said nothing, but Tamar could read the mistrust in her expression, a dislike bordering on hate. She withered under the girl's stare.

"Give the ceremony," Jane said to Brother Young. "I'll say my part. Tom must make his vows to me in God's sight, and let his soul be damned if he goes back on his word."

Tamar drew herself up, though her body was quaking. Her very soul seemed to tremble.

"And I," she said. "I will take my vow. And Thomas shall take his."

Let him answer to God if he breaks his word, she thought with a grim pang of satisfaction. *Let him answer to God for all of this.*

PART I

COME, YE SAINTS

1855–1856

1

TAMAR

The Atlantic Ocean
Summer 1854

The afternoon of the fifty-ninth funeral was calm and still; at least that much could be said for the day. The *John J. Boyd* rocked docilely on a flat sea, and the unvaried Atlantic spread around the schooner to every possible infinity.

Tamar Loader and her family had set sail from Liverpool eight weeks before, along with some five hundred converts to the Mormon church, the new American religion that had reached its arms across the ocean to embrace the poor and weary, the curious, the spiritually parched. When the *John J. Boyd* had first departed, Tamar's heart swelled with an optimism that seemed akin to the brisk winds that fattened the ship's sails. But the schooner had been due in New York almost two weeks ago. The summer wore on relentlessly. The ship had struggled across a sea that was by turns mirror flat and ravaged by tempests, and now New York seemed no closer than it had been from Liverpool's shore. Nor was Zion nearer—the sovereign land of God's creation, which the Mormons were building together in the far, fabled land of Utah Territory.

An unusual spate of summer storms had beaten the ship off course, and the captain—a singularly nasty man, possessed by an energetic hatred for all Mormons—had been obliged to re-chart the route time and again. Supplies of food and fresh water were dwindling. Passengers and crew alike were forced to subsist on rations that would scarcely have kept a mouse this side of its grave.

The depleted rations had taken a rapid toll on the travelers. Day after day, another old man or small child, or a woman who'd recently given birth, failed to rise from their bunk. The dead were sewn into old blankets and buried under the anonymous waves. Funerals had become as rote as morning prayers, and Tamar's eagerness for Zion gave way to a dull, heavy fear.

On that day, it was a little girl who'd perished—only nine years old, the light of her soul snuffed out on the cruel Atlantic, as easily as blowing out a candle.

Tamar stood shoulder to shoulder with her sister Patience, listening to the oratory. Knud Petersen, perhaps the most pious Mormon on the ship, presided over the service. The Danish man had emerged as a leader of sorts among the converts on the *John J. Boyd*. He could speak English as well as his mother tongue—which was well, for almost half the passengers were Scandinavians and could only communicate with their British shipmates by means of gesture and a few basic words.

Knud stood beside the narrow plank on which the dead girl lay, holding his hands above the small body, palms down, as if willing the child to sit up and draw breath. Someone had stitched the girl into an old blanket, securing a stout lump of coal at her feet as a weight. The prayer drifted from Danish to English and back again. The fact that Tamar couldn't understand half of the eulogy made no difference. She had already heard countless prayers for the dead—and endless beseechings for mercy, for deliverance. Death had visited the ship so often that it was practically a companion now. Tamar no longer dreaded it; she only wondered with distant curiosity when death would touch her more nearly. Would Patience be taken next? Or her mother—her father? Perhaps Tamar would soon find herself drifting above the deck of the ship, watching as her earthly body was sewn into a shroud.

Knud's prayer trailed off into silence.

"Amen," someone murmured in the crowd.

No one had the spirit to echo the sacred word. A few men helped Knud tip the plank upward, and the girl's body slid into the water with a meager splash. The silence was broken only by the listless flapping of a sail, the small metallic clink of chain or rigging. Not even the girl's mother wept. It was all too inevitable now, this horror of deprivation and loss. Fifty-nine dead, the food and water almost gone, and at least a week left to sail before the ship would reach New York.

By and by, the congregation dispersed. Most of the converts returned to their bunks, for, with so little food in their bellies, few had strength for anything but sleep. Tamar remained anchored to her place, watching the far-off horizon, its unrelieved grayness. Patience lingered at her side.

When most of the Mormons had gone below, the crew put up the sails and the *John J. Boyd* continued slowly west. Tamar and Patience gazed down into the waves, where a slap of spray broke now and again from the hull.

"Another one down into the depths," Patience said quietly.

"And so young," Tamar added.

"It's a shame. A proper shame." Patience had found her wellspring of anger. Tamar hadn't heard her sister speak with such emotion for weeks, not since the voyage had begun. "None of us deserves to end this way, tossed into the water like a bucket of fish heads."

"What else are we to do? You know we cannot keep the bodies for burial. Disease would spread, and the smell would make us all miserable."

"This ship stinks enough as it is," Patience muttered. "If Sir John knew how far we've fallen, he would be wrung by guilt. He would think better of his decision to cast Father out, I promise you that."

Tamar made no answer. She watched the horizon, but it was the same bleak sight she had seen for weeks on end. A familiar litany was running through her mind, too—the same preoccupation that haunted her since the provisions had run low. She was dwelling in the memory of all she'd lost—as she did every waking hour, leafing through a grim catalogue of heartbreak and surrender, a long enumeration of everything Tamar, her siblings, and her mother had sacrificed for her father's faith.

The new religion had swept like a fever through England. Its vision of one unified community—all members of the church striving together for a common, Christlike good—appealed strongly to those poor souls trapped in poverty. Too many families toiled without respite in the factories of London and Manchester. Tamar could easily imagine how the Mormons' promise must shine like a guiding light for the factory workers, the wretches of smog-choked cities. But she had never understood why her father had been so powerfully drawn to the Mormon faith.

James Loader was far from a factory man. His family had enjoyed a comfortable existence serving Sir John Lambert, the baronet of London. James had worked thirty years as head gardener at Aston Rowant, Sir John's sweeping seven-hundred-acre estate not far from the drudgery of London. Tamar and her brothers and sisters had grown up at Aston Rowant, surrounded by the tidy order of their father's gardens and the dark serenity of Sir John's wood. The Loader children had lived side by side with the baronet's sons and daughters, benefiting from the same education, enjoying a near-identical status to the heirs of the estate. It had been a charmed existence, to be sure—peaceful and idyllic, sheltered from the grime and noise and suffering of the city. And as they'd grown into their majority, each of the Loader siblings had seemed poised to enter society with great success, thanks to Sir John's patronage. Tamar and her two sisters had expected to make brilliant matches among London's upper crust, while her two brothers were poised to step into fine careers as barristers or bankers. Sir John had considered the

Loader children the next best thing to nieces and nephews, for James had been as dear to the baronet as if they'd been born of the same blood.

All that had ended two years ago, when Sir John had learned that James had been fraternizing with American missionaries.

I cannot allow any member of my household to shun the Church of England, he'd said frankly. *It simply will not do. I'll be held up on suspicion of heresy, James. You must drop these missionaries at once. If I hear you've been attending services at the Mormon chapel, I shall be forced to expel you from Aston Rowant.*

Why had her father thrown away such ease and opportunity for the sake of this religion? Tamar would never understand; she knew that by now. She also knew she could never admit her misgivings to her papa. She had joined dutifully in her father's plans to travel to America. Certainly, she had never considered remaining in England as her brothers had done. Papa's heart had broken when he'd finally realized he must part with his sons or part with his God, and if Tamar had taken her brothers' side, Papa would know that even his beloved daughter thought him to be what all of London society had called him: a fool. She could never wound him that way. She would follow him to the ends of the earth, rather than turn her back on his church.

If my place in London society had been the sum total of my losses, I mightn't be so bitter, Tamar thought. *But Edward . . .*

After they'd been cast out of Aston Rowant, the Loaders had made do as best they could in the city. Tamar and Patience had found a room in a boarding house on Cheapside, and there they had scraped by for almost two years, Tamar working for a dressmaker and Patience as a daytime governess for a pair of unruly boys. It had been a wearisome existence, and when Tamar had met Edward Fitz, a promising young banker, Patience had been almost as enthusiastic as Tamar was herself, encouraging her to marry Edward the moment he proposed.

Tamar would have loved nothing better. But Edward never raised the possibility until after her father had made up his mind to sail for

America and gather with the church in Zion. Tamar had known she couldn't spurn her father's religion, not even for the sake of a marriage. She had pleaded with Edward to join the church and come with her to the New World, but he had flinched away as if Tamar had struck his face, and had said, *I never thought you would be fool enough to fall for the Mormon chicanery. I'm afraid this must be goodbye, Miss Loader.*

"You've gone quiet," Patience observed.

"I was only thinking."

"About Edward, no doubt. You poor dear."

"I wonder if he still thinks of me," Tamar said quietly.

"How can he not? He wanted to marry you. When you insisted he must convert to Mormonism, I told you it was a dreadful mistake. Now I know I wasn't half forceful enough. I couldn't have imagined we'd be so long at sea, nor that we would find ourselves so wanting. I could wish you safely back in London, with sweet Edward to tend to your every need. Rather you and I should be parted forever than I should see you suffering on this ship."

"How can you wish it?" Tamar said. "I could never be parted from you—nor from our parents."

"You're twenty-two," Patience said. "I'm twenty-five. We aren't children any longer. In truth, I'm practically an old maid. We must make our own ways in the world; we mustn't cling like little girls to our parents."

"Why did you come along, then, if you despise Papa's church—if you think it preferable to break up our family and forge a life without our mother and father?"

Patience issued a hard stare. Thin as she was, with the dark circles of deprivation around her eyes, the cutting looks she favored were more knifelike than ever before.

"I would have stayed put like a sensible woman," Patience said, "if any man had asked for my hand. Edward Fitz offered you a way out of this mess, but I had no such offers. I could have begged charity from one of our brothers, but they aren't the barristers Sir John had once thought to make of them. They're butchers and builders now. They couldn't have spared a bob for my keeping. My only real choice was to cross the Atlantic. But you, Tamar—you could have had a better life than this."

"We'll find better lives in America."

"A country we do not know. We'll be strangers in a strange land."

"The Mormons will welcome us. You've read Zilpah's letters."

Their younger sister—two years Tamar's junior—had thrown herself wholeheartedly into the new religion. She had married a young Mormon weeks after Sir John had expelled the family from Aston Rowant. Zilpah and her husband had already crossed the Atlantic the previous summer—a much faster and more pleasant voyage than the *John J. Boyd* had managed. She had written almost every week, ecstatic with her new life, praising the charity and community of the church. Every one of Zilpah's letters had pleaded with the family to join her, that they all might be together in Zion.

"Perhaps the Mormons will welcome us," Patience said dryly, "if we live to see New York."

Tamar shivered in the brisk wind. "You're so terribly grim. We must all have faith—"

Patience flared again. "What faith? This isn't your religion, Tamar. Nor is it mine."

"I'm not *exactly* outside the religion. I'm trusting Papa's judgment, following where he leads."

"Blindly," Patience spat.

"God will keep us—"

"Like that little girl we tipped into the waves not an hour ago? How well did God keep her?"

Tamar turned away.

"Are you crying?" Patience sounded exasperated now.

Tamar faced her sister again, holding her gaze. Let Patience make no mistake: Tamar's eyes were as dry as her throat. She hadn't wept once since John Lambert had cast them down. Not when she and Patience had boarded in that cramped, flea-infested room at Cheapside. Not when Edward had cut her off so coldly, as if she had never mattered to him. It was Patience who'd wept bitterly at every turn in the family's fortunes. Tamar refused to waste her tears. God's will would be done, and she would keep her own faith in Him—though her faith might have little to do with Papa's church.

"We're both tired," Patience said. "And it's cold out here in the wind. Let us go back to our bunks and rest. That's better than quarreling, wouldn't you agree?"

Together, they made their way to the narrow cabin that had been their home for the past eight weeks. It was one of several identical cabins built into the hold of the schooner—each with two dozen small, hard bunks stacked double and lining the room. The bunks offered only tattered curtains for privacy. The air inside the cabin was close with the smell of sickness and unwashed bodies, but at least the room was warm. A small, freestanding coal stove was kept constantly alight near the cabin's door, emanating an insistent heat. A few whale-oil lamps swayed on their chains, lighting the thin, sallow faces that peered out from the bunks as Patience and Tamar entered.

The sisters' beds stood opposite one another, and close to the door. Patience clambered up into her bunk, which was above their mother's, and pulled her curtain shut. Tamar sat on the edge of her floor-level bed, listening to whispers and faint groans down the length of the cabin. Mama was sleeping. Tamar could hear her snoring lightly between the rustles and thumps of Patience settling in.

By and by, Tamar lay back and drifted into sleep. But she found no rest, for her dreams were all of Edward—first a simple memory of his tragic face when she'd asked him to join the church, then a haunting vision of a maze in some nighttime garden, where Tamar was searching for him. She could hear him calling, and panic was mounting in his voice, but she couldn't find him no matter how she dodged and hunted through the darkness. Finally, she dreamed of Edward striding along beside the ship, walking on the water with his long black mackintosh snapping in the wind. He'd stretched out his arms to catch her. He could save her from this misery. All she needed to do was jump—throw herself from the rail. Edward would be there, if only Tamar could find the courage to go to him.

She jolted awake, sitting up so suddenly that she almost cracked her head on the upper bunk. The ship was heeling, rocking on a swell. Another storm was coming.

But it wasn't the waves that had wakened her. It had been something nearer, something even more dreadful than a gathering storm. Men were shouting in the narrow hall outside the cabin door, and there was a scuffling sound as someone grappled for a hold.

"Get yer bloody hands off of me. I'll fight the damned lot, d'you hear?"

Tamar recognized that voice. It was the captain. He had made his distaste for the Mormons evident throughout the course of the journey, but now his words carried a special vigor of disgust. He was slurring, too.

What would that mean for the storm? Tamar asked herself grimly. How well could a rum-addled captain see his ship through the pitching waves and tearing wind?

She had no more time for worry. The cabin door flew inward. Women shrieked and children wailed; Tamar flicked back a corner of her curtain to watch. The captain loomed in the doorway. Light from a swinging lamp slid in devilish angles across his face.

"Another storm," he shouted. "You hear that? You feel the waves? Never a summer like this, not in all my years of sailing."

"Leave them be," Knud Petersen demanded from the passage outside. "That's a ladies' cabin, sir; a man cannot go inside."

"Ladies?" the captain burred. "Mormons aren't ladies. That's the trouble, see. This ship is cursed—cursed, I say! Never should have agreed to take vermin like you on board. God wants to sink my ship. Sink you all to the bottom of the sea!"

"You've been well paid for our passage," Knud said.

Tamar could see the Dane's large square hand on the captain's shoulder, trying in vain to pull him back into the gangway.

"Would have been in New York weeks ago, if I hadn't brought a lot of damned Mormons aboard."

From the confines of the passage, another man spoke up. "You would have been in Hell six weeks ago if you hadn't brought Mormons aboard."

Tamar recognized that voice, too. *Papa!*

"Step back," James Loader went on, "or Knud and I will haul you up to the deck and knock the wits back into your head with our fists."

Tamar cried out, "You mustn't, Papa!" He was a small man, slight of frame and gentle of spirit. He had been well fitted for gardening, and little else. If he challenged the captain to fisticuffs, he was certain to come out the worse for his efforts.

Knud's arm wrapped around the captain's chest, wrenching him back. But as the captain was dragged away, he spat another curse and kicked out hard with one salt-crusted boot. The little stove rattled, then tipped precariously on two of its iron legs. A heartbeat later, a red spray of embers scattered down the aisle.

Tamar threw herself back. The curtain fell, but it did nothing to shut out the screams of the women, the sudden cries of children. Footfalls like thunder rumbled down the length of the cabin as people attempted to flee. Shouts for blankets, to smother the fire, came from somewhere close by.

Then Patience was calling for Tamar. Her sister's voice rose to a frantic pitch—and then Patience said nothing at all, for she was screaming, a high, desperate sound of the purest terror and grief.

Tamar's curtain had been replaced by a flash of red. Heat slapped her face, shoving her back into the curve of the hull.

My curtain has caught fire. The thought came with a strange, drifting detachment. *The whole cabin must be ablaze. I won't get out of this. This is how my life ends. This is how I'll die.*

She could still hear Patience crying, and her parents shouting her name, calling for blankets to choke the flames.

"Papa," Tamar said quietly.

In an instant—in one ragged beat of her heart—all sound vanished. There was only the heat assailing her, the inescapable light of the fire. Nothing else, not even breath in her throat, nor fear nor regret in her heart. Tamar was suspended in a silent void, alone with the flames. Her eyes widened, and the glow surged to eclipse everything else, all thought, all memory.

She looked into the red brilliance of death and found a man gazing back at her.

His face was placid, his eyes both dark and gentle. Hair as long and beautiful as a woman's flowed down to where his shoulders ought to have been, but the only part of him that existed in that fire was his face, and his boundless serenity. He looked at Tamar with such love that the force of it struck her in the chest, made her cry out in ecstasy and wonder. She had never known a thing so pure as that love, that mercy.

For a moment, she thought she was looking at Edward, but that couldn't be. He had stayed behind in London. She wasn't in London now. She would never see London again.

I'll die now, Tamar thought calmly.

The man in the flames smiled. *You shall not.*

She could find no answer. The luminous stranger had sounded so certain, so confident, that Tamar felt it, too—a promise of renewal and salvation as hot as the fire itself. And there was more. The depth of his dark eyes seemed to well with love—a promise of love waiting somewhere far to the west, a love greater than any she had known, greater than any love she had hoped to find.

The last scrap of her fear burned away, and all her doubts turned to ash.

Fear not, the man said. *You shall be taken over safely.*

The next moment, he was gone.

The flames were gone, too—and the heat. Darkness swallowed Tamar, leaving only a violet echo of the flames behind her tight-shut eyes. She was coughing. She felt it first—her body doubled over and heaving, the tearing sensation in her throat. Then she could hear her own hacking and wheezing. And hands took hold of her; a fist tightened on the back of her bodice and wrenched her from the berth. She found herself on her feet—swaying, trembling, held up by stronger arms. Whoever held her upright gave her a light shake, and someone else was patting her from head to foot, checking for burns.

"She is well," Mama said, her voice small and tight with gratitude—with disbelief. "Not a hair on her head has been harmed, thank God."

Tamar blinked around the cabin. Knud Petersen was still grappling with a blanket; it smoldered and sent up wisps of smoke. The ruined curtain from Tamar's bunk was crumbling in the blanket's folds. Someone had righted the stove, and the burning coals that had spilled from its belly had all been extinguished, leaving only scorch marks along the floor.

When Tamar's coughing subsided, she asked, "No one has been hurt?"

"No one," Papa said. "Though I'd wager the captain will catch one of Knud's fists."

Tamar threw her arms around her father's neck. "Oh, Papa. I was so frightened."

But she hadn't been frightened—not once the man had appeared in the flames. She recalled his dark, sober eyes, his assured smile.

Was it a vision? she wondered. *Or a dream?*

"I want to go up on the deck," she said.

"You mustn't," her mother answered. "Not in this storm. You'll only catch your death, after such a shock."

"She needs fresh air," Patience said. "Goodness knows, we all need it after that bout of excitement. I could wring that man's neck—that drunkard of a captain. Let's wrap her in an extra shawl, Mama, and I shall go with her. She'll come to no harm with me looking after her."

Mama relented, and Patience bundled Tamar down the long hall to the open air of the deck. Tamar's limbs were still quivering, and she sank down on the first suitable perch that presented itself: a large coil of rope, damp with spray. Patience sat beside her, one arm around her shoulders as if she feared the wind might pick her up and blow her into the sea. The southern sky had blackened; the ship pitched on the angry waves. Wind-blown mist lashed her face. She closed her eyes, drinking in great, cold portions of the whipping wind, licking salt from her lips.

"Another storm." Patience sounded weary almost to the point of hopelessness.

"It makes no matter." Tamar spoke as if in a dream. Her own voice was distant in her ears as if her spirit had flown up, detaching itself from this present suffering. "We'll cross the ocean safely. We will stand on American soil."

There was no reply for a long while—only the whistling of the rigging, the shouts of the sailors as they wrestled with yardarms and lines. By and by, Tamar opened her eyes to find her sister staring, pale and shaken.

"What are you saying?" Patience asked. "Are you quite well indeed? You seem . . . affected, Tamar. Perhaps I was wrong to bring you here. We ought to return to the cabin."

"I'm quite well—though Mama wasn't entirely correct. My hair is singed." She lifted a golden-brown lock and sniffed it. "The smell is terrible."

"You won't notice it over the stench of sick," Patience said. "I suppose that's one small blessing."

"Something happened to me in that bunk."

"I should say so."

"No—listen, Patience, please. I shall try to explain, though I'm not certain I can. A man appeared. I didn't know him, and yet somehow I did."

"Knud?"

"Of course not; there's no mistaking him. This man was looking at me—looking *into* me—from the fire. He was inside the flames, and yet he seemed not to feel them at all."

Patience was silent, watching her sister with a tense and fearful expression.

"He told me," Tamar went on, "that we would be taken over safely. I know it's true. I can feel it right down in my bones—in my soul, I suppose. It's true, Patience."

"That we'll reach New York? That we'll survive this . . . trial?"

Tamar watched the storm clouds, searching for the right response to her sister's desperate queries. The horizon wore a heavy mantle of black, and the sea below was a sickly purple shade. The color reminded her of bruised flesh. A tongue of lightning licked down to the water. Tamar knew she ought to have been terrified. Yet though the ship was rocking, and the wind was keening around the masts, and though the storm was gaining on them with all the fury and speed of God's judgment, still there was no fear in her heart.

"All of it is true," she finally said. "Everything we've left behind—our place in society, and Aston Rowant, and our brothers. Even Edward. We've done as we were meant to do. There's a purpose to our suffering. A reward better than any of us can imagine waits for us in Zion, if only we have faith enough to reach it."

Patience frowned. "You sound like Papa now, with all his talk of Zion. I thought you were no adherent to this church."

"I wasn't," Tamar said. "Not truly. Not in my heart. But I am now. What I saw in there, in the flames . . . I can't help but believe."

She noted the disappointment in her sister's sharp eyes. Patience was readying her tongue for a good and proper lashing. But the scolding never came. Patience pressed her lips together, turned her face to the sea. Whatever she thought of Tamar's shifting faith, she kept it to herself.

After a long pause, Patience said, "I could wish for your certainty, for I haven't much of my own—not when I look at those clouds and feel this wind. How are we to survive?"

Tamar took her sister's hand. "Whatever befalls us, it will be for some true purpose. We mustn't lose sight of that fact."

~

The *John J. Boyd* sailed through four more storms before it came in sight of America. When a boy high on the mast cried out, "Land! Land ho!" Tamar was on deck with several other women, draining the last of the rain from a few old barrels, which was all the fresh water the schooner had left.

She hurried to the rail. The women pressed shoulder to thin shoulder, squinting into the glare for some glimpse of the blessed shore. More voyagers emerged from the cabins, hobbling into the light. In minutes, the deck was crowded, and when the unmistakable blue slab of solid ground appeared on the horizon, the *John J. Boyd* erupted into joyful cheers. Every voice raised a hymn to Heaven. They shouted thanks to God.

Tamar alone made no sound, for wonder had stilled her very soul. The vision in the flames had been no fancy. She had been comforted and guided by one of God's own messengers—perhaps by the Son Himself. The heat of her testimony burned in her heart, swelling to cut off her breath.

Her eyes blurred with tears. They ran down her cheeks, into the corners of her mouth. They dripped from her chin. It was the first time she had cried since her trials had begun, and yet she wept in awe, never fear nor grief.

She felt thin arms encircle her waist and turned to find that Patience had embraced her. Tamar rested her forehead against her sister's shoulder, sobbing with gratitude. Her shoulders heaved; her body shook while the songs and prayers of deliverance soared up past the sails, into the bright new sky.

"You were right," Patience said. "Thanks be to God, Tamar, your vision was true."

2

JANE

Parrish Canyon, Utah Territory
September 1855

Jane crouched on her heels in the mouth of the gulch, sheltering under a broad willow. The canyon was all color and movement around her, the gold and russet-red of autumn leaves blending into a harmonious blur, stirred by a gentle wind and undercut by the cool blue stone of the gulch's wall in shadow. A twig snapped in the undergrowth, and Jane tilted her head quickly, aligning her weak eye with her strong one. The mad blur of the world slid into temporary clarity. A deer was poised on the far side of the canyon road, tense with surprise, its large ears straining toward her.

Jane smiled, relaxed. Her vision lost itself once more in a confusion of soft edges and merging color. She could just make out the deer picking its way through the brush, a multiplicity of slender legs and switching tails cleaving through the shapeless forms of leaf and shadow. There was no sense in fatiguing her eyes to focus on the deer, to watch it walk away in perfect limpidity. With its duplicate bobbing backs and its graceful movements, the creature was just as pretty through Jane's marred vision as it would have been if she'd seen it clearly. She was used to looking at the world this way—through a muddle, a dazzle of indistinct color. Jane's eyes troubled other people far more than they ever troubled her.

The late-September morning was lively with birdsong, and even the dry-smelling undergrowth rustled with the comings and goings of small lives—the shrews and chipmunks who foraged with frantic energy among fallen leaves, and the snakes who hunted them. Throughout Salt Lake Valley, every living thing was making ready for the winter to come. And there was no denying that winter would soon arrive. Jane could smell it on the air every morning—a sharp, smoky promise of cold. Summer was over, and no mistake.

Her family had traveled the long, hot trail from the village of Winter Quarters, far to the east in Nebraska Territory, reaching the shore of the Great Salt Lake only a few weeks before. Now they would rest in the foothills high above the valley, above the lake itself—a vast plane of hazy blue that stretched across the valley floor to the distant mountains, purple and small, on the far horizon. Next summer, they would press on westward, for no one lingered in Salt Lake Valley except the Mormons, and neither Jane nor her family were members of that church.

Rather, Jane's family had been drawn to the trail by the bright promise of California. Her father, a farmer who'd lived all his life in Virginia, had dreamed of finding a fortune in gold—or, failing that, he'd hoped to put down roots in the fertile lands along the Pacific coast. He had spoken often of planting orchards that would go on yielding fruit long after his death. But Jane's father hadn't planted a single tree before death had claimed him. They'd been on the trail only three weeks—scarcely out of Virginia—when he'd fallen from his horse. He'd broken his neck, and that was that. Jane had helped her mother bury him under a pine tree along the trail, and then they'd pressed on, rejoining the wagon train, which was miles ahead by the time the digging and the crying were finished.

Jane had been only nine years old then. One way and another, her mother had carried on, bringing both of her small daughters safely to Winter Quarters, the waypoint where Mormon travelers congregated to rest their teams and replenish their supplies. There, Jane's mother had claimed a recently vacated cabin, settling in to finally grieve her husband's death.

A year of weeping and despair had followed, and Jane had been left with little time for anything but work. She had kept house, caring for her younger sister, Sarah Ann. She'd seen to it that Mother roused herself from sorrow long enough to eat the food Jane cooked, and she'd even planted a small garden behind their cabin once she'd understood that Mother meant to stay in Winter Quarters for a good, long time.

The demands of tending house had kept Jane from fretting too much over her own lonesome state, or the whispers and stares of the children she met. She had no need of friends, no liking for anyone her own age—save for Sarah Ann. Her sister was the only soul in all the world who never remarked on Jane's wandering eye, never called her hurtful names, or laughed at the sight of her. Hard work around the cabin had been Jane's refuge in those days, sheltering her from her mother's grief as well as from her own.

They might be in Winter Quarters still, if Mother hadn't met Elijah Shaw, a carpenter from Kentucky who'd likewise found himself waylaid at the Mormon village, his trek to California interrupted by a badly injured leg.

Mother and Elijah had found comfort in one another's company, for they were each rare birds in Winter Quarters: no Mormons yet still bound to the trail. By Jane's twelfth birthday, Elijah had become her stepfather, and by the time Jane was thirteen, she had a new baby brother, little William, who had his father's dark, curly hair.

A new marriage and a new baby had revived some of Mother's pluck. She and Elijah had decided to take to the trail once more in the spring of 1855. Neither Jane nor Sarah Ann had wept to leave Winter

Quarters behind, for it was a cramped, muddy place, and felt rather impermanent—all its residents changing with the seasons as new wagon parties struck out West and new waves of travelers arrived from the Eastern states. Jane had long since come to feel as if her family were the only certain thing in all of God's creation. If it suited her mother and Elijah to press on toward California, then Jane was pleased to put Winter Quarters at her back.

If she'd known how the trail would sicken her mother and her little sister, Jane would have planted her feet in the Nebraska mud and refused to move one step from the old cabin's door. She would have insisted they remain in Winter Quarters for another year, or two, or ten—however long it took Mother to regain her health after little William's birth. Jane couldn't say whether it was the birthing itself, or the demands of nursing the baby, but something had sapped her mother's vitality on that long wagon journey to Salt Lake Valley.

Worse still, Sarah Ann had also weakened on the trail. The girl had always been prone to fits of coughing and wheezing, or strange spells where the simplest acts seemed to drain away all her pluck. Sarah Ann was small and delicate for her age—twelve years old now, but the size of a child far younger. Long before they'd reached the Great Salt Lake, Jane had begun to fret over her mother and sister, day and night.

A long spell of rest will do us all some good, she told herself, not for the first time. *We'll have three seasons to recover our strength, and next summer, we'll travel all the way to California as easy as ringing a bell.*

Till the summer came, Jane would work as hard as she ever had before, fetching and carrying to spare Sarah Ann, cooking and cleaning so her mother need think of nothing except tending the baby. Jane was strong enough to bear it. She'd always been tough as rawhide and ten times as useful, as her stepfather liked to say.

She kept her eyes on the narrow, uneven road that cut between the steep walls of the Wasatch Mountains, up into the pale-green scar of Parrish Canyon. In the three weeks since Elijah had built their small cabin at the canyon's mouth—with the help of some Mormon men from the nearby village of Centerville—Jane had grown familiar with the comings and goings of the people who lived farther up in the foothills. Today was market day in Centerville, the half-formed hardscrabble town on the shore of the lake. At any moment, the settlers' wagons would begin rolling past with their loads of autumn vegetables and other goods for sale. When she heard the distant rumble of a wagon's wheels, she scrambled to her feet, tilting her head once more to align her eyes. A large dray was coming through the stunted oaks and willows, pulled by a fat gray horse.

Jane stepped to the edge of the road where the driver couldn't fail to see her, clutching an armful of old rag bags against her chest. She and her mother had stitched those bags from scraps of cloth they'd foraged in Winter Quarters. The bags weren't much to trade, but they were all Jane had of any value or utility. She'd started a small garden on the slope beside the family's new cabin, but the rutabagas and parsnips had only just begun to sprout. They would do no good till November, and Jane needed vegetables now. She didn't care whether the man driving that wagon was a Mormon or a Catholic or a follower of Mohammad. If he would trade those shabby old bags for some of his vegetables, she would sing praises to any version of God the man preferred.

The driver reined in his horse. "Well, hello there, miss. You ain't lost, I hope."

"No, sir." She kept her face turned partly away, hoping he wouldn't notice her eye. "I live here, right where the canyon opens out. That's our house, over yonder."

"You're Elijah Shaw's little girl."

Jane didn't bother to correct him. "I've come to see if you'll trade for some of your vegetables, sir. We . . . we can't get down to the market square today, but we're in awful bad need of some roots or cabbage, or . . . or anything that isn't meat and biscuits."

Jane's limbs began to shake at the mere thought of cabbage. She'd been feeling weak and useless of late—no match for her work, yet the demands of keeping house, caring for the baby, and tending the garden only weighed more heavily on her young shoulders as autumn advanced. Now she craved fresh green food with such intensity, she felt giddy over the prospect of a turnip or a handful of mustard leaves.

Mother and Sarah Ann needed the nourishment even more desperately. Mother's stomach troubled her a great deal; sometimes she couldn't keep down the food Jane cooked. Her milk had dried up, too—but thank goodness, William was getting by on porridge. The baby wasn't exactly thriving, but Jane was keeping him alive handily enough. Elijah had mentioned that morning, as he'd headed down the slope to hire himself out to a gang of Mormon builders, that he thought he might get a milking goat in lieu of pay. A she-goat with a full udder would go a long way toward easing Jane's worries.

The driver eyed her with a sober expression.

She held up the patchwork bags so he could see them, how large and well-made they were. "I've got these bags to trade. They're properly sturdy. You can carry a lot with them; we used them all along the trail from Winter Quarters."

"Come now, miss. Put your bags away. I won't take all you've got left in this world."

Her face burned. Was it so obvious that she was in a desperate state? Mother would be ashamed if she knew the neighbors looked on her family with pity.

"I've got some carrots here," the driver went on, "and a few apples. You can have whatever you can carry in your apron. I won't take a thing in trade; I won't hear of it. Wouldn't be Christian, I say."

Jane dropped her bags in the dirt and held up her apron. The man filled it with carrots, small red apples, and a few onions. He even lowered a large cabbage atop the load. Jane nearly lost her grip under the weight, for her hands were still shaking with hunger or excitement. She managed to keep hold of what the man had given her.

"Thank you," she said breathlessly. "Oh, thank you so very much."

He touched the brim of his hat. "Don't mention it." The man picked up his reins again, then hesitated, glancing down the slope toward Centerville. "You might . . . er . . . you might seek Mrs. Ricks down at the village, if you chance to find yourself there. Tabitha Ricks. She's a real good healer, and the closest thing we have to a doctor this far out of Salt Lake City. She's mighty knacky with herbs and the like. Mrs. Ricks can tell you what all you can eat right here in the canyon—if you ever find yourself inclined to go foraging."

Jane stepped back so the man could drive on. Then she hurried home with her treasures.

After she'd stored the vegetables in the coolest corner of the house, she cut up some of the carrots, sliced a few leaves of the cabbage, and stirred them into the soup she'd left to simmer on the hearth fire. There'd been nothing to put into the soup except the bones of a grouse, which Elijah had killed the day before. Sarah Ann was singing to baby William on the girls' bed while Mother slept in her own bed against the opposite wall.

Jane hurried back to the canyon to fetch the bags she'd dropped—goodness knew when they might come in handy again—then perched on an empty crate beside the fire, stitching her patchwork as best she could through her blurred vision, watching as the light in the cracks of the shutters mellowed from the pale blue of morning to the gold of afternoon. The soup smelled rich and wholesome by now, the carrots having mingled with the pickings on the grouse bones. When Mother began to shift and murmur, Jane laid aside her work and dipped a bowl of broth from the kettle. She made sure to ladle up a few nice pieces of carrot and cabbage, too.

"My goodness." Mother pushed herself up on trembling arms and leaned against the headboard. "What have you been cooking? It smells delicious."

"Only a soup I made from the grouse we ate yesterday."

Jane proffered the bowl, but when she saw how weak Mother looked, she thought better and held the bowl herself. She tipped it carefully as Mother sipped from the rim.

"How do you feel today?" Jane asked.

"Better, I think. I'm hungry, and that's a change."

She drank more broth while Jane did her best not to fret. The fact that she had an appetite was encouraging. Most days, Jane had to coax her to eat a few paltry crumbs. But the circles around her eyes were growing darker by the day, and there was an alarming thinness to her face, a sharpness to all her features. Whatever sickness plagued her, it was making itself known—demanding, *I'm here. You can't pretend you don't see me.*

Jane sat and talked for a spell, raising the bowl now and then to feed Mother a little more broth. Sarah Ann brought the baby over, and the two younger children cuddled up against their mother, William drifting off to sleep in the crook of her arm while Sarah Ann rested her head on her shoulder. Mother told stories of her childhood in Virginia—the same tales Jane had heard a hundred times before, but she listened now with something sharp and poignant in her chest. The peace inside the cabin both comforted Jane and unsettled her. Her mother seemed regretful and distant today. Jane almost felt as if she were saying farewell.

As the afternoon deepened, Elijah came in, stamping his boots and brushing sawdust from his sleeves. He'd found work with one of the building companies, after all. Mother greeted him, and he turned to her with his mouth open as if to speak. But when he saw her face—when he saw her there with the children gathered around—he said nothing.

A tension of words unspoken hung in the air. At length, Jane asked, "Have you found a goat for William?"

Elijah blinked. He glanced at Jane as if surprised she had spoken. Then he stared at Mother again, and without a word, he turned and left the cabin.

"Let him go," Mother said faintly. "Let him be alone with his thoughts."

Jane had no intention of leaving her stepfather to his thoughts. Now more than ever before, she felt the urgency of their situation—a winter in the mountains bearing down, with no food in their pantry and little hope of getting more. She sprang from the bed, chasing Elijah out into the copper light of evening.

He had wandered several yards down the slope. The cabin and the great immovable wall of the mountains stood at his back. And Jane was at his back, and Mother. He was staring out over the narrow strip of valley, the small town with its banners of woodsmoke just beginning to rise, the glaring expanse of the lake—water bluer than cornflowers under a cloudless sky, stretches of pale violet to mark the salt pans where nothing would grow.

Jane stumbled to a halt some paces away. He must have heard her approaching, but he didn't turn.

"Elijah," she said. "Did you get a goat for William, or not?"

His shoulders rose and fell—a deep breath or a sob. Jane crept another step closer, in awe that a man could do such an astonishing thing as this—crying.

"Elijah?"

He turned then and looked at Jane directly. His face was hard, his eyes bitter. Jane flinched, heart lurching painfully in her chest. Her stepfather had never looked at her that way before—angry, hurt, ready to lash out.

"She's dying," Elijah said.

The words struck Jane like a blow. She staggered back, clutching at her stomach. Elijah walked away—not to the cabin, nor down toward the settlement, but to the road, which he followed up into the dark mouth of Parrish Canyon.

She watched him till the underbrush and the slanted shadows consumed him. She seemed incapable of movement, incapable of thought, transfixed by the feel of the sun on her back and the sight of the teeming shade between the canyon walls—the busy leaves of willow and sage moving, moving, the dapples of light and dark where moments before her stepfather had been. It couldn't be true. Mother, dying? Surely she hadn't traveled all this way only to die on the trail, just as Jane's father had done.

There must be something I can do.

There was always something Jane could do, some work to occupy her hands and head.

What had that man in the wagon said about a doctor in the village?

Mrs. Ricks. Tabitha Ricks. I'll go and find her. She'll cure whatever has been ailing Mother.

She didn't tell her mother or Sarah Ann where she was going. Nor did she wait for Elijah to return. She fetched the mule's bridle from the old shed and wrestled it onto the stubborn creature's head, then climbed up the corral fence so she could swing a leg over the animal's back. Soon she was riding down the long road to Centerville with her skirts pushed up, the afternoon sun hot on her unaccustomed knees.

It took the better part of an hour to ride to Centerville. By the time Jane arrived, the market was finished and the farmers who'd come from far-flung places were loading up their unsold wares, preparing to drive back home before night set in. She didn't see the man who'd given her the carrots and apples that morning, but she called out to everyone she passed.

"Pardon me, sir. Pardon me, ma'am. Where can I find Tabitha Ricks?"

Someone directed her toward a large whitewashed house on the northern edge of town. Centerville was a good deal smaller than Winter

Quarters had been, and Jane found herself outside the healer's front gate with merciful speed. There was no one to be seen, save for a young boy digging with a sharpened stick at the far end of the garden, near a corner of the house.

Jane slid from the mule's back and tied its rein to the fence, then made for the front door, picking her way between beds of herbs and strange flowers. Her skirt brushed against the unfamiliar plants, which released their scents—sharply camphoraceous or sweet like lemons and licorice. Bees hummed above the beds and blundered, pollen drunk, across the path.

Jane had gone only halfway to the door when a head appeared above a row of purple coneflowers. The figure had straightened suddenly from where she'd been stooped, but she was so small, her eyes and her large black sunbonnet were all that could be seen above the flowers. Startled, Jane tipped her head so she could see the figure clearly. At first, she thought it was a girl but soon she realized she was looking at a grown woman. The lady in the black bonnet stood no taller than Jane—in fact, she might have been shorter. But though she was undoubtedly young, there was nothing girlish about her keen eyes or the sober line of her mouth. The tiny young woman watched Jane with grim expectation.

"Do you know where I might find Mrs. Ricks?" Jane asked.

"You've found her," the other answered.

Jane felt the ground moving slowly out from beneath her. Little by little, she was slipping into a pit of despair. She had imagined—had hoped—Mrs. Ricks would be a mature, matronly woman, gray-haired with a wise countenance. She'd come looking for a thoroughly experienced woman well versed in the ways of illness and sensible enough to cure any affliction. This slip of a girl couldn't be Centerville's only healer.

"I—I need a doctor," Jane stammered.

"I'll have to do, I'm afraid."

"Tabitha Ricks. I'm looking for Mrs. Tabitha Ricks. Is she your mother?"

The woman gave a wry chuckle. The bees that circled her dark bonnet seemed to swarm with greater vigor, as if they, too, were amused. "Child, my mother died in Kentucky when I was but five years old. Tell me what the matter is. I'll help if I can—and odds are good that I can. I'm not much to look on, but I do know my business."

Jane told what she could of her mother's illness—how she seemed to grow weaker by the day, and now could scarcely eat. How her face was changing as if death were trying to break free from inside.

"It came on suddenly," she concluded, "or at least it got worse since we stepped off the trail for the season."

Tabitha listened in perfect silence, her sharp eyes narrowed and trained on Jane's face. If Jane's wandering eye gave her a turn, she was gracious enough not to show it. When Jane had said everything, Tabitha called to the boy who'd been digging near the end of the garden.

"Charles Kimball, go and saddle my horse. I'm riding up to Parrish Canyon. Be quick, boy; there's no time to lose."

Jane had thought her heart couldn't beat any harder, but when she heard the urgency in Tabitha's voice, it gave a terrified lurch.

"Don't faint," Tabitha said.

"I'm not about to."

"You are; I know the look. Sit on the ground if you must, but do not faint. I must rely on you to lead me to your mother. Go get on your mule once your head stops spinning. I'll fetch my herb bag. We'll ride as soon as Charles brings my horse."

~

They rode from Centerville to the mouth of the canyon in near silence, Jane bareback on the rawboned mule and Tabitha on a spotted, unrefined mare—an Indian pony, which despite its diminutive size still

38

looked too big for the small woman. Whenever Jane stole a glance at Tabitha, she found the healer watching the road with a hard intensity. Jane had no stomach for asking questions about her mother's condition. Tabitha's focus was all Jane could bear, for the healer's stark resolve spoke plainly enough in a language beyond words.

The best Jane could offer by way of conversation was to blurt out, halfway through their ride, "My stepfather thinks Mother is dying."

"She may well be, at that," Tabitha answered. "I won't put honey on the truth. You must be brave, for we know not the hour. But your stepfather could be wrong. I'll know for certain when I see her with my own eyes."

They arrived at the cabin just as the sun was setting, throwing a golden blanket over the valley and the lake beyond. The canyon was a deep slash of purple shadow, and between the imposing shoulders of the mountains, the stars had begun to show themselves in a dusky sky. Sarah Ann, wrapped in one of Mother's shawls, was wandering the rows of the new garden with William in her arms. She was pointing to the sprouts at her feet, trying to interest the baby, though he squirmed and whined and reached up his hands for Jane.

"Has Elijah come home?" Jane asked her sister.

"He's inside with Mother. He told me to take William out of doors. Said he wanted to talk with her alone."

Sarah Ann looked at the healer.

"I've brought someone up from the settlement," Jane said, "to help make Mother well again. Her name is Mrs. Ricks. Say hello, Sarah Ann."

Sarah Ann said nothing. She only stared, half curious and half afraid, as Tabitha slid from her pony and took the leather satchel from the horn of her saddle.

Jane dismounted, too, and took Tabitha's rein. "I'll see to your horse. Go on inside, Mrs. Ricks. Sarah Ann, you stay out here with me."

Sarah Ann followed Jane to the creek. While the horse and mule were drinking, she peppered Jane with more questions than could ever be answered. Jane mostly kept her silence. She could do almost any task, and do it well, but how could anyone explain to a child—to a soul as tender and trusting as Sarah Ann—that Mother might be dying? They might soon find themselves orphans, both their parents torn away by the damnable trail. There was little Jane could do about it. Certainly, there was nothing she could say.

When the animals had drunk their fill, Jane took the baby from Sarah Ann and allowed the girl to lead Elijah's mule back to its corral. Jane kept hold of William with one arm and led the healer's spotted pony with the other hand, moving slowly through the blue veils of the coming night. There was a bite to the air, a smell of frost. Only a few crickets still bothered to sing in the grass.

Jane remained on the slope outside the cabin as night came on. The chill made her shiver, for she'd brought no shawl when she'd ridden to town. The cold didn't matter. All that mattered was this terrible, cramped agony of waiting. Through her fog of dread, a curious, distant appreciation crept in—for the moon coming up over the distant mountains, for its shining whiteness on the surface of the lake. Even blurred, the sight struck her as something holy, something she must remember all her life.

This is the way the moon looked the night I found out Mother was dying. It was beautiful, and bright, while everything around me was dark and sad.

Sarah Ann brought blankets from the cabin. The girls wrapped themselves together, their arms around one another and the baby. Jane told stories to pass the time, though she didn't know what stories she told. Her mouth moved and the words came out—familiar words, one of the fairy tales Sarah Ann had always loved—but Jane never heard a word herself. She kept her eyes on the rising moon till she heard the cabin door open and close behind her.

Tabitha stepped out, her leather bag slung over one shoulder, the black bonnet in her hand. Her mousy hair was disheveled, wisps pulling out of her braid and catching the moonlight in a silvery halo.

"Take the baby inside," Tabitha said to Sarah Ann, "and see if you can't interest your mother in some bread or soup. I've given her a dose of medicine to soothe her stomach. Her appetite will be good in another hour or so."

After Sarah Ann had gone, Jane asked, "You've given her medicine? She'll be well now?"

The healer sighed. She looked down at her long skirt brushing the grass. "It's as your stepfather feared. I'm sorry, girl. Your mother is dying."

"Jane," she answered faintly. "My name is Jane."

"Of course. I'm sorry."

Silence stretched between them again—not the strained, expectant silence of their ride but a different sort of quiet, heavy with acceptance.

At length, Tabitha said, "I've seen afflictions like this before—usually caused by a growth of some kind inside the body. I couldn't feel any such growth in your mother, but nevertheless, the signs are clear."

"Isn't there anything to be done?"

Jane had to ask the question, though she knew the answer already.

"Not even the best doctors in Salt Lake City can save a person who has sickened so far and in this way. The best we can do now is to ease her pain till God calls her home."

"How?" Jane had begun to weep. She only realized it when she heard that word coming from her throat, strangled by a sob. "How can I take away her pain or make her comfortable when I know . . . when I know she'll be . . ."

"There are medicines for it. I'll teach you how to use them. I'll teach you other things, too—how to talk to her, how to ease her into God's arms. How to make her feel certain that you and your sister and your baby brother will be strong enough to survive without her. That will allow her to pass more readily into the world beyond. I'm known for such things, in Centerville and elsewhere."

"I thought you were a healer," Jane said. "They told me . . . that man told me . . . you were as good as a doctor."

"I can heal common maladies," Tabitha said patiently. "And there's no better midwife between here and Winter Quarters. I'm proud of that work, Jane, but those aren't my only gifts. God also fitted me to help souls cross from this life to the next. Your mother is suffering now, but you can take away some of that suffering and give her ease."

"I don't know how to do it."

"Of course you don't—not yet. I'll show you the way. I'll ride up often and talk with you, teach you what I know. You'll find it's a gentle and loving task, once you learn how it's done. And I'll be there to guide you."

Jane nodded. What else could she do?

"Give me a leg up into my saddle," Tabitha said.

When the healer was mounted, she looked down at Jane. The moonlight softened her stern face.

"You must be strong," Tabitha said.

"I'm always strong," Jane answered.

3

TAMAR

Iowa City, Iowa
Spring and Summer 1856

Tamar stood at the window of Zilpah's small home, gazing out across the quiet streets of Iowa City to the broad blue river at the edge of town. Spring had flourished into bright and hopeful color. Lilacs bent over paling fences and swayed at the crossroads, flaunting their clusters of purple flowers. Tamar breathed in deeply, imagining she could smell the sweet perfume although she was inside, helping her sisters bake the weekly bread and prepare the evening's supper.

Iowa City was the western terminus of the railroad, the farthest boundary of American civilization. Beyond the river, one could find only an occasional rustic settlement separated by countless miles of prairie, and the villages of the Indian tribes. From this small town, the Loaders would set off into the wilderness with Zion as their destination.

Since her vision on the ship—that man in the flames, his peacefully assured countenance—Tamar had longed for Zion with all of her father's passion. After they'd landed in New York and taken up residence in a shabby tenement, she had gone on dreaming of God's kingdom in the far west. The family had lived almost two years in New York, packed like kippers in a tenement flat, all of them working six days a week and saving every cent they earned for a wagon and team to carry them across the plains. Those had been hard, hungry months, but bright fancies of Zion had fortified Tamar's spirit.

Yet now, as the date of departure loomed ever closer, Tamar found herself reluctant to put Iowa City at her back. The town was such a gentle, pretty place, and once they'd crossed the river, they must travel more than a thousand miles through barren grassland and untamed forest until they reached Salt Lake Valley.

When the Loaders had stepped off the train at Iowa City, Zilpah had been waiting to greet them on the platform. Her husband, John Jacques, had been at her side. Tamar hadn't set eyes on her younger sister since Zilpah had boarded her own ship in England almost four years before. The sight of her had affected Tamar as strongly as her vision on the boat had done. Zilpah's radiant smile and sable-dark curls had been as beautiful as Tamar had remembered, and her eyes had sparkled with the same love of mischief she'd had in childhood. Tamar had thrown herself into her younger sister's arms—and only then noticed the swell of her stomach. Zilpah had been five months with child on that April morning. She'd made no mention of her precious hope in any of her letters to the family.

John Jacques had welcomed the Loaders enthusiastically, though he'd scarcely known his in-laws before he'd brought Zilpah to America. Tamar had found her brother-in-law jolly and warm from the start, with a loud, infectious laugh. His accent was all Liverpool—not London, like his pretty little wife and her sisters. There would have been a time when the Loader girls would have balked at the thought of marrying a Liverpool man, but the years since being cast out of Eden had taught them humility.

A short walk had brought them from the depot to the Jacques home—a quaint, two-story affair of pale sandstone, with a whitewashed fence around a modest garden. It was no grand mansion, yet Tamar had stared around the small parlor and examined the kitchen with awe bordering on giddiness. There were only three bedrooms, so Patience and Tamar must share a bed again, as they'd done in the tenement. But after that grim, crowded existence, Zilpah's little house seemed as grand as Sir John's manor.

The rains of April had given way to a mild green warmth, and the Loaders had settled into Iowa City, finding their friends among the church, making their first preparations for the coming trek. There was no shortage of hands to help with any task before them—and Tamar had often found herself drawn into sewing bees and biscuit-baking parties, or impromptu jamborees where eggs and vegetables were pickled and preserved amid laughter and song.

"Are you daydreaming, Tamar?" Patience said, kneading dough on Zilpah's table with flour to her elbows.

"She was thinking how much she'd like to smell those lilacs at the crossroads," Zilpah said.

Tamar smiled. "How did you know?"

"It hasn't been so very long since we were girls together at Aston Rowant. I remember your ways—your dreamy spells, all your longings to go out wandering in the wood, or to idle away the day beside the pond. Dear old Aston Rowant. I miss it every day."

"I wouldn't mind swimming in the pond, myself," Patience muttered. "That was always a good way to cool oneself on the warmest days. I fear it will be dreadfully hot this summer. I don't know how we're to manage."

Tamar had noted the difference in climate with more than a little trepidation. The weather in New York hadn't been so very different from that in England. But here in Iowa, the heat was already brutal, and May had scarcely begun. The river that ran through town engendered a steady breeze that cooled the streets and freshened the gardens, but when Tamar had ventured out to distant farms, she had found the heat nothing short of hostile. The sun beat down with savage fists, and a piercing glare reflected from the grass or from the pale, hard-packed roads. Tamar had wondered with growing unease how she and her family would fare on the open trail, with summer still ahead.

Zilpah drained the basin where she'd been washing dishes and approached the table with a weary sigh. She reached for one of the chairs, but Tamar took hold of it first, pulling it out so her sister could sit.

"You needn't be so quick to wait on me," Zilpah said.

"Nonsense," Patience answered shortly. "You don't rest nearly enough, considering your condition."

"I've plenty of strength to keep up my duties. I don't mean to be a burden to John, in any case."

Tamar noted how Zilpah rubbed surreptitiously at the small of her back. She was six months along now, and this would be her first child. Surely the pregnancy was tiring, especially as the heat increased.

"It's a right good thing you've opened your home to us," Tamar said, "for you as much as for the family. Patience and I can ease your burdens; you never need trouble yourself over John. Mama can help, too, and I daresay she'll be a great hand when your time comes, for I'm sure I know nothing about bringing babies into this world."

"But we'll be on the trail by the time your baby comes," Patience said. "You'll have to rely on one of the town midwives for help."

"But hasn't Papa told you?" Zilpah said. "John and I shall travel with you. We shall all enter the valley together. I only wish our brothers could be with us. Then we should truly be a family united."

Patience stopped her kneading. "Whatever do you mean—coming with us? I've never heard such an absurdity. Look at yourself; you're only three months away. You can't take to the trail; it's out of the question."

Tamar laid a hand on Zilpah's shoulder. "Better that you and your husband should wait for next year."

"Listen to the two of you, squawking like a pair of geese. If John and I were to wait, you would only tell me the baby is too small to risk on the trail, and I must wait another year still. I've pined for my family more than three long years. Now that we've found our way back to one another, I don't mean that we should be parted."

Tamar said, "It's far too dangerous—"

"For nine years now," Zilpah broke in, "the church has sent wagon companies from here to the valley. The guides know their business well. It takes perhaps seventy days to make the journey—sometimes less. Even in extremity, we'll certainly reach our destination before my time comes. And though I've heard it's not exactly pleasant to ride in the back of a wagon, I feel certain I can manage. I would rather be rocked and jounced along a dusty trail, wedged between a barrel of corn and a crate full of old clothes, than say goodbye to my sisters again. And our parents; they aren't growing any younger."

Tamar said, "Our parents aren't so old that you need fret over them yet."

"But neither do I like to waste more years apart. I'm young and healthy, and I've had little trouble with my condition. I can have the baby in Zion as well as in Iowa City."

"And if the journey doesn't proceed as usual?" Patience said. "What if you're caught on the trail when your time comes? One can imagine all sorts of horrors that might befall a company in the wilds of America— storms, flooding rivers, packs of wolves. Marauding Indians. To face all that while caring for a newborn—"

Zilpah tapped Patience on her flour-dusted wrist, as if she'd made a jest. "Nonsense. Storms are all but unknown during the summer. The men will have their rifles, so we needn't fear the beasts, and as for the Indian tribes—they've become great friends to Mormon travelers. They're eager to trade with us. We've even heard tell of friendly Indians offering their service as guides. I tell you, the worst any of us will face on this journey is the monotony of long travel. Now put it out of your heads, both of you; my mind is quite made up. I shall leave Iowa City when you do."

"I suppose," Tamar said slowly, "that God won't allow any serious harm to touch us, since we shall be on a holy pilgrimage."

Zilpah beamed. "My thoughts precisely."

Tamar felt the prickle along her spine that meant Patience was staring.

When she glanced in her elder sister's direction, Patience was indeed looking daggers. She whisked a linen towel from the table, wiping the flour from her hands with a vigor of disgust. "Tamar," she said in a voice too sweet to be trusted, "may I speak with you in the garden?"

Tamar stifled a sigh and followed her sister out of the sandstone house, across beds of daisies and herbs. At a corner of the fence, as far as they could get from the kitchen window, Patience took hold of Tamar's upper arm and pulled her close.

"Are you mad?" Patience hissed close beside her ear. "What are you thinking, encouraging Zilpah to risk the trail?"

Tamar tugged herself free. "She's set her mind; you heard for yourself. There's nothing I can do to influence her now—not one way, nor the other."

"You told her that God wouldn't allow harm to touch her. On a trail nearly fifteen hundred miles long! Through untamed wilderness!"

Tamar was accustomed to ducking the barbs Patience fired from her tongue. It was easier to allow her sister's countless outrages to pass her by without piercing the armor of her conviction. But now Tamar found it wasn't as simple as it once had been to ignore that needling. She bristled, drawing herself upright.

"How do you know but that I wasn't correct? God can perform miracles—"

"Heaven preserve me," Patience muttered. "This faith nonsense has run entirely out of hand."

"Nonsense?"

"A little faith is a good thing. Too much is a poison to common sense. Papa threw away our futures and a perfectly good home for the sake of his faith. We risked our lives at sea for the sake of faith, lived in shameful squalor in New York—"

"I would do it all again," Tamar insisted. "I've seen what I've seen. I've felt what I've felt—"

"Your reliance on faith over sense will lead you straight into peril, along with Zilpah and her baby."

"My convictions are what they are. I cannot change them. Nor would I if I had the power to do so. I can't regret what I've suffered in the name of faith."

Tamar clenched her jaw. More words were straining in her throat, desperate to be spoken.

If I regret a moment, then why have we suffered? There must be some meaning to this pain. For if we've lost everything and God has made no greater design, then I could never bear the agony of this ruined life.

She refused to give voice to her thoughts, however. Patience would only hold those words over Tamar's head for the rest of her days, ready to use her doubt as a cudgel.

When she could manage to speak without betraying herself, Tamar said, "I told you of my vision. It meant something—what I saw that day on the ship. I haven't come all this way for a fancy, and I was no fool to leave Edward behind."

Patience gave an abrupt laugh, little more than an exhalation. The river wind tugged her hair from its bun, blowing the fine brown wisps around her face. She looked half wild, her eyes too piercing, her smile too satisfied. "Who are you hoping to convince, Tamar? Me, or yourself?"

~

The heat gathered, day by day. Tamar grew sluggish and weary in her work. Her head throbbed every afternoon, and whenever her duties of baking or sewing brought her close to Patience, that dreadful prickling sensation seemed to crawl over her skin, from scalp to heels, burning like nettle rash. It was only a manifestation of her sister's obstinance, Tamar knew. For in a rare moment when they could speak without anger, Patience and Tamar had mutually agreed to keep their quarrel over faith and common sense well away from Zilpah and their parents. Yet all those sharp words and pointed challenges must come out, sooner or later.

All too soon, the month of May was nearing its end. On an especially warm and humid evening, Tamar and Patience returned from a stroll—which they'd spent quarreling—in the last flush of sunset. Tamar paused in the garden, dabbing sweat from her brow with a linen kerchief. She found she couldn't stop staring at the sandstone house. The lamps were already glowing in the lower windows. Somehow, Zilpah's home seemed to be gazing back at Tamar with an air of unpleasant expectation.

Patience, who had drifted several strides ahead, said brusquely, "Why have you stopped? It's time for supper."

"I don't know," Tamar said. "I feel uneasy."

"Is it another of your visions?"

Tamar ignored the sneer. She pushed on toward the house, shouldering her sister aside, forcing Patience to hurry in her wake.

Inside, the family had gathered at Zilpah's table, but no one had touched the roasted chicken and boiled peas that had been laid out for their supper. Papa was studying a newspaper with a furrowed brow. John had taken Zilpah by the hand as if to comfort her.

"What is it?" Tamar said. "Has something gone wrong?"

Papa sighed, letting the newspaper fall to the table. "Word has made its way round the city that I've intended to buy a wagon and team."

"Of course you've intended it," Patience said. "How else are we to travel to the valley?"

"It seems," Papa said, "wagons are no longer in mode."

"In mode?"

It was John who explained. "There are now so many brethren and sisters seeking to make the journey . . . the church can't pay for wagons. The best the church can afford is wooden handcarts—one cart for every five people."

"Handcarts?" Patience burst out. "They expect all of us to make the journey on foot, dragging carts behind?"

"It's the best that can be managed now," Papa said quietly.

Patience tossed her head. "This folly is none of our concern. We worked ourselves to the bone in New York—and made do in that dreadful tenement house—so we could afford a wagon and team. We shall travel in a wagon, and the rest of the church can make out as best they can."

Papa looked rather shamefaced. "I've said as much to the bishop, for he told me once already that we must pull our handcarts like the rest. I said I had money enough to afford a wagon for my family, and I intended to make the journey properly outfitted. It seems I've erred in judgment."

He pushed the newspaper across the tabletop. It was a copy of the *Latter-day Saints' Millennial Star*, the paper printed for and by the Mormon church. Tamar picked it up and read. Among the advertisements for trail supplies and columns giving notice of marriages and deaths, one forceful headline stood out in boldface letters: *Brother James Loader Guilty of Apostasy?*

A chill ran through her from head to heels. She read the item in stark disbelief, heart pounding in her throat.

Father Loader, formerly of Aston Rowant, Oxfordshire, England, conveyed his family safely to New York in answer to the Lord's call to Zion. What a man suffers in New York is between himself and God, yet now it seems Father Loader has brought his family out of one part of Babylon only to settle in another part of Babylon. He has rejected President Young's instructions to all Saints to travel by handcart into Zion. We fear that such disobedience must be the first stirrings of apostasy.

"How can they print such lies?" Tamar demanded. "You're no apostate. After all this family has suffered, after all we've lost in the name of our faith—"

"Your faith," Patience interjected.

Mama made a small sound in her throat. Patience's doubts had troubled the whole family, and this seemed an especially raw time for more of her agitation.

"I cannot stand to be accused of apostasy," Papa said quietly. "I will show them better. We are going to Utah with all the rest of the Saints, and I will pull the handcart if I die on the road."

A brief silence fell.

Flatly, Patience broke it. "You cannot mean it."

"Indeed, I do."

"What of our labor in New York, Papa? Almost two years saving and suffering so that we might afford a wagon and a strong team. And now you mean to make us pull carts as if we are livestock ourselves."

"We must walk with our handcarts, or we shan't go at all."

"Good," Patience said. "Then we'll stay where we are like sensible people."

Tamar sank into her chair. "What of Zilpah? She can't be expected to walk all the way to Zion—not in her state."

"None of us shall walk to Zion," Patience insisted.

No one in the family answered. Tamar found she couldn't look at her elder sister, though she could feel the force of her affronted rage.

"There's no cause for concern." Zilpah was smiling, but Tamar noticed the tension around her eyes. "They say handcarts move faster than ox-drawn wagons, anyhow. We'll reach the valley all the sooner on foot. I shall be settled in long before the baby comes."

"We can't defy the bishop," Tamar said to Patience. "Read the paper for yourself if you doubt what we must do. The *Millennial Star* has all but declared Papa an apostate. Think what it will mean for us. If we were to travel in more comfort than our poorer brothers and sisters, we would only reap resentment."

"Let them resent us!" Patience cried. "Why should I care?"

Tamar scowled at her. "Would you start your new life in the valley already branded a heretic?"

"I'm afraid Tamar has the right of it," Papa said. "We cannot set ourselves above the others, and a poor start we would make if we arrived in Zion dragging all the resentments of our neighbors behind us. I'll send word to the bishop—reassure him that we will consecrate our money to the church and go on foot to the valley."

Patience stared for a long moment, but her dark eyes were as vacant as if she saw nothing—as if the family had already vanished from her world. At length, she said quietly, "I can't do this. I shall not do it. Go to your Zion without me. I want nothing of this madness—nothing."

She turned abruptly and headed for the door.

Tamar startled herself by rising from the table and following her sister out into the twilight—not to argue, this time. She had no intention of quarreling now.

"Patience, wait. Please stop."

Patience did not stop. She lifted her skirts and hurried on, down the garden path to the picket gate, out into the road.

Tamar rushed to catch her. The night had begun to ring with the music of frogs. The sound seemed to isolate everything so that Tamar and Patience moved through a world of lonesome distance, where everyone was too far, everything beyond the reach of comfort or certainty. All Tamar could be sure of was her sister, and Patience was slipping away.

She caught up to Patience at the river's edge. She had stopped below a great, spreading willow, staring down at the water as it flowed past. The reflection of emerging stars blinked and shifted along the current.

"Patience," Tamar said when she had regained her breath.

Her sister looked up with an expression of such agony, such hollow-eyed loss, that Tamar nearly cried out in fear.

"Why can you not see?" Patience demanded. "Why can you not understand what folly this is?"

"It can't be so terrible as you fear. Hundreds have made the journey already. Thousands."

Patience covered her face with her hands. She made a small, ragged sound, very much like a sob. "You've all gone mad. Papa and Mama and you. Zilpah, too. Our brothers were right to part ways. I ought to have stayed in London."

Tamar reached out tentatively, laying a hand on her sister's arm. She could feel Patience trembling.

"We will reach the valley. God will protect us—"

Patience let her hands fall. She hadn't been weeping; her eyes were dry, and they burned now with a dark intensity like fever. Like rage. "I don't have your faith, little sister."

"I still pray that you will find it."

"Much good may your prayers do me."

"I hope they shall do you some good. I don't like to see you this way—"

"Angry? Furious at your mad reckless insistence—"

"Frightened."

"I am frightened. I won't deny it. I'm frightened I'll lose everyone I love. I've already lost my home and my brothers. What have I left in this world, except for you and Zilpah and our parents? And where shall I go, how shall I support myself, when you all go trotting off to your promised land like lambs to the slaughter?"

Tamar drew a sharp breath. "You can't mean to part with us. Not after we've come so far together, after all we've suffered, side by side."

Patience considered the river again, a swath of dark satin unrolling through the night. The frogs chorused madly around them, and the stars went on burning, eternal and unconcerned.

At length, Patience said, "God help me, I don't know what I mean to do. I find myself in a strange land. I would rather be led to the block than march out into that wilderness. But it may be a worse fate to be parted from my family here, where I am a stranger."

Tamar offered her arms. Patience moved toward her, one slow step and then another, until Tamar could wrap her in an embrace.

"I've no conviction left," she muttered against Tamar's shoulder, "if I ever had any to begin with. But still, I don't wish to be abandoned."

"Will you come with us? Will you trust in me, and in Papa, and in the long experience of this church? Will you believe that we are strong enough to walk without falling?"

Patience sagged in her arms, leaning heavily against her shoulder. "I'll go with you, God help me. But I will believe only in what I see with my own eyes."

4

JANE

Parrish Canyon, Utah Territory
June 1856

"I've found it," Jane called. Her voice rang down the canyon, rebounding from the pale-yellow walls. "Tabitha, I've found the dock!"

She could hear a crackling of twigs as Tabitha made her way up the creek bed. Jane didn't wait for her companion. She pulled her skirt and petticoat up between her legs, tucked them snugly into the tie of her apron, and splashed into the shallow creek. Water flowed in over the tops of her boots, but she didn't mind. The cold bite of the mountain stream was a welcome refreshment in the summer heat.

As she waded out on the far bank, Jane tilted her head. The double image slid into a single dock plant, tall and robust, its glossy leaves ruffled along the edges. Jane plucked a leaf and tasted it. The tart flavor of lemons filled her mouth. By the time Tabitha joined her, Jane was grinning in triumph. She hadn't been wrong. Even at a distance—even with her poor sight—she had identified the first curly dock of the season.

"Well done, Jane." Tabitha had one small hand wrapped around the dried rattlesnake's tail that she wore on a cord around her neck—a good-luck charm, she'd told Jane once. She released her grip on the withered brown charm and reached into her apron pocket. A moment later, she withdrew a pair of iron scissors and began snipping dock leaves. The fresh, bracing scent of the plant's sap hung in the still air. "Now tell me—how is curly dock used?"

"Other than eating it," Jane said, munching another leaf, "you can bruise the leaf and put it on a rash or a nettle sting."

"And when powdered?"

"Toothache and swelling of the gums."

"And what use is the root?" Tabitha asked, still selecting the choicest leaves and dropping them in her foraging basket.

"The root . . ." Jane hesitated.

Tabitha had lectured her on the uses of curly dock the last time they'd met, more than a week before. Jane had listened intently, as she always did, but the daily demands of caring for Mother, Sarah Ann, and little William often left her weary and forgetful. William was walking now, and Jane had to look lively to keep the mite out of trouble.

She scowled as she snapped off a few dock leaves for her own basket. What had Tabitha told her of the root? Surely, she could remember. After all, it was one of the remedies Tabitha had said they might try for Mother's illness. This was an important herb; she must recall every use and property.

"I remember now. It clears accumulations of bile and lymph. That makes it good for the liver and for painful joints."

"Excellent. And for the bowels?"

"Stoppages and piles," Jane said.

Tabitha tucked her scissors away. "You're learning quickly. You'll be a healer yourself, one day, unless I miss my guess. Now don't take too many leaves, or you'll kill the plant. Leave enough on the stalk so it will have strength to regrow."

Jane could feel herself glowing as they waded back across the stream. She held her foraging basket against her stomach and grazed the dock leaves with her fingertips. They rustled faintly as if whispering to her. She wondered whether it could truly be possible that a girl like her could become a woman like Tabitha, learned and confident, sought-after for her knowledge and wisdom.

Surely my eyes will keep me from becoming a healer.

All the same, she couldn't help slipping into a daydream. What pride she would feel, to be the one whom people called upon in their hours of greatest need. How kindly she would deal with all those who sought her help. She would be as sensible and charitable as Tabitha herself, never withholding the least aid while speaking frankly of what one must expect from every illness and treatment.

If Jane had had her preference, the canyon and the valley would be long behind her now. She would be living with her family in California, all of them happy and whole. But when the spring had come and Mother still hadn't recovered her full strength, Elijah had said there was nothing to be done but sit tight for another year and hope for the best.

Jane would have given anything to see her mother back to her old vim, but since she had to linger in illness, at least Jane had had the comfort of Tabitha's company—and the benefit of her knowledge. Tabitha had called at least once a week, for the canyon was home to some of the most critical herbs in the healer's apothecary. After she'd examined and treated Mother, Tabitha always took Jane up the road and into the shady gulch for a lesson in foraging and medicine. Jane had come to anticipate the healer's visits with giddy excitement. Those precious hours shone with the light of learning; she could feel a world of possibility opening around her, growing wider with each lesson and every success.

And though the winter had been hard on Mother—so hard that several times Jane was convinced she would certainly die—the warmth of spring had restored a little of her strength. Perhaps, Jane thought, her extra work with herbs and poultices and medicinal teas had been of real use.

I might keep Mother strong enough for another season or two. And if I can become a healer myself, perhaps I might find a remedy for her ailment.

She might even cure her sister—whatever unknown malady kept Sarah Ann small and frail no matter how Jane fed her up. Sarah Ann's coughing fits had never abated, and sometimes she was struck by spells of dizziness and weakness.

But there must be a remedy for her, too, Jane told herself. *Perhaps someday I'll find it.*

Half of Jane's heart scolded her for a fool. Tabitha had made it clear that even though Mother had seemed to rally her strength, a sickness caused by an internal growth could be unpredictable. The other half of Jane's heart clung to that fragile hope. Recovery was unlikely, perhaps, but "unlikely" wasn't the same as "impossible."

They left the trail behind and stepped onto the road, a line of two hard-beaten wheel ruts that ran from the foothills up the cool trench of Parrish Canyon, into the stony heights of the Wasatch Range. There they let their skirts and petticoats fall, and Jane set her basket on the ground to stretch her arms above her head, luxuriating in a patch of sunshine.

"You're perkier than usual," Tabitha observed.

"I'm happy; that's why."

"Pleased with your knowledge of the dock plant?"

"I'm pleased if you are."

Tabitha gave her an affectionate look. "You know you've done well." Abruptly, she changed the subject. "Your mother was sleeping when I looked in on her, so I haven't examined her yet. Tell me—how has she fared since my last visit?"

"She's still weak," Jane admitted, "and she has trouble eating now and then. But she's stronger than ever she was this past winter."

Tabitha nodded. There was something hesitant in her eyes.

Jane forestalled her. "I know what you're about to say. You're going to remind me that Mother is still quite sick and may not survive."

It amazed her that she could speak those words without weeping. When had she learned to discuss her mother's condition without fear?

Perhaps Mother's suffering had simply become commonplace—and Jane's suffering, this long, terrible suspension of waiting.

"I don't want your hopes to soar up only to come crashing down," Tabitha said gently.

"God *does* perform miracles."

A corner of Tabitha's mouth pulled up in a wry expression. "Sometimes He does. Anyhow, Jane, you'll need all your best wits about you soon. You'll be more on your own than ever before when it comes to treating your mother."

Jane picked up her basket, held it tightly against her chest as if it were a shield. "Why? Are you leaving the valley?"

"Heavens no," Tabitha laughed. "I'm going to have a baby soon. Haven't you noticed?"

Tabitha smoothed back her full skirt. Jane tipped her head, clearing her vision as best she could—and noticed the swell of Tabitha's stomach.

"I hadn't seen," she admitted. Silently, she cursed her eyes. If she couldn't even notice when a woman was with child, what sort of healer would she make?

"It's all right. Goodness knows I'm small, and these petticoats fluff me out like some ridiculous lapdog. One can be forgiven for failing to notice."

"When will the baby come?"

"Late autumn. I'll be getting bigger now at a rapid pace, and it will be harder for me to ride. I'll need to restrict myself to the most urgent calls. I'm afraid you won't see me much till after the baby is born—and then probably not for many months. Not till he can suck from a bottle of goat's milk."

Jane shook her head as they walked on toward the canyon's mouth. Tabitha had been such a regular companion on those weekly walks along the creek, it was hard to think of her in any other setting. Certainly, Jane couldn't picture that stoic, commanding woman rocking a baby in her arms, cooing with a mother's adoration. Tabitha had never spoken of her home life before; she was always focused on the matter at hand, whether it be Mother's illness or the plants they gathered or the lessons she delivered on ailments and remedies. Yet Jane should have expected that Tabitha would don the mantle of motherhood, sooner or later. She had first known the healer as Mrs. Ricks, after all—though Tabitha had never spoken of her husband to Jane.

"You're startled by my news." There was no mistaking the amusement in Tabitha's voice.

"I've only known you as a healer" was Jane's explanation. "I never pictured you as a mother."

Tabitha laughed. "But I've been a mother all this time. This will be my second baby. I've a little girl already—Catherine. She's two years old, and a handful. I think she'll like having a brother or sister to play with."

"Who tends her when you're gone?"

"Mrs. Shelby, my neighbor. Truly, Mrs. Shelby's daughters do most of the tending. They like to play with Catherine, dress her up and put flowers in her hair. Thank goodness for willing neighbors, or I'd have retired from my practice when Catherine came along. Someday soon, I must find a woman to live in the house with me and Mr. Ricks. A nice, friendly widow or a spinster who doesn't mind tending children. Otherwise, I see no way to continue my work. I can't rely on the Shelbys forever."

"I'm sure Catherine will be glad of the new baby," Jane said. "I've always loved having a little sister and brother."

"And you're good at the job—a sensible, reliable girl. Those are the best traits in an older sister."

Her words carried the weight of experience. Jane looked at her eagerly as they followed the wheel ruts downslope. "Do you have a sister?"

"Two, both older than I—though I haven't seen them or heard from them in many years. I think they've long since forgotten I exist. I left my family when I was sixteen, you see. I was determined to come to

Deseret. They were just as determined to stay in Iowa. We didn't part on the happiest of terms. I've had no word from them all these years."

Jane asked, "Deseret?"

"Have you never heard the name? It's what members of the church call this valley. The whole territory, in fact. The United States calls it Utah, but we have our own name for the land."

"Sometimes I've heard the Mormons call it Zion," Jane said, "but never Deseret. Of course, my family doesn't go to church on Sundays. We read our Bible at home. Elijah says that's good enough for God."

Tabitha chuckled. "I daresay it is good enough. Your family isn't Mormon; there's no reason to expect you to sit through our Sunday services."

The mouth of the canyon spread wide around them, and the willows gave way to the cleared field. The oats Elijah had planted rippled in a warm wind, softly green and dancing.

The gentleness of sunlight on the field bolstered Jane's spirit. The day had been a good one. She saw no reason to beat back the hope that was rising in her chest, singing in her heart.

Recklessly, she said, "Maybe we would have gone to your church, sooner or later, but there's no cause to get too comfortable in this place. Once Mother is well, we'll pull up stakes and move on to California."

"Jane . . ."

She could hear the caution in Tabitha's voice. The healer was always ready with a warning that Mother might not survive. Jane knew Tabitha only wanted to keep her expectations in check so her heart wouldn't break when the dreadful day came—*if* the day came. But surely it couldn't hurt to nurture a little hope alongside all of Tabitha's stark sensibility.

Finally, Tabitha sighed. She wrapped an arm around Jane's waist and headed toward the cabin. "You poor, dear girl."

Before they reached the cabin, Elijah stepped outside, dressed in the canvas dungarees he wore to work the oat field. He lifted his hat to Tabitha. "Mrs. Ricks. Always a pleasure to see you."

"And you, Mr. Shaw. This girl of yours impressed me yet again with her sharp mind."

Jane blushed at the praise.

"Janey is smart as a whip and twice as quick." Elijah put a hand on her shoulder. His face was a blur to Jane, but she could hear the pride and warmth in his voice. "And if I worked half as hard as this kid does, my oats would've grown twice as high by now. I'd best be about my business."

He lifted his hat again and set off, whistling, toward the shed.

Jane helped Tabitha saddle her little spotted mare, then gave her a leg up. They said their farewells, and the healer set off down the long, dusty road.

Jane lingered on the stoop of the cabin, watching as Tabitha vanished into the glare cast by the lake and the bright summer sky. The wind moved among the oats, bending the supple stems in waves of silver and green. The day was bright with promise.

5

TAMAR

The Mormon Trail
Summer 1856

Tamar could hear jeering and laughter long before she spotted the village of Williamsburg on the open Iowa plains.

"Do you hear them?" Patience walked several paces ahead, leaning into the knotted rope that ran over her shoulder. The rope's other end was tied to the crossbar of the family's handcart, between Tamar and her father, who pulled between the shafts. "They think us fools. Perhaps they have the right of it."

"Pay them no heed, Patience. It's they who'll be proved fools on the day of judgment."

Papa spoke with such placid assurance, Tamar believed he was entirely untroubled by their predicament. His decision to forgo the wagon and team had brought him serenity. That was more than could be said for any other Loader. Tamar's mother had walked three days without raising a single complaint, yet her feelings were plain to read whenever Tamar caught sight of her face. Sometimes Mama wore a mask of anger, sometimes bafflement, as if she couldn't quite understand how she'd found herself on this hot, endless plain, with nothing to do but walk from sunrise to sunset. Zilpah professed a faith greater than fear; she smiled whenever someone was looking in her direction, but when she thought herself unobserved, her hand strayed to the ponderous swell of her belly, and the smile fell away. John, who pulled his and Zilpah's handcart, never seemed to take his eyes off his wife. He watched Zilpah with a wary expression, ready to drop the crossbar in the dust if she so much as stumbled. Patience muttered all the time, when she wasn't cursing or kicking stones. And though Tamar had kept her thoughts to herself, she could feel her frown as if it had been permanently scored into the substance of her flesh—carved so deeply that even her soul was scowling.

Papa was a small man. The work of pulling a handcart loaded with the family's possessions was harder on him than on other men. Tamar and Patience had agreed that they would help with the cart, so as to spare their aging father as much as they could. John had even insisted that some of the Loaders' supplies must be added to his cart, to spare his father-in-law the worst of the labor. Papa never complained. He never even sighed. At night, when the company assembled and the long string of travelers condensed into one great circle of tents and fires, it was he who fortified the family with praise and encouragement. When relentless morning came, he chivvied them all from their bedrolls, eager for another day, ready to walk ever closer to Zion.

That morning, word had made its way through camp that the company of weary travelers would pass through a newly founded town sometime after midday. Williamsburg had only just been built, but the village had grown up around a sturdy log bridge spanning Old Man's Creek. The company of 250 Mormons—outfitted with fifty handcarts, several pack animals, and two wagons full of rations and other communal supplies—would count itself blessed to use that bridge, rather than dragging their burdens through another icy current and over a bed of jagged stones. Yet as they neared Williamsburg and the derisive shouts of the townspeople hung like vultures in the sky, Tamar knew the Mormons would be denied access to the bridge after all.

Another half hour of toil brought them close enough to Williamsburg that Tamar could see the village as well as hear it. A dozen small shacks were clustered around the red-painted front of a hard-goods store, and a thin strip of smoke trailed up from a forge. There was the bridge, too, spanning the blue-shadowed depression of the creek. The residents of the town had occupied the bridge, sitting along its length, swinging their legs easily above the water.

One of the company's scouts, a Scandinavian boy with copper hair, came striding down the length of the column. "We'll ford upstream," he called as he passed. "Secure your carts for the crossing."

"Go and take the rope from your sister," Papa said.

Tamar blinked at him. "Shall I send her back to help you pull?"

"No. I'll manage well enough until we're beyond the town."

"The cart is too heavy for you to pull alone."

"This cart doesn't weigh as heavily on me as shame weighs on your sister."

Tamar held his eye for a moment. She wanted to refuse. Neither she nor Patience was any bigger than their father, but by working together, at least they could spare his body the worst of the work. John pulled his and Zilpah's handcart by himself, but he was a good deal taller and broader than Papa—and was decades younger.

"Go ahead, then," Papa said. "We're strong enough, between the two of us, to pass by this den of serpents."

Tamar ducked below the crossbar and strode ahead to where Patience was trudging with the rope. She could make out words from the villagers now. They burned like a slap across the face.

"Beasts! Look at the beasts! Like oxen, they are."

"Give me the rope," Tamar said.

Patience did not look around. Nor did she answer, except to shake her head. But there were tears rolling down her cheeks and hanging from her sharp chin.

Tamar took the rope without asking again. Patience's hands went loose on the knot; she drifted aside with a loud sniff while Tamar positioned the rope over her own shoulder and leaned into the line. The knot bit into the bruise she had already earned from yesterday's hauling, but she didn't ease up. She meant to take as much strain off her father as she could manage, at least until the company had moved beyond Williamsburg.

Little by little, the Mormon company made its way down into the shallow ravine where Old Man's Creek ran broad and cold. When the Loaders descended into the ravine, one of the boys on the bridge stood up and whooped at Tamar like a bullwhacker driving his team. He mimed cracking a whip in the air above her head. She kept her eyes fixed to the ground, shielding her face behind the brim of her sunbonnet. No one from Williamsburg would see the tears standing in her eyes.

They mock us because they fear us. They haven't enough faith of their own, and they know they are men without conviction. God will try them and find them wanting. They know what awaits when they stand before the throne to receive the final judgment.

Comforted for the moment, she paused beside the creek to remove her boots and stockings. John was already leading Zilpah across. Holding her skirts high with one hand, she clung to her husband's arm as they waded into the water side by side. At least the creek was no more than knee deep; that was the sole advantage in making the journey so late in the summer. The waterways were easier to ford, though Tamar had often found herself wondering whether deeper streams might be preferable to the brutal heat of July.

Once Tamar had tied her skirts above her knees, Papa pulled his handcart into the water. Tamar set her palms against the rear of the cart's small bed and pushed. She gritted her teeth as she stepped into the creek. The first few paces in the boggy shallows were no trouble, but as they maneuvered deeper and the current picked up, a bitter chill wrapped around her bare legs. Her toes went numb, even as she groped for a foothold among the slime and stone of the creek bed.

"Cold," Papa called back, "but good for the feet. I used to soak my feet in an ice bath after a long day of gardening on Sir John's estate."

Tamar didn't reply. She couldn't trust herself to unclench her jaw, for fear a hysterical shriek might come bursting out—or a wail of misery. But the frigid water had eased the pain of her blisters. There was little dignity in thrashing along with legs bare to the thigh, but she did feel a rush of energy. Pulling the cart was so dreadfully monotonous that she hadn't realized how sleepy she'd become. Now she wondered at her own weariness. Never had she imagined that mere walking could prove so tiring. Three days into the journey, and her bones felt as steady as a jelly; her back was bent and aching, like the bones of an old hag.

We've more than a thousand miles yet to go, she realized. *No one can walk so far. This is a fool's errand.*

All of Patience's darkest warnings had so far proved true. This pilgrimage was an act of humiliation, and far more dangerous than Tamar had imagined it could be. Men may have ridden the trail between Iowa and Salt Lake Valley dozens of times, but they were experienced scouts, conditioned for life on the open prairie. Most of the pioneers were too old or too young for such a rugged existence—or were like Tamar and her sisters, women who'd been used to life in England and Europe, which even at its most rustic had borne no resemblance to the hardships of the trail.

As the handcart reached the shallows of the opposite bank, Tamar scrambled forward and ducked below the shafts, throwing her slight weight against the crossbar. She and her father pulled together, dragging the cart up the steep slope of the ravine.

Their cart was identical to all the others in the company—a short-sided box, four feet by four feet, balanced between two great wheels. At the front, two straight shafts supported a crossbar for pulling or pushing, depending on terrain. The carts had been assembled by men of the church and were made entirely from joined wood—no iron, for every nail and pin would mean more weight. Each cart must carry enough clothing, quilts, tents, and cooking utensils for five people. At least the rations were transported by wagon, so Tamar and her family were spared the necessity of dragging their food to Zion. Goodness knew, the burden was heavy enough as it was.

Some half mile away from the unfriendly town, a large stand of willows promised welcome shade. The families who had already crossed were hauling their dripping carts toward the willows. The scrub would make a fine windbreak for the nightly camp, and though the day was still young, the disappointment of being mocked and insulted by the townspeople already weighed heavily on many hearts. An early stop and a proper rest would do the whole company good.

Patience took up the rope again, and soon they reached the grove of stunted willows and pushed their way through. Half the company was already there, preparing for a hard-earned rest. As was the nightly custom, the party had ranged into a loose circle. Handcarts stood tipped forward, resting on their shafts, while men and women bustled about, raising canvas tents, digging firepits into the sod, or hanging the kettles they'd filled with creek water on iron tripods for the night's cooking.

Soon Tamar and Patience had raised their tent beside Zilpah's, which Mama was helping to stake out against the wind. John was striking his flint over a small firepit. Papa had already retired to the tent, and Tamar was content to leave him to his rest. They would all be stronger for a few more hours of sleep, their bodies and wills fortified for the long road ahead.

When their work was finished, Tamar, Patience, and Zilpah sat in the trampled grass, watching the camp grow around them.

"Can it be possible that we've walked only three days?" Patience said. "It feels like a thousand years."

Tamar sighed, luxuriating in stillness. "I've heard it said that just when one thinks one can't possibly go on, strength comes suddenly like a blessing from Heaven, and all weariness falls away."

"That's a miracle I should like to see," Patience muttered.

"The women back in Iowa City told me I must walk as often as possible," Zilpah said. "It makes babies come easier."

"Jolly," Patience said. "Then I expect you'll wake one morning to find your babe already sleeping in your arms, considering how much walking you've already done."

Despite the long rest that evening, Tamar felt no stronger when sunrise came. Her back and legs protested when she tried to rise from her bedroll, but when she saw her father already up and securing the load on the handcart, she forced herself to stand even while her body cried out for more sleep.

She plodded on for two weeks before the rejuvenating spirit found her at last. Strength and assurance flooded in, and she was able to walk with her head up, pushing the handcart's crossbar with ease while she took in the vast, sweeping plain, a sea of golden grass under a great, arching sky of flawless blue. She was still weary, her back and legs tight with a persistent ache, but she never grew so tired that she longed for a rest before the company circled its carts and halted for the night. She was filled with her sacred purpose, all her thoughts turned toward Zion, imagining the moment when she would stand in the dry hills to gaze down upon the Eden her chosen people had made.

However, the spirit of mercy that had granted new strength to Tamar and the rest of her family had withheld its blessing from Papa. He alone, of all the family, remained in a state of constant exhaustion. Each night, he was first to collapse in his bedroll, scarcely propping himself up long enough to spoon down barley porridge or a soup hastily boiled from a smoked joint of beef. In the mornings, he still rose without complaint, but he climbed from his bedroll slowly, limbs shaking, eyes squinting—a man far older than his years.

"He's diminishing before our eyes," Patience whispered one morning while she and Tamar rolled up their tent.

"And Zilpah is bigger than ever," Tamar said. "There's no hope we'll reach the valley before her time comes."

"She must see the truth—she and John both—yet every time I've asked what she means to do, Zilpah won't answer. She still believes her baby will be born in Zion."

"How long can it be before she is delivered? Six weeks?"

"Eight, if we're lucky," Patience said. "Surely there is a good midwife in this company. I'll make it my business to find out. There might be a doctor among us, too, who can recommend some fortifying medicine for Papa."

Patience spent the day stalking up and down the column, speaking to every woman she met and imparting the urgency of Zilpah's circumstance. By the time the evening camp was made, she'd found a certain Sister Whitaker, a big, broad woman with a silver braid, who had midwifed for decades and knew a little of the herbalist's art, as well. Sister Whitaker was the best the handcart company could do for a doctor.

"We'll call on her when Zilpah's time comes," Tamar said. "And if Papa doesn't improve in another day or so."

That night, Tamar woke with a start in the black chill of her tent. The air was close with the smell of sweat and the trapped breath of her family. She lay still, stiff muscles shivering, staring up into the darkness. She had no sense of the tent's peak above her—only a thick, heavy blackness that seemed to extend into eternity. A light shuffling sound came from somewhere close by—then the slow rhythm of padded feet. A creature was moving through the trampled grass, a sly, cautious beast. She heard a rumbling growl.

Wolves!

She didn't know whether to remain in her bedroll or get up—try to drive the animals away. If she revealed herself, would the wolves run, or turn on her with flashing fangs? Yet if she remained cowering in the tent, might they not tear through the canvas and fall on Patience or Mama? Or on her father, so weak and defenseless, his strength almost gone?

No one else stirred. The padding of those wolven feet came nearer, circling the tent. She heard the click of a claw against stone, the whisper of a tongue sliding over a furred lip.

Tamar rolled from the tangle of quilts, quickly, before she could talk herself out of such foolhardy action. She crawled to the tent flap and pushed herself out into the night, rose to her feet, all exhaustion burned away, strong and upright as a pillar of stone.

The night bit with sharp teeth. Her cheeks and eyelids were cold; her arms wanted to wrap around her body, but she wouldn't allow herself to shrink—not when those beasts were close by. The sky must have clouded over while she'd slept, for the darkness was almost complete. Only a faint, silvery, sideways glow illuminated the nearest tents—a low moon, blurred behind a veil of cloud. Not even embers from the cook fires still burned. The darkness was almost complete. She was gripped by a dizzy sensation of rising—the ground pulling away, her body detaching from this world and lifting up, up into the cold nothingness of the sky.

Tamar tried to call out. "Help." Her voice was scarcely a whisper. "Help us, please. We need help."

There was no answer, only a vibration in her chilled feet. The sensation crawled up through her bones until it shook her very heart. It was a growl. The wolves were still circling, and they were near. She stared into a black and fathomless world, hoping to see a kindly face, a hand extended to grasp her own. She found only the small, golden lights of the animals' eyes watching her. The wolves drew in, closer and closer still.

Tamar shut her eyes and prayed.

When she opened her eyes again, she was lying on her back, on the grudging comfort of her bedroll. The quilts were pulled up to her chin, and the peak of the tent was just visible overhead, grayed by the first touch of dawn. Patience was breathing steadily beside her. On the other side of the tent, she heard Papa turn over slowly, murmuring as he settled once more into sleep.

Tamar eased herself up and slid out into the new day as quietly as she could manage. She bit back a groan, for her body—though more energetic than it had been on those first days of the trek—still felt bruised and battered and far older than her twenty-three years.

Where was the painless strength that had gripped her last night when she'd risen to drive back the wolves? And what had become of those beasts? She had no memory of confronting them. Nor could she recall returning to the tent.

Perhaps I only dreamed it.

But when she scanned the ground, she found a track impressed in the dust, unmistakable even in the meager light. She stepped on the wolf's print, grinding it under the sole of her boot. She scuffed it until all trace of the animal had vanished.

Tamar was the only member of the company who had yet risen. She wandered some way apart from the camp to attend to the needs of the body. When she returned, the first true light of morning had colored the sky a pale pink, and a low trace of clouds lingered along the western horizon. The camp had just begun to stir—men stretching and yawning, women attempting to stir their firepits back to some utility. There might be just enough time to heat the previous night's barley mash before the company rolled on again. The mash went down easier warm than cold.

She paused outside her family's tent. She could hear Mama and Patience speaking in low, urgent voices, too quietly to make out the words. She reached for the flap, but before her hand could touch it, Patience flung it aside and peered up at her, pale with concern.

"Papa is in a bad way," Patience said. "He can't fight his way out of his bedroll, though goodness knows he's trying. He simply can't continue. He must have more rest, or I'm certain he'll die."

"Don't say such a thing."

"This is no time to lose your wits. You've seen for yourself how he has weakened. But the company will go on, with or without us."

"We can't be left behind, Patience. We've no food; all the barley and salted meat is on those supply wagons."

"We must speak with the company leaders, convince them to leave us with three or four days' worth of food—"

"Oh no, Patience! There are wolves in this place. I've seen their prints. If we don't keep up with the company, the wolves will tear us apart."

Patience pinched the bridge of her nose for a moment, breathing deeply as if to rein in her temper. "I don't know what's to be done, Tamar."

"You and I can pull Papa on the handcart."

"Not for long, we can't. Not if we hope to keep our supplies—the tent, our blankets, our pots for cooking. Even if Mama were to help, I doubt we could haul Papa and the rest more than ten miles, fifteen at most. And I won't see our mother reduced as our father has been."

"We're to meet with another company in two more days," Tamar said. "The Martin company. Surely you've heard the sentry boys talking about it. Martin has more supplies, more carts, more men to help us pull."

"Yes," Patience said. "That's it. Yesterday, while I looked for a midwife, I heard some of the men talking about the Martin company. They've a special wagon for invalids. Anyone who's fallen ill, or who's been injured or bitten by a snake, is bedded down on that wagon. If we can get Papa to the Martin company, he can ride with the other invalids."

Mama emerged from the tent at that moment. She looked from Tamar to Patience in pleading silence, her eyes too large in her thin face.

"We won't fall behind," Tamar insisted, taking her mother's hand. "Patience, wake John and Zilpah. I've a plan that will see us through, at least until we meet with Martin's company."

The Loaders worked quickly while the rest of the camp struck their tents and tied their belongings to their carts. In short order, Tamar and Patience had shifted the contents of their handcart to John's, save for a few blankets. With John's help, they lifted Papa from his bedroll and laid him on the bed of the empty cart, tucking and rolling the blankets around him, doing their best to bolster his frail body.

"There's no need for this," he said. But his voice was thin and hoarse, and his hands were shaking. Tamar found she couldn't meet her father's eye.

When Patience and Tamar took up the crossbar together, their father commanded them to stop.

"I can walk," he insisted. "I won't see my daughters work like mules while I do nothing."

"Not another word out of you," Patience answered sharply. She pulled the cart into sudden motion; Tamar had to trot a few steps to keep up. "You lie there and rest your bones, and don't pester us with your old man's mumbling."

"It's for the best, James," Mama said.

He reached over the rear of the cart and took her dry, thin hand. "Amy. I'll be on my feet again; you see if I'm not."

"Mama," Tamar said, "walk ahead and ask after Sister Whitaker until you find her. She's an herb-woman. She might have some remedy for Papa."

John had enlisted the help of a boy, the son of another family, some fourteen or fifteen years old. Together, they managed the overloaded cart while Zilpah walked along beside them. Tamar could see her younger sister glancing now and then at the towrope, which was looped and tied around the crossbar.

"Don't think of it," Patience warned.

Zilpah was defiant. "I'm strong enough to pull."

"You've got a belly full of baby," Patience said.

Tamar stared at her sister in disbelief. It was an astonishing indelicacy, to speak so frankly of Zilpah's condition. It was positively American.

"Have mercy," Patience said flatly to Tamar. "We're hundreds of miles from civilization, and you still think to mind your manners?"

"Let her pull," Tamar said.

"I will not."

Tamar jutted her chin at her elder sister, then loosened the rope herself and tossed the knotted end to Zilpah.

"If her time comes early, you're to blame," Patience said.

"If we can only reach Martin's company before then, we can put Zilpah and Papa both on the invalids' wagon. Then the baby can come whenever it pleases."

They fell into place near the back of the company's long line. Papa grumbled as the handcart rattled over uneven ground, but the girls kept up their pace. Tamar's legs burned with the effort; her back and shoulders were stiff long before midday. But as the sun rose higher and the fly-buzzing heat of afternoon pressed in, fear bore down on her heart, heavier than the weight of her father in the cart. There were wolves in the wilderness—hungry beasts waiting to claim whoever fell behind.

Tamar and Patience managed to cling to the rear of the company for a full day before their strength began to wane. Tamar toiled at the crossbar, telling herself that the pounding in her head was only the heat and lack of water—sensations to which she had grown accustomed—even as her eyes blurred and her arms shook, even as her feet stumbled and her steps slowed. Patience spoke quietly all that weary day, murmuring encouragement, insisting that Tamar could manage a few steps yet, and then a few more. Tamar's breath came harder and hotter. She couldn't seem to raise her eyes from the hard, barren ground, no matter how Patience cajoled her to look up, to fix her gaze on Zion.

By the time the sun had begun to set, red as blood through a haze of distant brush fires, Tamar dragged her heavy head up to see that she and her family were all but isolated on an empty trail. They had fallen behind. The end of the column was half a mile or more in the distance, the slowest of the travelers just gaining the company's circle for the nightly camp.

"We've lost them." Tamar's throat was dry, her voice like a rasp against wood.

"Nonsense," Patience said. "The camp is just ahead. You only need a good night's sleep. You'll go on stronger than ever in the morning. Now come; one foot in front of the other. We're almost there. You can do it, Tamar."

Like an ox, she moved when Patience goaded her and stopped when told. She was aware of nothing, save the desperate heat in her head and chest, and a strange vibration running through her body—a visceral quiver, as if the substance of her very flesh were seeking to burst apart. She was a rag worn to nothingness, all rents and holes. Only by the force of her sister's will did she remain in a single piece—and by some obscure mercy from on high, the threadbare grace of God.

Distantly, she was aware of her sisters helping her duck from beneath the crossbar. Patience made her sit on the ground beside Papa while Zilpah hurried across the camp to fetch Sister Whitaker with her basket of herbs.

"I must get up," Tamar said thickly. "Help . . . raise the tent."

Papa laid a trembling hand on her wrist. "Be still, my girl. You've worked enough this day. John and that boy he's found will help your mother raise the tent. It won't do for you to make yourself sicker."

"I'm not sick," she said, and knew she was lying.

In time, Sister Whitaker arrived and looked Tamar over.

"It's mountain fever," the herb-woman said. "There can be no doubt."

Mama gave a wordless cry.

"Don't fret, Sister Loader. The odds are good that your daughter will recover. Most who are stricken by mountain fever are fit again in three or four days."

"Most?" Mama gripped Tamar's hand. "Can you give me no better hope? And what of my husband?"

"A good strong tea of coneflower morning and night should help him recover his strength. Though it's best if he rides on the cart for a few more days, till the herb has had time to do its work."

Sister Whitaker rose from her crouch, knocking dust from her skirt with an energetic hand. Tamar tried to look up at her face, but her neck ached from the fever and the low afternoon sun was much too bright. It surrounded the herb-woman's form in a brilliant halo.

"You might consider staying here till Tamar is fit to go on," the herb-woman said. "I've advised several families to stay put and care for the sick among them. Tamar isn't the only one who's been stricken by mountain fever, and Sister Ashton is due to give birth any day now." She turned toward Zilpah. "You aren't far from the blessed hour yourself, young lady, unless I miss my guess."

"Surely I've weeks yet," Zilpah said.

Sister Whitaker raised a single brow skeptically. "I haven't been a midwife thirty years for nothing. The time is very close for you; I know the signs. It may be that you've counted the days wrongly. It happens more often than you might guess—especially with women as young as you, and with a first baby."

Zilpah clutched at her belly. Her face had gone quite pale.

"We can't linger here," John said. "The supply wagons—"

"I've arranged with Brother Cluff to dole out five days' rations for everyone who must stay behind."

"Will five days be enough time for Tamar to recover," John asked, "and for us to regain our place in the company?"

"God willing," the herb-woman said. "You must all add a dose of prayer to the medicine I'll give you."

After she had measured out the remedies for Tamar and Papa, Sister Whitaker took her leave, and a silence fell over the miserable group. Tamar wanted to speak—urge them all to keep up with the company, reassure them she only needed one night's rest. The words wouldn't come. She was mired in the relief of sitting, the comfort of hard ground. And weariness was dragging her down, down toward sleep.

Dimly, she was aware of Patience speaking. "We haven't got a choice. We must make camp here with the other invalids, and hope God answers our prayers, for once."

The next morning, Patience pulled Tamar to her feet and wrapped her arm around her shoulders, holding her upright while the company rolled on without them. A short distance from the trail, a stream cut deeply into the sere earth. Stunted willows and cottonwoods clung to its banks. The Loaders hauled their supplies to the sparse mercy of the shade, then remade camp as best they could with a handful of other unfortunates. The stream was little more than a trickle clouded by silt, for summer was at its brutal peak—but at least it was water. Those who weren't tending to the sick and injured dug pits near the bank, which filled with seep-water clean enough to drink. Others made snares to trap the animals that would come by night, drawn to the water. John and some of the sounder men took their rifles and set off into the tall grass, searching for game.

This strained, fretful industry went on around Tamar, dipping now and then into her fevered half awareness. Images passed before her eyes, when she could bear to open them—luminous men in white raiment, beckoning with outstretched hands, and birds flying backward through the air. The Beast of Revelation came striding over the yellow plain, parting ripples of heat mirage with its terrible body. All seven of its leonine mouths were hungry; they grinned at her and called without words. Across these fitful visions, harsh reality would sometimes pass—a woman walking by, carrying a pail in which someone had been sick, or a boy's boots moving from left to right, mud to his ankles from the seep pits. Once a devil menaced Tamar with his whip, but before the lash could cut her skin, Patience bent over her bedroll to press a wet cloth against her forehead, and the devil dissolved in a burst of red, the fragments of his goatish body flying apart like the shards of a dropped vase. And when the fever receded and lucidity crowded in, Tamar knew herself and her family to be trapped in a Hell just as dire as any the fever dreams had revealed. They were castoffs, forgotten pilgrims huddled in a vast, uncaring wilderness, begging deliverance from a distant God.

On a blue evening, while a flush of the day's remembered light still hung lazily in the west, Tamar pushed herself up with trembling arms and sat, rubbing her eyes, counting the tents and handcarts that remained under the willows. Surely the invalids' camp had been larger than this. More than half the former inhabitants had vanished. The night was quiet, save for the low murmur of a woman praying.

She stared out at the darkening plain. Stars were coming out, five and six at a time in a blue-velvet sky. She felt no stronger than she had before, yet something had compelled her to sit up and take notice of the world, rolling on in its eternal course. There were riders coming down the trail. Two riders on gray horses, traveling from the west.

"Patience." Tamar could scarcely speak above a whisper. "Patience, come quickly. Do you see?"

Patience had been stirring the embers in a small firepit. She turned when Tamar spoke, and must have seen the riders at once, for she lurched to her feet. "John! Someone is coming!"

John strode out of the camp with his rifle at the ready, but soon led the riders toward the willows. He was grinning and laughing, and all who were fit enough to stand went out to greet the newcomers. Tamar rolled onto her side, straining to hear over the pounding of her heart.

"These good men have come from the church," John said. "From God himself, thanks be. These are the apostles Franklin Richards and John Taylor."

A mutter of awe went through the ragged encampment. Tamar couldn't see the men's faces from where she lay, but their voices carried through the cool night, easing her heart like balm to a wound.

"We've come from Winter Quarters," one of the apostles said. "The first members of your company arrived some two days past. They told us we'd find you here, in need of aid and blessing."

"We've brought enough food to see you all to Winter Quarters," the other said. "The town is but thirty miles to the west. Brother Martin has arrived with his company. You'll go on with him to the valley."

"Then we'll have more hands for the work," John said, "and more strong backs for the pulling."

Patience's sharp voice cut through the hopeful murmurs. "How can you say *we*, John? We're stranded here. I see little hope we might reach Winter Quarters with Tamar and my father so poorly. And Zilpah's time comes closer every hour."

"Perhaps we can help in that way, too," the second apostle said. "Show us who's still ailing, Sister, and we'll do what we can."

Patience led the men to Tamar's bedroll. They sank to their knees beside her. Between the dim starlight and the blur of her fever, she could scarcely make out the apostles' features. She could discern that one was in his middle years, with a half-grayed mustache that swept down around his mouth, while the other was at least ten years younger, dark-haired and bright-eyed.

The younger man took her hand. "You've been ill, Sister Loader. Can you rise?"

"She can't," Patience said. "It's all she can do to sit up now and then, to drink a little water or broth."

Her voice broke suddenly, all the habitual coolness falling away. Tamar realized with a slow-dawning surprise that Patience was crying—weeping as if Tamar had already died.

"Please. I cannot lose her. You don't know what we've suffered, what we've sacrificed to come so far, and all because she believes."

The elder apostle glanced over his shoulder at Patience. Mildly, he said, "You don't believe, Sister?"

Before Patience could answer, Tamar felt the elder man's hand on the crown of her head. A moment later, the younger apostle rested his palm above her brow.

"Tamar Loader," the elder said, "I bless thee in the name of the Father, and the Son, and the Holy Ghost. You shall be healed. You shall rise and walk into Zion. This I do command of thee in Jesus's name. Amen."

"Amen," the younger man murmured.

The apostles withdrew their hands. Tamar held her breath, waiting for some great and miraculous change. The moment hung suspended in the twilight . . . and finally crumbled. She felt no better. The only difference was a tingle on her scalp where their hands had rested.

The men moved on to bless Papa in his turn—then to the other stranded souls. Tamar's tongue prickled; her mouth tasted of copper, of bitterness. These men stood among the Twelve Apostles, the highest authorities in God's restored church, save for the president and Prophet, Brigham Young. They held the power to call down miracles, and yet the fever continued to beat at her from the inside. Her head still throbbed, her limbs quaked. They had spoken a sacred blessing over her sickbed, and yet she lay in misery.

She was too weary to think, too ill for grief. She slipped gratefully into sleep, heedless of the tears that matted her lashes.

6

JANE

Parrish Canyon, Utah Territory
Late Summer 1856

Along the verge of the wagon road, tall grasses and wiry summer weeds leaned together in faded drifts. The first asters of the year had opened like small, earthbound stars. Jane reached into the tangle of crackling stems, plucking the pale flowers. Sage and thorns scratched the backs of her hands, but she paid the marks no heed. She hardly felt the clawing of those dry twigs, and when she'd gathered a proper bouquet, she looked at the fine red lines along her knuckles and wrists with dull surprise. What did the scratches matter? They would heal. What did anything matter, now?

She made her way slowly up one rut of the road, past the canyon's mouth, and into the mercy of its shade. The slope climbed toward the heart of the mountain. Jane saw nothing of the cottonwoods and willows, the lacework of shadow and light below their mobile, whispering branches. She saw only the narrow path she had walked twice a day for the past week—the trail to the crooked pine where less than a week before the small family had laid Mother to rest.

Elijah had wanted to site the grave closer to the cabin, but Jane had insisted they find a pine tree to mark Mother's eternal bed. Back in Virginia, they had buried Jane's father below a pine—the only monument he would have, save for the hasty cross someone had lashed together from a couple of broken planks and a scrap of rope. Jane had insisted that Mother should be buried beside the same kind of tree. The stunted bristlecone in the canyon bore little resemblance to the lush green pine that had marked Father's grave so many hundreds of miles to the east. Mother's tree was all red trunk and desperate, reaching arms—but it was a pine, and Jane couldn't help entertaining the sad, fanciful thought that now her parents would be united in the world to come, finding their way back to one another through the roots and branches that surrounded their graves.

She gazed up at the bristlecone for a moment, watching the branches stir in a placid breeze. She could almost imagine that the wind through the needles sounded like her mother's voice—the warm, gentle whisper of Mother in the night, bending over Jane's bed to soothe away some nightmare, some childish fear. But that was only a fancy. The wind was nothing but wind, and Jane would never hear her mother speak again. Not this side of Heaven.

Among the bristlecone's roots, the red earth still looked freshly turned, and the mound rose insistently from the ground. Elijah had made a better cross for Mother than the one Father had received. He'd fastened the two narrow planks with an iron nail and had carved her name into the wood. *Martha Thomas Shupe Shaw, 1824–1856.*

Jane laid the asters at the foot of the cross. The wind picked up, capricious as canyon breezes often were. The flowers scattered at once over the naked ground, but Jane didn't try to gather them. She didn't want this, anyhow—to have laid a bouquet on her mother's grave. To have lost her mother with such cruel haste and stark finality. She didn't want to be an orphan.

She sank to the ground, settling back on her bottom and hugging her knees to her chest. Overhead, the branches went on sighing. The shade was cool and quiet, the heat of summer driven back by the high canyon walls. It would have been a pleasant spot for resting and thinking, if only her mother weren't lying below that frank red mound.

I wish Tabitha would come.

Jane hadn't seen the healer for several weeks. No doubt her pregnancy was too far advanced for casual riding, and Tabitha was reserving her strength for the most urgent calls. Not for the first time, Jane considered sending for Tabitha by way of the next man who came driving down the canyon road—begging the healer to come and talk, to share her wisdom. Even silent comfort would have been welcome, for Jane could find neither sense nor peace without Tabitha to confide in. But she couldn't bring herself to do it. Tabitha had other concerns. Mother hadn't been her only patient; the countryside was full of sick and injured people who needed the healer. Jane was just one girl, of little consequence. One girl without her mother.

She lingered almost an hour beside the grave. Such had been her habit every day since Mother had drawn her final breath. Each day, Jane asked herself crossly why she did it, what good it was to anyone to sit and weep beside a mound of earth—or to sit and stare at nothing, devoid even of thought, as empty inside as an old dry well. No answers ever came. She climbed to her feet and brushed the dust from her skirt, then marched back along the trail to the canyon road, scowling over her own laziness. There was plenty of work waiting at the cabin. Supper must be cooked; the garden must be tended. And Sarah Ann needed Jane. The baby needed her, too.

Jane was the only parent the children had left now, for Elijah had faded almost to nothing since they'd laid Mother to rest. He was useless around the house, standing and staring at the walls as if he'd heard someone speaking from the other side. Sometimes when Jane addressed him, he never answered at all. Elijah had always been a kindly stepfather, but now Jane wondered where his intentions lay. Would he go on looking after her and Sarah Ann—who, after all, were not his children?

Seems likely Elijah hasn't thought so far ahead, she told herself. She couldn't imagine him working out what the future might hold. He didn't seem to believe in a future at all—not anymore. Elijah drifted aimlessly through his days as if it had been he who'd died, not Mother. As if he were the ghost.

Jane's thoughts crept through her head. She felt dulled by grief and exhaustion, all her former sharpness worn away to a blunt, useless edge. *How am I to wake him from this dream, and make him see that we need him? He must come around before autumn, before the snow starts to fall. We need his work—his pay—to buy food and warm clothing.*

Autumn wasn't far off now. The asters had been proof of that. And once the summer was gone, the long, brutal cold of a mountain winter would quickly descend. Jane must prepare now for the season to come.

She lost herself in a tally of all the clothes she and Sarah Ann had left—and as she wrestled her sluggish mind toward this new task, some of her grief and anger receded. Now that Mother was gone, they could cut up her old dresses to make new, and Mother's old shawls would do for wrapping against the cold.

Jane preferred these straightforward calculations to dwelling on the loss. If she was piecing together a plan for survival, then it didn't hurt so badly to think, *Now that Mother is gone.* The absence became only another certainty, another great hard stone of reality. She couldn't move the monolith of grief from her path, but she could blaze a trail around her grief and use it as her landmark.

When she returned to the cabin, she could see the soft blur of Sarah Ann and William at the edge of the garden. Sarah Ann was holding the baby by his hands, encouraging him to walk among the rows of bush beans and the trailing squash vines. William squealed and laughed as he toddled side to side. Jane smiled, struck by a poignant sweetness. She was glad William was too small to realize what he had lost. He would grow up without the burden of this sorrow.

On the western slope, silhouetted against the blue of the lake, Elijah moved slowly through his field. Jane could make out some long-handled tool, a hoe or a rake, trailing from one of his hands. It dragged and snickered through the waist-high oats.

She turned abruptly away from the sight of her stepfather in the field. She had come to a decision—suddenly, without having truly thought at all. She must send word to Tabitha Ricks—not asking her to come, for Tabitha had her own concerns, but merely informing her in straightforward, businesslike terms that Mother had gone to God. Mother had been Tabitha's patient. She deserved to know what had happened.

Jane tried to assemble the note in her mind while she entered the cabin and blinked in its warm dimness, struggling to adjust her eyes after the summer brightness outside.

I am writing to inform you that Martha Shaw is dead. I am writing to inform you that my mother, Martha Shaw, is dead. I am writing . . . my mother is dead.

How could anyone write such words, commit them to paper and make them real—let alone speak them aloud?

She would do it, though. This was her work now, her most important task, and Jane never shirked her duties. When she could see again—as well as she ever saw—she crossed the single room to the bed that had once held her mother. Now it only held Elijah at night, and then Jane often heard him tossing and sighing, beyond the mercy of sleep. Mother's old writing box was under the bed, Jane knew. She knelt and groped under the frame, pushing aside the old carpetbags stuffed with winter clothing, the wicker basket that held William's blankets and diaper cloths.

Her fingertips found the smooth surface of the letter box. She caught its corner and worked it, inch by inch, toward herself, and when she could grip it properly, she slid the box out into the dim half-light. The lid was carved with vines and flowers encircling Mother's initials: *M. S.* The *S* had stood for Shupe, not Shaw—Jane's own name, her father's name. The box had been a gift from Father, long ago, in Virginia, before he'd caught the mad idea to try his luck in California.

Jane traced the initials with a finger, then opened the lid. Inside, the bottle of ink was tightly stoppered, and the old quill pen lay waiting across a few blank sheets of paper. Mother had taught Jane how to read and write—their favorite way of passing time together in Winter Quarters—though Jane had found both reading and writing weary tasks, thanks to her uncooperative eyes. She hadn't tried to scratch out a single word in well over a year, but surely the rudiments would come back to her now, in her hour of need. Her handwriting had always been a fright, Jane knew, and it would be far worse now, rusted by long disuse. With luck, however, she would scrawl clearly enough for Tabitha to understand.

Jane carefully removed the stopper from the bottle of ink, setting both on the floor. She tipped her head and squinted at the nib of the quill. It seemed sharp enough for writing. Then she licked her finger and picked up the first sheet of paper in the box . . . and paused. As the paper came away, it revealed another below, this one covered in unfamiliar writing.

A prickle of caution moved up her spine. She took that sheet, too, and with her head cocked at an awkward angle, she read the paper laboriously. It was the first draft of a letter.

My dear friend Oscar,

I am writing to you from Utah Terr., or what the Mormons call Deseret. I got here with my wife and small family two summers past after leaving Winter Quarters by wagon train. It is a pleasant enuf valley but I am afraid work is not as good here as a man might hope to find. Only due to my not being a Mormon myself. I am welcomed as a builder for the most part but unless I join their church there aint a lot of hope of my doing much else to earn my pay. I am farming some but my home stead is off a space from the nearest town and it's hard to get by.

My dear wife Martha did not live, alas. She was taken by a slow illness, and very cruel. I write to you to ask if there is work for a fellow back in Nebraska. Assuming I can get back to you, Oscar, with the children, who are a heavy burden indeed.

Do write and tell me what prospects you see if I can find some way to return. I wait anxious for your letter so don't sleep on sending it.

Your friend

Elijah Shaw

The letter fell from Jane's fingers. It drifted like a fallen leaf, wafting this way and that until it settled again in the wooden box.

The children, a heavy burden indeed.

Never before had Jane considered that Elijah had already made up his mind—and that he would be dissatisfied at caring for a brood of young ones, two of whom were not his own.

If he takes us back to Nebraska, what will become of us then? Surely he won't keep us—not if we're a heavy burden.

Hastily, she returned the ink and quill to the box, and shoved it under the bed. The letter to Tabitha was forgotten. She staggered to her feet and picked up the first useful thing that came to hand—the little corn broom that rested against the stone hearth. She began sweeping the cabin's floor, though she'd swept it once already that morning. No matter; a second sweeping had never done a floor any kind of harm. There was work to be done in the cabin, in the garden outside, in the field—she would go across to the oat field, take Elijah a dipper of cool water from the stream, a bite to eat. She would ask him what work he had for her to do, what tasks she could perform to ease his burden, to make herself as useful as her stepfather would like.

She mustn't be a burden now. There was no telling what might come if any of the children weighed too heavily on Elijah's mind.

~

The day was gentle, even cool, between the steep flanks of the canyon. When Jane tipped back her head, the sky was a narrow band of blue, the deep and even azure that only shows itself during the peak of summer's heat. She smiled as she made her way down the canyon road, head thrown back, watching that perfect blue as it dashed and bent and curved between the canyon walls like water tumbling in a brook. She could almost convince herself that the chattering of the creek was the sound of the sky—a river's current flowing overhead.

She swung her basket easily in one hand, despite its weight. Elijah had complained of a toothache that morning, and had asked Jane to leave off her usual work and to search instead for the goldenrod root that could ease his pain. Jane had gone eagerly enough. Since her discovery of the letter, she had applied herself more determinedly than ever before to keeping house for Elijah. That had meant less time in the canyon, foraging for the handful of plants that Tabitha had taught her to use. She had sorely missed those hours of peace and solitude, the whispering company of wild things, relief from the monotony of her daily routines.

It hadn't taken long to find an ample patch of goldenrod. The plant preferred the cool, wet climate of spring, but the canyon held sufficient pockets of shadow and dew to keep goldenrod growing well into summer. She'd dug a useful supply of the long cream-colored roots, but had found she was in no great hurry to return home. She had passed the morning foraging for more herbs to replenish her small cache of medicinal powders and teas. She had even gathered a few seeds from useful plants, hoping she might coax them to grow nearer the cabin—along the bank of the creek, perhaps, or in the shade of the great, rustling willow behind the mule's corral.

Now her basket was full, and the sun had crossed its meridian. Jane could tarry no longer. Delightful as the day had been, there was more important work waiting at home. The children needed their sister. Sarah Ann was as stunted and thin as ever, her breathing and color still subject to sudden decline. Jane never liked to leave the baby in Sarah Ann's care. What should become of them both if the girl were taken by one of her fits while Jane was foraging and Elijah was working the field?

As she left the canyon, the full heat of day tightened like a fist around her. She paused to pull her bonnet up, shielding her eyes from the glare. In the stillness, she heard a murmur of voices from somewhere just ahead. Jane blinked, struggling to align her eyes. A buggy stood in the yard with a sorrel between its traces. The buggy's polished black sides were clouded by dust, but the grime of travel couldn't conceal its fine lines. It was an expensive vehicle. She had never seen such a conveyance before—not anywhere near Centerville.

Someone has driven all the way from Salt Lake City.

Surely only city folk could afford such a luxury. But what possible business could city folk have with Elijah Shaw?

Jane hung back, far enough from the cabin that she could make out her stepfather's tone but not his words. There were two other people with him—a man who spoke in a deep bass rumble and a woman with a high, sweet voice. That lilting, motherly speech wrung Jane's heart with longing.

Elijah and the two strangers came around the corner of the cabin and approached the buggy. Jane kept very still, reluctant to draw their attention. Elijah moved with obvious hesitation. The other man held a tall black hat in his hands, and the woman who walked beside him wore a dress of deepest red. There was a decadent sheen to the fabric. Her golden hair was curled and pinned high on her head. She was a rich man's wife, Jane understood—and she was carrying a baby in her arms.

Elijah and the other man helped the woman climb up into the buggy. Then the strange man ascended, took the reins, and extended a hand for Elijah to shake. The sorrel began to move, wheeling slowly around in the dry, trampled yard.

Only then did Jane understand. The basket of herbs fell from her hand.

"Wait!" she cried. "Don't go!"

She ran, hoisting skirt and petticoat above her knees, but the buggy rolled out onto the road as the sorrel began to trot faster than Jane could run. Still she pounded through the heat, desperate to catch the buggy, though her breath was already a fire in her lungs. She could taste blood at the back of her throat.

"Wait!" she screamed. "Come back!"

"Janey!" Elijah moved to stop her as she passed the cabin. Jane spit a curse at him and ran down the slope, but it was no use. The buggy was already far beyond her.

She staggered to a halt, letting her skirts fall, bracing her hands against trembling knees. Jane heaved for breath, choking on tears—on the bitter taste that had come up into her mouth. She could hear Elijah moving cautiously toward her, his feet dragging through the dust. She rounded on him.

"How could you? How could you do such a thing, you . . . you cruel, mean devil!"

"Janey, please."

He was reaching out for her now as if he thought to take her gently by the shoulders. She slapped his hands away.

"Your own son! He's your son, and you gave him away like . . . like a dog or a lamb!" She reeled back. The buggy was lost to sight down the hill, but she could see a faint banner of dust rising from the road.

"William!" Jane screamed. "Come back!"

"I had to do it. Don't you see?"

There was pain in his voice, a great, strangling pain that made his words sound weak and small. Jane felt no pity for him. There was no room for pity alongside her grief and rage.

"Little William needs a mother," Elijah went on. "I can't care for him proper—not like a mother could. And you can't do it, Jane—not on your own, young as you are. It breaks my heart to part with him, but it's best for him, in the end. He's my son. If I don't do what's best for him, then what kind of father am I?"

A dread so vast and cold seized Jane that for a moment she was struck to silence, unable to comprehend exactly what she feared—unable to put that terrible, instinctive panic into words. She saw nothing but Sarah Ann's face, and her arms felt guiltily, shamefully empty because they weren't holding her sister.

She whispered, "What have you done with Sarah Ann?"

"Nothing," Elijah said.

Jane ran again—toward the cabin this time, dodging around her stepfather. She could hear him racing after. Jane shouted her sister's name, though her throat was red raw.

Elijah managed to catch her at last, snaring her around the middle. She collided with his thick forearms; the breath was wrenched from her body. There were stars dancing where the foothills and the cabin should have been.

Elijah held her while she fought for breath.

"Hush," he murmured. "Hush. Sarah Ann is sleeping. She had another of her dizzy spells this morning, so I gave her that tea you got from Tabitha Ricks. She's inside, Jane, I swear. She hasn't gone anyplace. Don't wake her. Don't give her the news while we're both in such a state."

When Jane finally managed to suck in some air, Elijah let her go. She stood shaking and gasping as the tears coursed down her face. She could hear him sniffing, too—then a ragged sob, quickly stifled.

She spun to face him, clasping her hands, a pleading gesture. "Don't send Sarah Ann away. Or me. Please don't separate us; I can't bear it."

He only looked at Jane, his jaw slack, his eyes dull and red.

Jane had to break through his fog of despair. She had to make him understand. Sarah Ann was all the family she had left. If she lost her sister, it would be the end of everything. In a blink, she understood what she must do. However much she mistrusted her stepfather now, she would keep sweet at all times, and work without tiring. She would give Elijah no cause to consider sending Sarah Ann off to some other woman, some unknown mother. Jane would be mother enough for both of them now.

"Let me keep house for you," she said. "I'll do any work you like, but let me care for Sarah Ann. She won't be a burden to you, I promise. Nor will I. But let us stay together at least till next summer, till you're ready to take to the trail again."

"The trail," Elijah said, as if he'd never heard such words before.

"Please."

He stared at Jane a moment longer. Then he nodded and turned away, and set off slowly toward the mouth of the canyon.

By the time autumn arrived, Jane had become rather handy at caring for herself and Sarah Ann without troubling their stepfather. She trained herself to wake before the dawn so she could stoke up the hearth fire and start breakfast cooking in near-perfect silence while Elijah still slept. She had him fed and out the door to his field—or to the building companies down in the valley—while the morning sun still hung blushing and low above the Wasatch peaks. The rest of her days were a blur of activity, setting Sarah Ann to whatever small tasks the girl could manage on her own, caring for the mule and the hens, washing Elijah's clothes, or bringing in the harvest from the garden.

As the days shortened and the nights grew colder, the garden demanded ever more of Jane's attention. There were still plenty of squashes to pick and cure, and beans to shell and store for winter eating. The summer-dried earth must be harrowed and softened, for when the first rains came, the seeds of winter vegetables must be planted straightaway so they could put down sturdy roots before the bitter frosts arrived.

At the edge of the garden, on a clear September morning, Jane breathed in deeply, savoring the crisp, vegetal scent of the nearby trees, the shy little ferns that grew in the shade among their roots. Somewhere back in August, she had passed her fifteenth birthday. *I'm a proper woman now—grown up to a respectable age, and doing a woman's portion of the work. Elijah has no cause to complain.*

Since that terrible day when the carriage had driven off with William in another woman's arms, Jane had taken great care never to cause her stepfather the least grief or inconvenience. She never asked for anything, unless it couldn't be avoided. She even drove a rickety dogcart to town once a week, selling whatever small excesses she'd raised in the garden, so Elijah never had to trouble himself with the market. Sometimes the girls would go days without setting eyes on their stepfather, except when he left the cabin early in the morning and came home long after dark, weary from a hard day's work. That suited Jane perfectly. The less Elijah had to think about the girls—the fewer opportunities he had to weigh their burden—the likelier it was they could remain together.

She wiped her hand on her skirt and reached down for the mattock, ready to resume her work. A flash of movement caught her up short—a bolder, darker stirring among the ripple of heat waves. She aligned her eyes, staring sideways. A rider was coming up the hill. For a moment, her heart gave an eager bound, for she thought it might be Tabitha. But the horse was much too tall to be Tabitha's Indian pony. And now Jane could see that it was a man riding up the canyon road.

She lingered at the edge of the garden, curious and in no hurry to swing the mattock again. Perhaps, she thought, the stranger would ride up into the ravine, bound for some lonesome habitation in the cooler heights of the foothills. But no—the red horse left the road and came plodding down the lane that ran between Elijah's dusty yard and his field of waist-high grain.

As the rider approached, Jane lowered her face by habit, for she never liked strangers to see her too clearly. The horse's front hooves appeared before her and stopped in the dust. She waited for the man to speak.

"You're Elijah's girl," the rider said.

She answered without looking up. "He's my stepfather, sir."

"Is he in?"

"Yes—in the house. You can go and knock, if you please. You may tie your horse to the hitching post under the willow. The shade is good there."

The horse didn't move, nor did the man speak again. After a long moment, Jane turned up one side of her face, just enough so that she could peer through her strongest eye past the brim of her bonnet.

The rider was a man in his late twenties—large, broad-shouldered, with a dark beard trimmed close to his jaw. He had removed his hat to speak to Jane, and his hair was damp with sweat. He watched her in expectant silence, blue eyes lit by an intensity she didn't understand.

Quickly, she lowered her face again. Her cheeks burned, though she couldn't imagine why she ought to feel ashamed.

"Elijah is inside," she repeated.

"Do you know," the man said quietly, "I'm going to marry you someday."

At once, a swell of affront rose in her stomach. Who did this stranger think he was, to say such bold things to a young woman—to a girl! He was mocking her. He had to be—making sport, as the boys back in Winter Quarters mocked her for their amusement.

Jane looked up, making no attempt to hide her eyes. She stared at the man directly, forcing him to confront her flaw.

She had expected him to laugh, or to make some cruel remark. He never said a thing—only went on gazing at Jane with that same strange intensity, a certainty and a resolve that stirred her fury and fanned the flames even hotter.

"Is that so," Jane said. "Well, I wouldn't marry you if you were the last man on earth!"

The rider chuckled. "The very last?"

"And no mud left for God to make another. Go on and talk to Elijah, if you've come to see him, for I won't speak another word to you."

She snatched her mattock from the ground. For one giddy moment, she was tempted to brandish it at the stranger, but she didn't want to spook his horse. The horse had done nothing to offend her. Jane turned her back ostentatiously and stalked away.

She lost herself so deeply in the garden—and in her work—that she never knew when the rider left, nor whether he'd spoken with Elijah after all. She only knew that when she paused some hours later to drink from the creek, her arms and back ached more fiercely than they usually did, for she'd been wielding the mattock for hours with concentrated fury. The sun was mellowing now. The sky was a deeper, gentler blue. It was three o'clock, perhaps later, and she had eaten nothing since breakfast.

Jane drank another cupful, letting the cold water pinch and sharpen her belly. She went to the cabin to hunt up some biscuits and apple jelly. Sarah Ann was outside, knitting a new pair of wool stockings in the shade of the willow.

"Was a man here?" Jane asked. "Younger than Elijah, with a short black beard?"

"He came and went hours ago," Sarah Ann said.

"Have you left any biscuits in the tin, or did you eat them all?"

"There's plenty left. And Elijah wants to speak with you. He told me to send you in if you ever came up from the garden."

Jane stepped inside, feeling rather light-headed. She took two biscuits from the tin, split them with a knife, spread a generous portion of jelly on each. She was about to take a bite when Elijah emerged from his shadowy corner.

"Janey. There you are."

She returned her biscuit to the plate, watching Elijah in silence.

"Do you know who that man was, came up this noon?"

"I've no idea," she answered rather shortly.

"He's Thomas Ricks—a fellow who's well thought of down in Centerville."

Jane waited. Something hard and pressing seemed to fill her stomach, pushing back her hunger. *Ricks—that's Tabitha's last name.* He must have been a brother or a cousin, Jane thought.

"What do you suppose he came to talk to me about?"

Elijah asked that question as if he were concealing some wonderful surprise—as if at any moment he would reveal a delight that would set Jane to squealing. She could feel her cheeks burning again. She wouldn't speak of what that man had said to her out there in the garden.

"I suppose he came to buy some wheat," she said. "To stake a claim on the crop before anyone else could."

Elijah gave a hearty laugh. His glee made Jane want to kick him.

"He did make an offer on the wheat," he said. "But more than that: he offered to marry you."

Elijah wore a foolish grin. It was clear he was expecting her to clap her hands or swoon dead away. She only went on staring.

"Well, what do you say, Janey?"

"I say I've never heard of such nonsense in all my life."

"But, Jane—"

"I don't like that man," she went on, "and I'll never marry him. You can tell him I said so."

"But he's a perfectly respectable fellow."

A respectable man doesn't ask a fifteen-year-old girl for her hand. Jane said nothing aloud. She only bit into her lunch, never taking her eyes from Elijah's face.

"You ought to give real consideration to the offer," he said.

"I've no doubt that if I were to marry, it would free you up to do whatever you please. Wander off to California, or back to Nebraska— wherever the wind might blow you."

"I've got no itch to wander. And anyhow, you should be more sensible, Jane. Think of your prospects. Not many men will be glad to take you, what with your . . . your eyes being as they are."

Her hands had gone numb. Her very self had gone numb. She let the tin plate drop; it landed on the table with a crash, sending biscuit crumbs scattering. Jane spun on her heel and hurried away—back outside to the coolness beside the creek.

By the time the willow shade closed around her, Jane was gasping with offense. She squeezed her eyes shut—her damnable, cursed eyes. She tried to hold back the tears, but they fell all the same.

Of all the mean, heartless, half-witted things Elijah could say . . .

She spat in the grass. It didn't make her feel any better, so she spat again, this time with more energy, but the result was the same.

So Elijah wanted to parcel her off like some troublesome stock. Sell her along to another man, for him to deal with. And a Mormon, of all things!

Of course, nearly everyone in the valley was a Mormon. Still, Jane had no liking for the idea. She could never be a Mormon's wife. They seemed pleasant-enough people, but she didn't belong among them.

I'd just bet Elijah would push me out the door and into some Mormon's hands. Never mind that I don't know a thing about these people, nor them about me. I'd be one less burden for Elijah to carry. That's all that matters to him now.

Jane wouldn't have it. She would cling to Elijah like a burr. She would hang from him like a millstone around his neck. Let that serve him right, for what he'd done to William.

She could hear Sarah Ann stirring in the willow shade. A moment later, the girl's small hand slipped into Jane's.

"What's the matter, Janey? Why are you crying?"

Jane shook her head. There wasn't a word of explanation she could think of—not that would preserve her dignity.

"I hate him," she muttered.

"Elijah?"

Jane nodded. Then she mustered her resolve, wiping the tears from her eyes. There was work to be done. No time for crying.

"Is your knitting finished?"

"Almost," Sarah Ann answered.

"We must work even harder than we've worked before. We must be useful to Elijah, and never vex him."

"Of course." Sarah Ann sounded confused.

"Come." Jane sank down in the grass and picked up the knitting. "I'll help you."

"There's no need. I can do it by myself."

"You won't be by yourself—not ever. I'm going to stay with you for good, Sarah Ann. Do you hear me?"

She blinked at Jane, startled and perhaps a little frightened by her sister's vehemence.

"We'll be together forever," Jane insisted. "If I have to be an old maid, and work in a shop or as a teacher to care for you, then I'll do it. And if Elijah thinks I can't manage on my own, then I'll just show him. He'll see. I'll show him how hard I can work, and then he can choke on it, for all I care."

7

TAMAR

The Mormon Trail
September 1856

The morning after the apostles visited the invalids' camp, Tamar woke late and lay quietly on her bedroll under the willows. She watched as light and shade moved in shifting patterns over the flattened grass. Her father lay facing the creek, which was all but dry now, and he was so still that Tamar wondered, with a sudden, sinking chill, whether he'd passed into the Lord's arms while she had slept.

She sat up quickly. Papa stirred at the sound. Relief flooded her, leaving her trembling—and she realized it was a different kind of shaking from that which had gripped her all those long days of illness. In the thrall of mountain fever, she had felt insubstantial—more mist than bone, and likely to blow away on the first strong wind. Now she seemed entirely herself again, or nearly so. All the pieces of her being had drawn back together, a unified whole. The worst of the illness was behind, and only the future lay ahead—the future, and the miles she must walk before she would reach Zion.

Papa rolled over and met her eye. When he smiled, she remembered the gardens at Aston Rowant—Papa moving easily between the beds of lavender and bergamot, a pail in one hand, his trimming shears in the other. The bees and the little white moths used to float around his shoulders, drawn by the scent of cut herbs that clung to his old woolen jumper. The insects would drift lazily, luminous in the afternoon light—a halo around her father's head.

"You're looking much better," he said.

"As are you. Do you feel well?"

"Quite." He grinned, sitting up carefully on his bedroll. "I've been up and about, in fact, since dawn. You've only caught me having a lie-down. I feel like a new man, thanks to the apostles' blessing."

"I am almost good as new, myself."

Tamar could have scolded herself. She had fallen asleep believing the blessing had done nothing at all. A wave of shame ran through her. Silently, she prayed.

Forgive me, Heavenly Father, for doubting Your power, and the power and wisdom of Your priesthood. I won't make the same mistake again.

"I do wish we could say as much for everyone in this camp," Papa said quietly. "Poor Sister Ashton. She tried her best, but she was too sick, too weak."

Tamar pressed a hand against her heart. It seemed to have stopped beating. "Her baby?"

Papa shook his head.

"How could I have slept through it all?" she said. "Imagine, lying here oblivious while another woman . . . while she died, and her child with her."

"You aren't to blame," Papa answered gently. "You could have done nothing for her, in any case. When God wills, we all must go. And she was surrounded by others who gave her what comfort and strength they could, Tamar. Your mother, your sister—"

"Not Zilpah, I hope."

"No. John and I kept her well away. But she knew, of course. She understood what it meant when we heard no baby's cry."

"I know I shouldn't murmur against God," Tamar said. "Against His design. The Lord knows best. All is according to His plan." *And I've only just resolved myself to a perfect faith. Oh, why is it so hard to cast doubt aside?*

"But . . . ," Papa said.

"But it doesn't seem fair," Tamar admitted. The shame of her weakness—this sinful inability to accept the Lord's design—was almost enough to make her weep. "It isn't right that a girl so young should come to this end. And the baby—what sense in taking its life, too? It might have lived and brought some comfort to its poor father."

"You're right," Papa said quietly. "It isn't just, nor sensible. And all may be according to God's design, but we are only human. We can't know the mind of the Almighty. It isn't for us to understand."

"Oh, Papa, this has all been too hard. I believe, yet my faith isn't perfect. I've seen miracles with my own eyes—I have felt them—and yet when I think of Sister Ashton and her baby . . ."

"If it were easy to get to Zion, then the act of going would mean nothing at all. The harder a sacrifice comes, the greater its worth in Heaven."

"What can God want with such a sacrifice? How can this sorrow please the Lord?"

"I don't pretend to understand God's mind. I know only that I am His faithful bondsman. I go where He directs me and do as He commands, trusting all the while that I shall have my reward. And if He requires me to die in service to His design, then I shall die with a light heart and an easy mind." He paused. Crickets sang in the momentary silence. Finally, Papa said, "I pray that Sister Ashton held the same conviction in her heart."

"Poor Zilpah. She must be so frightened. Where is she now?"

"She's been all day beside the stream."

Tamar clambered to her feet, took a few experimental steps toward the creek bed. Her legs quivered from disuse, and her back was stiff from lying so long in her bedroll. But an undeniable energy flowed through her body. It was the first time she'd risen and walked by her own strength since her family had joined the invalids' camp. How many days had she lain there, felled by the terrible fever? Five—six? Perhaps more. Mountain fever was a harsh disease, and yet it had released its iron grip at a touch of the apostles' hands.

Every doubt that had plagued Tamar since taking to the trail had burned away in the fever's heat. God was drawing her ever closer to the valley. And when she stood in Zion at last, surrounded by the faithful, Tamar would claim her reward. The happiness she had forgone as Edward's wife waited somewhere ahead, multiplied tenfold, shining with the light of holy ordinance. She would reach the valley for certain. The apostles had told her so, and she believed them now.

Patience came striding out of the willows, somber and ready as ever. "Merciful Mary, but it's good to see you on your feet. If I had to haul you up one more time so you could use the chamber pot, I felt sure my back would break."

"You and Mama cared for me so tenderly."

"Surely you didn't think we would leave you to your own devices."

Tamar embraced her sister. When she tried to let go, Patience held her all the tighter, so Tamar wrapped her again in her arms. They remained that way for a long while, taking comfort in one another's presence, reassuring themselves that nothing had parted them yet.

At length, Patience stepped back. "You smell like you fell into a midden heap."

"So do you."

They shared a laugh, but the merriment slipped rather quickly from Patience's face. "Now that you're no longer delirious, we need to discuss Zilpah."

"She must be miserable now. Papa told me about Sister Ashton."

"Come and sit with Zilpah awhile," Patience said. "She's in a bad way. She needs company. I fear to leave her alone too long with her thoughts. Mama is helping tend the sick, and John has gone to help Brother Ashton. The wretched fellow can't be left to dig that grave on his own."

Tamar made her way through the thicket of willows. She found Zilpah sitting on a fallen tree, her back turned to the camp and all the grief it contained. Zilpah's shoulders moved slightly as she drew breath, but otherwise she was as still as the tomb.

She didn't turn as Tamar came through the dry grass, but when Tamar sank down on the fallen tree and put an arm around her sister's shoulders, Zilpah said, "I was a fool not to listen to you and Patience when you told me to stay in Iowa. I thought God would bear me up. I thought my faith would give me wings, and I would cross the distance as easily as a bird in flight. I thought we would have reached the valley by now, and I would be safe when the baby arrived, but we've been so dreadfully slow."

"Forgive me."

It was all Tamar could think to say. If she hadn't taken the fever—if she'd had strength enough to pull the handcart just one day more—they would be in Winter Quarters now, resting comfortably, regaining their strength for the next push out into the wilderness. Zilpah could give birth in a proper town, surrounded by midwives and physicians, with clean blankets to swaddle her baby, without the specter of wolves and other beasts slinking through the darkness.

Zilpah shook her head. Tears broke from her lashes. "You aren't to blame. I am. And God is to blame."

"You mustn't say it."

"I don't know why I ever left, Tamar. That is the truth."

"Why you left Iowa?"

"England. What madness possessed me? What fever infected us all? I look around at this endless plain, and I know this is real, yet still, it seems as if I must be caught in a nightmare. I don't understand how I came to be here, and in such a state. How did I ever believe this was a thing I must do?"

"You're strong enough," Tamar began.

Zilpah cut her off. "I'm not. I never was. From the first day, it was too much to bear. But I kept on, believing . . . I know not what. Believing I would find some reward in Zion. Now I know the truth. The only reward I shall have is a shallow, lonely grave—"

"No, Zilpah—"

"—here in this wasteland, where no one will come to mourn me. And I've condemned my baby to the same fate. What kind of mother am I?"

Tamar stroked her sister's back. She could feel Zilpah's ribs beneath her hand—the frailty of her body.

"Sister Ashton's fate is not yours. God will spare you yet."

Zilpah turned suddenly to face Tamar, her eyes hard and mocking. "Will He? How has He spared any of us?"

A crackle in the brush made Tamar spring up from the cottonwood. It was no circling wolf—only Mama and Patience moving through the rippling grass. A wave of dizziness swept through Tamar—relief, she wondered, or the lingering effects of the fever? She swayed, and Patience hurried to her side.

"Go back to your bedroll and rest," Patience said. "You'll do us no good if the fever takes you again. Now go; don't argue, or I'll drag you to bed by your hair."

Tamar gave Zilpah one final, lingering look, memorizing her fine features, the dark curls that had pulled free from her braid to fall around her face. Her skin was still porcelain smooth, even smudged with the grime of long travel. Zilpah stared back, eyes wide with a plea or an accusation.

Spare her, Heavenly Father, Tamar prayed. *Whatever strength you have given me—whatever miracle of healing You have granted—let it pass to my sister. Let us not leave Zilpah here in a lonesome grave. Let our whole family stand together in Zion.*

~

Zilpah's time came the following day, just as the sun passed its meridian. Tamar and Patience had been debating, in hushed and urgent tones, whether they ought to press on toward Winter Quarters. Brother Ashton had departed that morning, leaving his handcart behind, stumbling out onto the trail with only a rucksack full of the most basic supplies. The only families who remained at the invalids' camp were the Oakleys and the Jensens, each still nursing their fevered ill.

"I can pull Brother Ashton's cart," Tamar insisted, "with our supplies. When Papa begins to feel weak, you can pull him on our old cart, and John will pull Zilpah."

Patience grunted in derision. "You aren't yet steady enough to walk from here to the seep and back. Pulling a handcart is out of the question."

"I'll bear up. If we can get Zilpah to Winter Quarters, she can give birth in a real town with midwives to care for her and the baby. Surely I'm strong enough to walk thirty miles—"

An unmistakable cry cut their argument short. They stared at one another for a dreadful, suspended heartbeat. Then they both ran toward the willows.

They found Zilpah crouched beside the fallen cottonwood. Mama was already at her side, urging her up, pleading with her to take shelter in the shade. When she rose, shuddering, Tamar could see that the back of Zilpah's skirt was wet from the burst waters.

Zilpah labored only four hours, and the baby came as easily as any firstborn has ever done. The new mother wept in fear and screamed in pain, but she kept up her strength, and when the tiny boy arrived, he was red and vigorous, crying lustily enough to please any midwife.

Mama withheld her joy until she was satisfied that the afterbirth had passed in a single piece. Then she rocked back on her heels, wiping the sweat from her face with a grimy sleeve.

"Zilpah will live," she said to Tamar. "So will the child. Thanks be to God for His mercies."

Tamar had been kneeling beside her sister, bathing her brow with a damp cloth. She made as if to rise, for too many weeks had passed without any cause for celebration, and she longed to bring the joyful news to John and Papa. A wave of dizziness pushed her back to the ground. She crouched on hands and knees, trying to conceal her distress from her sisters and her mother.

"I told you." Patience towered above, a monolith of shadow against a too-bright sky. "You're still too weak from the fever to do much of anything. You sit and rest, Tamar. I'll find John and give him the news."

For once, Tamar did not argue. She watched Zilpah suckle the tiny newborn for a few blissful minutes. Zilpah was smiling now, all of yesterday's terror forgotten. She hummed gently, tracing the shape of her son's red cheek.

A murmur of voices at the campsite drew Tamar's attention. She stood—more slowly this time—and made her way toward the commotion. Patience hadn't located John or Papa yet. She was lingering at the edge of the camp with those members of the Jensen and Oakley clans who were well enough to move about. All were shading their eyes with their hands, gazing to the west, where a small wagon was trundling toward them.

The stranded travelers could only pray the wagon was driven by a friend, not an enemy. But as the vehicle came closer, solidifying out of the rippling heat waves, someone recognized the man who held the reins and called out to him in greeting. It was Brother Joseph Young, son of the prophet Brigham Young—one of the leaders of the original company that had set out from Iowa City some six weeks before. Brother Young lifted his hat in greeting as he neared the camp.

"I'm glad to find you all still here," he said. "Cluff and Taylor sent me back to carry the sick to Winter Quarters. We must leave the town in four more days, you see, if we're to make it through the mountains before the snows arrive. We'll load everyone who's too ill for walking into the wagon. The rest must walk along beside."

"One of my sisters has just given birth," Tamar said, "within the past hour. She needs care—as does the baby. May I ride with her?"

Patience took hold of Tamar's arm. "You're still too sick, yourself, to care properly for Zilpah. And our father is weak, Brother Young; you must allow me to ride in the wagon. I shall care for all three members of our family."

"I'm sorry, Sister," Young replied. "This is only a small wagon, and so many are stricken with the fever. Whoever rides must care for themselves till we reach Winter Quarters. There isn't room for any other arrangement."

"Then the Loaders will remain," Patience said.

Tamar rounded on her. "Are you mad? It's nearly thirty miles to Winter Quarters."

Patience began pulling her back toward camp. "Thank you, Brother Young," she called over her shoulder. "Do tell us if we can be of any assistance while the rest are helped onto your wagon."

When they'd drifted some twenty paces away, Patience said quietly, "Don't be a fool. We can't allow Zilpah and the baby to ride cheek by jowl with a lot of feverish Oakleys and Jensens. She and the baby might take bad air from them and fall ill themselves."

"Yet now we must force her to walk those thirty miles to Winter Quarters."

"We've the Ashton handcart, and unless I miss my guess, another cart or two will be left for our use. If we spread the weight of our camp and our sick among four carts, we can move much faster than we've done before, even with you wobbling like a colt."

Tamar opened her mouth to argue. She promptly shut it again. Patience was right; she could see that plainly enough.

"I'll agree," Tamar said at length, "provided Papa rides in a cart as often as we can manage. He can't walk more than five miles at a time, and even that is asking too much."

"I will pull him," Patience said. "And when he insists on walking, I'll pull you. Yes, Tamar—I won't hear of you going on foot the whole distance. We'll find some way for all seven of us to fit in a single tent."

"We'll be terribly crowded," Tamar said.

"But our loads will be lighter, with only one tent to haul. We'll divide our other supplies between two carts and make each as light as possible. Mama will pull one—though I hate to make her work so hard—and you and Papa will trade off with the other. John must pull Zilpah and the baby all the way to Winter Quarters. She won't be much good for walking, not for days yet."

Thus decided, they set out along the creek to bring John the happy news. There was no further need to negotiate the next day's plan. Determination had set between Patience and Tamar like mortar solidifying between two blocks of stone. The sisters rarely agreed on anything, but when they were united in a single purpose, no one in the Loader family could stand against their will.

That night, long after the Jensens and Oakleys had departed with Brother Young, Tamar did her best to sleep. John and Papa hadn't let the cook fire burn down to coals but had stoked the flames instead, piling on fallen limbs and summer-dry brush. Now it was almost as large as a bonfire, the flames leaping six feet high, sparks snapping and rising, driving back the coyotes that circled in the tall grass.

At dawn, the Loaders distributed the barest necessities among four carts. Zilpah was lifted onto one with the baby in her arms, while Papa insisted that Tamar should ride for the first few miles at least. Before the sun had cleared the horizon, they were moving steadily west, the old campsite dwindling behind. They kept up their spirits by suggesting names for Zilpah's little son.

"The baby ought to have a properly religious name," Tamar suggested. "After all, we are on a holy pilgrimage. Why don't you call him Alpha? He is the first of your sons."

"Oh yes," Patience muttered, "and when you've decided you've borne enough children, you can call the last Omega. Those in between shall be Jehovah, Elohim, and Jesus."

Zilpah ignored the cutting remark. "Yes, it suits. Alpha—I think that is his name."

As afternoon gave way to evening and the air began to cool, riders appeared on the horizon. Brother Young had returned—without his wagon—and he was accompanied by Brother Cluff, the man who'd led their party from Iowa City. Three more young fellows rode behind them.

"Howdy," Cluff called, raising a hand. "We saw a big fire burning through the night and rode out to learn what it meant."

"It was ours," John said. "We were set about by animals, but no harm done. Tell us—how much farther to Winter Quarters?"

"Eight miles, I should say."

Tamar gave a startled laugh. "We've walked twenty-two miles in a single day!"

"Would that we all might stay and help you pull," Joseph Young said, "but we're searching for Brother Ashton. He hasn't turned up at Winter Quarters. The poor fellow must be dazed by grief; he might have lost the trail. With any luck, we'll find him before the Indians do."

Cluff and Young left two companions behind—a welcome blessing, for the young men took over the hauling of the carts. Tamar sighed and stretched as she walked beside her sister, working the tension from her shoulders and back.

When the afternoon had grown late, Tamar said, "How many hours from Winter Quarters do you suppose we are? Have we time to rest again? There's a shady spot by those standing rocks—do you see?"

Patience squinted through the evening glow. A pale sandstone outcropping rose abruptly from the earth some sixty feet off the trail. There was a pool of inviting shade around its base—but as Tamar looked, something moved in the shadows, something fast and determined. Her heart leaped. Reflexively, she drew a sharp breath as if to scream, but such fear transfixed her that she couldn't make a sound. Only then did her thoughts resolve from the sudden flare of instinct.

Indians!

At least ten men were rising from the shade. They loped easily across the distance with bows in their hands.

The Loaders halted. Papa clambered down from his handcart. Though his back was bent and he moved slowly, he stood with the other men, shoulder to shoulder between the women and the approaching natives. John kept his rifle across his chest. A strained silence fell. Even the larks in the tall grass had ceased their evening song.

The Indian men ranged into a loose ring, circling the handcarts, calling to one another in their unfamiliar tongue.

"Now, see here, fellows," John said. "We want no trouble."

If any of the strangers understood English, they gave no sign of it now. Tamar realized she had taken her sister's hand. She held tightly to Patience, trying to make some sense of the rapid, flowing language. Were these men from a friendly tribe—one that traded with Mormon travelers? Or did they have some hostile intent? The men looked powerful, well built—certainly better fed than any Mormon. Each wore his hair cut short along the scalp, while long black locks flowed down their backs, adorned with feathers and beads.

"Don't make any sudden moves," one of Cluff's men advised. "They're Omaha."

"What does that mean?" Papa asked. "Are they from a dangerous band?"

Cluff's man had no chance to reply, for one of the strangers approached the cart in which Zilpah was cowering. He wore his hair in two braids, one of which sported an eagle's feather. He peered over the edge of the cart, searching Zilpah's face with an expression of curiosity that almost bordered on tenderness. Zilpah, for her part, huddled around little Alpha, trying to shield him with her body. Tamar could hear her sister's ragged breath.

The man with the eagle feather spoke to her in a cajoling tone. He reached out one hand, but Zilpah shook her head, wrapping herself more tightly around the baby. Alpha gave a mewling cry.

The other Indians chuckled. One passed some casual remark to his friends, and their laughter grew. Tamar sensed something derisive in those men—a certainty of their own strength, amusement over the frailty of the travelers.

Another Omaha said something short and dismissive to the fellow with the feather in his braid. The one with the feather shot back at once, harshly, gesturing at Zilpah and the baby. Clearly, he would suffer no harm to a mother and her newborn, but the others in his group didn't seem to approve of his mercy. A few of them challenged the man with the eagle feather. One even went so far as to raise his bow, brandishing it like a club. But the man with the feather stood firm in his authority, gesturing again to poor Zilpah while he spoke. The others relented at last and withdrew, muttering and casting dark looks at their leader.

The man with the eagle feather waved westward down the trail, speaking calmly to the Loaders and their companions. No one in their party could understand the Omaha tongue, but they needed no further urging. They set off at once, moving as quickly as their handcarts would allow.

Tamar looked back many times as they fled. The man with the feather remained on the trail, watching them go—and perhaps keeping his own men from pursuing with their bows and knives. Tamar was grateful for that man with his obvious authority. Despite the stories she'd heard of friendly tribes, she was certain the other Omaha men had intended no kindness toward her family.

When it seemed clear that they had escaped for good, Zilpah began to sob, clutching Alpha against her breast. Mama was weeping, too.

"A narrow escape," Patience said. "Thank goodness that man has a tender heart."

"You sensed it, too?" Tamar whispered. "They would have attacked us, but for the fellow with the feather in his braid."

Patience made no answer, and Tamar was grateful for her silence.

The miles passed swiftly. When the sun was settling toward the horizon, casting its long red glow into the travelers' eyes, one of Cluff's men said, "We'll be at Winter Quarters in no time. Look—there's the river."

No body of water was evident on the trail ahead, but there was a uniform line of stunted trees, green against the unrelenting dun of the summer prairie. The band of trees stretched from north to south, as far as Tamar could see in either direction.

"That will be the Missouri," John said.

"There's a ferry to take us across, and then we'll be in the town proper. The old company is there—joined up with Captain Edward Martin. We'll share in his supplies and make the remainder of the trek in a company of more than a thousand. What do you think of that?"

"I think we had better get to Winter Quarters before we count our chickens," Patience said.

As dusk came on, the Missouri revealed itself through the line of the trees, a dark satin ribbon snaking through the night. The air was sweet with the perfume of fresh water, the perpetual greenness of the willows—a welcome contrast to the bone-dry, dust-choked smell of the prairie. Lamps to mark the ferry landing glowed in the distance. The safety of civilization was but a stone's throw away.

As they proceeded toward the landing, a strange, angular hulk of splintered wood asserted itself from the dusk. They drew closer, and now Tamar could see the broken wheels, the shattered axle, the staved-in sides of a Conestoga. As they passed the wagon's wreckage, three dark mounds stood out against the dim silver twilight. Someone had made hasty crosses from broken planks. There were no names carved into the wood, but hanging from one cross was a woman's bonnet.

"Indians, do you suppose?" Patience asked quietly.

Tamar only shook her head. She remembered the conversation she'd had with her father under the willows. *If it were easy to get to Zion, then the act of going would mean nothing at all.*

Trembling, she turned away from the ragged crosses.

I shall not be among those who are sacrificed, she promised herself. *The apostles blessed me. They told me I should walk into Zion.*

She would see the valley yet, even if Heaven itself conspired against her.

~

In the town of Winter Quarters, on a bluff above the river, the Loaders were assigned a cabin while the captains of the handcart companies finished their preparations for the last stretch of the trail.

The town was much smaller than Iowa City had been—and it certainly couldn't compare with the stark gray majesty of New York—but despite its modest size, it was a thriving center of industry, flourishing amid the trade routes of fur trappers and local tribes. The place had been founded some ten years past by Brigham Young as a waypoint for pioneers headed for Salt Lake Valley.

Travelers were housed in cabins along the western edge of the bluff. The plank walls were cracked, the roofs thatched with sagebrush, and the bunks inside short and narrow. Still, after more than a month on the trail, the decade-old shack might as well have been a palace.

The Loaders rested three days in their cabin—three blessed days during which none stirred from their bunks unless necessity demanded. On the fourth morning, Brother Cluff announced that the company must move on.

Tamar rose from her bed entirely restored. All remnants of the fever had vanished, and a new strength flowed through her like some wondrous elixir, every beat of her pulse lifting her spirit and urging her to press on. As she helped her family pack their two handcarts—they had surrendered the spare carts to Edward Martin, captain of their new company—she noted the same vitality in her parents and sisters. Even Patience found no cause to grumble.

Captain Martin was a somber, methodical man with a dark beard and searching eyes. As the summer waned, he led his company of nine hundred souls, two hundred handcarts, and eight supply wagons west from Winter Quarters. Once the great column of travelers was underway, Tamar seldom set eyes on Martin again, though they often heard his trumpet blowing, a sound that preceded the arrival of his messengers—young boys who rode mules and ponies up and down the long line of pioneers, calling out news or announcing how many hours remained until camp circled for a night of rest.

A week after leaving Winter Quarters, the low blue suggestion of mountains appeared on the horizon. For days, those peaks remained as distant as ever, always beyond reach, like a magic castle in a fairy tale that is seen but can never be entered. Then the sere plains gave way to a softer, greener landscape. Creeks and rivers became more plentiful, though they were still shallow enough to ford. Only then did Tamar realize that the mountains were clearer on the horizon, growing taller with each passing hour. They shouldered up from the earth like drowsing giants half roused from slumber, and the uniform blue of their color dissolved into variegations of blue-green forest and blue-violet shadow, touched here and there with the luminous bluish-white of permanent snow.

The Loaders traveled well those first two weeks, taking turns in the shafts of their carts. Even Zilpah resumed her towrope, holding the knotted line over one shoulder while Alpha nestled in a sling against her breast. But as the Rocky Mountains loomed ahead, Papa's health began to falter once more.

At first, Tamar failed to notice that he walked more slowly and stumbled more than he ought. It wasn't until one of Martin's messengers called out the day's instructions, then turned his pony to trot back up the line of pioneers, that Tamar thought to look over her shoulder. Instead of the long, steady snake of the great company, there was nothing behind but a few other ailing families and the endless stretch of trail, reaching back to its vanishing point among the waving grass.

"Patience," Tamar said, "we're practically the last in the column."

Patience gave her a scornful look. "Did it take you so long to notice? We've brought up the rear since morning."

Tamar considered her father, pulling at the crossbar beside her. His breath was heavy, his eyes dull. She didn't like the way his arms quivered, nor the heaviness of his feet as they dragged in the dust. But camp was only another hour away. Surely a good night's sleep would restore his strength.

The following day, however, Papa was so weak and slow that the Loaders found themselves far behind the last cart in the column. He refused to allow them to rearrange their supplies so he might ride once more in the cart.

"If we stop, we'll lose sight of the company," he said. "On we go, and no complaining."

Yet as afternoon settled into evening, the tail of the company vanished in the glare of sunset, and they found themselves alone on the trail.

"What are we to do?" Mama said.

Patience stopped walking. Tamar, pulling beside her, was forced to stop, too.

"We must make camp on our own," Patience said. "They can't be so very far ahead, but if we press on, we might lose the trail. We shall rest for a spell and go on just before dawn breaks. If luck is on our side, we'll find the company as they're putting out the morning fires and packing up their carts."

"I don't like to camp alone," Mama said. "We must have a fire, but this is Indian country. A fire will draw attention, and we haven't the numbers of the company for safety."

"Your mother has the right of it," Papa said. "We must press on and reach the camp. We haven't far to go; I'm sure of it."

"I do believe it's safer to press on tonight," John said slowly. "Though God knows, it's a Devil's bargain."

Patience let out an explosive breath. "If we must march on like a pack of fools, we'll do it quickly. Papa, you shall ride in the cart, and let us hear no more of your protests."

And so they pressed on as sunset faded and twilight settled across the land. The mountains vanished in the gathering dark. A wind picked up, biting through Tamar's sleeves, and a veil of ragged clouds obscured the stars. Only a sallow patch of moonlight showed in the sky, faltering and dimming behind the clouds. The vast, open landscape of prairie and foothills no longer existed. There was only the night, drawn in close enough to strangle, revealing nothing of the world ahead or the trail behind. All they could see was the ground at their feet. Tamar felt as if she were walking along some precarious ledge. At any moment, she would put her foot wrong and plunge over the precipice. She would fall into the greedy, all-consuming dark.

When they crossed a shallow stream, Mama filled the cook pot and held the dipper so everyone could drink without stopping. The water was ice cold, tasting of granite and snow. She stirred some of their flour rations into the little water that remained, making a thick and flavorless paste. Tamar ate the cold paste with one hand and pushed the crossbar with the other. She could hear her father murmuring on the cart's bed as he sank into a fitful sleep. Each time the wheels jolted over a stone or a rut, he gave a quiet grunt, but he never seemed to waken.

The wind shifted, bearing down from the north, carrying a smell of smoke.

"Campfires," Tamar said hopefully.

Patience shook her head. "That's wood burning—trees and brush. It doesn't smell a thing like the buffalo chips we burn in camp."

Soon a sickly reddish glow tinted the sky at Tamar's right hand. Then the crest of some distant black hill fell away, and she could see the brush fire burning along the contour of a ridge. It lay like a great, malevolent worm, vivid and menacing. Tamar couldn't tear her eyes from the fire as they pressed on into the night. Only when another unseen hill blotted out the ridge did she face to the fore—and even then, an echo of that hellish light remained before her eyes. She couldn't blink the memory away.

Tamar never knew how she kept walking through the endless void of night. But when the black sky gave way to a soft grayish blue and the first birds began to call among the sage, they came upon the Martin company as the camp's great circle was disassembling—the women kicking loose soil over their cook fires, the men lashing rolled tents and bundles of blankets to their carts.

"I could sing for joy," Tamar said.

Patience exhaled. "And I. Never could I have guessed I would feel so glad to see a filthy, stinking camp again."

The Loaders rested a few hours in the ruin of the campsite, sleeping directly on their mats with no tent above their heads. At midmorning, they pressed on, eyes fixed to a distant pinpoint, the tail end of Martin's column. A wisp of dust proved that the company was only just ahead. Even their inadequate rest had done them all some good—everyone save Papa, who still drifted in and out of consciousness. As the day wore on and mountains towered ever closer—as the foothills began to rise around them, the ground sloping upward underfoot—his condition remained unchanged.

Sometimes Tamar could hear him muttering over the monotonous creak of the cart's axle. He spoke to people who weren't there—his sons, the brothers Tamar missed so dearly, who were safe at home in England. And Sir John Lambert, the master whom Papa had served loyally for thirty long years—the man who had cast the family out for this dangerous new faith. Sometimes she heard her father scolding Sir John, scorning him for his cruelty. At other times, she could hear him weeping, pleading with his master to forgive him, to take him back into service for the sake of his wife and children.

Mama walked beside the cart, positioning herself to cast a narrow column of shade over her husband's head. It was the best any of them could do to shelter him from the pounding sun. Whenever he was strong enough to sit up, Mama made him drink the creek water she collected at every crossing, and eat a little of the flour paste, too. Tamar could hear her mother speaking softly to Papa, soothing his half-conscious fears, singing to ease him into sleep. Her throat was tight with the effort of holding back tears.

When they reached the campsite that evening, Tamar eyed her father on the bed of the cart. He lay curled and small, eyes tightly shut, his limbs drawn in as if he were cold—yet the day had been warm and humid. His lips moved as he spoke or prayed, but he made no sound.

A cold hand seized her heart. She stared down at her father, accepting what was to come even as she denied it.

"Go and help Mama with the tent," she said to Patience. "Get it up quickly. One of us must stay with him. He mustn't be left alone—not now."

When Patience had gone, Tamar pried one of her father's hands free from where he'd clutched it against his body. It felt withered and bony, like the gnarled claw of some strange bird. He was already transformed into a thing she couldn't recognize. This frail, broken creature—this had never been her father, the man who had walked among flowers with a halo of bees around his head. This helpless, human thing bore no resemblance to the man who had bounced her on his knee when she'd been a child—who had kissed away her hurts and dried her tears and promised to protect her from every harm. In her heart, her father was more permanent than the earth and sky. Surely no world could exist without him in it.

"Amy," he whispered.

"It's me, Papa—Tamar. Your girl."

"My girl." His voice was cracked and dry, almost not there at all. "We will go to Zion, Tamar. We will gather with the Saints . . ."

"Yes, Papa. We shall." She could no longer keep her tears at bay. They spilled down her cheeks, flowing like all the rivers they had crossed together. "We shall walk into Zion, just as the apostles said."

He drew a long breath. It rattled in a way that sent a terrible chill coursing through Tamar's body.

"Patience," she cried, "come quickly. There's no time—no time!"

They had only just finished raising the tent. John took Papa in his arms and bore him inside. Once he was laid on his bedroll, Tamar cradled his head in her lap. The family crowded around, gripping Papa's arms, stroking his hair, patting his chest as if their hands might hold his spirit to the earth.

"You know," he said faintly, "I do love my children so well."

"Yes, James, I know it," Mama told him. "And they love you."

He never spoke another word. His final breath was small, hesitant. His chest didn't rise again. They had been in camp no longer than a quarter of an hour. The noise of the night's gathering was still going on around them—mothers calling to their children, girls singing while they worked, men laughing and shouting to one another across the great circle of the camp. None of the other travelers knew a life had ended. A spirit had fled to Heaven, to lie in sacrifice at God's indifferent feet.

Tamar looked up, stunned by the swiftness of the loss, the finality. She found Patience at the foot of the bedroll, staring back, hard-eyed and hateful.

Tamar breathed her sister's name.

Patience gave her no chance to say more. She bolted up and scrambled from the tent.

Tamar eased her father's head from her lap and hurried after. Outside, she could see her sister in the dusky light, dodging through a crowd of children, making for the far side of the camp. Tamar ran in pursuit.

She didn't catch up to Patience until they were well beyond the circle. Only when Patience fell to her knees amid the stunted juniper and gray sage could Tamar finally reach her. She knelt, trying to take her sister in her arms, but Patience pushed her away. She held her stomach as if she might be sick, rocking where she crouched, mouth twisted with silent grief until, finally, one great, agonized cry tore free. Patience keeled forward. She fell across the ground, facedown in the dust.

Gently, Tamar took her by the shoulders, trying to ease her up.

"Leave me be," Patience wailed.

"Please, don't take on so. You must be strong—"

"Why?" Patience screamed the word with all the fury of a gale, though she was still lying on the ground. "Why must I be strong? How can anyone be strong enough for this?"

"You mustn't fall to pieces. Not with so far yet to go."

Patience pushed herself up to hands and knees. She rocked back onto her heels, keening, her face turned up to the blank sky. Tamar held her tightly, rocking with her. Their tears fell together on the parched ground.

They went on weeping in one another's arms until the sharpest edge of grief was dulled. Finally, Patience drew a long, shuddering breath. She let it out slowly.

"This was all madness," she said softly. "It was and is madness."

"Never that," Tamar said. "There's a reason for—"

"Stop!" Patience rounded on her, red-faced. "For God's sake, stop this, Tamar! There is no reason for any of this! Wandering off into the wilderness like a pack of purblind fools! We've been cast out of our home; we lived in shameful poverty in London and New York. We weren't even permitted a wagon, which might have spared our father's life! What purpose does this serve?"

"It serves God's purpose."

Patience lurched to her feet, stark against the dim sky. "What kind of God does this to His chosen people? Who would worship such a cruel, unfeeling master?"

"But I *saw* Him. My vision on the boat . . ."

Tamar reached up with trembling hands, but her sister stepped back.

"*You* saw a vision—or so you claim. I have seen nothing—nothing but my family torn apart and suffering for the sake of a foreign faith!"

Tamar managed to catch the hem of her sister's skirt. She clutched it desperately, unwilling to let Patience slip farther away. "We must go on believing. Don't you understand? If we don't believe, if we don't find some purpose in all this terrible loss . . . then we've lost every scrap of what we once had for nothing. For nothing!"

Patience hadn't calmed herself—not exactly—but she was standing still, waiting for Tamar to say more.

Tamar struggled to her feet. Her whole body was shaking from the shock of the loss and the cold of approaching night. From the terrible energy of grief. She wanted to fall to the dust, as Patience had done. Instead, she forced herself to stand upright and meet her sister's eye.

"If we don't make some godly purpose for our grief," Tamar said evenly, "then our father died a fool. I love him too much to allow it. I won't hear anyone call him a fool—not even you."

She reached out cautiously, offering her arms. Patience fell forward with a whimper, allowing Tamar to catch her. She all but collapsed against her, shaking with silent sobs, leaning into Tamar's grim determination, which was all she had to offer on that barren plain, beneath an empty sky. They held each other until twilight faded and the crickets sang a dirge in the long, dead grass.

8

JANE

Centerville, Utah Territory
Autumn 1856

The ferns had curled away to brown slumber, and the sunflowers had long since faded from the fields. The dogcart rumbled and jolted down the hill, skimming past the dry verge of the canyon road. When she reached level ground on the valley floor, Jane clucked her black mule to a steady trot. The contents of the cart rattled around her—the goods she'd collected to sell at the Centerville market, sacks and clay jars full of dried beans and peas, several large squashes with hard blue rinds. Jane had debated for days over whether she ought to sell the surplus from her garden or preserve it all against the coming winter. She had put by a good store of food already, but one could never be sure how long a winter would last, nor how harsh it might be. Extra beans and pumpkins in the larder meant no one would go hungry during the long, snowy weeks between late October and the spring thaw.

But Jane was also in sore need of thick wool yarn to knit jackets for herself and Sarah Ann. Both girls needed new boots, too, and sturdy cotton cloth for patching the holes in their old skirts and blouses. And, of course, Jane must find a way to pay for the herb-woman's services—assuming Tabitha knew what ailed Sarah Ann, and could treat the illness successfully.

Jane was determined to find all the money she needed on her own, without troubling Elijah.

Guiltily, she eyed her cargo as the cart sped along the road. Some of Elijah's old tools were tucked among the pumpkins and dried peas. They were only small chisels and mallets, which Elijah hadn't touched all summer long. He wouldn't miss them, and likely would have given Jane permission to sell them if she'd asked. But she'd been too frightened to broach the subject.

The less he must think about our care and feeding, the better.

She didn't intend to see Sarah Ann spirited off to Salt Lake City for some other family to raise.

By early afternoon, Jane had sold everything she'd brought to the market, though she suspected word might make its way back to Elijah that his chisels and mallets were fine tools. She would have to explain her dishonesty—but the valley's building companies wouldn't be active till springtime. With any luck, he wouldn't know a thing about it till then. Meanwhile, she'd raised enough money to buy all the yarn and cloth she needed at Smoot's Mercantile.

Jane stood beside her empty cart, tilting her head to admire her earnings. The three one-dollar banknotes were crisp and pretty, printed with the images of a herd of cattle, an Indian, and a white man. The words "Deseret Currency Association" stood out boldly on the bills. Deseret—that was the name the Mormons had given to Utah Territory.

When she inspected the four coins she'd earned, her heart raced, for they were real gold. The bright metal flashed in her palm.

Seven dollars was an obscene fortune—more value than Jane had traded for in all her months in the valley. Yet she knew it would be just enough to see herself and Sarah Ann through the winter—and even then, they must cut close to the bone.

She put the coins in one pocket and her banknotes in the other, then made her way to Smoot's Mercantile to find her wool and cloth. After she'd bought her yarn and a yard of patching cotton, three gold coins remained. She hoped the gold would be sufficient for a final errand in town.

Jane remembered the way to Tabitha's home; there was no need to stop and ask for directions. The whitewashed house with its broad, teeming garden was much as she recalled, though the brilliance of summer had faded, and the medicinal plants in the garden had shed their flowers. Jane tied her mule to the fence and made her way up the central path to the healer's door.

She knocked, but for a long while, there was no answer. Perhaps Tabitha had gone off to treat some ailing person—or perhaps she had moved to Salt Lake City or left the valley altogether. But no—her garden was too neatly tended, despite its spent, autumnal appearance. The healer was still in Centerville, even if she wasn't presently at home.

Just as Jane made up her mind that the house was vacant, the door swung open. There Tabitha stood, unmistakable in her small stature with that strange snake's rattle hanging around her neck. The healer looked harried and strained. She held a squalling newborn on one hip and another small child clung to her skirt.

"Oh," Jane said. "I'm sorry; I . . . I've come at a bad time."

"Why, Jane Shupe," Tabitha said. "You're a welcome sight. You haven't come at a bad time. Or, at least, there's no good time anymore—not with two babies to look after. Is someone in need? Have you come down to fetch me?"

"No," Jane said, "at least—not urgently. I hoped to speak with you, though. I'd like your advice, if you have the time." She added quickly, "I have money to pay you. Three dollars. I hope it's enough."

Gently, Tabitha bounced the baby. She gave Jane an assessing look, taking in her wind-tousled braid and her worn-out boots. "Come in, girl, if you don't mind the noise and mess. We'll talk about pay later."

Tabitha led her to a small but beautifully appointed parlor. Three armchairs with tufted canvas backs were ranged around a braided rug made from bright rags. Several half-height bookcases stood along one wall, the tops of which were covered with jars and bottles of colored glass. Each jar held dried leaves, powders, or liquid tinctures. Afternoon light blazed in through the window, striking Tabitha's apothecary, sending a rainbow of splintered light up from the jars. When a breeze stirred the tree outside, the light shifted and moved among the containers of herbs and remedies. Luminous spots of amber, green, blood red, and cobalt blue danced along the walls.

Below the window, where most parlors might have boasted an elegant sideboard or even a piano, a rustic pine workbench stretched from corner to corner. On this surface was heaped every stem and root Jane could imagine. Some, she recognized from those idyllic hikes with Tabitha in the canyon—the glossy dark leaves of coneflower, bundles of gray sage, the soft, pale inner bark of willow. Mortars and pestles and scales were pushed against the wall; small clay pots stood at the ready to be filled with measured doses. Bundles of herbs hung drying against the windowpane, and the parlor was redolent with a pleasantly herbaceous smell, softly green and comforting.

"This must be where you prepare your remedies," Jane said. "It's wonderful."

"It is," Tabitha agreed, "when I can find time to work. I was already hard-pressed when little Catherine came along, but now that Junior is here"—she nodded to the baby in her arms—"I've had less time than I'd prefer. Still, I manage. My work is too important to be neglected. Now and then, some women from the church pitch in, tending the children or cooking my supper so I can see to the sick and injured. Sit wherever you like."

Jane took the chair that faced the workbench. She was fascinated by its implements, its commingled order and disorder.

Tabitha sat opposite and propped the baby on her shoulder. She gave his back a few expert pats. The baby let out a burp, then settled contentedly against his mother. The small girl at Tabitha's feet toppled onto her bottom, but before she could cry over the fall, she found a leather ball on the floor and rolled it toward Tabitha's foot. Tabitha nudged the ball back to her daughter.

"How have you been, up there in the hills?" Tabitha asked. "I've missed our rambles along the creek."

Jane almost answered with automatic cordiality, *We've been fine, thank you.*

But that wasn't true. It was only Jane's habit to deny her own suffering, to make believe all was within her control. How else could she keep Elijah satisfied? Sarah Ann was not fine—that was the plain truth. She was puny and weak, much frailer than a girl of thirteen ought to be. And Jane had nothing under control—not one thing in all the world, if she were honest.

She said, "We've been having a hard time, my sister and I. And you were such a great help when my poor mother was sick. She died, you know, last month. I meant to send you a letter, but I never found the time to write."

"I wish I could have spared her life," Tabitha said quietly. "At least you and I eased her way into the next world."

Tabitha watched Jane for a long moment. Jane tipped her head as subtly as she could manage, trying to read the healer's expression. Tabitha wore a thoughtful look—and a pensive one, as if she could discern the full breadth and depth of Jane's awful predicament. To find such sympathy and care in another's eyes struck Jane with a pang of gratitude. She could feel tears coming, and blinked them away, unwilling to show any weakness before a woman she respected so greatly.

"This little one will finally sleep, I think," Tabitha said. "Let me go and lay him down. I've got hot water in my kettle, too. I'll bring you a cup of nice lemon-balm tea, if you've time to spare, and we'll have a proper talk. Watch Catherine while I'm gone, if you will."

Jane was left alone with the little girl, who sat pawing at her ball on the braided rug, gazing up at Jane with solemn eyes. She felt rather anxious in the girl's presence. William had been near Catherine's age when Elijah had given him away. Jane wondered whether her lost little brother could remember her or Sarah Ann. Perhaps somewhere in the distant corners of his memory, he had a soft recollection of his mother—her gentle spirit, the tender love she'd given to all her children.

Tabitha came bustling back to the parlor, brighter and more energetic now that the infant was out of her arms. She carried a simple clay cup in each hand. The steam that rose from those cups had a sweet, inviting fragrance.

"It's rather nice to have company." Tabitha passed a cup to Jane. "My husband has been away for several days now. He's a sheriff in the valley, and he's often gone—dealing with disputes over land, over cattle, that sort of thing. Though, lately, he's been absent even more. Brigham Young relies on him a good deal. It's the unrest, you know—folks are getting anxious out in the smaller settlements, on the fringes of Deseret, and where there's tension, there's conflict."

"The unrest?" Jane asked.

Tabitha blinked at her over the rim of her cup. "I suppose you wouldn't know a thing about it, living up in the canyon as you do, and not being a Mormon yourself. How much do you know about the politics of the United States, Jane?"

"Just about nothing, I guess."

Her face burned with shame. Tabitha must think her a fool, and if there was one person in all of Centerville whose esteem Jane craved, it was she. Jane sipped her tea to cover her embarrassment. It was bright with the taste of lemons.

"You know there's a president in charge of the whole country, I suppose—just as we've a president here, in Brigham Young."

Jane nodded.

"Well," Tabitha went on, "a new man is to be elected president this very autumn. We don't know yet who will win the contest, but if James Buchanan comes out on top, we could face a heap of trouble, here in our quiet valley. It seems Mr. Buchanan has made the Mormon religion a proper plank of his campaign. You know, I suppose, that there has been much argument for many years over the practice of slavery."

"That I do know," Jane said eagerly.

The question of abolition had plagued America since before Jane's birth, and in recent years, it had become such a bone of contention in far-off Washington that even Jane had gained some slim understanding of the conflict. Politics barged their way from the Eastern states to Salt Lake Valley, and when Elijah was in a talking mood—which wasn't often—he shared what news he'd gleaned from his workmates on the building companies. Jane knew the men who led America were sharply divided over whether certain states ought to continue holding Black people in bondage, or whether they all must be freed as a matter of principle and human rights. The conflict seemed to sour, year after year—and now Jane wondered whether those who predicted a war between the states might be proved right after all.

Jane said, "That business between the Northern and Southern states is awfully far away. It can't touch us in Deseret."

"That's so," Tabitha agreed, "as long as Buchanan doesn't take the White House. But he has insisted for months that the slavery practiced in the Southern states is one and the same with—"

Tabitha seemed to catch herself. She looked away from Jane, taking a long draught of her tea.

"With what?" Jane prompted.

Tabitha chewed her lip for a moment. "With . . . certain practices among our people. It's ridiculous, of course, for the two are not the same. But this Buchanan fellow has convinced his entire party that the

Mormons out in Utah Territory are committing the very same sins as those who've enslaved the Africans."

"I don't understand. What practices do you mean?"

Tabitha waved a hand, brushing away her concern. "Nothing for you to fret over. After all, you're no Mormon. And even if Buchanan should win and carry on with his spurious accusations—well, Brigham will handle it." She took on a decidedly wry tone. "Love Brigham or hate him, he does seem to have an uncanny knack for getting himself out of trouble—and the whole church along with him. But enough talk of politics. It's always a disagreeable subject, and I fear I've worried you needlessly over the election. Very likely, you're right—whatever happens in Washington won't touch us here. Let's turn to the matter at hand. Tell me what brought you here today."

"It's my sister, Sarah Ann. She's still terribly weak and frail, and she can't seem to grow, no matter how much I feed her. I don't know what else to do for her. I thought maybe if you examined her, you might know how to treat the sickness."

"I see," Tabitha said. "Describe her symptoms for me."

"Her what?"

"The way she behaves; the ways in which you sense there is something amiss."

Jane took a deep breath, considering her words. Then she set about naming all of Sarah Ann's frailties—her stunted size, her too-thin body, the way she often gasped for breath, even when she hadn't exerted herself. Sometimes her fingernails and lips turned blue, Jane said, and she was often very tired, though she did little work, except sewing and knitting.

When Jane finally fell silent, Tabitha nodded thoughtfully and sipped her tea again. "I've seen such ailments before. Sometimes the cause is very serious indeed, but often it's simple to cure. It will take time for the remedies to work, however. There's a tea you must give her twice a day, and see that she drinks it all. And she *must* have as much red meat as you can manage, Jane. If you can't get your hands on red meat, then the darkest possible greens will do. And good orange pumpkin flesh in the winter."

Jane instantly regretted the pumpkins she had sold at the market.

"There's a broken pane of glass in our shed," Jane said. "I think I can set it up in my garden so the glass will trap the heat of the sun. Even in winter, I might be able to coax some chard to grow there—maybe a little mustard."

"Clever," Tabitha said. "I never would have thought to use glass panes in a winter garden, but I can see now how it might work."

Tabitha led her to the workbench, where she measured out the proper herb, then poured it into a clay pot with a tight-fitting lid. She talked all the while, describing how the herb must be brewed at just the right temperature and for the right length of time to properly extract its potency. Jane took the pot in her hands, gazing at its doubled image. Her spirit lightened for the first time in weeks.

"Look at you." There was obvious affection in Tabitha's voice. "How hungry you are for knowledge, for good work. I was like you when I was your age—when I first became a healer's apprentice. I could use an apprentice now, myself. I've so much to manage on my own, between the children and my practice—and with my husband so often away, your help would be more than welcome."

Jane glanced up. "Me?"

"You've the right temperament to become an herb-woman yourself, and I've already seen you at work in the canyon. You're a sensible girl—a girl with wits. What do you say?"

"I . . . I don't know. I would like to do it, but I don't think I could leave my sister alone."

"She might come with you down the hill to my house—in fair weather, anyhow. Perhaps she would be good company for the children while you and I are working."

"I must think it over," Jane said slowly. "I'll have to see how she fares with this tea you've given me. If she gets stronger . . . perhaps."

Tabitha smiled. "Perhaps. We'll give it till the spring, shall we? You can make your decision then."

"Thank you, Tabitha. Oh, thank you so much for everything."

"Call again, Jane, whenever you have need."

Jane left Tabitha's home just as the sun began to set, casting a long, lingering redness over the lake. She untied her mule quickly and climbed into the dogcart, hurrying toward the canyon road and home. She was eager to give Sarah Ann her first dose of tea and a good portion of boiled greens. Surely Tabitha was right, and the cure would be simple, once effected.

It wasn't till Jane was halfway up the hill, with Centerville falling into dusk behind her, that she realized the three gold coins were still in her pocket. Tabitha had never raised the question of pay.

Jane considered Tabitha's offer over the weeks that followed, while the bright blaze of autumn leaves turned to dull brown and the canyon winds gusted them off across the valley. The garden yielded the last of its harvest. She gathered her seeds for next year's planting. There was no telling yet what might come with the spring. If Sarah Ann responded to the remedy, then Jane might apprentice herself to the herb-woman after all. By the time the autumn cold had settled decisively over the foothills, Jane's prospects seemed rosy.

Sarah Ann disliked the bitter taste of the tea, but the treatment—and a good helping of stewed greens with every supper—did seem to have some effect. The girl was still as thin as ever, but she was perkier, more energetic. Now and then, she even helped Jane in the garden, pulling up the spent vines of autumn peas, digging turnips from the soil with her bare hands.

Jane began to feel confident enough in Sarah Ann's health that she often caught herself spinning fantasies while she worked—bright plans for a hopeful future. She might serve two or three years as Tabitha's apprentice, then take Sarah Ann south to Salt Lake City, where she would begin a practice of her own. She would find a little house at the edge of the city—nothing extravagant, only two small bedrooms and a pretty parlor like Tabitha's. There she and her sister would live out their days in comfort and dignity. In time, they might find William and reunite the family. Jane would be the head of the household, and neither her brother nor her sister would want for anything that she could not provide.

Jane leaned on the handle of a hoe in the crisp October sunshine, watching Elijah work the mattock at the edge of the wheat field. He labored as steadily as he ever did, with his usual indrawn silence. Jane would let him know, when the time was right, that she'd had an offer from the healer—a real opportunity, a chance to step out from under his charity. Soon she and her sister would be no burden to Elijah Shaw.

He won't mind so much that I sold his tools if he's certain I'll be out of his hair for good and all.

Sarah Ann gave a sudden laugh from the midst of the turnip patch. Jane looked around, smiling, for it had been a long time since she'd heard her sister sounding so energetic. Sarah Ann had pulled a round golden turnip from the earth—a huge root, almost the size of her head. She held it up for Jane to see. Her cheeks were pink, her eyes as bright as evening stars. Jane knew, looking at her sister's rosy delicacy among the brown dullness of October, that everything would come out right, after all.

A sudden, harsh cry jerked her around so quickly, her hoe fell into the weeds. Elijah was staggering at the edge of the field, clutching his head with both hands.

Jane ran to him, calling his name, demanding to know what the matter was. He never answered till Jane was at his side, clinging to his elbow. His eyes were screwed shut, and a string of spittle ran from his lips.

"My head!" Those words grated like steel over stone. "The pain!"

Jane was no healer yet, but still, she could tell that this was no ordinary headache. He needed help, and quickly.

"Get inside and lie down," she told him. "I'll ride to town and bring Tabitha."

Elijah gave a feeble nod. He began stumbling toward the cabin, still clutching his skull with both hands. Jane hoisted her skirts and ran for the corral where the black mule waited. There would be no time to hitch him to the cart. There would scarcely be time for the bridle. She must ride bareback, as fast as she could induce the stubborn animal to run.

"Help Elijah get inside," she called to her sister. "I'm going to Centerville—"

Sarah Ann screamed—a piercing sound, terrified. Jane whirled about to stare across the empty slope. At first, through her blurred eyes, it seemed as if Elijah had vanished. Then she noticed a low brown smudge in the grass. He had fallen flat, facedown against the earth.

Jane ran again to her stepfather's side.

"Elijah!" She dropped to her knees beside him, shaking his shoulder, pummeling his back. "Elijah, say something! Speak to me!"

He made no answer. A strange, growling animal sound ripped from Jane's throat, half despair and half rage. He couldn't do this now—leave them alone. Not now! She clenched his hair in her fist, turned his head sideways so she could see his face. He had fallen so hard that he'd broken his nose. Blood poured down over a slack mouth. His eyes were open, yet they saw nothing, and when Jane released his hair and placed her palm softly on his back, he was very still.

She rocked back onto her heels, staring up at the cold sky. Dead. Elijah was dead, as suddenly as that. Her last source of money in all the world; the last protection she had, a young girl alone in the foothills with a sickly sister to tend.

I'll have to bury him at the edge of the garden, she thought, so calm and dull inside that for a moment she wondered if she had died along with him. *I can't drag him farther than that, and Sarah Ann is still too weak to help with the work.*

She could hear her sister sobbing in the turnip patch. Slowly, Jane rose to her feet. She stood over Elijah's body, looking down at the motionless blur, the great, heavy weight of him.

I must go and get the shovel, she told herself sensibly.

There was work to be done—now as ever. Jane would do her duty. When had she not? Duty and work, first and last. Duty and work, for her sister's sake. She was all Sarah Ann had left now in this world.

9

TAMAR

The Mormon Trail
Autumn 1856

There were trees in the foothills—bristlecones and low, stunted oaks—but no time to fell them, no time for splitting lumber. Without a coffin, the family had no choice but to wrap Papa's body in one of their thin quilts, laying him to rest in a hastily dug grave not far from the circle of the camp. And then they moved on—always onward, the trampled ring of the former campsite fading and vanishing in the grass, the simple cross Tamar had made from fallen branches dwindling to a dark slash behind her, then a speck, then nothing at all when she looked back over her shoulder.

The whole family walked in a blunt, heavy silence for days after his death. Tamar was unaware of anything, save for the grief that dragged like chains behind her. She performed the dull routine of the trail as mindlessly as a fragment of wood caught and carried by a river's flow. Rising from her mean bed, striking the camp, taking up the crossbar of her cart to plod along the same bare, hard-worn trail. The slow rhythm of her feet, the relentless ache of her body. Yet the agony of her heart eclipsed every other pain.

It was the cold that finally brought her to the surface of her misery. One gray afternoon, the notion that her hands had grown stiff and clumsy slipped in past her ruminations. She blinked and looked at them where they gripped the crossbar. Her knuckles were red, and when she tried to open her hands to flex and stretch them, she found that her fingers moved with a peculiar slowness.

I'm cold, Tamar realized. *Not only my hands but all of me.*

She lifted her gaze and found that she was in the mountains proper. Forests of low-growing pines clung to the hills, which had drawn in close to the trail. Beyond, scarps of pale stone jutted from the dense green of wind-sculpted trees. The ground had sloped up gently enough that she hadn't truly noticed the change in elevation—nor the strain of pulling uphill—but she could feel it now, a redoubled burning in her legs and back. Her breath rose in clouds. Her ears ached from the chill.

One of Martin's boys was trotting down the length of the column, shouting out the time. "Four hours yet to go," he said from the back of his pony. His breath, too, was a silver plume, and twin puffs of steam drifted from the pony's muzzle.

"Where are we?" Tamar called to the boy.

"In the Laramie Range, Sister. There's one last river crossing ahead. Then we'll have our camp for the evening."

"A river crossing?" Patience demanded. "Surely not, in this cold."

"We aren't likely to see many days warmer than this," the boy said. "Summer's behind us, but we've only twenty more days to travel. Then we'll be in the valley."

The boy trotted away.

"We can endure twenty more days," Mama said, pacing along beside the handcart. But her voice was as dull as Tamar felt inside. Papa had been the most enthusiastic of them all, the most determined to reach the valley. Without his eagerness, twenty days would pass like an eternity. It seemed so absurd a length of time that Tamar laughed under her breath. *Twenty days or twenty thousand. It's all one to me, now that he is gone.*

Long before they came within sight of the North Platte River, the first snow of the season arrived. It came first as a dusting of tiny crystals, almost too small to be noticed, yet the flakes stung Tamar's face when the wind blew between the high reaches of the Laramie Mountains.

It will pass, she told herself. She leaned into the crossbar, dragging the twin weights of grief and necessity up the slope of the trail, but as the company snaked to the summit of a ridge, the snow condensed into large white flakes, whipping around Tamar with dizzying speed. She tried to fix her gaze on the foremost ranks of the company, but the snow had drawn a veil across the world. She could see no more than five cart lengths ahead.

Martin's boys called through the blowing storm, voices muffled by the weather. "Halt! Halt and take shelter under your carts! We'll wait out the storm in place!"

Patience helped Tamar lower the crossbar to the ground. Her hands were as stiff as ever, her fingers clumsy and locked around the damp wood.

"This may be the first sensible decision Martin has made for weeks," Patience said. "He can't think to ford the river in this cold."

Tamar and Patience retrieved their blankets and woolen shawls from the bed of the cart, then crouched and scuttled under the tilted bed with Mama between them, each wrapped in a snow-crusted quilt. John and Zilpah huddled below their own cart, with Alpha thickly swaddled in his mother's arms.

"I don't know what you think we ought to do about the river," Tamar said, "other than cross it."

Patience snorted. "We ought to go back—that's what."

"All the way to Iowa City?"

"Of course not. We must return to Winter Quarters."

"After how far we've come? And what about this snow?"

"We're at a high elevation now," Patience said, "but if we return to the plains, we may have weeks yet before we see another snowfall. Surely that will give us time to find reasonable shelter—or to build cabins, if we can't reach Winter Quarters before the snows overtake us."

"Pass the winter in cabins," Tamar sputtered. "And what food shall we eat? Would you have us starve?"

"We shall either starve or freeze," Patience said bluntly. "Make your choice. At least, in cabins, the men might hunt—"

"We can't go back." Tamar couldn't look at her sister. She kept her attention fixed on the storm, the flakes pouring down in cascades, the snow gathering around the edges of their cart—one inch, then two. "We shall go to Zion, and we shall do it together, for our father's sake. You know my feelings. I won't suffer him to be called a fool."

Mama flung a hand from her blanket, holding it like a wall between Patience and Tamar. "Stop this arguing, for mercy's sake! All we have now is each other."

Little by little, the storm slackened. Then the snow ceased altogether. The order to proceed was passed down the length of the company, and the pioneers emerged from the scant shelter of their handcarts—sluggish with cold, groaning and coughing in the bitter air. The need for shelter had delayed them by almost an hour, and the going was slower than usual with several inches of snow on the trail. By the time they passed the summit of the ridge and descended to the bank of the North Platte, evening had almost come.

The fording of the river was a long and harrowing chore. Once the supply wagons were hauled out on the opposite bank, Martin ordered some of the mules unhitched, and by this method, the frailest travelers were carried over the river. Mama, Zilpah, and the baby were among them, but Patience and Tamar were obliged to haul the family's cart across the North Platte.

"I shall pull," Patience said, "while you push from behind."

Tamar nodded, bracing her arms against the rear of the cart while Patience splashed into the water. She could hear her sister gasp—then Patience uttered a shriek of distress. But she never slowed. The cart surged forward, and Tamar pushed with all her strength, gritting her teeth to keep from crying out as the water soaked through her boots and dragged at her skirt, slashing her legs with a knifelike cold.

She scrabbled for purchase on the slick stones. She could hear Patience sputtering and sobbing—then a gulp and a cough as the water came up to her chest and splashed into her mouth.

"Push!" Patience cried.

Tamar dug in with numb feet, praying for a surge of strength as the freezing water wrapped around her waist. She gave the cart one hard shove. It rocked forward more than she'd intended, and the wood of the bed suddenly vanished below her unfeeling hands. The cart rolled up quickly from the center of the river, but Tamar had already lost her balance. Her arms pinwheeled, beating at the surface of the water for purchase. She toppled forward into the icy current.

Searing cold closed overhead. She heard nothing but a strange, distant gurling and the pop of stone striking stone. Her body thrashed by instinct, fighting the weight of her wet skirt as it dragged her down to the rocky bed. She twisted below the surface, saw a mobile gray light hanging somewhere above, and clawed toward it. The next moment, she burst from the water, roaring desperately for breath even as the current sucked her under once more.

"Save her!" Mama's desperate scream mingled with the churn of the river. "My daughter—save her! She'll be drowned!"

Tamar fell back into the water, fighting, thrashing, but her limbs were growing more useless by the second. And that inexorable cold was all around her now, *in* her, biting down to her bones, filling her marrow with an inverse fire. She must give in; there was no sense in struggling, no use trying to survive. God demanded His sacrifice, and Tamar, like a fool, had placed herself on the altar.

Something seized her by the back of her dress—a hard hand so powerful she thought for a moment it was the Lord Himself dragging her up to Heaven. But she broke the surface, sucked in a desperate breath, and found more hands gripping her wrists and ankles. She had been caught up by four of Martin's men. They kept her head above the water, hauling her to the opposite bank.

They left her lying on the bank and plunged back into the water. Evidently, Tamar wasn't the only one who'd fallen. The moment the men were gone, her family crowded around.

Mama wept as she bent over Tamar. "Thanks be to God, she's alive."

"She won't remain so for long if we don't get her out of these wet clothes," Patience said—still dripping herself.

"Pull her to her feet, John," Zilpah said, "and help her walk. Captain Martin is setting up camp only a few yards away, beyond that stand of pines. We must get our tent up quickly. We can warm her in there."

John pulled Tamar's arm around his neck. She leaned on him heavily as they crept away from the noise and terror of the crossing. A half-seen sunset was fading between the trees, and the air grew colder by the moment. By the time the Loaders had rounded the pines and found the evening's campsite, their clothing had begun to freeze on their bodies. Tamar's skirt was stiff and white with frost. When John let go of her wrist and ducked from beneath her arm, her sleeve made a sound like shattering glass.

The family managed to raise their tent with astonishing speed. While John returned to the river for the other cart, Tamar and Patience were pulled into the tent and stripped of their frozen garments. Mama and Zilpah had both remained dry on the back of a mule. After a brief and urgent consultation with one another, they agreed to remove their underskirts and aprons, wrapping them around Patience and Tamar, who stood blue and shivering in the center of the tent. Finally, Zilpah pushed their half-clothed bodies together and wrapped them in two blankets.

"That's the best we can do for the moment." She eased her sisters to the ground. "Once John returns and finds something dry for himself to wear, I'll have him light the buffalo chips I've kept from the prairie. We can burn the chips in my little tin trail oven. It might do to warm us for the night. And, of course, we shall all sleep under common blankets."

Patience managed to speak through her chattering teeth. "But your husband—"

"We've more pressing concerns than modesty, just now," Zilpah said.

The trail oven proved an effective tent warmer, thanks to the supply of dried dung Zilpah had so carefully preserved on the prairie. The chips smoldered, giving off a foul odor, but they burned as warmly and as long as the best English coal. The tent held enough heat that the soaked clothing, which Zilpah had pinned up along the peak of the canvas, thawed and began to dry. Drops of water fell just past the place where Tamar and Patience were huddled together. Whenever a droplet landed on the tin oven, it hissed and raised a coil of steam.

"You'll have warm, dry clothes again by morning," Mama said. "That's one small blessing we may count."

Just before full dark came, the ration woman visited their tent, doling out their allotment of flour and smoked bones.

"The crossing is finished," she announced. "No one was drowned, thank God, though we had plenty of near misses." She reached into the tent to squeeze Tamar's shoulder. "You aren't alone in your trials, Sister Loader."

"A great relief," Tamar said wryly.

The snow came and went throughout the night. When they woke, they found the mountain valley buried under a white blanket more than a foot deep. The company managed to travel only seven more miles that day before Martin was forced to call an early halt. Too many were falling ill after the terrible crossing of the North Platte. The invalids' wagon was overfilled, and the leaders of the company fell to arguing over what was best done, and who ought to be held responsible.

While the men griped and bickered, Patience and Tamar wandered a short distance from the camp circle, prodding with sticks into drifts of snow, hoping they might uncover a viable stand of greens or a hibernating hive full of honey—anything to supplement their sparse rations.

"We don't know what to look for," Tamar said. "We might be trampling atop all manner of food, and never know it. This isn't like foraging for mushrooms in the wood at Aston Rowant."

"Quiet," Patience said. "I think I've found something. Come and help."

Tamar hurried to her sister's side. Patience was kicking at a knee-deep mound, batting the snowdrift with her stick. She uncovered something wet and dark—a fallen log, Tamar thought at first. Then she saw the stiff spikes of fur, the flattened sag of what had once been an animal's belly. It was a large, dead creature buried by the snow, ribs showing through the ruin of its hide.

"Patience, no!"

"Oh yes," Patience answered grimly. "Meat is meat, out here in the wilderness."

"But it's rotted. The corruption will poison us."

Patience kicked away more of the drift. She uncovered the head of a buffalo calf, its eyes long since picked out by scavengers, its mouth frozen open.

"Beef head soup," she said calmly.

Tamar reeled back, clutching her stomach.

"Once we've got it boiling away in the kettle, we won't be able to tell the difference between this and the head of a freshly killed calf."

Patience was right. Tamar knew it. A good, rich broth and a few hearty pieces of boiled cheek or calf's brain would do them all much good. She swallowed the bile rising in her throat and crouched beside the carcass, then drew the small work knife from her apron pocket, as Patience had done. Together, they cut the head from the frozen body and stripped off the stiff, corrupted skin.

They carried their grim prize back to camp between them, each holding one of the dead creature's ears. Mama, emerging from their tent, gave them a startled look, but she raised no protest—only nodded and set to work on a fire of chips and green wood. Before long, the head was boiling in the kettle and pale fragments of meat were dropping from the skull. Tamar added handfuls of wild sage and juniper needles, hoping to disguise the flavor of decay. By the time their supper was ready, the oily broth still tasted faintly of corruption, but none of the Loaders turned up their noses, drinking down the horrid soup until their bellies protested.

The next morning, they woke to the sound of grief. Across the camp, women wept and children wailed, and men spoke in low, bleak tones over the still bodies of fallen companions. Tamar wondered how many had died in the night. She stared around the miserable camp, trying to count every tent at which the mourners hung their heads. The company must have lost at least a dozen souls. But there would be no digging of graves—not in this frozen ground. The dead must be left for the snows to claim. Or stacked like cordwood on the wagons as their food stores dwindled. The bodies could be carted away. Borne off to some secret place where the living might make some use of their flesh.

Tamar's stomach clenched with hunger, a pang strong enough to sweep away all her wits, all her senses save for that lone sensation, the gnawing emptiness that demanded to be filled. A thought flashed into her mind—quick as a strike of lightning. She discarded the black hunger in disgust and horror the very moment it appeared. But the fact that she had entertained such an abhorrent notion filled her with a deep, shuddering remorse.

I shall never do something so devilish. Never. I'll gladly starve before I'll let the flesh of my fellow man pass my lips.

But even as she swore her oath, her stomach cramped and cried out its ceaseless, gruesome command.

To distract herself from that dreadful fancy, she left her family to pack the supplies and went looking for Captain Martin, hoping to learn what lay ahead. They'd been only twenty days from Zion. Surely their deliverance was still close at hand. A word of encouragement from the captain would give her the strength to go on.

She found Martin near one of the supply wagons, which was filled now with weeping, muttering invalids. He was deep in conversation with the company's scouts. Tamar hung back, waiting her turn to speak.

"How many have we lost overnight?" Martin asked.

"Nineteen, that I know of," a scout answered. "The number may yet rise."

"And our rations?"

"We've twenty days' food left. Nothing more than that."

"We must cut our rations by half, then," Martin said. "Eight ounces of flour per man and woman, four ounces to a child."

Tamar staggered away from the gathering of brothers, one hand pressed to her mouth to hold back a cry of disbelief.

Nineteen dead. And there may still be more.

She stared at the camp as it disassembled in the gray dawn light. Never before had she seen her fellow travelers as she saw them now. Everywhere she looked, men and women were huddled in thin rags, their backs bent, their bodies angular where the bones pressed through. Those whose boots had been worn to nothing by the summer's long walk had tied rags around their feet as some pathetic protection against the biting cold and cutting ice. Some carried children in their arms who'd grown too weak to walk. The poor little ones hung in limp surrender, eyes staring into a cruel white world but seeing nothing, nothing at all. A few people already showed black stains on their cheeks, noses, or fingers—the first marks of frostbite. Everywhere she looked, her fellow travelers moved like souls caught in a nightmare. And the sky was heavy with clouds, the snow almost knee deep. There would be more snow yet to come. Tamar could smell it on the air.

A new chill racked her. It had nothing to do with the cold.

There are hundreds of miles between us and the valley. Shall any of us live to see Zion?

~

The company struggled on for more than a week while the sky bore down with its dark, bitter clouds and relentless snow. They could manage only a few miles each day before storms forced them to stop, and even in the afternoons, the ground was often too frozen to drive in their tent pegs. The pitiful company spread out their tents as best they could, climbing under the canvas, where the weight of snow piled upon their bodies, pressing them down as if into their graves. Each morning when the pioneers climbed from their frigid beds, fresh word went around the camp that more had perished in the night. Tamar had stopped counting the dead when the tally passed 150.

Those who'd succumbed were packed into one of the old supply wagons, for it was empty now of their precious flour and barley. She had seen bodies being carried from the tents to the makeshift morgue. Sometimes the cloth of a ragged trouser or shirt had been torn, and the stiff flesh beneath was pink and raw. Those were no wounds made during life; Tamar could tell at a horrified glance. The edges were neatly sliced as if by a butcher's knife. She swallowed her disgust and tried not to condemn those who had given in to the dark temptation. For those who'd partaken of the damnable rations, Tamar could feel only pity, not scorn. She prayed each night for mercy upon their souls. In the mornings, she looked into the haggard, staring eyes of her fellow pioneers—faces going black from frostbite, bones as sharp and distinct as the words of God—and tried not to wonder who among them had eaten well the night before.

At least most of those who'd sunk into temptation had kept the shame to themselves. One night, Tamar was wakened by the screams of a child—then shouts and curses from a man. She crawled stiffly from her bedroll and peered outside the limp tent. In the pale moonlight, she saw a young father brandishing his rifle as he chased a crouched and huddled figure across the circle of the camp. A woman burst from a tent, holding a child in her arms. The girl was weeping with pain and terror, and the mother shouted, "That beast came into our tent. I caught him gnawing on my girl's fingers!"

Patience was lingering close by, pressed against Tamar's shoulder.

"Why wouldn't he have gone to the supply wagon?" Tamar said quietly. "There are a few pounds of flour left. Why try to . . . try to eat . . ." She couldn't force out another word.

"Perhaps his mind has broken," Patience whispered. "Broken for good."

The man with the gun pursued the hunched creature beyond the ring of tents, out into the forest. As the fleeing figure left the camp, he glanced back over his shoulder. Tamar caught his eye—and shuddered. Patience had the right of it. Those eyes were wild and staring, all spark of humanity gone.

"For pity's sake, come away from there." Patience pulled her back from the tent's door.

Tamar returned to her blankets. She listened for the report of the rifle, but it didn't come. She never saw the wild man among the company again. She supposed the once-human creature had been driven into the wilderness to meet his final judgment alone.

On the ninth day after the river crossing, Martin veered off the trail into a cove of steep limestone cliffs. The snow was falling thick and fast, blowing sideways into the pioneers' faces. Within that natural shelter, the wind didn't tear quite so fiercely, yet the snow still fell, reducing the vast white world to a circle of suffering. Within the dismal ring, Tamar was conscious only of her own misery and that of her family—the searing pain of cold that never left her extremities, the stiffness of her limbs, the resigned torpidity of heart and mind.

The travelers tried to raise their tents as best they could while Martin selected a few men to go scouting beyond the mouth of the cove. John was among the chosen, for he'd borne up better than most. By afternoon, he returned to camp with news that he'd found an abandoned fort not far away.

"It's a small affair," he told Tamar. "Only a few shacks and a one-room cabin enclosed by an old stockade. The company passed it on our way into the cove, but I suppose none of us could see it through the snowfall."

The fort was near enough that the sickest and most badly frostbitten could be carried there in handcarts. They would be tended under shelter somewhat better than half-collapsed tents.

"If only the fort were large enough to house us all," Tamar said.

She watched her brother-in-law depart to help with the transportation of the invalids, and added silently, *Some of us might have hope of surviving this hell, if we could find better shelter.*

They had traveled not quite sixty miles from the North Platte River, with hundreds of miles yet to go and the harshest weather still ahead. Winter had thrown open its arms to catch them all in a deadly embrace.

Not even a miracle, not even God Himself can save us now. Tamar accepted the truth with quiet acquiescence—no grief, no sorrow, for grief and sorrow had already grown so great around her that they encompassed all things. She crouched in the darkness of her sagging tent. With stiff red fingers, she fed the last precious fragments of buffalo chips into the tin oven. She told herself: *Patience had the right of it all along. We never should have left London. We were doomed from the start.*

That evening, Martin's bugle sounded thinly across the cove, summoning all who were hale enough to walk. Zilpah made as if to rise, but Tamar stayed her with a hand on her shoulder.

"It's warmer in the tent—though, goodness knows, not by much. Keep Alpha here. You must remain, too, Mama, and help care for the baby."

The poor mite needed more than warmth. Zilpah's milk was beginning to dry. Tamar had heard her sister weeping on their mother's shoulder, pleading with Mama to help her find some way to keep the milk flowing. Alpha was still too young for pap, even if they'd had any pap to feed him.

Patience lay on her side, eyes open but seeing nothing, staring into dim shadows. She made no move to rise. Perhaps she hadn't heard the bugle at all; perhaps, by now, Patience was in a place beyond hearing, a place where suffering couldn't reach her.

Outside, Tamar found that evening had come. The overcast sky had lost the diffuse luminosity of day, and long blue shadows stretched from one wall of the cove to another. The snow had slackened. She could make out more of the encampment now. The tents, half staked, were drooping on their poles. Canvas that had browned with prairie dirt was crusted by snow. Tamar shuddered at her first clear sight of the camp in nine days' time. So few tents remained. The dead must number well above two hundred.

She made her way slowly across slick ground to the wagons, where some half of the remaining pioneers had gathered to hear the captain speak. He'd climbed up to the bed of the nearest Conestoga; he was already addressing the ragged crowd by the time Tamar joined their ranks.

"You've all been marvelously cooperative," Martin said, "with my decision to reduce our rations from one pound of flour to half a pound. I'm grateful for your sense of responsibility to the whole. But as you can see, we find ourselves in a still more difficult situation. We pray for a change in the weather, but we may be stalled here for some days yet. Men who are able to hunt have gone out searching for game, and we've been reduced in numbers somewhat since crossing the river. Yet even if our hunters meet with success, still I fear our rations may not hold out till we reach the valley."

May not? Tamar choked back a bitter laugh.

"We must cut rations again," Martin said. "Four ounces per person, regardless of age."

A murmur of protest went up from the crowd, but it never rose to a clamor. They were all too weak and exhausted for much opposition.

From somewhere to Tamar's left, a man asked, "How much longer must we stay here, Brother Martin?"

"Till the snow stops. We may press on when we can see a mile or more into the distance, but even then, it will be slow going."

A woman cried out, "We can't go on like this!"

"We must turn back," another agreed.

"Peace." Martin lifted his hands. When silence had returned, he said, "I've sent riders ahead. We aren't so very far behind the company that Brother Willie led out of Winter Quarters a few days before we departed. If our riders can catch up with Willie, we may divert some of their supplies for our use. We may—"

"Look!" A man at the far edge of the crowd pointed toward the mouth of the cove. "There comes a rider now!"

They all turned to see a lone figure mounted on a thin, dark mule.

"That must be Joseph Young." Martin waved a hand above his head—an effort that left him panting. "Brother Young! We're here!"

Young was smiling by the time he reached the wagons. He swung down from his saddle and shook Martin's hand with vigor. "I bring good news," he said to the crowd. "My father, President Young, has learned of our plight. He has organized a rescue party, complete with plenty of provisions for every traveler—food, warm clothes, blankets, wood for fires. Best of all, there are wagons enough to carry us all to the valley."

A gasp ran through the crowd—then a ragged cheer.

Brother Young shouted above the din. "We must only press on twenty-five miles more."

"Twenty-five miles?" Tamar said. Her cheeks burned against the cold; she hadn't intended to speak up, but now it seemed she couldn't stop herself. "At the rate we've been traveling, it will take five days to go so far—perhaps more than that. We're weak and hungry, and so many of us are down with frostbite. How can we pull our carts twenty-five miles on four ounces of flour a day?"

"Sister Loader," Young said, "surely you have more faith than that."

Tamar could find no answer. Faith had carried her this far—all the incomprehensible distance from her home, from the man she had loved, from civilization itself. Faith had taken her father away—the kindest, gentlest man that God had ever made, whose only desire had been to build God's kingdom on Earth. Faith had deposited Tamar and what remained of her family in a frigid tomb, and then it had vanished without a trace.

What faith ought any of us to have now, she thought bitterly, *as we watch our loved ones die in the cold as God withholds every mercy?*

But she could say nothing. The most she seemed capable of doing was staring up at Brother Young, hard-eyed and silent with shock.

"We'll pray that God will send us sun to melt away the snow," Martin said. "And with knowledge of our deliverance only a few miles down the trail, we'll eat heartily once more. A pound of flour for every man and woman, and in the morning—"

Tamar never heard the rest of his declaration. She was stalking back across the cove toward her family's tent before she'd even realized she'd turned her back on Brother Martin.

She found Zilpah sleeping with the baby bundled tightly beside her. Mama was stroking her hair. Patience had roused herself somewhat, sitting wrapped in her blankets, but her eyes were as distant and dull as they'd been before. John had gone out with the hunting party and hadn't yet returned; it fell to Tamar to pass along Martin's news, and Brother Young's, as well. She would rather have kept it to herself, for surely there could be no hope that the company could reach the rescue wagons. Yet soon the story would be circling the camp. That fragile, futile hope would kindle like fires in the dark, and the family would only take Tamar to task for having kept the news to herself.

"But I don't believe we'll make it twenty-five miles," she said after she'd done her duty and shared the tale. "The snows are here to stay. We've had no relief in more than a week. The weather will only grow colder as we ascend the mountains. Our best hope—if we've any left at all—is to stay put and pray the rescuers will find their way to us."

"Tamar is right." Patience spoke in a low, monotonous tone. "There's no point in going on. Whether we go or whether we remain— we're dead, either way. All that's left is to bury us."

Mama stared at her for a long moment, lips trembling. Her hand had stilled on Zilpah's hair. "Thank God your sister is asleep. I shouldn't like for her to hear you talking that way."

Patience only sighed in answer.

"You say we'll be given a pound of flour each?" Mama went on. "Then Zilpah must have as much as she can eat. That will keep her milk flowing awhile longer. The rest of us will eat only a little."

By nightfall, John had returned empty-handed, and Tamar fell into a mercifully dreamless sleep. She woke to a feeling of certainty deep in her chest—not a knowledge that all would be well but rather a determination to speak to her sister, to tell Patience that she'd been right all along. The warnings she'd given in Iowa City should have been heeded from the start. God had outfitted Patience with sense a good cut above the common, and yet the people she loved most had spurned her—casting her admonitions aside, like Cassandra in days of old.

She lay on her bedroll, staring at the yellow glow of the tent walls, the cold morning light, while the sounds of the company striking camp went on around her. She tried to marshal her thoughts and the dregs of her strength, tried to organize the words she must say to her sister, but words and thoughts were half-formed things, flitting beyond her grasp, fading into nothing before she could see them clearly.

"Tamar. *Tamar!*"

Mama spoke with such urgency that Tamar bolted upright on her bedroll. Her head was swimming from hunger, but she stared in alarm around the confines of the tent. Zilpah and John were still curled in their blankets, and beyond them, Mama had sat up, too. She was clutching her blankets to her chin as if they were a shield against some unseen attacker.

"What is it, Mama?"

"Patience is gone!"

Tamar scrambled from the tent, into the blue glare of morning. She turned in a slow circle, staring around the forlorn ring of the encampment, searching for her sister's pale form. The sky had cleared overnight. Now it hung above the cove in a curious, intense blue—the blue of a painted vase dropped and falling, a brittle, shattering color. A sob rose in her chest. Her sister was nowhere to be seen.

She has wandered into the trees, Tamar realized with a sinking sickness. That was the way so many had died since the snows had come. They left their tents in the middle of the night and walked out into the wilderness as if summoned by some terrible, compelling voice. They went out alone to place themselves in death's cold hands while their loved ones slept on, unaware.

Or she met with that wild man in the forest—the one who tried to eat a child while she had yet lived.

"A beautiful day, Sister Loader," someone called. Tamar didn't see who, nor did she care. "Our prayers have been answered. Feel that sun! We'll reach the rescue wagons for certain, now."

"My sister," Tamar cried. "Have you seen her? Where is she?"

Someone took her by the shoulders. "Easy, now. What's all this weeping for?"

Tamar blinked and scrubbed at her eyes. It was Brother Cluff who held her—the former leader of the company.

Before she could make a reply, Cluff said, "Best get your family packed and ready to move on. We'll make good time in the sunshine."

"We must stay," Tamar said vaguely, glancing beyond his shoulder, searching for any sign of Patience.

"Nonsense. Handcarts are more maneuverable than the rescue wagons, especially in snow."

"We mustn't leave!" Tamar tore herself from his grip. "Patience! Where can she be?"

She spun away from Cluff, stumbling over compacted snow, making for the dense forest of pines that ringed the edge of the cove. Patience was in those trees, surely. She was already gone, blue and still, but Tamar would find her. She would tell Patience that she'd been right all along, that this had been one great, unforgivable folly—even if she must say it to her sister's lifeless body.

"Patience!" The name came tearing from her throat as she struggled toward the dark line of the wood. Her eyes were blurred by tears, but she could make out that dark band of shadow, and she drove toward its waiting darkness, determined to find her sister, to stay beside her body until death came for them both.

Just as the pines closed overhead, Tamar heard her name—then a pair of thin, strong arms wrapped around her, pulling her tight against a familiar bosom.

"Come now, Tamar. There's nothing to fear."

She reeled back and stared into her sister's face. Patience was gazing beyond her, into the depths of the camp and the brilliant, sun-struck day. Her face had lost all its sallowness; her cheeks were flushed now, rosy with excitement. And though her eyes were as sunken and dark-ringed as anyone's, they burned with a fire of inspiration.

Tamar took her hands. Then she patted her way up Patience's arms to her shoulders, then to her face. This was no vision, no angel. Patience was alive and standing before her.

"Thanks be to God," Patience said, still watching the camp with a rapturous expression. "I have had a vision."

"You've . . . what?"

Now, at last, Patience met her eye. She smiled, reassuring and warm. "I met a man in the wood. I'd gone into the trees to . . . I don't know why, now. I simply knew that I must go. I was walking alone as the sun came up, and the light was falling down through the treetops. And there before me stood a man."

"One of the brothers," Tamar said.

"No. He hadn't come from the camp. He simply appeared before me—one moment there were only trees, and the next, he was standing in a great shaft of golden light, watching me and smiling. He didn't look a thing like the men of the company. He wasn't thin and suffering, nor was he dressed as we dress. He wore a robe of white."

Tamar watched her sister in silence, recalling her own vision on the schooner—the man's face emerging from the flames, his peaceful countenance, his gentle assurance.

"He asked if I were Patience Loader, and I told him I was. He nodded, and said, 'I thought it was you. Travel on; there is plenty ahead.' Then he turned and walked away. But I saw that his feet never sank into the snow, nor did he leave any prints. He was like Jesus." Tears had gathered in her eyes. "Walking on the water. Oh, Tamar, you were right. You were right all along. A thousand times, I thought you and Papa were too foolish for words, but it was I who was a fool. It was I who did not see. I understand now. I see it all so clearly."

She took Tamar's hand, began striding eagerly toward the camp and the handcarts. Tamar stumbled as she tried to keep pace, flailing through the deep snow.

"We must go on," Patience said. "We must build the Kingdom of Zion."

10

JANE

Centerville
Autumn 1856

Once she had stoked the fire and seen that the tinderbox held enough dry wood to last the day, Jane dragged the old, padded chair from its place beside the window to the hearth. She set Sarah Ann's sewing basket near the chair and draped one of the small lap quilts her sister had made across its arm.

"There." Jane brushed her palms together. "Now you can stay put where it's nice and warm till I come home."

"I don't want to stay by the fire. And I don't want to sew. Sewing is dull."

"Nonsense; you make beautiful quilts. Why, I guess yours are the prettiest blankets in the whole valley."

Sarah Ann took a hesitant step toward the hearth. "Truly?"

"Of course it's true. Come spring, we might sell your quilts in town. Maybe we'll make enough money to buy a carriage—and a horse, instead of a mule. Wouldn't that be fine?"

"I'll need more cloth soon, if I'm to make more quilts. I've nearly run out of Elijah's old shirts." Sarah Ann sat, and the shabby chair gave an alarming groan, even under her slight weight. She tucked the lap quilt around her legs. "More thread, too."

"I'll buy more thread for you today at Smoot's." Jane had enough pennies for a spool or two, though she had precious little money for anything else. She bent over Sarah Ann, knotting their mother's old shawl more tightly below the girl's chin. "Remember not to stir from this spot, unless it's to put another stick of wood on the fire."

Sarah Ann's eyes glinted with mischief. "What if I have to answer the call?"

"Use the chamber pot. You mustn't go to the outhouse. It's too cold today."

"And if I'm hungry? Can I stir from this spot if I'm hungry?"

"There are biscuits in the tin," Jane answered, busying herself with her own shawl and the fur-lined deerstalker hat she'd found in Elijah's trunk. "There's cheese in the pantry, too. And remember, at midday, you must—"

"Drink my tea," Sarah Ann said. "I know, Janey."

Tabitha's herbal treatment seemed to have reached the peak of its abilities. Sarah Ann was no longer improving—still small as a mouse and thinner than a rail, and whenever Jane touched her sister, she was half afraid the girl might snap like a twig. All the same, Sarah Ann had gotten no worse in the two weeks since she'd first started drinking the remedy. The two weeks since Elijah had died.

Jane left a kiss on her sister's cheek, then stepped out into the fierce cold of a late-October morning. The light lay pale and low across the fields Elijah had cleared. The snow was unmarked down the curve of the slope, except by a few small blue depressions—the hoofprints of deer and the fanned-out marks where owls had dropped down to snatch the small creatures that scurried under the snow.

When springtime came, the field would beg to be planted with wheat or oats. Jane knew she might make a good profit from the sale of the grain—if she could manage the field. That seemed out of the question. She had neither time nor skill to plant and maintain acres of wheat. She could tell already that caring for her small garden would eat up the better part of her strength—and the garden would produce just enough food to keep herself and Sarah Ann alive for another year.

The cold bit into her lungs and needled her exposed skin. She followed the path her own feet had made to the stock shed and the soiled, trampled corral. Halfway there, her face turned as it always did, eyes fixing on the double image of the dark wooden cross just beyond the sleeping garden. Jane never could come within sight of Elijah's grave without staring—without remembering the day he'd died.

Almost as soon as she'd had him under the ground, Jane had raided the cabin for any money or valuables her stepfather had left. She'd found a few things worth selling—an old pocket watch on a brass chain. His work boots, which were far too big for Jane's feet. She'd sorted through the rest of his tools, keeping only what would serve her around the meager little homestead. Everything else, she'd taken to the Centerville market. Within a couple of weeks, the last of Elijah's possessions had been converted to banknotes and more of those miraculous gold coins.

Jane had guarded her small cache of money, dipping in only when necessity demanded. But even before October was out, she had realized she must find work in town. And since she would be forced to work, the apprenticeship to Tabitha was out of the question. Jane had let that dream go with a sigh—but only one. Her mind was made up. She would work to support herself and her sister, and be grateful she had the chance to earn a little pay. She wouldn't mourn the future she once dreamed of. Those had only been dreams, after all. This life was the stark reality.

Jane rode the old black mule to Centerville, pushing her mount as quickly as she dared up the slick road till she reached the red shop front of Smoot's Mercantile. There, she slid from the mule's back and led him to the rear of the building. Smoot kept a small corral in the alley, along with a lean-to for housing the animals of his customers who were forced to ride many miles from far-flung settlements.

Jane turned the mule loose in the corral. Just as she was closing the gate, Smoot leaned from the rear door of his shop, bald head flushing as red as the painted clapboard.

"You're late again, young lady."

"I'm sorry, Mr. Smoot. The road was slicker today than usual. I had to go slow—"

"Don't stand there talking about it," he barked. "Get a jump on, you lazy girl."

Jane hung her fur hat on a peg beside the back door and set to work with her usual focus. Smoot was never stingy with his firewood, so the stove had filled the shop with a pleasant warmth. Her fingers began to thaw while she sorted and tallied the goods that yesterday's customers had brought for trade. There were well-cured winter squashes, bushels of dried corn and beans, even nails and simple tools made by the local smiths. She pried open a crate to reveal kiln-fired pots and dishes packed in layers of straw, all made from the distinctive white and bluish-gray clays of the valley. Another smaller box contained a dozen glass jars, full to their bale lids with the fragrant seeds of anise, fennel, and black nigella—local substitutes for more exotic spices like cinnamon and pepper, which one could find in abundance east of the Missouri River but only rarely in Deseret.

Jane had heard visitors to the shop discussing Brigham Young's plans to build a rail line that would connect Salt Lake City to the Missouri. Not only would a railway make it far easier for new church members to reach the valley, but it would bring a full range of goods for local merchants to sell. No longer would the Mormons be forced to make do with whatever they could produce by their own labor. Spices, steel, china, molasses, factory-woven cloth—the countless luxuries of civilization would finally be theirs.

Maybe we can take a train back to the Missouri River, Jane mused, *Sarah Ann and I. We can leave this rotten place behind, get to a real city where I've got more prospects, where there are doctors and proper medicine for Sarah Ann.*

Or maybe the railway would run right through the valley, farther west to California. Then she and Sarah Ann could finally reach the land their parents had dreamed of, and with no more trouble than how do you do. She thought of California while she worked—the hills sparkling with gold, the valleys sweet with orchards and vines.

The bell on the front door rang, snuffing out her bright fantasy. When she looked up from the crates of pottery, Jane found midday light flaring on the frosted windowpanes, casting a bright halo around the man who'd entered. His tall, broad body was a dark silhouette, his face obscured by the brilliance outside.

"Well," Smoot said, coming out from his back room, "if it isn't Brother Ricks. It's an honor to see you, sir."

The man gave a small, bashful laugh. "You talk as if I'm some kind of hero, Brother Smoot."

"I know a respectable fellow when I see him. You've been called down to the city often, Brother—we've all noticed, here in Centerville, and we're all right proud that one of our own is so esteemed by President Young."

"You don't know the half of it," the man said wryly. "You've heard about the rescue party President Young sent into the mountains, I guess."

Smoot's voice took on a grim reverence. "Those poor souls, stranded and suffering in the snow. My wife and I have been blessed to contribute to the rescue effort. We sent along several smoked hams and a few bushels of wheat. I only wish we could have spared more."

"I'm to ride out in five days' time," the man said. "Brigham has charged me with leading the party back to the valley." He didn't sound pleased about it.

"What an honor! You'll distinguish yourself yet again. You've already given Centerville a right good name in the president's eyes, but it seems Brigham isn't done with you yet."

"It seems he's not," the man answered. "It'll be hard work, and urgent. All those desperate people, sick and suffering with the cold, most of them half dead already. I wonder that Brigham hasn't found a worthier man to lead the party home."

Smoot pounded him genially on the back. "There's no worthier man in all of Deseret. You're humble, Tom, as befits a man of God—but you oughtn't to be *too* humble. Take a little of your well-earned praise and believe that Brigham knows what he's about. The president and Prophet wouldn't misplace his trust—not with the Almighty to guide him."

Tom Ricks. Why did that name prick at Jane's memory?

At first, she thought she must have heard the man's name in connection with Tabitha. Perhaps he was the healer's husband, whom Jane had never met—the sheriff who was often called away to settle disputes across the valley. But this man sounded too young to be a sheriff, and anyhow, the surname didn't signify. Centerville was filled with folk who shared last names—Smoots and Allreds, Jepsons and Kimballs and Rickses. This man might just as easily be brother-in-law or cousin to Tabitha.

Then she recalled the summer and Elijah's first crop of wheat. The rider who'd appeared at the edge of the garden on the tall, chestnut horse. The man who'd outraged Jane by insisting he would marry her someday.

She flinched back, hiding behind a freestanding display of pantry goods. Jars of honey stood along the upper shelf in orderly ranks. She peered between the amber vessels, moving carefully to keep the display between herself and Tom Ricks as he approached the counter. It was the same man. Even with her double vision, Jane recognized his broad face, the strong cheekbones, the narrow blue eyes and dark beard.

"Before I head into the mountains," Tom said, "I've got another errand on Brigham's orders. I wonder if you've got any plows in stock."

Smoot was startled. "Plows, in autumn?"

"Anything made of steel, really. Brigham has sent me out to buy up all the steel I can find and send it along to the smiths of the valley. We'll be fashioning what we need for the summer and fall—knives, swords, bayonets."

"Merciful Heaven," Smoot said. "You can't mean—"

"I'm afraid so. Letters have arrived in the city, bearing the news we've feared. James Buchanan has won the presidency, and Brigham thinks it likely he'll send the army marching on Deseret."

"Surely it won't come to battle," Smoot said. "We're so awfully far from Washington. How can Buchanan think it worthwhile?"

Tom made a small huffing sound. It might have been a laugh. "The way I see it, Buchanan has put his own back against a wall. He's worked so hard to convince all those back East Gentiles that the Principle is akin to slavery, and now our ways have become a matter of states' rights. He has put our church directly in the way of a compromise between North and South—a compromise that might avert civil war."

The Principle? Jane thought. *What on earth does he mean?*

"We never asked to stand between North and South," Smoot said darkly. "We've taken ourselves all the way to the back of beyond—to a desert, no less, with a lake of brine, not even fresh water! All so we might live beyond the reach of federal laws and meddling senators. And now look: we're dragged against our druthers into this abolition mess! Pshaw. That's what I say."

"I don't claim to know God's purpose," Tom said. "All I know is that this must be a part of His plan. The United States has been dancing along the edge of civil war for years now. If God wishes the Mormon people and our Principle to determine whether America goes toppling over that cliff, then so be it."

"Careful now," Smoot said quietly. "My shopgirl is about somewhere. We must be careful how we talk. I don't know who in this town knows about the . . . the *doctrine* . . . and who doesn't."

Jane willed herself to perfect stillness, scarcely daring to breathe. She hadn't the least idea what doctrine the men were discussing, but it held no interest for her in any case. She was much more concerned about being caught eavesdropping. Smoot would turn her out for certain if he knew she was listening in on men's talk.

After a moment, Smoot said, "Still as the grave. Jane must have slipped outside."

"Buchanan will have to come and stamp out the Principle with his own boot," Tom said, resuming his tirade, "but he won't find it as easy as he supposes. Brigham has already resurrected the Nauvoo Legion."

Smoot whistled softly through his teeth. "Our old militia, back together again. Now that's a sign of the times."

"The Legion may not have to face the army after all—so I pray. But we'll be ready if the time comes. Brigham and his best are already assembling troops and drilling men. Might be, that's why I've been picked to lead the stranded handcart party home. No one else could be spared. But till I ride for the mountains, I've been tasked with scouring the northern end of the valley for every scrap of metal that can be spared. You'll tell me if anyone brings in good tools for trading, won't you? Brigham has given me plenty of money to pay a fair price."

"You can bet I'll tell you," Smoot said. "I'll do my part to support the Legion. Every man in Centerville will do the same."

Jane huddled behind the shelves while Tom said his farewell. Grimly, she resolved to pray as hard as any Mormon that no real conflict would arise between the Nauvoo Legion and the United States. She had a heavy enough burden as matters stood now. The last thing she needed was war erupting all around her.

She did need Tom's money, though. She recalled Elijah's plow, safely stored in the shed behind the cabin. The steel colters were in fine condition.

When Mr. Smoot had returned to his stock room, Jane dodged across the shop and out the back door. The cold assailed her with its usual force, for she'd forgotten her hat, but she hurried through the alley and around the corner of the building, almost colliding with Tom Ricks as he made his way north along Main Street.

"Beg your pardon, miss," he said, touching the brim of his hat.

Jane looked up at him, making no attempt to hide her eyes. "I heard you asking after a plow."

"Well, if it isn't little Jane Shaw."

"Jane Shupe," she said with icy emphasis.

"You've grown up, I'd say."

"What else ought I to have done with my time?"

That took the smart remarks right out of his mouth. He gave an apologetic smile.

"I've got a plow to sell," she said. "I'll let it go cheap. Ten dollars. You can have it anytime you like—tonight, if you please—but you must come and pick it up. I can't bring it downhill to you."

"I'm much obliged, Sister Shaw—pardon, Sister Shupe." He paused, eyeing her more sharply. "Wait a minute, now. Wouldn't it be your stepdaddy's plow? I don't imagine he'd be glad to hear you're making deals over his equipment."

"My stepfather is dead."

Something softened in his eyes. The spark of amusement faded to a deep, hollow sadness. "There's been too much death among our people of late. You poor thing. I suppose you went and got yourself a position with Smoot, is that it?"

Jane nodded.

"Don't say another word. Get back inside before old Smoot notices you're gone. I'll bring the sleigh up to your place tonight about an hour after sunset. How does that sound?"

True to his word, Tom arrived in the shank of the evening, just as Jane and Sarah Ann finished their supper of bean stew and hard biscuits. The sky was still a deep indigo when Tom came sweeping up the hill. Twin lanterns swung from the sleigh's curved footboard, casting a globe of yellow light against the gathering dark.

Jane welcomed him inside and offered to fix him a cup of herbal tea to warm his bones. It seemed the only polite thing she could do, and instinct told her that hospitality would put Tom's ten dollars in her pocket faster than any of her usual displays of vinegar.

He accepted the tea graciously and sat sipping at the table while Jane washed the supper dishes in a pail. He looked around the cabin with its stark emptiness, frowning unless he chanced to meet Jane's eye—and then he gave her a pitying smile that was almost timid.

She wanted to growl at him, *Haven't I done well enough, considering my circumstances?* But it wouldn't do to put the man on his back foot.

Sarah Ann was thrilled to have company. No one had come to the cabin for months, and even then, the visitors had only been men seeking to buy Elijah's grain. She chattered to Tom, asking him questions about the town, about his sleigh and the tall red horse that pulled it. Then she took out her sewing basket to show him her patchwork.

"Aren't you a busy bee," he said, holding one of her neatly stitched squares up to the candlelight. "And what a fine hand you've got for needlework. I don't think I've seen the like in all the valley."

Sarah Ann stared at him for a long moment. Finally, she said, "Janey says so all the time, but I reckoned she was only being nice."

"You ought to enter one of your quilts in the fair next autumn," Tom said. "I guess you have as good a chance as anyone at winning the top prize."

After Sarah Ann had packed her squares away, Jane put the candle inside its glass and led Tom through the deep-blue night. In the stillness of the shed, the plow stood ready for his inspection, but he only looked at Jane with a troubled frown.

"I don't mean to intrude," he said, "but your sister is . . . a sickly little girl."

Jane drew herself up. "I take good care of her. Haven't I kept her fed and clothed all on my own since Elijah died?"

"Now, Sister Shupe, don't take me wrong. You've faced some trying times, no doubt. You've done an admirable job of caring for your sister. But she looks so frail."

"There's naught to be done about it," Jane said rather coldly, "except for us both to carry on. Now, Mr. Ricks, will you buy my plow, or not? I could use the money, for Sarah Ann's sake."

He did buy the plow—paid Jane ten dollars in gold coin from Brigham Young's treasury, then added five more in paper banknotes, which he took from his own pocket. Jane shook her head, but Tom tutted and folded the bills in her hand.

"Charity is my duty," he said. "My service to the Lord."

She couldn't look at him. She didn't want him to see the shame in her face, nor the elation. "Thank you for your generosity. I see you are a true Christian man."

"You didn't think so once." He sounded amused. "I seem to recall the words 'and no mud left to make another.'"

Jane was glad for candlelight—too dim and dancing for Tom to make out the flush along her cheeks. "Do you need help wrestling this plow into the back of your sleigh?"

"I think not. I can manage. You get that child into bed where she can't catch a chill. I'll see you by and by, Sister Shupe."

Jane didn't see Tom Ricks again until three days later. He entered Smoot's Mercantile while she was busy behind the counter. She'd been filling small paper cones with ground cumin and mustard seed for Mrs. Allred, who was drumming her fingers impatiently on the rim of her shopping basket.

Smoot called from the back room, "Good to see you again, Tom. Have you come in to ask after more steel? I think there have been a few small tools, brought by for trade."

"In truth, Brother Smoot, I've come to speak with Jane."

Startled and gripped by a sudden blush, Jane turned her face to align her eyes. Tom had removed his hat and was clutching it against his heart—a gesture of apology.

Jane lowered her face again, tying the spice cones with twine as quickly as she could manage. She didn't want to spill their contents across the counter, which would only try Mrs. Allred's patience even more. Jane tallied the prices and marked the sum in Smoot's account book, then said to Mrs. Allred, "Come again."

When the shop was empty save for Tom and herself, Jane stepped out from behind the counter and approached the man, her stomach tight with apprehension. "Has something gone wrong with the plow?"

"No, not that. I've been thinking for days about your little sister."

Whatever Jane had expected, it hadn't been this. She could do nothing for a long moment except stare up at Tom. His eyes flicked toward the curtained partition that separated the back room from the shop itself, but Smoot was still absorbed in his own affairs.

Finally, she managed, "Why should you think about my sister at all, sir?"

"I've been unable to get the poor girl out of my head."

"Poor girl?"

"Please don't take offense; I mean you none, I swear. Jane, there's something dreadfully wrong with your sister. She's far too small for her age, and anyone can see how thin and weak she is."

"We haven't much," Jane said icily, "but we do have enough to get by. I don't starve my sister, sir."

On the contrary, Jane often ate less than she wanted so that Sarah Ann could fill her stomach. And she struggled and fretted over the garden, adjusting her panes of glass to grow the dark greens Tabitha had prescribed. Jane contented herself with the pickings on a bone while Sarah Ann ate the full portion; she begrudged her sister nothing.

She knew Tom's dreadful suspicion was correct, though. Sarah Ann was too small and weedy for her thirteen years. Even with Tabitha's remedy, there were days when the girl could hardly walk to the outhouse and back without losing her breath.

"No one can care for a child as tenderly as you've cared for Sarah Ann," Tom said. "Look at you now—working as a shopgirl instead of playing or sewing pretty dresses or going to dances, as any girl your age ought to do. All for your sister's sake."

Jane scowled. She could feel his point still unmade, pressing like a needle into her gut.

"I can't stand to see anyone suffer while I do nothing to help," Tom added. "I mean that for Sarah Ann and for you. Haven't you worked hard enough?"

"I don't follow your meaning."

"If you'll allow me to take your sister into my home for proper care—"

Jane sucked in a hard, cold breath. The force of it was like a fist in her chest, pounding against her ribs. "Into your home?"

"Let me explain—"

"You want to take my sister away from me!"

She was dimly aware that her voice had risen—she was on the verge of shrieking at the man. She tried in vain to marshal her wits, but outrage and fear, a two-headed beast, had stirred to life inside.

"You don't understand."

"I understand plenty, Tom Ricks! I see how you're trying to separate us. And I won't stand for it, do you hear? You can't take my sister away from me! Not you nor anyone else!"

"Here, what's all this?" Mr. Smoot had appeared from the back room. He glowered over the counter. "This is one of Brigham Young's most trusted men, and you think to treat him with such disrespect?

Shouting and carrying on like a wildcat in a sack? I won't have it, Jane. You march yourself home and don't bother coming back to my shop. Such impropriety as I've never seen in all my days! You're dismissed!"

There was no more air in the room, no strength in Jane's body to draw it in. She stared at Smoot while her heart thundered in her ears. Then she spun on her heel and ran for the shop's front door.

"Wait, Brother Smoot," she heard Tom saying, "don't be so hasty—"

Then Jane was outside, slipping and skidding on the compacted snow, hurrying for the alley and her old black mule. She had the mule bridled and was already up on its back before she realized she'd left her fur hat inside, hanging on the peg beside the door. It was the only warm hat she owned, but she couldn't go back inside. Not now, not after what Smoot had said.

Jane kicked her mule into a fast walk. As she swung out onto Main Street, Tom emerged from the shop, holding up his hands in entreaty.

I'll certainly never speak to you again, Jane thought viciously. *You fool of a man, you intruder, you thief in the night!*

The mule shouldered right past the great hero of Brigham Young's esteem. Tom was forced to step back. She caught a glimpse of his face as she passed. His mouth was half open, his eyes wide and dazed—a stricken expression. A guilty look.

She didn't say a word to him as she fled Centerville. She wouldn't speak to him again, not if he were the last man on Earth.

11

TAMAR

The Mormon Trail
November 1856

The clear day made travel easier than it had been since Martin's company had crossed the North Platte, for after ten days of wind and snow, even autumn's marginal sunshine warmed limbs and bodies that had grown stiff from cold. The company managed twelve miles that day before evening forced them to halt in a grove of white-shrouded pines.

"A better distance than we've covered in recent days," Patience said—relentlessly optimistic, forcefully determined. She'd been a changed woman since her encounter with the robed man in the forest.

Tamar pounded in the tent stakes with quivering arms and made no reply. Twelve miles was a better distance, to be sure, yet they had covered only half the stretch of trail that lay between themselves and salvation. Anything could befall their company in the meantime. The storm might return, with a greater fury than before. Some hostile tribe might descend on the weakened party. And hour after hour, more people found themselves crippled by frostbite and other injuries. Some dropped to their knees between the shafts of their carts, too weak to go on. The two invalids' wagons would soon be overfull. If there weren't enough faithful who could stand on their feet, let alone pull the hand-carts, then twelve miles might as well be twelve thousand.

She slept, though she never felt herself sliding down into that hollow pit, the merciful unawareness from which too many never returned. One moment, she was conscious of the challenge she had thrown so casually into the face of the Almighty. The next, she opened her eyes and the tent was gone—its cold, constricting walls, the dense, fetid smell of nighttime breath.

Tamar found herself in a brightly lit room. The walls were white, but touched by morning sun, softly golden and eager at the window. Everything she saw was warm, feathered around its edges by a mellow glow.

She recognized the place. It was her bedroom at the cottage in Aston Rowant. She was lying in the old bed, a deep feather tick that cradled like her mother's arms. She turned her face on the pillow, looking at the familiar washstand with its Tyrol pitcher and basin. Through the window, she could hear bees humming among the lavender. She inhaled the gentle perfume of her father's garden.

"Sweetheart."

Suddenly Edward was there, standing at the foot of the bed, smiling as only a husband may do when his wife is half undressed beneath the bedclothes.

"It never happened, then," Tamar said. "The ship, and New York. The journey with the handcarts. And Papa—poor Papa out there on the plains."

She sat up, letting the quilts fall away so Edward could see her in her nightdress, the delicate ruffled collar and the rose-pink ribbons of silk, the lace bodice that revealed as much as it hid.

Thank God, it had all been some dreadful nightmare. They hadn't lost Aston Rowant; Tamar was in the cottage now, waking from a dream, and home was as real as it had ever been. She had lost nothing. Edward was there before her. Edward—her husband.

She blinked, rubbed her eyes with a stiff, cold knuckle. Edward had doubled somehow. One moment, she'd been looking at him alone—his easy, reassuring smile, his debonair manner—and the next, there were two of him standing at the foot of the bed.

One of those figures changed with startling speed, in the space between one heartbeat and the next. He was no longer Edward but a different fellow—a stranger, some years older than Tamar yet still rather young. He was tall, broad of shoulder, with a wide face and hard cheekbones, a round, coarse nose. His mouth was hidden behind a heavy beard, but Tamar had the impression that he was smiling with Edward's same familiarity. A husband's smile. The stranger's eyes were narrow and pale, a sharp blue-gray. Ice gray.

"Who are you?" Tamar demanded, pulling the blankets up to cover her shame.

She tore her gaze from the strange man, looked at Edward for some reassurance. Edward was still smiling, but now he was looking through Tamar, or beyond her, into a great and uncrossable distance.

"Who is this? Edward, answer me. Who is that man beside you?"

The light on Edward's shoulder, on the side of his face, blurred and warmed. The edges of his body dissipated. He was a mist now, fading, fading.

She cried out in alarm, reaching for him.

But it was the stranger who raised his hand in response. The tips of his fingers brushed Tamar's. A fire ran up her arm, into her pounding heart.

She jolted awake and found herself sitting up on her bedroll.

"Are you well?" Patience had already risen, and was crouching on her knees, folding her quilts. The pale light of morning was shining through the peak of the tent.

Tamar looked around the shelter. The rest of the family had already gone.

"Where is Mama?" Tamar said.

"Cooking up what little remains of our flour ration. Thin gruel again for breakfast."

There was no more sarcastic sting to her words. The vision in the wood had solidified her resolve, and now Patience had donned cheerful acceptance like some warm and brilliant cloak.

Tamar threw aside her blankets, scrambling toward the flap of their tent. "I must speak with Mama. It can't wait."

She found her mother and Zilpah beside their handcart, stirring the family's pot. From a few damp sticks of wood, they had coaxed just enough flame that the gruel barely steamed in the morning air.

When Mama looked up and found Tamar approaching, she straightened from the paltry fire. "Merciful Heaven. What has upset you so?"

"I've seen him."

Tamar was quaking like an autumn leaf, and not only from the exertion of leaping up on a long-empty stomach.

"God sent me a comfort and a knowing," she babbled. "He might have punished me for my doubts, but instead, He sent me a knowing— I know now, Mama; I *know*!"

Zilpah stared at Tamar with concern bordering on fear. "Patience," she called, "what is she talking about? Can you make any sense of this?"

"None whatsoever," Patience said calmly. "You had better slow down, Tamar, and tell us what you saw."

"My husband," Tamar answered at once. "Edward was there, and he smiled at me, but then he vanished, and only the other man remained. He touched my hand."

She lifted her right hand, looking at the snow-chapped fingers with wonder. She could still feel the fire of his touch. It was burning all through her soul.

"So you had a dream about a handsome fellow," Zilpah said dryly. "It's a wonder you've any strength for such fancies, given our state."

"He wasn't handsome. At least, not very. And this was no fancy, nor was it a dream. It was a vision, I tell you—a sign from God. I doubted, but I doubt no more." She took Patience by the arm, pulling her close. "We didn't come all this great distance in vain. Everything we've suffered—everything we've lost—"

"I know," Patience said simply. "We're both certain now—Tamar and I."

"That's some small consolation," Mama said quietly, stirring the pot again. "Perhaps someday soon I shall be given to know that this was no folly."

As Tamar had foreseen, the afflicted had nearly doubled in number overnight, and there was a great deal of difficulty with the invalids' wagons. Martin's company was unable to move on until several hours after sunrise. The remnants of the food cache had to be parceled out among some of the handcarts. Tamar felt certain the starving pioneers would help themselves to the communal supply once they were spread out along the trail, free from the supervision of the captain's men. She made up her mind to forgive the inevitable acts of theft before they'd even occurred. Who among that party would have the strength to resist eating whatever food that was placed before him? Anyhow, forgiveness came easily when one had certainty of salvation—for Tamar knew, to the very center of her spirit, that the dream had been a gift from God. A revelation of the man whom she would marry, the promised love that waited for her in Zion.

As she trudged through the snow that morning—feet burning from the cold, body in agony from relentless toil—she thought of the stranger's face. She saw again his placid countenance, the unsurprised awareness with which he had looked upon her. She thought of his touch, and her fingers still recalled the warmth of his skin. Whenever she stumbled and the old commonplace terror gripped her—a flash of panic that she would never rise again, that her bones must be left under the snow while the company plodded on—Tamar remembered that man. She saw his faint smile, scarcely detectable through the tangle of his beard. Then she rose to her feet and carried on, for she couldn't die there. She had seen her husband's face, laced her fingers with his. She must marry that man, whoever he might be—and so she went on walking, dragging the cart through mires of mud, through the endless stretches of cold white valley, closer to Zion step by dogged step.

Just after midday, when the sun was glaring from a comfortless sky, Martin's bugle sounded, and a voice cried down the length of the trail. "Wagons! I see wagons ahead!"

"Can we have reached the rescue party so soon?" Mama asked.

"There were twelve miles at least to travel this morning," John said. "I'd wager we've gone no more than three or four."

The bugle whined again, commanding a halt. Tamar and Patience shared an eager look.

"The rescuers have come to us," Tamar said. "Thank God, we are saved."

The company reassembled in its customary circle along the bank of Greasewood Creek. At the heart of the ring, some twenty wagons stood waiting with fresh, fat mules in the traces. Well-muscled, round-faced men—clearly, no victims of privation—were stacking crates and baskets on the ground beside the wagons while Martin organized the travelers into lines. Everyone was to receive new, warm clothing and food from Brigham Young's storehouses.

Tamar and John helped Zilpah to the ground, where she leaned against her cart's wheel, cradling Alpha against her chest.

"Stay and rest," Tamar said. "John, you remain with Zilpah. Keep her spirits up; she looks too tired and ragged, and it won't do for her to slip away now when deliverance is at hand. Patience, Mama, come with me. We can carry enough supplies for the whole family."

They took their places at the end of a clothing line. The travelers were thin and haggard; they made a startling contrast to the men from the valley, so plump and energetic they seemed almost ethereal, like beings from another world.

We've grown used to the sight of ourselves, Tamar mused, *walking skeletons that we are, scarcely able to stir our bones.*

Yet despite ashen and emaciated bodies, the company's collective spirit soared. They sang as they waited—"Come, Come Ye Saints" and "Hail to the Twelve." Tamar joined in, lifting her voice with elation. She could as soon have stopped her own heart from beating as stopped herself from singing along.

We will onward to the valley,
speed your way, make haste and come;
that, ere long with joy and gladness,
we may bid you welcome home.

The valley men passed woolen clothing and new boots and hard-tack biscuits to the pioneers, looking with pity at blackened fingers and noses, at ruined feet showing through bundles of frozen, bloodstained rags. But the pioneers felt none of their suffering—not now, with sacks of flour heavy in their hands and warm stockings for their children's feet. The blue afternoon seemed to shimmer with laughter, and women moved with the music of grateful prayer.

As Tamar edged closer to the head of her supply line, a rider trotted past the company's outer ring, making straight for the central wagons. She stopped singing as the rider approached, staring at his face with a sudden, peculiar intensity. No conscious thought had crossed her mind. She was merely transfixed by the man as he reined in his tall red horse and swung down from the saddle. He was a giant—taller than anyone present, with shoulders like those of a bull. His dark beard had grayed at the ends—not with age but from the frost of his breath. Despite the effect of the frost, Tamar could see that he was young, little older than herself.

One of the rescuers approached the rider, reaching out a hand to shake. "Brother Ricks. What news from South Pass?"

"Eighty more wagons have arrived," the tall fellow answered. "I saw them with my own eyes. Once we get these folks over to South Pass, there'll be room for everyone to ride in wagons all the way to the valley."

"You were right, then, to press on. We might not have found these poor wretches in time if we hadn't done as you suggested and taken the wagons east. I'll be sure Brigham Young hears about the part you played when we return to the valley."

The rider leaned back comfortably against a wagon wheel, accepting the praise. He folded his arms across his barrel chest with an air of self-satisfaction. Tamar's gaze was still fixed to his face, as if sewn there by an invisible hand. Piece by piece, she assembled the puzzle of the rider—his wide cheekbones, his fat nose, the narrow, pale eyes. She sucked in a startled breath, and an instant later, his casual glance passed over Tamar, moved on . . . then returned to her face with a new, keen attention.

She knew him then. A great thunder of certainty ran through her and left her trembling, left her ears ringing from the blast.

She reached out blindly and found her mother's hand.

"That's him—the one from my vision. That's the man whom I shall marry."

The company crowded into the rescue wagons and rode some ten miles farther to South Pass, where they were assigned to less cramped accommodations for a final journey through the Rocky Mountains to the basin of the Great Salt Lake. It took the better part of a month to traverse the high passes and ferry across rivers winter-fat and November cold, but though the wagons rocked and pitched, it was such a novelty not to walk that Tamar never complained—nor did anyone else in her wagon.

The lengthy ride was even a peculiar kind of blessing, for sometimes she had occasion to speak with the dark-bearded rider when his scouting duties didn't take him too far from the trail. On those days, he would walk his horse easily beside her wagon, and she would lean from the box with one elbow out in the cold, enthralled by his stories, spilling out her own tales of the long journey from Aston Rowant.

Tamar soon learned his name: Thomas Ricks. He'd first gone to the valley nearly ten years before—when, at the age of nineteen, he and his family had fled Nauvoo in the turbulent years just after the death of the first Prophet, Joseph Smith. Thomas called Deseret his home ever since, and assured Tamar that it was a place of surpassing beauty—not only in the grandeur of its fields and mountains, its vast, shining lake, but also in the spirit of fellowship that flowed through all its inhabitants.

"Zion is already a paradise," he said, "as lovely as ever Eden must have been. And yet we'll make it prettier still. The more Saints who gather there, the better we can nurture the land. One day it'll flower like a desert rose, no matter the season."

Like a desert rose. Tamar cherished those words, turning them over in her head whenever Thomas rode far in his scouting duties, or when she lay among her wagon-mates at night, listening to the whisper of their breath and the patter of wind-blown snow against the canvas arch. *Like a rose in the desert.* Something was unfolding inside her, opening tentative petals to a new, unaccustomed warmth.

In the mornings, if by chance she caught Thomas's eye, she would wave to him, and her cheeks would burn with pleasure when he raised a hand in answer or called her name. Patience clicked her tongue, half astonished and half amused at Tamar's boldness. Mama admonished Tamar to remember her manners—they may be rescued souls riding in pioneer wagons, but they were still English ladies, and must recall propriety. Tamar only laughed in reply. Thomas would be her husband someday. No one knew it yet, save for Tamar herself and the God who had promised her a great and lasting love. But the thing was as good as done. She was on the verge of claiming her reward, the treasure she had earned through suffering and sacrifice.

The month faded away. Winter came in earnest—short, sharp days of ice and wind, long black nights when the stars drifted like the flakes of a blizzard. On the last morning of November, the wagons trundled to a final rise and paused at the crest of a ridge.

"There it is," Thomas said, halting his horse beside Tamar's wagon. "The valley—our home."

Tamar craned her neck, struggling to see past the gathered wagons to the holy land beyond. She caught a flash of light on water, a fleeting glimpse of the lake between a Conestoga and its team.

"This won't do," she said. "It won't do at all. I can't see a thing from here."

Tamar made her way to the wagon's rear gate, stepping carefully over the outstretched legs of her family and their traveling companions.

"Where are you going?" Patience demanded.

She made no answer but climbed over the gate, scrambling down the rickety ladder steps to the frozen ground below. Her limbs trembled with the effort. She wondered whether she would ever recover her strength after those long months of destitution on the trail.

Thomas spoke to her, but Tamar didn't answer him, either. She staggered through the milling riders, slipping between the wagons, striving to break free. The gleam of light on water drew her on.

"Here, now—what are you doing, Tamar?"

She glanced around. Thomas was jogging to her side. He reached out as if he thought she might be on the verge of falling.

"You're still too weak to go wandering off alone," he said.

"I'm quite well, Mr. Ricks. I'm hardier than you think, having survived all these months on the trail."

"You are, at that," he answered, quietly amused. "If you insist on walking, then take my arm. I won't have you falling under a wagon wheel."

She hesitated only a moment. She could feel the warmth of his body, smell the wool of his wrappings on the crisp air. Suddenly shy,

Tamar found that she couldn't look into his eyes, but she did slip her hand around his well-muscled arm. He was solid and real, the only certain thing in a world that had for too long seemed all shadow and illusion.

"Take me through this crowd," she said. "I want to see the valley."

They made their way through the company until they stood alone on the blowing ridge. The land fell steeply into a white basin—a broad and bountiful land as safe as the fortress of Heaven. She could see the growing city, the small outer villages clustered on the distant floor like gray patches on a pale quilt, and Salt Lake—a vast sheet of beaten silver—lost itself among the far blue mist of distant mountains.

"You've seen it," Thomas said. "Now let me escort you back to the wagon. You really are too weak for walking; I can feel you shaking."

"When I was stricken on the trail, two of the apostles chanced to find us. They blessed me. They told me I should yet walk into Zion. I don't mean to make a liar of my God."

He made no reply, but Tamar could feel his eyes on her face. Finally, she tore herself away from the sight of that blessed land—her goal, at last; her father's dream made real. She gazed up at her companion. Thomas was watching her with a curious intensity, those keen blue eyes fixed upon her as if he stared at something precious or holy.

"Walk with me," she said. "Go with me into the promised land."

PART II

In Deseret's Sweet, Peaceful Land

1856–1857

12

Tamar

Salt Lake City and Centerville, Utah Territory
Winter 1856–1857

Just after noon, 104 wagons carried the forlorn survivors of the hand-cart companies into the heart of Salt Lake City. The broad streets and right angles made such a contrast to the long months of tangled wilderness that Tamar was quite overwhelmed. After walking halfway down the ridge on Thomas's arm, she'd been satisfied, and had allowed him to lift her back into the wagon. Now she let her head fall into her hands and wept, assailed by a barrage of emotion. The currents of relief, astonishment, awe—and most of all, a great, hollow grief for her father—merged into a single force inside her chest, a flood that could only find its expression in a torrent of tears.

"Look up, Tamar. See the temple."

It was Thomas who spoke. With an effort, she swallowed her sobs and scrubbed her face on a grimy sleeve. She found Thomas riding beside the wagon once more. There was no mistaking his smile, even through the dark thicket of his beard. She looked past him to a great, empty lot strewn with pale blocks of stone. A black rectangular void had been cut into the earth, at least as wide as St. Paul's Cathedral in London, stretching the entire width of the city block.

"It's only a foundation now," he said, "but you can picture it in your head. The tall spires, that pearly stone shining in the sun, right here in the heart of the city. It'll be a sight to behold one day—a fitting monument to the kingdom we're building, a place where all people will pull together, holding all things in common."

The wagons halted in a ten-acre expanse of snow just down the road from the temple's foundation. Crowds had gathered around the edges of the vacant lot, on foot and in buggies, while small flocks of smartly dressed women moved among the people, making notations in the little books they carried, shouting instructions to the assembled city folk.

"Union Square," Thomas said. "Under ordinary circumstances, you newcomers would camp right here till you'd arranged accommodation. But I guess these aren't ordinary circumstances. The snow doesn't make for fit camping, anyhow. The local Relief Society has raised a whole army of volunteers to take you folks in and keep you sheltered through the winter. You see the ladies with notebooks? Those will be your Relief Society leaders. You'll all be in capable hands; you'll want for nothing till you've found your feet and can make your own way. Now I must be off. President Young and his men will want my reports of the trail and the rescue."

Tamar reached for him—though, on his horse, he was too far away for her to take his hand. "Shall I see you again?"

He touched the brim of his hat. "I'd count on that, if I were you."

The Loaders and their wagon-mates clambered down from the bed. A woman in a red felt coat approached. Her breath fogged the air as she muttered over the notebook she carried. The Relief Society woman informed them that the apostle Franklin Richards would house John and Zilpah, while Patience and Mama would be sent to live with one Bishop Thorn.

Zilpah spoke up timidly. "Must our family be separated?"

The woman raised a brow. "I'm afraid there aren't many homes large enough to host entire families, my dear. Once the rescue party met you on the trail, a few riders returned to the city with a list of every soul who departed from Winter Quarters—and everyone who was lost along the way. We've done our best to keep families together, but space is limited, as you may well suppose. However, you needn't worry. No one will prevent you from visiting as often as you like—and, of course, you shall reunite every Sunday at church. And," the woman added rather pointedly, "it's a great honor to be hosted by an apostle and his wife."

Tamar put an arm around Zilpah's shoulders. "You remember Brother Richards. He's one of the men who found us on the trail just before Alpha was born. He blessed me. And Papa. Please," she added to the volunteer, "where shall I stay? My name is Tamar Loader."

The woman scanned her list again. "Ah, here you are. Tamar, you shall be the guest of Thomas Ricks in Centerville."

She drew a sharp breath. Suddenly she felt as if her feet had left the earth, as if she were floating up into the white sky.

"Centerville," Mama exclaimed, "where is that?"

"Only a short jaunt to the north."

"But we can't be parted! I mustn't lose my daughter, too!"

Mama was weeping now. Patience pulled her hastily against her chest, casting a pleading look at Tamar.

There was nothing she could say. It rent her heart to see her mother in distress, and yet to live with Thomas . . . to dwell beneath his roof, a guest in his home, free to know him better, to learn his habits and his ways . . .

This is God's hand at work. If I am to have my long-sought reward, then I must do as the Lord wills.

"Tamar," Patience snapped.

"I . . . I don't wish to interfere with the Relief Society's efforts."

"You might wipe that foolish grin from your face, at the very least."

"I'm sorry." Tamar schooled herself to a more sober expression.

"What did you tell me back in Iowa City?" Patience demanded. "You said we ought not to part, especially after we'd gone so far together and suffered so much. Now we've come farther still, and suffered . . ." Patience seemed to choke on her words. At length, she marshaled her feelings and scolded on. "Yet here you are, champing at the bit to flit off to some unknown town, leaving us alone in a city of strangers."

"It isn't as bad as all that." Tamar patted her mother's back. "We shall still visit one another, shan't we? We must be grateful for the charity we've been given. By and by, we'll come together again. Perhaps it won't even be so long. Perhaps we'll be separated only a few weeks—"

"Surely," Patience broke in, "with our father gone, Bishop Thorn can make room for Tamar under his roof."

"No," Tamar said quickly. "These good people have gone to great trouble to find shelter for so many desperate souls. We must cause them no further difficulty but go wherever we find charity and make no complaint."

The Relief Society woman gave Tamar an approving look.

Tamar took her mother's face in her hands—that dear, warm, pleading face, so thinned and haunted by the trail. "I will be well, Mama. I promise you that. And I shan't be separated from you—not truly."

"But to know that you're so far away, in another town entirely . . . !"

"Have faith. God will put us each where He means for us to be. And I know He will not separate us—not for good, and not for long."

The woman with the notebook called a young girl from the crowd and sent her running to fetch the carriage that would transport Tamar to Centerville—to Thomas's home. Soon the girl was back, flushed and panting. "Follow me, miss, if you please. The carriage is just over yonder."

Tamar bade her family farewell, then set off across the crowded park on the heels of the errand girl. As she turned back to wave at her mother and sisters one last time, she scolded herself to keep the eager smile from her lips. It wouldn't do to let her family see that her heart could bear the separation. They would think her unfeeling. In truth, she had felt a cold stab of apprehension at the thought of separation. But she also knew that God had offered a sacred covenant. The love she yearned for waited only a short carriage ride away.

The errand girl left Tamar beside a rather shabby buggy with a spotted pony in the traces. The pony stamped and lashed its tail while a small figure fussed with its harness. The horse's mistress worked with her back to Tamar, and watching her—hearing her confident, self-assured voice as she spoke to the animal—Tamar was startled out of her lovestruck reverie. The figure before her was dressed in faded madder skirts that reached all the way to the ground—a grown woman's style of dress, yet surely this tiny figure was that of a child, no older than ten or eleven years.

Perhaps here, girls wear long skirts from the time they can walk, she mused.

Then that strange personage turned and peered up from the edge of her bonnet. Despite her diminutive size, she was clearly a woman. Her face was still unlined by age, yet she possessed an unmistakable air of wisdom and long experience—almost of cynicism. She looked upon the world with a self-assurance no giddy girl could affect. Tamar placed her age at twenty-five or -six, more or less of an age with herself.

"You're Tamar Loader?" the small woman said.

"I am."

"Very good. Climb aboard; we can make it back to Centerville before the roast burns."

Once Tamar and the fey little driver were seated side by side, the pony wheeled about and headed smartly down the road. They slipped past the temple's foundation, then the blocks of the city with their neat storefronts and clapboard homes. Salt Lake wasn't as grand or as busy as New York had been. Even Iowa City, though comparable in size, had possessed a greater air of establishment. Yet Salt Lake was a pretty and welcoming place, even in the bleakest part of the year. Smoke rose from stone chimneys; rosy-faced children played in the snowy gardens, calling and waving as the buggy passed. And beyond the pin-straight roads, that impossible expanse of water glittered in the sun.

Tamar settled back on her seat with a long sigh. She hadn't a thing to her name—only the clothes on her back, which were threadbare and stained, hardly worth tearing into rags. Yet now she felt rich as any queen. She had come to the end of a long, sorrowful trail and found herself in a land of order and simplicity, of growth, of joy. A place with a future, where love could flourish.

"You'll be wanting a good bath when we get home," the driver said. "And some proper clothes. None of my old dresses will do for you; I'm much too small. But I've found a few women in Centerville who've been happy to offer their things."

Something in her words caught at Tamar. Fear stirred to life inside her. Why did this woman speak of clothing and baths and roasts in the oven when Tamar was meant to stay with Thomas, as his guest? As his future wife?

"I'm sorry," Tamar said. "I've been dreadfully impolite. It's the long journey, you see. I never thought to ask your name."

There was a brief pause. The driver flicked her reins and clucked to the horse. Tamar's heart hung in a terrible suspension between one beat and the next, between the awful knowing and the inevitable confirmation.

"I'm Tabitha Ricks," the woman said. "Thomas's wife."

December ripened toward Christmas and the new year. Snow drifted deep across the valley, blanketing the steep foothills and the high wall of the Wasatch Mountains. The far edge of the lake was lost in silver cloud; it seemed to Tamar as if the water went on into an unknowable eternity, or plunged off the precipice of the world, and nothing lay beyond except a colorless void. The road to Salt Lake City became impassable unless one had access to a sleigh. She would find little opportunity to visit her family until springtime came.

She had earnestly tried to find contentment as a guest in the Ricks home, but each day, as she worked silently beside Tabitha, disappointment dragged more heavily at her heart.

Tabitha was delighted to have another woman present, for she'd already given Thomas two fine children—Catherine, who was two years old, and Thomas Junior, a fat, giggling infant. Tamar found she couldn't entirely like the children, though they doted on her and even preferred her gentle touch and soft English voice whenever they needed soothing. Yet Tamar couldn't look into the children's faces without a stab of pain.

They should have been mine, she thought miserably each night when she tucked them into their cradles. *It's I who was promised to Thomas—I who should have borne his children.*

By day, she worked steadily to ease Tabitha's burdens. It was the least she could do, as repayment for the woman's generosity. By night, when Thomas returned from his duties as sheriff of Centerville and the nearby settlement of Farmington—or from his forays to the city, where he often met with Brigham Young—she sat at the supper table with eyes downcast, picking at her meal, listening while husband and wife talked over their day. How she hated the familiarity that existed between them. How she envied Tabitha her right to touch his hand, or pat his bearded cheek with affection, or laugh with him as she and Tamar cleared away the dishes.

"Our guest is always so quiet," Tabitha observed one night, smiling sidelong at Tamar. "She's good company by day, but she'd be better company still if she would gossip."

Thomas answered offhandedly, "The English are always reserved."

He went on bouncing the baby on his knee, his back half turned to Tamar.

Look at me, she pleaded in her heart. *Look at me the way you did on the trail. I know I didn't imagine it. I know my vision was true.*

Yet Thomas paid no more heed to Tamar than to the motes of dust spinning in the lamplight around him.

Each night, when the house was tidy and the children were asleep and the man and his wife had gone to their shared bed, Tamar shut herself in the small room behind the kitchen where her poor, narrow pallet was kept. She curled beneath the quilts, weeping into her pillow until exhaustion carried her away—but even in dreams, she remembered the yellow room in the cottage at Aston Rowant, Edward speaking her name, Edward fading away while only Thomas remained.

When time permitted, she wrote letters to her family in the city—Tabitha was as generous with her paper and ink as she was with everything else. Tamar told them of the lively church at Centerville, the joyful meetings on Sundays and the gay dances the ladies' society arranged. There had been two dances already that winter, and Tabitha had insisted Tamar must go to each one.

"So you can meet a nice fellow," Tabitha had said, "and entice him to court you."

She wrote to her family of the snowy countryside, the shops in town, the work she did for Tabitha's sake. But Tamar couldn't bring herself to write a single word about Tabitha herself—nor Thomas, nor the children.

Patience and Mama both responded with regularity, and Zilpah even managed a hasty note now and again, though she was so busy with Alpha as he grew. Yet despite their cheerful words and all assurance that Tamar was loved, she felt as lonely as an island in a vast, cold sea. The colorless winter spread all around, and in the gray haze, there was no horizon, no future to which Tamar could fix her sight.

At least the young women of the Centerville church were good company. They were quick to greet Tamar if they saw her out walking, and when she came to the dances, they flocked around her, laughing and teasing as if they'd all been sisters from the cradle. Their sorority was enough to distract Tamar from the worst of her sorrows—at least while the company lasted. But when she returned from a walking party or from a meeting of the Centerville Relief Society, and caught sight of Thomas by the fire—Thomas smiling at his wife with their little daughter in her arms—then all the bitterness flooded back in, shaming Tamar to her soul.

On the Sunday before Christmas, she perched stiffly beside Thomas in the church pew, eyes fixed on the bishop, scolding herself to stop dwelling on her dismal ruminations and pay closer attention to the sermon. The bishop was reading from the Book of Mormon, the First Book of Nephi.

"'For behold,'" he recited, "'I have refined thee; I have chosen thee in the furnace of affliction.'"

Suddenly she could feel the warmth of Thomas's body beside her own. A terrible flood of longing crested in her heart. The man she loved must remain forever beyond her reach. She would go on dancing with other men, disporting with the other unmarried women of the church as if she were goods on sale in a shop window—but it was all a fancy, all a lie. In her heart, she belonged to Thomas, and yet she could never live as her heart demanded.

This is my furnace of affliction, she realized, dizzy and sick. *The fire of this agony will render me to nothing.*

"What is it, Tamar?" Thomas said quietly. "Are you well?"

She blinked in surprise. She was on her feet, though she'd never intended to move, let alone to stand. The congregation had fallen silent around her. Even the bishop had paused in his sermon.

At that moment, Junior began to fuss, and Tabitha turned her attention to the baby. Tamar seized the opportunity, slipping down the line of the pew as quickly as she could manage. She hurried from the meetinghouse, out into the glaring cold, and waded across the yard to the old willow that stood behind the building. The tree's golden branches were stark against the sky. There was an old carved-stump seat below the willow, half buried now by snow. Tamar sank onto the seat and keeled forward, burying her face in her hands. A wind rattled the naked branches overhead, but the only other sound was her lonesome weeping—a small, muffled misery against the vastness of winter.

"There, there, dear. Why are you crying so?"

Tamar sat up quickly. Four young women had followed her from the meetinghouse—all members of the friendly group who'd adopted Tamar as one of their own.

"I . . . I didn't hear you approaching."

"No doubt," her friend Eleanor said. "You've been crying fit to wake the dead."

"It's nothing. I'm sorry to have upset you."

Mary cast a wry glance at the others. "Nothing, is it? Come now; no one weeps this way over nothing."

"Yes," Eleanor said. "It's plain something has gone dreadfully wrong. There's no use pretending otherwise. Out with it. Be sensible, now."

Tamar laughed bitterly. "That's the trouble, I'm afraid. I'm not sensible at all. And I'm afraid you'll all think me wicked once you know the truth. Oh, girls, my heart is broken. I've learned to care for Thomas—and once, on the trail, I'd thought God had promised me to him. But it's no use. I should have known he'd have a wife. I was a fool not to ask whether he was married back on the trail, before I'd learned to care, but everything was so desperate and hard, and Thomas seemed the only good thing in all the world. I just went on doting shamelessly on that man, and now I've lost my heart to him. I'm afraid I'll never get it back. And I know I can never love another—never, never!"

She covered her face again, too ashamed for her friends to see. What a dolt they must think her now—what a simpleton!

For a long while, no one said a word. Tamar withered inside. Now that her friends knew how daft she was, they would want nothing more to do with her. She had lost the only good society she'd had since coming to Centerville.

I should have listened to Patience and Mama. I should have made the Relief Society keep us all together. At least I wouldn't be so lonely, now. I would be far from Thomas and Tabitha, and I wouldn't be made to see them together, day in and day out, knowing I can never have him.

When the silence stretched on, Tamar ventured a glance at her friends. She thought she would find herself alone with the girls beating a hasty retreat across the snow. But all four had remained. They looked at one another furtively. Eleanor locked eyes with Mary and gave a subtle jerk of her head as if to say, *Go on; you tell her.*

"What is it?" Tamar asked.

Mary chewed her lip, glancing toward the meetinghouse. "Perhaps . . . perhaps God wasn't wrong, after all."

"He does most usually get things right," Eleanor added.

"I mean," Mary said, "perhaps your vision was a true one."

Tamar sniffed. "What are you saying, girls?"

"We . . . that is, some of us . . . ," Eleanor began.

Nancy cut in. "Things aren't done the same way in Deseret as they're done elsewhere. This is Zion, after all—the Lord's kingdom."

Tamar stared from one to another. They were bouncing on their toes, kicking at the snow, brimming with nervous energy. Eleanor smiled at Nancy, embarrassed, almost giddy.

"It isn't uncommon," Eleanor went on carefully, "for a man to take more wives than just one."

What were they speaking of? Tamar could find no way to respond. She must not have understood Eleanor's meaning. Surely God's own righteous people did not engage in adultery.

"Not everyone," Mary added. "And only when a man is called specially by the Lord to live the Principle."

Tamar shook her head, bewildered. "The Principle?"

"Of plural marriage," Nancy said casually. "The Blessing of Jacob. The Way of Abraham. He had four wives, you know—Father Abraham."

Tamar drew a long, shuddering breath. She groped for words, but none came.

"It only makes sense," Mary said. "We came to the valley to restore the original religion to the earth, far from the laws of fallen man. We know from the Bible that all the most righteous men had more than one wife."

"So they could multiply their houses like the stars," Nancy said.

"You're telling me," Tamar said carefully, "that Mormon men marry several women? At once?"

"Not all the men," Nancy corrected.

"So you see," Eleanor said, "perhaps your vision was true. Perhaps someday Thomas Ricks will be called to take another wife. Then you can be his without any guilt. It's no folly. You were given a revelation of what's yet to come."

Tamar lurched to her feet. The girls fell back from her, muttering.

She marched toward the meetinghouse without another word, but she heard Nancy say behind her, "Drat! Catch her, someone. She mustn't tell!"

Eleanor called, "You mustn't speak of it, Tamar—not to anyone! It's a sacred thing, not to be discussed."

The meeting had been dismissed by the time she reached the hall. She only nodded when Thomas asked whether she was well. She couldn't meet his eyes—nor could she stand Tabitha's sympathy, the healer's probing questions. One way or another, Tamar managed to convince them both that she was hale—it had only been a passing fit of melancholy, some grim memory from the trail.

At supper, she was as silent as ever, and that night, she sat on her bed, staring at the paper and ink on her small corner table. If only she could write to Patience to ask her counsel. Patience had always possessed a sturdy sense, a straightforward reckoning with facts. And since her own vision on the trail, in the snowed-in cove during the worst hour of desperation, Patience had believed in the restored gospel with all her heart.

She will tell me if this is righteousness or sin.

Tamar crept to the writing table and sank down slowly on its little three-legged stool. She picked up her quill . . . and then let it fall from her hand.

What if Patience declared unequivocally that this practice, this Principle, was nothing but the foulest iniquity? Had they come all this way, lost their home and their father, only to find themselves stranded among devils?

Patience mustn't know. She'll be angry with me—ashamed. She'll say we must leave at once, go back to New York. And I can't face the trail again. My spirit isn't strong enough to bear it.

Tamar remained awake that night, kneeling beside her bed, praying for the wisdom to discern saintliness from sin. But her thoughts remained as shrouded in haze as the far shore of the lake. No matter how she pleaded with God to spare her this suffering and tell her plainly what she must do, she found no certainty, no relief.

Endlessly, she strayed into recollections of Thomas on the trail—his firm presence, the strength of his body, the way he had found her with his eyes that day when the wagons came. She remembered that first sight of the valley spread out below the final snowy ridge. She and Thomas had stood apart from the rest, side by side, gazing down on the promised land.

Weary, shaking from despair, Tamar struggled up from her knees and crept quietly through the sleeping house, out into the white garden. The clouds had cleared overhead. A half-moon rode high and distant in the ink-dark sky, attended by a multitude of stars. A faint rosy flush was spreading above the Wasatch peaks. Dawn would soon come, and Tamar had had no sleep. Nor had she had any answers from the Lord.

In the cold clarity of a winter morning, her thoughts assembled into some semblance of order. If she had known the Mormons were disposed to this shocking behavior, she never would have listened to their preaching. She wouldn't have left London, even if it had meant remaining with her brothers and parting with her parents forever. Yet here she found herself, in the Mormons' Eden. She had made her sacrifices along the trail; for better or worse, God had taken note of Tamar. She couldn't accept this immorality—it flew in the face of propriety. Nor could she understand how her heart could bear it—the pain of sharing Thomas with Tabitha. His wife. His first wife.

And yet she couldn't stop herself from loving him.

She stared up at the moon. The chill brought tears to her eyes, blurring that sacred light and smothering the stars.

God has called me to this life for a purpose of His own. I can't deny what my heart desires. I will be Thomas's wife, if he will have me—even if it means I must live in shame, even if it means I must hide the truth from my family. Even if my heart will break to know that Tabitha has gone first where I most desire to go. God's will be done.

She heard the scrape and squeal of the front door opening. She turned quickly, half afraid, for she didn't want anyone to see her this way, weeping with her poor soul bared, already committing to an unthinkable sin.

Thomas had come out onto the step. He was wrapped in his winter coat, watching Tamar with that same intensity he'd shown on the ridge above the valley when she had asked him to walk with her into Zion.

All her fears departed in that moment, scattering away like a flock of birds. She watched him cross the garden, trudging through the snow toward her, closing the distance between them.

I am as ore in the fire, she thought, waiting for her husband—yes, her husband; she was certain now—to reach her side. *God shall refine me in the furnace of my affliction.*

"Tamar. You're up early."

His voice was harsh with some emotion she couldn't understand. She watched his eyes—those narrow, sharp blue eyes that seemed to see through veils into the depths of her heart.

"I never slept," she said. "I've been praying. For guidance. For understanding."

"As have I."

"I've been praying to know the difference between righteousness and sin."

He nodded, drew a long breath, let it out slowly in a cloud of mist. Thomas stared out over the lake. The moon's reflection shivered and broke on the water.

"You came to speak with me," Tamar said. "To tell me—"

"There are ways of living. In this valley. In this world."

He hesitated. In the morning stillness, she heard him swallow hard. His hands moved restlessly in the pockets of his coat.

At last, he went on. "I felt as if I should get up from my bed and come out to the garden. I knew I would find you here."

She waited. She watched the lake as he had done—the moonlight, the settled blue peace of the coming day.

He said, "The purpose of Zion, Tamar . . . the work we do here . . . is to restore God's true church. The ways of the true religion aren't the ways of men. That's to say, not the ways of common men, in the cities—like New York, like London."

She turned to him abruptly and held his gaze. His brow furrowed as if her nearness caused him some deep inner pain, but he didn't look away.

"If you're asking me whether I'll be your wife—your second wife—I will do it, Thomas, and gladly. I will live the Principle with you, if this is God's will. You've only to name the date, and I will come to you, as Rachel came to Abraham."

13

JANE

Centerville
February 1857

The money from the sale of Elijah's plow held out almost till winter's end. On that dismal ride home from Smoot's Mercantile, with the cold nipping at her bare head and ears, Jane steeled herself for even leaner weeks to come. She resolved to make do with her fifteen dollars till spring was well underway and the garden was in, for then she wouldn't need to fret so much over food and warm clothing. When the roads had cleared of ice and snow, she could take Sarah Ann's lap quilts to town and sell them door to door. She might cut firewood in the canyon and sell it in bundles along the road. All manner of opportunities might present themselves if she could only stretch those precious banknotes through the winter.

In the end, it wasn't Jane's money that gave out first. It was her spirit. One morning, late in February, she woke to find that Sarah Ann had already risen from their bed and was fixing breakfast on her own—a porridge made from the last of Elijah's oats. Jane tried to rise, too. She tried to speak, but a leaden dullness had settled across her spirit and pressed her body down into the old straw tick. Her heart and head alike seemed plunged into a thick, heavy silence.

One clear thought remained, and it repeated endlessly against the void. *I'm not likely to find another position—not in a store, nor in any woman's home.*

Word had surely made its way around Centerville—rumors of Jane's outburst at the mercantile. No one would hire the short-tempered girl who'd dressed down Tom Ricks—especially not now that he'd emerged as a great hero who'd played a critical role in rescuing the stranded pioneers.

She lay staring at the weak morning light around the cracks of the shutters. Spring was still many weeks away. When the garden emerged from beneath its blankets of snow, she must prepare the soil and plant it, and pull weeds and tend new growth. She must haul wood from the canyon, food from town, see that Sarah Ann took her medicine each day. The weight of all that work, the endless responsibility, bore down upon her young body till she felt her bones grinding to dust, till she felt as old and used up as a broken clay pot.

I can't do this on my own. It's all too much for one girl to bear.

Jane didn't try to blink back her tears or wipe them away. She let them fall on her thin pillow and made no attempt to quiet her sobs, though she knew the sound would alarm Sarah Ann. When her sister came to hold her hand and soothe her tears away, Jane forced herself to sit up. She could only move very slowly, as if age or illness had stiffened her limbs.

"I must ride to town this morning," she said woodenly. "There's someone I must speak to—the sooner, the better."

She hadn't any idea where she might find Tom Ricks, though she had a notion that the healer Tabitha must know where the man lived. They shared a surname, after all. They must be relations of some kind; perhaps Tabitha had married one of Tom's brothers. Mounted on the black mule, with a shawl wrapped around her head to keep off the worst of the cold, she ventured down the hill toward Centerville.

By the time she reached the valley floor, her stomach was tight with apprehension. The mere thought of showing herself in the village filled her with shame. She felt certain there were faces peeping from behind lace curtains, voices muttering, *There goes the girl who sauced our hero, the girl who screamed like a kettle at Tom Ricks.*

She would go straight to Tabitha's house—speak to no one on the way. She would pretend there was no one else in all the world, even if someone called to her, even if boys mocked her from the storefronts and yards.

As the black mule plodded closer to town, Jane repeated the plan in her head to steel her spine. She became so engrossed in her own thoughts that she didn't hear, at first, when a man called her name. Nor had she known the man was there, for she had fixed all her attention on the town ahead, its low blue shadows against the snow, the haze of gray smoke hanging over its rooftops.

"Sister Shupe. Jane!"

The voice became more urgent, sharp enough to cut through the tangle of her thoughts. Her body jerked in surprise, and the mule, uncertain what its rider intended, stopped in the road and lashed its tail.

Jane turned slowly, peering back over her shoulder. There was Tom Ricks, of all people, several paces behind her on the side of the road. He was standing at the end of a long lane between two fenced fields, and he was waving at Jane as if to a friend. A coil of hemp rope was slung across his body. At the far end of the lane, a small red house squatted beside a peak-roofed barn.

"Sister Shupe, won't you stop and speak with me?" Tom called. "I owe you an apology, and I'd like to give it, if you please."

She swallowed hard. She had no desire to speak with Tom, nor to look at him, nor suffer his useless apologies. And yet this was the very reason why she'd ridden to Centerville. Like it or not, she was obliged to talk to that man. He was the last hope Jane had.

She turned her mule and made her way back to the lane.

Tom looked up at her with a timid smile. "I'm glad to see you looking so well."

"Not looking too thin and starved, I hope," she replied acidly.

Too late, she recalled herself. She would do Sarah Ann no favors if she put this man off.

She forced herself to soften. "You seem well, too. Is that your house, back there along the lane?"

Tom glanced over his shoulder. "No—no, it's Brother Ellison's place. The ropemaker." He patted the coil across his chest. "This is only part of the order Brigham has put in for the Legion's use, but Ellison won't have more rope ready till the end of March. I could have driven my sleigh over, I guess, but it was such a pleasant morning. I thought a walk would do me some good. And I guess it has done me good, for here I've come across you—just when I most needed to speak with you."

She had no idea how to respond—if indeed Tom expected any reply. She only sat, hands flexing on her reins, waiting in the strained silence.

"I'm terribly sorry about your job," Tom said. "I tried to convince Brother Smoot not to be so hard on you. I told him you're in sore need of pay. He wouldn't hear it, though . . . and I'm to blame. I feel plain miserable about it. If there's any way I can help you and your sister now—"

"There is one way," Jane broke in. The words dragged, but she must speak now or not at all. She knew she would never find the courage to dive into this folly a second time. "You told me once that you would marry me. Do you remember?"

He drew a long breath, turning away to gaze out across the snowy fields to the distant town.

"Well?" Jane said.

"I recall it."

"Now is the time. You *must* marry me, and take my sister in, for I can't keep Sarah Ann on my own. I need a husband to support me. Sarah Ann needs a brother."

He looked up at her then, holding her eye—unflinching, undeterred by her strange appearance, just as he'd done when he'd stood at the edge of her garden and made his absurd proposal.

"I see," Tom said. "Very well."

Jane felt rather baffled by the response. He had accepted her outrageous demand too readily. She'd thought he might laugh at her, rebuff her in some way. She'd been prepared to convince him by pointing out how hard she worked, how much experience she'd already gained at running a household. Instead, he merely seemed to be waiting for her to say something more.

"So I'll do it," she added at length. "I'll be your wife, and cook and wash for you, and tend your house, and I suppose . . . I suppose I'll have your children, if God wills it. But only under one condition. You must never separate me from my sister. She's all I have in this world. I won't be parted from her."

"Is this really what you want? To be my wife?"

"I want to keep Sarah Ann safe. Whatever I must do to help my sister, I'll do it willingly."

Tom scratched his beard. Not looking at Jane, he said, "There's a difference, I think, between wanting and willing."

Her throat constricted. Was he rejecting the offer? She couldn't allow that. "You once *wanted* to marry me. Do you still, or not? Tell me outright. I haven't any time to waste—nor breath to waste on useless talk."

He laughed then—not the uncertain chuckling men sometimes used when they'd been caught in foolishness or fraud, but a full, hard laugh, with real amusement. He rocked back on his heels, gripping the coils of rope in his fists.

"What's so funny?" she demanded.

Tom cleared his throat, trying and failing to drive the grin from his face. "Only that you said to me, 'I wouldn't marry you if you were the last man on earth.' And now here you are, coming to me with this . . . proposal."

A bitter taste rose in her throat.

"I'm sorry," Tom said. "I shouldn't have laughed. I wasn't mocking you, I swear. Listen—you don't want to be my wife. That much is plain. You and your sister can live on my charity till you find a man who strikes your fancy."

"I won't live on anyone's charity. I'll make my way honestly in this world."

He took a step toward her, his face serious now—and earnest. "There's nothing dishonest in accepting help."

"I don't need help for a month or a year. I need stability. Sarah Ann needs it. I need a reliable income . . . and a man who's respected enough to find work and keep it. As for finding some other fellow who strikes my fancy, what use is there in such an idea, for a girl who looks as I do?"

Tom said nothing. His features blurred—not only from Jane's wandering eye but from the tears that had come so suddenly. She blinked them away, refusing to let them fall.

"You're sensible," he ventured at length, "and resilient. I admire strength in any person—especially someone as young as you. I'll marry you, Jane Shupe, if that's your will. And your sister may live in my household, where she'll be safe and well cared for. I give you my word on that."

Something seemed to burst inside her, like the lancing of a tender boil. It brought a rush of pain and disgust, but also relief. She would be all right now. The hardest part was over.

Jane wiped her eyes on her sleeve. "I'm glad to hear it. When shall we have it done?"

"Have it done?" Tom repeated. He laughed again—but softly now, a thoughtful kind of humor. "Can you be at the church on the twenty-seventh of March, two hours after noon?"

"If that's what you wish."

He reached into the pocket of his work-stained canvas jacket, withdrew a few banknotes, and offered them up to Jane. "This ought to keep you and your sister fed until our wedding day."

Jane hesitated only a moment. She took the bills, folded them quickly, and slipped them into her sleeve. "Thank you, Tom. You're generous, as always."

14

TAMAR

Centerville
March 1857

Tamar remained perched on an embroidered footstool, humming a meandering tune, until both children had settled into sleep. When their gentle sighs filled the room and there was no more shuffle and stir from their wicker cradles, she laid aside the knitting she'd been working, stitch by careful stitch—a winter cap for Thomas Junior, woolen and warm, the yarn dyed a charming shade of green. She leaned over the baby's cradle, imagining what he would look like in the cap. The color would become him, complementing his eyes, which resembled his father's more each day as he grew.

She could love the baby and little Catherine unreservedly now. The sight of their faces no longer pained her, for, with acceptance of Thomas's proposal, she had the promise of her own children shining before her, a guiding lamp in the darkness. She brushed the boy's cheek with a fingertip, ever so gently, careful not to wake him.

Tamar gazed down at the girl. Catherine's black curls spread over a pink-frilled cushion, and she'd thrown a fist up beside her angelic face. Tamar tucked the child's hand back under the edge of her patchwork quilt, blew her a kiss, then quietly left the nursery, closing the door behind.

The moment Tamar was outside that precious room, the peaceful spell lifted. She could hear Tabitha working in the kitchen, sorting through pans and muttering while her small boots clipped to the pantry and back again. Tamar knew she ought to be with Tabitha now, lending a hand to lighten the work, but she found herself more reluctant than ever to speak to her hostess, or even to keep silent company with Tabitha. Since that dawn when Thomas had asked her to be his second wife, Tamar had felt distinctly uneasy in Tabitha's presence.

Or *had* Thomas asked? She leaned against the nursery door, watching the toe of her boot as she prodded at the hallway's runner rug. She couldn't remember now just how the arrangement had come about. Oh, she could recall the emotion of the moment with a perfect, diamond clarity—a great warm rush of happiness, a settled comfort that seemed at once both newly arrived in her soul and planted there before the foundation of the world.

After the dawn had broken and the moment had passed, however, certainty wasn't such a decided thing. The days and nights that followed were fraught with doubt. This Principle that Thomas had espoused—it may have been the old Abrahamic way, but the days of Abraham were long gone. Tamar still felt half sinful when she contemplated her wedding day, which was all too quickly approaching.

By now, she understood the source of her turmoil. She couldn't see her position clearly—not with regard to Tabitha—and every hour pulled her closer to the snare of this unconventional marriage.

If only I could ask Patience for her advice.

That was out of the question, of course. Thomas had stressed the importance of maintaining their sacred silence. Even here in the Eden of Deseret, the church had deadly enemies. There was some new president back East—Buchanan—who was looking for his chance to bring the whole United States Army down on the valley. "Even here," Thomas had told her soberly, "we can't be too careful how we speak of the Principle, and to whom."

If only Tamar could find some way to discern what Patience knew of this custom without coming right out and admitting the truth. Perhaps her sister had already learned of the Principle. Perhaps Patience, too, was engaged to be married as second wife or third to some righteous city man eager to take her hand. Then there would be no danger; Tamar could speak freely. Oh, if only she could *know* what to expect from the wedding, from her future as Thomas's second wife.

And least of all did Tamar know what she could expect from Tabitha.

Did Tabitha know of the proposal? Was she aware of the impending wedding, to be held only a few days hence? Surely Thomas had prepared her. Perhaps Tabitha had even thought of this marriage herself, encouraging Thomas to take a second wife to help with the children and the housework.

I may be fretting over nothing. Perhaps Tabitha put this idea into Thomas's head. Perhaps she thinks of me as Sarah thought of Hagar. After all, I've been as a servant to Tabitha all these months, and gratefully so.

The next moment, Tamar suppressed a shudder of foreboding. Sarah cast Hagar out, in the end. The handmaid and the child Ishmael were left to wander the desert, alone and suffering, exiled by the first wife's wrath.

If only she could find some way to raise the subject, to ask after Tabitha's feelings without violating Thomas's gentle command to tell no one, to speak not at all of the Principle.

The crash of a dropped pan pulled Tamar from her reverie. Tabitha muttered a curse in the kitchen. Tamar was needed, always needed to lighten the work and smooth the way. She cracked open the nursery door, peering inside to be sure the noise hadn't awakened the children, but the dear little ones slept on.

In the kitchen, she found Tabitha just beginning to knead a great batch of dough for their weekly bread. Flour was scattered across the table, and Tabitha, small though she was, worked with a vigor and concentration that seemed to indicate that the first wife might just as easily pound and pummel and slap Tamar on that hard tabletop if she took half a notion.

That was the trouble. Tabitha possessed such an imposing personality that she might as well be six feet tall—or tall as a temple spire. Tamar liked the woman heartily, yet she also quailed in her presence. Tabitha's work as the village herb-woman had given her an air of authority, and her independence added a layer of untouchable awe to her countenance. Well did Tamar know that Tabitha, alone among all the women of the valley, had no real need for any man. She could support herself from her own earnings, if circumstances should ever demand it. Tamar couldn't help but feel inadequate beside her hostess's great strength of character and steely determination.

"Thomas won't be here for supper tonight," Tabitha said. "Nor for two days at least."

"I never asked about Thomas," Tamar said quickly.

Tabitha chuckled. "I know you didn't. I was referring to the dough."

Tamar glanced down at the pale ball yielding and caving under Tabitha's hands. Now that she looked more closely, she could see it was a smaller portion than Tabitha usually prepared.

"He'll be in the city for a few days," Tabitha went on, "working with Brigham Young and the Legion."

"More of this Legion business." Tamar began gathering up the implements she knew Tabitha would no longer need—the flour sifter, the tin measuring cups, the crock of butter. "I know Thomas has insisted we'll have nothing to fear from this business with President Buchanan, but still, I can't help feeling anxious. If there were truly no threat from Buchanan, then President Young wouldn't have called up the Legion in the first place."

Tamar felt rather proud of the ease with which she could discuss such things—speaking of Nauvoo's old militia as if she'd been born a native of the Illinois Mormon stronghold. Of course, most talk in Centerville had revolved around the Legion since Tamar's arrival. Every conversation turned, sooner or later, to speculation on what the summer might bring. Buchanan was growing more insistent that Deseret must bend the knee to Washington, while Brigham Young stood fast in his insistence that freedom of religion would be honored.

"There'd be nothing to fear," Tabitha said, "if some of these men would give up their scandalous behaviors and return to proper, civilized conduct."

Tamar had been rinsing the measuring cups in a pail of water. She paused with her hands submerged. Now was her opportunity to raise the subject she had long avoided. She must do it at once, or not at all—for it didn't seem likely the chance would come again.

"Do you mean the Principle?" she asked carefully.

Tabitha glanced at her over her shoulder. "Where have you heard talk of the Principle?"

"From some of the unmarried girls at church." It wasn't exactly a lie. "I suppose they were gossiping shamefully, and I ought not to have listened, but how can one resist listening to such a tale as that?"

Tabitha gave a disgusted grunt. "Such a tale, indeed. Yet if the men would abandon this notion, there would be no more threat from Buchanan or his army. We'd be left in peace; we'd be free to manage our lives and our church without interference. Until the Principle is no more, we'll continue to live under threat of invasion."

"Do you . . . do you suppose it's true?"

"That depends on what you mean by *true*," Tabitha said. "Do I think it's a fact that some men have taken more than one woman as wife? I don't merely think it; I know. You forget, Tamar: I'm the midwife of these parts. No baby is born within ten miles of Centerville without my knowing it. And there have been too many so-called unwed mothers for my liking. Do I think it's true that the Principle derives from God—that it's part of the restoration of true religion?"

Tabitha said nothing more, but the way she pounded the dough with her fists spoke eloquently enough.

"I . . . must go to the well," Tamar said faintly.

She took the pail and left the kitchen in haste. Water slopped over the rim onto her boots, but she never slowed.

Outside, she emptied the pail onto a patch of Tabitha's garden, then pressed herself against the house, biting her knuckles to keep back a cry of distress. She had her answer, and no mistake. Tabitha couldn't possibly have approved of the coming marriage. In fact, she certainly knew nothing about it.

How am I to live with her once the wedding is done? I can't keep this secret from Tabitha forever.

The trail had done its best to break Tamar's spirit, but she had prevailed over that adversity. This, however, was a snare that she knew her poor heart couldn't survive.

Three days later, when Thomas returned from the city, Tamar watched uneasily for an opportunity to speak with him alone. It came that night, after the supper dishes were cleared away and the children were bathed and dressed in their nightgowns.

"Aunt Tamar will tuck you into bed," Tabitha said to Catherine. "I must make up a medicine for old Brother Richards. His cough has been troubling him again."

"I don't want Aunt Tamar," Catherine insisted. "I want you, Mommy!"

Tabitha shared a confused glance with Tamar. Usually, the children preferred Tamar's ministrations at night. There was no accounting for the changeable tastes of a two-year-old, however. Tabitha thought better of an argument. She shrugged and took Junior in her arms, then led Catherine down the hall to the nursery.

"Thomas," Tamar whispered once they were alone. "I must speak with you. Now, if you please. I'm afraid it can't wait."

Thomas had been lounging in a stuffed chair beside the parlor fire with a book in his lap and his stocking feet stretched out comfortably before him. At the urgency in Tamar's voice, he set his book aside and drew himself up.

"Tabitha knows nothing of our plans," Tamar said quietly. "Of our wedding."

"You haven't told her yourself, I hope."

"No. I've done as you've asked and said nothing of . . . our particulars. But naturally, the subject of the Principle has arisen. How not, with the Legion drilling down in the city and President Buchanan making his threats?"

He sighed. "It's true that I haven't told Tabitha yet. I've been praying to know when the time is right. God hasn't answered me yet, and with so much work down in the city—Brigham and the Legion, one thing and another—"

"But she must know before our wedding day. We can't surprise her. I respect her too much to hurt her that way. I can't help imagining how I would feel to have another wife thrust into my life, my marriage, without even a warning so that I could prepare myself . . ."

Tamar trailed off. Thomas's cheeks had reddened, and it seemed as if he could no longer meet her eye.

"You must trust that God knows His business," he said at length. "We may not understand His workings. But all is done according to His design."

Something hard settled in her stomach. She couldn't recall the last time she'd felt so downtrodden, so discouraged in faith.

And then she could recall it. A memory returned with sharp, painful clarity—the hard bedroll, the shade under the willows, the ache and delirium of the fever that had racked her body and distorted her thoughts.

She remembered the apostles crouching beside her, laying their hands on her head. They had blessed her, and yet it had seemed as if their blessing had had no effect—as if all their great and holy power had been only a rumor, a sham.

But when morning came, Tamar had risen renewed in body and spirit. She had prayed that day, more earnestly than she'd ever done before, promising the Lord that she would never again doubt the power of the priesthood. And here she was, doubting the Lord's will, and doubting the guidance of her future husband, who, after all, held the sacred priesthood, as did all men of the church.

Like a worm in the core of an apple, a memory twisted deep in Tamar's heart. She thought of Patience in Zilpah's garden, long ago in Iowa City—Patience muttering among the daisies, *A little faith is a good thing. Too much is poison to common sense.*

No, Tamar told herself. *I swore to my Lord that I would doubt His ways no longer. The Almighty sees the grand design; He will not guide us falsely.*

She lowered her head in obedience. "Just as you say, Thomas. I will trust that God knows best and has the matter well in hand."

Tamar resolved herself to fret no more over Tabitha. She would leave the matter in Thomas's hands. God would tell him, when the hour was right, to teach Tabitha the path of righteousness. Tamar need only look forward to her wedding day with a joyful heart, as any bride should do.

15

JANE

Centerville
March 1857

The morning of Jane's wedding dawned dismal and gray, the sun hidden behind a wall of dense cloud. A recent spate of rain had melted the worst of the snow, and Jane stood in the door of the cabin, still wearing her old flannel nightdress, watching the sky with a sense of grim amusement. It was a long ride to Centerville. Very likely, she and Sarah Ann would be caught in a downpour. The bride would arrive at the meetinghouse soaked to the bone, looking like a half-plucked chicken.

There was nothing for it but to keep on, one foot in front of the other. If she arrived at her own wedding bedraggled and wet, what did it matter? Tom Ricks wasn't marrying Jane for her looks, anyhow. They might as well start as they meant to go on.

She closed the door resolutely, then opened the wooden chest where she and Sarah Ann kept their clothing. Pawing through the old gray skirts and faded blouses, she found the single pretty dress she could claim as her own, pulled it out from under the rest, and shook out the wrinkles as best she could. Jane laid the dress across her bed. It was made from fine cotton, once madder red but faded by age to a soft rosy pink. The bodice was pin tucked and decorated with a V of off-white linen lace, and small, delicate ruffles were gathered at the collar and cuffs. She hadn't looked at the dress in years, preferring to keep it buried out of sight below the more workaday garments she'd made and remade for herself and Sarah Ann. The dress had belonged to her mother, who had worn it at both her weddings—first to Jane's father, then to Elijah.

"It'll look fine on you," Sarah Ann said.

Jane spun to face her sister, a lump like guilt rising in her throat. She had explained everything to Sarah Ann, of course—the necessity of this marriage, how it would benefit them both. Sarah Ann had accepted the news in good cheer. She had liked Tom Ricks when he'd come to buy the plow. Yet still, Jane felt as if she were doing something not quite chaste. She was selling herself, driving a bargain for her companionship—for her body, too, she supposed—like some head of stock in the market square.

Sarah Ann passed a plate of food to Jane: a ladleful of the bean stew Jane had cooked the night before, reheated over the morning fire, and a hot soda biscuit with a slice of cheese melting between its halves.

"It isn't much of a breakfast," Sarah Ann said, "but I guess after today, we'll eat like queens."

"I wouldn't expect that, if I were you. Tom isn't a rich man, but he is honest and generous. I'm sure he'll keep us well. Better than we've managed up here in the canyon, anyhow."

Jane ate mechanically, never tasting the food—which was just as well, for it had been bland the night before and likely hadn't gained any savor overnight. All her thoughts were on the man she would marry in a few hours' time. She wondered whether it was true, what she'd told Sarah Ann. Tom wasn't stingy, and he'd been quick to apologize after he'd cost Jane her job. But making amends wasn't exactly the same thing as being honest.

I don't know this man at all—not really. And yet I must live with him as his wife.

The thought made her so apprehensive, she couldn't manage to clear the plate. She tossed the remainder into the grass for the crows to pick and busied herself with dressing. Sarah Ann, too, put on her finest—only a dull brown skirt with a linen shirt and a blue-checked pinafore. They were serviceable clothes, not pretty and certainly not fit for a wedding.

The girls put out the fire, then took the small bundles of necessities they'd made the night before and slung them on their shoulders. The remainder of their belongings would stay in the cabin till Jane sent her new husband up to fetch her things.

"It's time to go," she said.

Sarah Ann paused on the threshold, staring down at the valley—at the little village that would be their world now. "I don't like to leave this place," she said. "Mother's grave is so near, and this has been our home for so long—the two of us, Jane. Everything will be different now. We'll be more than two."

"Needs must," Jane answered gently.

She put a hand on her sister's shoulder and led her to the corral.

The weather held till the girls reached the outskirts of Centerville, riding side by side in the rustic dogcart. Then the cold rain came beating down, drifting across Main Street in billows of gray. By the time they reached the meetinghouse and hitched their mule to the rail outside, Jane's hair was plastered to her head and her shoulders were dark from the downpour. At least Sarah Ann was dry beneath her wrappings. Goodness knew what a bad chill might do to her, delicate as she was. Jane led her under the eaves and unwound the shawls and scarves.

"Do I look all right?" Jane asked, pushing her dripping hair back from her brow.

Sarah Ann gazed at her soberly for a moment, then burst into laughter.

Jane couldn't help smiling, too. It was all so absurd, so hopeless. She might as well find some amusement in the twisting and turning of fate.

"We might be early," Sarah Ann said. "There's no telling what the hour is; I can't find the sun at all."

"We might be late, for all we can say. Let's go inside. It's dry in there."

They made their way to the meetinghouse door, hugging the log wall to avoid the rain. Jane eased the door open as quietly as she could, fearful she might draw more attention than she liked.

She had never been in the Mormon meetinghouse before; her family hadn't belonged to the church, and after Mother and Elijah had died, Jane had found an hour of prayer each Sunday sufficient communion with God. She'd grown used to working through the rest of her Sabbaths—which she knew was a sin, but she figured the Lord would forgive as long as she only did necessary work and kept her thoughts repentant. Sunday nights, she recited whatever Bible stories she could remember for Sarah Ann's benefit, which was the best approximation she could make toward keeping the Sabbath holy.

She hadn't set foot inside any kind of church for years—not since her earliest memories—but despite her lack of experience, Jane thought the Centerville meetinghouse was an unusually plain affair. An uncarpeted aisle ran between two rows of spartan benches. No one occupied those seats; evidently, Tom hadn't bothered to invite his friends and relations to the wedding. On either side of the room, two narrow windows were set into the log walls, admitting a weak gray light, by which Jane could just make out a pair of figures standing at the far end of the hall—Tom and the preacher, she assumed.

Or was it three people she saw? With her uncooperative eye, Jane couldn't be certain.

She blinked, tilting her head. The blurred images slid together, the scene at the end of the aisle snapping into sudden, terrible clarity. There was a preacher, indeed, standing behind a simple pulpit with one hand resting on his Bible. And there was Tom before the altar—unmistakable in his height and broadness, the darkness of his beard.

He was facing a woman, holding both of her hands. She was several years older than Jane, with features as dainty as those of a china doll. Her skin was smooth and fair, her cheeks glowing with an eager flush. Golden-brown hair swept back from her brow, covering her ears with two rounded puffs. Her dress was cut plainly, but it was the ethereal blue of forget-me-nots, and a crisp linen kerchief showed at the neck, framing her face. She was gazing up at Tom with a smitten, tremulous expression. Jane knew in an instant why that woman was standing at the altar, and what her radiant glow signified.

Jane halted so abruptly that Sarah Ann collided with her back.

"Sit there." Jane passed her bundle to Sarah Ann, pointing to one of the rough-hewn benches. But she never looked away from Tom and that woman.

At the sound of her voice, Tom glanced down the aisle, then smiled when he recognized her. "Here she is—the other girl I mentioned, Brother Young."

"Other girl, indeed," Jane fired back. "I'd like to know exactly what's going on here, Mr. Ricks. I turn up for my own wedding only to find the groom making his vows to another bride!"

The woman in the blue dress was staring at Jane. Her cowlike eyes held a wounded startlement. "Thomas, I don't understand."

Jane marched down the aisle, prickling with shame over her wet, ragged appearance.

"This man," Jane said, "this *cad* told me to come to the church on this very day, at this very hour, and he would make me his wife. Did you forget which bride you'd promised yourself to, Tom Ricks?"

He dropped one of the blue lady's hands, reaching for Jane as if he intended to pull her up to the altar, as well. Jane stepped back. She wouldn't suffer his touch.

"I should have realized," Tom said carefully. "Of course, you don't understand the custom, Jane. You've never been to church, as far as I've seen—and even most who count themselves among the fold have yet to learn of the Blessing of Jacob."

"The blessing of what?"

"This is our custom. It has become so ordinary to us—to the men, at any rate—I never thought to ask myself whether you'd already heard. Whether you'd be unpleasantly surprised . . ."

He gestured weakly at the woman in blue, who was looking from him to Jane and back again with an increasingly distraught expression.

The preacher cleared his throat. "If the lady doesn't like the thought of being—er—involved in such an arrangement, then I can't proceed, Brother Ricks. Not with her, anyhow. Sister Loader has already given her consent."

"Yes," the blue lady said. She was musical, unmistakably English. Yet despite the sweetness of her voice, there was an air of desperation in her words. "I will marry you, Thomas; my mind is already made up. No force on Earth or in Heaven can dissuade me."

"I'm sorry, Jane," Tom said. "I should have prepared you for what you would see—what it would mean to marry me. Of course, if you'd rather not, I understand. As Brother Young said, no one will compel you. You may still have my charity, if you wish. But—er—you must keep this a secret. It's a sacred covenant, you see. We don't discuss the practice with those who aren't already called to the work. Do you understand?"

Jane felt as if the floor of the church were yawning below her feet, as if she were plunging down into a cold black chasm. She whirled and ran from the meetinghouse.

"Janey, wait," Sarah Ann called weakly behind her.

Jane threw open the door and plunged out into the rain. It lashed her body, the bitter cold cutting through her mother's dress and chilling her to the pit of her stomach. She stormed toward the dogcart and her patient, shivering mule. *California,* she thought. *We'll go to California, Sarah Ann and me. We'll leave this mad valley behind, and—*

She heard a ragged cough behind her. Then one of the deep, shuddering gasps that always signified the beginning of one of Sarah Ann's wheezing fits. She spun again, racing back to her sister, who was stumbling through the rain without any of her wrappings.

"What are you doing?" Jane demanded. "You can't be outside in this weather, not without something warm to wear."

Sarah Ann couldn't answer. She only coughed again, harder this time and red-faced.

Fear burned in Jane's gut, so hot it drove back the chill of the morning. She turned Sarah Ann around and marched her back into the meetinghouse, where the girl stood shivering and panting for her breath.

Thank God, Sarah Ann recovered herself before one of her dreadful fits could take hold. But it had been too near a thing.

She needs a better home than I can give her, Jane realized with a sinking dread. *And we'll never make it to California—not till she's better. Not till I've found some cure.*

She glared up the aisle once more, at Tom and his trembling bride. *That man can give Sarah Ann more than I ever can. Anyhow, a long ride back to the cabin in this weather might sicken her beyond all hope of recovery.*

Once Sarah Ann was seated again, Jane marched up the aisle and faced Tom squarely, ignoring the woman beside him.

"I won't let you go back on our deal," Jane said. "You will marry me, Tom Ricks. You'll keep your word to me and to my sister. And I'll see to it that I get what's due to a wife—every scrap and crumb of my due."

She stepped close to the other bride, staring her full in the face. The pretty English flower flinched at the sight of Jane's wandering eye, which only filled Jane with grim satisfaction.

"Give the ceremony," she said to the preacher. "I'll say my part. Tom must make his vows to me in God's sight, and let his soul be damned if he goes back on his word."

16

Tamar

Centerville
March 1857

Tamar wanted to scream, to tear at her hair. She wanted to throw herself on the floor and weep, but she willed herself to perfect stillness as the bedraggled girl joined her at the altar, reciting her marriage vow in a cold, mocking voice. She hadn't the least idea who this hot-tempered, venomous young thing might be. Tamar had never seen the girl before—not at church, nor at the dances or other social events where young unmarried women gathered. She certainly would have remembered Jane, with that unsettling cast to her eye and a pertness that could even put Patience in her place.

It's all one to me, she told herself, fixing her gaze on her husband's face. *I knew he was a married man when I accepted his proposal. What does it matter if he's married to one other woman, or two, or a dozen? I shall do God's will with a grateful heart. I shan't question the ways of the Almighty.*

But though she told herself that Jane made no difference, still Tamar's eyes burned and her heart beat painfully in her chest. This was her wedding day. She had resolved to share Thomas each day to come— share him without bitterness or discontent. But this day should have been sacred to Tamar alone—the one day she would have her husband entirely to herself.

She closed her eyes briefly while Thomas recited his portion of the vows to the stiff-backed girl. A memory of the trail returned with such vividness that for a moment she thought herself still on the plain, struggling toward Zion. She recalled the river crossing, her feet sliding on stones, the ground vanishing beneath her. She could feel once more the river's icy grip, the current dragging her under. Cold lanced into her bones.

Tamar opened her eyes with a start. She wasn't in the river. This was the meetinghouse, and she was holding Thomas's hand. He was real—her marriage was real, as was his love. The girl beside her changed nothing.

The door to the chapel crashed open once more, and with such force that Tamar cried out in alarm.

"Thomas Ricks—you scoundrel. Betsy Smoot told me to hie to the meetinghouse and see what trouble you were up to. I didn't believe it could be true. I never would have thought you could do such a thing."

Tabitha came storming down the aisle, rain blowing in behind through the swinging door.

"Let me explain," Thomas began.

Tabitha cut him off ruthlessly as she gained the altar. "I'll just guess you can explain, like all the other men in this town who take to this abomination."

"It's no abomination; it's a calling from God."

She laughed bitterly. "It's always a calling, isn't it? No man is quite fool enough to tell his wife, 'I've taken a fancy to another girl.' No—it's always a sacred calling, a blessed covenant."

Jane had gone rigid at Tamar's side. "His . . . wife," she stammered. "Tabitha is your wife?"

"My first wife," Thomas said.

Tabitha's mouth pinched as if she wanted to spit. "I'm your *only* wife, you deceitful wretch."

Brother Young broke in smoothly. "The matter is already decided, Sister Ricks. Thomas is married to both these women before the eyes of God. It can't be undone."

Tabitha rounded on Jane, fury giving way to pained disbelief. "You." She was almost asking, almost pleading. "Little Jane Shupe."

"I didn't know," Jane said. "I swear, Tabitha. I never knew he was already married. If I'd known, I never would have—"

"And you." Despite Tabitha's diminutive size, when she turned her cold countenance on Tamar, she seemed to tower with authority and offense, a great black fortress of hate. "I take you into my home, allow you to sit at my hearth and eat at my table as if you were my own sister, and this is how you repay me?"

Tamar never knew where she found the strength to speak, for her very spirit seemed burned away by the blaze of Tabitha's rage. "If you would but allow Thomas to teach you the Principle—"

"Don't open your mouth in my presence, you hussy."

Tamar's throat went dry.

"Talk," Tabitha shouted, whirling to face her husband—*their* husband. "Speak, oh, wise man, you who hold the keys to the priesthood. Tell me why you never asked my permission before you took another wife. Two wives, and one of them still a girl!"

Thomas groped for the words that would soothe her anger.

"Go on," Tabitha barked. "I'm waiting to hear your wisdom! Why don't you teach me the Principle, as your trollop suggested?"

Tamar could no longer hold back her tears. It was painful enough to learn on her own wedding day that Thomas would have more wives than Tabitha and herself. But to be so crassly insulted by this woman whom she had loved and respected—who had offered Tamar comfort and companionship after the long ordeal of the trail, when she was isolated from her own family. This woman, whose home Tamar had kept as if it were her own, whose children Tamar had minded and kissed and held in her arms. Tabitha's naked hate was too much to bear. She covered her eyes and wept.

"That's it," Tabitha said. "Hide your face. Hide your shame, if you think you can."

At last, Thomas found his words. "Leave her be. After Brigham called me to live the Principle, I prayed for days—for weeks, in fact, asking the Lord to show me how I ought to raise the matter with you. I asked Him to tell me whether I must ask your permission—and I would have asked, Tabitha, and given you the choice. But He wouldn't allow it. I knew it would cause trouble when you learned the truth. I can't pretend to understand what God means by this calamity, but we're in the thick of it now. We must find some way forward, all of us together, for that's what the Lord wants. It's what He expects us to do."

"It's what God wants." Tabitha's voice dripped with sarcasm. "It's always God's plan."

An insistent pressure welled in Tamar's stomach. For a moment, she feared she might be sick. Then that surge of emotion became words in her heart—a line of scripture. She was meant to speak in that moment, for good or ill, whatever may come.

"For behold," Tamar said quietly, "I have refined thee. I have chosen thee—"

Before she could complete the scripture, Tabitha's hand licked out, fast as a strike of lightning. The slap cracked across Tamar's cheek. Her ears rang with a high, whining sound.

"Find some other place to house your harem," Tabitha hissed at Thomas. "Your Jezebels won't set foot beneath my roof again."

"Tabitha means what she says." Thomas helped Tamar climb up into his carriage. "I can't bring you back to the house—not till she's come to accept our situation."

Tamar hunched in the front seat, shivering from the day's chill as much as from her distress. It seemed as if Tabitha had taken the bleak downpour with her when she'd stormed out of the meetinghouse, for the rain had stopped and a feeble blue sky was showing itself and hiding again behind the racing clouds. The biting wind relieved some of the pain in Tamar's reddened cheek.

She fixed her gaze on the half-obscured mountains along the lake's farthest shore while Thomas wiped the worst of the rain from the buggy's rear seat. He lifted the young girl into the carriage. Then he gave his hand to the other—Jane. His third wife. Tamar couldn't watch him do it, couldn't bear to see Jane's fingers entwining with his as she ascended to her seat. The mountains were like dream castles drifting behind a low shelf of cloud.

Thomas stepped up and took the reins. The buggy jolted into motion, and the horse's hooves made a hollow heartbeat sound on the muddy road. Tamar turned her face as the carriage moved, the better to keep her eyes on the mountains beyond the lake. It was easier than looking at her husband.

"I set up a fine little house for Jane," Thomas said, "a few lots down from ours. From mine and Tabitha's. From . . . that house."

He didn't seem to know how to say it, how to admit that his home was Tamar's, too—that she had lived with him as any member of his family would do. She was his family still—and now she belonged to him more completely than ever before.

"You and Jane must live together till Tabitha comes around," he went on. "God willing, it won't take long. Perhaps only a few days. I'll pray for her—and with her. I hope she'll soon be made to see the sense in this arrangement."

"The sense," Jane muttered from the rear seat. "Indeed."

"I think you'll find the house pleasant enough," Thomas went on, paying no heed to Jane's bitterness. "Several men of the church helped me furnish it, and their wives contributed everything you might want, or so I hope—quilts, dishes, even food in the pantry. Of course, if you find anything is lacking, you've only to ask. I'll provide whatever you need."

"Did those women know they were furnishing a home for a second and third wife?" Jane asked sharply.

Thomas glanced at her over his shoulder but didn't answer.

"And how ought we to ask for the things we need?" Jane went on. "Shall we brave Tabitha's wrath to get to you?"

Tamar didn't want a separate home. She didn't wish to live apart from her husband. She didn't wish to leave the only home she had known since coming to the valley. Whatever tension existed now between herself and Tabitha, surely it wouldn't be helped by distance. She and Tabitha needed to talk—to discuss this state of affairs. Tamar knew she could make the first wife understand that this was part of God's plan for them all, if only she could speak to her in confidence, tell her about the visions she'd been granted on the ship and on the trail.

Most of all, Tamar didn't wish to live with this woman . . . this *girl* whom Thomas had never mentioned, not once.

Yet she knew if she raised an objection now, it would only further strain a situation that could scarcely be called tenable. She thanked Thomas politely and watched the road ahead.

The buggy drove on, north through town, past the two-story white-washed home that had been Tamar's until this fateful day. They passed three more houses. Then Thomas pulled up a short lane that led to a small log home almost at the edge of the settlement. A disused hen coop stood to one side, and near the front door, a row of flat-topped stones had been arranged in a bench of sorts. There was no garden, but Tamar could see that a decent patch had once been plowed and likely planted. It wrapped around the southern and eastern exposures. A few farms lay beyond, and past those fields, still brightened here and there by the remains of snow, the valley swept on along the shore of the lake, and the Wasatch Range rose up, steep and near.

Thomas set the brake and climbed down. He lifted the girl child from the buggy first, before he'd even offered his hand to Tamar.

"What do you think of your sister's new house, Sarah Ann?" Thomas asked.

"It's finer than our cabin was," the small girl replied.

He gave her a fond smile, patting her wet brown head. "You'll like the inside better still. I found a good horsehair sofa for you and set it up beside the kitchen stove. It'll be a fine, warm place for your sewing. Come; let's have a look at the rooms."

He helped Tamar and Jane from the carriage and led the way inside. "I'll go back for your mule and cart, Jane," he said, "and I'll fetch your things from the cabin this evening. Tamar, I'll bring your belongings, as well. Now tell me what you think of the house."

Tamar had to concede that it was a pleasant home. The main room was spacious, marrying parlor and kitchen with a good-sized table between. Glazed windows in every wall let in ample light. Although there was no proper hearth, there were two large iron stoves—one in the kitchen for cooking, with an oven attached, and the other on the parlor side. Someone had lit the kitchen stove in advance; Tamar could hear the metal tinging and crackling as it expanded with the heat. The stoves must have cost a great deal of money, for they'd been transported from the East via wagon—and no proper wagon trains had come to the valley for more than a year. With such luxury as dual stoves, the house would stay cozy and dry, even in the depths of winter.

The women of the church had been generous with their donations. Bright rag carpets covered the floor. A newly made pine cabinet held a full array of dishes and pottery. She could see kettles and cook pots hanging from hooks along the kitchen wall, and beside the cooking stove was the horsehair sofa Thomas had promised to little Sarah Ann—freshly carved legs like a lion's paws, canvas upholstery neatly tufted and dyed a fetching blue. Whoever had made the sofa—no doubt someone in Salt Lake City—knew his craft well, and surely charged a pretty penny for the work.

Brigham Young must have given Thomas a great reward for his heroics on the trail, Tamar thought. *Or perhaps the people of Zion love him so well that they'll give him almost anything for the asking.*

On the eastern wall of the house, three doors led to additional rooms—none of them large, by any means, but their smallness would prove an asset, come winter.

Tamar knew she should have been grateful for such a lovely home. A part of her was grateful. But the larger part was embittered. This wasn't how she'd pictured her existence as a married woman. *How can a wife live apart from her husband?*

"I only put a bed in one room," Thomas admitted, "for I hadn't expected Tamar to need this house, too. I figured you might turn the other rooms to some purpose of your own, Jane—sewing, or candle-making, or whatever occupation you like. At least till you're old enough for children. I'll set about finding another bed today. With any luck, I'll have something suitable before nightfall, but if all else fails, I'm afraid one of you must make do with the sofa."

"One of us?" Jane planted herself in front of Thomas, staring up at him with that strange, crooked tilt of her head, that roaming eye. "What about Sarah Ann?"

He cleared his throat. "I think it's best if I take Sarah Ann to my house tonight, and perhaps for a few days after. Tabitha needs to examine her."

For one shivering moment, no one spoke, but Tamar could feel the very atmosphere of the log house constricting as if Jane were drawing down the wind itself, filling her spirit with a wild, howling energy.

"You will *not* take my sister from me."

Jane didn't so much speak those words as pronounce them, her voice ringing with a marble hardness that took Tamar aback. How could any female creature—especially one so young—command such fury?

"Now, Jane, listen to me."

"I will not listen to you. I won't hear a word. You deceived me; you trapped me in this pit of sin with a vow I made before God—a vow I can't break. And now you think to take my sister? You promised me! You gave your word that Sarah Ann would stay with me."

Jane seized her sister by the arm, wrapping the girl in a viselike embrace. Sarah Ann clung just as fiercely to Jane. There were tears in the younger girl's eyes.

Tamar's heart broke for the poor child. She was so small and frail. Very likely, this commotion would further damage her constitution.

"Jane," Thomas said firmly, "think back to our conversation. I told you Sarah Ann would remain in my household, and so she will. I haven't gone back on my word—nor will I ever; you can count on that. If you recall, I offered you charity, but you insisted on marriage out of your own stubborn pride."

"Out of need."

"Sarah Ann must come with me," Thomas said, "for this night at least. Where else is she to sleep? There's only one bed and one sofa here—"

"She'll sleep in the bed with me," Jane said. "We've done it many times before."

"It's narrow. You won't sleep well, all knees and elbows in one another's ribs."

"I don't care. We'll make do."

"She needs medicine." Thomas was cajoling now, almost pleading. "It's plain to see—for goodness' sake, Jane. Let Tabitha care for the girl. You know she's an excellent healer."

Those words broke down the great, towering wall of Jane's anger, though Tamar couldn't understand why. The girl crumpled around her sister, weeping freely into the child's damp hair.

Tamar moved cautiously toward the girls. She felt as if she were approaching a mother bear with a cub. "Tabitha is a wonder with herbs.

Why, I've lived with her four months, and in that time, I've seen her cure all manner of maladies."

"I can't allow it," Jane sobbed. "Not after her temper at the church today."

Sarah Ann wailed, "I'm frightened, Jane!"

"There, there," Thomas said. "She's angry, I'll grant you that, but she's angry with me—not with you, Sarah Ann."

The girl began to wheeze between her sobs. Then she coughed, red-faced.

"No," Jane said, thrusting the girl out suddenly, holding her by the shoulders so she could look into her eyes. "No, Sarah Ann, you mustn't. Not now. Breathe. Come on; breathe."

The poor child's eyes were glazed with panic. Her thin chest heaved as she struggled for her breath, and a dreadful rattling came from her throat.

A terrible chill ran through Tamar's body. She had heard that sound before . . . when her father lay dying in the back of a handcart.

"Thomas," she said, "get the girl to Tabitha straightaway. It can't wait!"

Thomas said nothing more but scooped Sarah Ann into his arms and headed for the door.

Jane threw herself after them. "No!"

Tamar grabbed Jane by her waist. The girl twisted in her arms, clawing at Tamar's wrists and the backs of her hands. She tore great, painful gashes with her nails, but Tamar did not relent. She was stronger than she looked, and well did she know it. The trail had made her body thin yet powerful, and she had learned how to endure the worst agony without flinching. Jane was a tall girl, sturdy for her age, but she couldn't free herself from Tamar's hold, no matter how she struggled.

"Let them go," Tamar said calmly. "You must, Jane. He'll take your sister to Tabitha, and she will treat her gently. I would stake my life on that. She may be furious with both of us now, but she won't turn Sarah Ann away. She is always kind to those in need."

Jane seemed not to hear. "Please! Sarah Ann! I'm sorry!"

There was no mistaking the terror in her voice, the desolation. Tamar ached with pity.

Through the log walls, she could hear the buggy rolling away, the horse cantering down the lane. Only when she was certain Thomas had a proper head start did she release her grip on Jane.

The girl flew to the door, then out into the lane. Tamar followed more sedately. She watched as Jane stumbled to a halt halfway to the road, sobbing and shaking. The carriage was already diminished in size, its wheels throwing up a wake of mud as Thomas rushed the child to Tabitha's care.

"Come now," Tamar said gently, approaching from behind.

Jane reeled away, heaving. She vomited bile into the weeds beside the lane.

"Oh, you poor dear."

For all her misgivings and shocked betrayal, Tamar couldn't help being stirred to kindness. She tried to pull Jane's braid back over her shoulder where it wouldn't be fouled.

Jane knocked her hand away.

Once the fit of gagging had passed, Jane straightened and stumbled toward the house. "This must be a bad dream," she muttered. "I'm in a nightmare, that's all."

Tamar followed her back inside, talking softly as she went. "It's no dream. Would that it were. You must think of your sister now. She is safe with Tabitha . . . even if you and I are not."

Tamar shut the door and leaned against it, watching Jane with no small amount of caution. The girl stopped in the middle of the parlor, staring at the wall. Jane was volatile, clearly—and half mad with grief. Tamar wasn't sure whether she ought to approach her again, or even speak. The backs of her hands burned. She glanced down. Jane had left her mark; red scores ran from Tamar's knuckles to her wrists, the skin welted and fire hot.

When Jane finally spoke, she was so composed, so quiet, that the fine hairs lifted on Tamar's arms.

"I feel dirty. I feel as if I'll never be clean again."

"You . . . didn't know they have this custom?" Tamar asked hesitantly. "The men of the church, I mean."

Jane shook her head, still staring at nothing. "We've lived in this valley almost two years. Perhaps I ought to have known. I suppose I never paid enough mind to Mormon ways. I've been . . . busy. Since I was a small girl. Working to take care of my sister and . . ." She faltered, then drew a shuddering breath. "Anyhow, I'm not one of them—one of you. I'm not a Mormon."

Tamar was taken aback. She hadn't considered that anyone might have come to Zion for some other purpose, without the aim of restoring the true church. She hadn't thought that this deep mountain sanctuary might just be a valley, to some. Or a pit. A trap.

"The worst of it is," Jane went on, "I've always thought so highly of Tabitha. She helped me—when my mother was dying, and after. She even offered to make me her apprentice. But I never imagined Tabitha might be Tom's wife. There are so many people in this place who share a name—all the Smoots and Youngs and Rickses. I thought she and Tom must be related somehow, of course, but I never imagined they might be husband and wife. Because, you see, Tom told me once that he would marry me. I thought he was a bachelor, and Tabitha was his cousin or an in-law. What else should I have believed? In all my life, I never imagined anything like this. Such wickedness."

It's no wickedness, Tamar wanted to say. *The Principle is a sacred covenant, an act of worship . . .*

She knew Jane would take no comfort from those words—or worse, the girl would mock her for believing what Thomas had taught. The knowledge that she was setting herself apart as a handmaid of the Lord had comforted Tamar through the final weeks of winter as she'd waited for her wedding day. She didn't feel like a blessed handmaid now. She felt lost and forgotten. She felt like a fool.

"The worst of it is," Jane began—but she couldn't go on. Her body convulsed as she wept again, and all at once, Tamar was uncomfortably aware of the girl's wet dress, her limp, rain-soaked hair. She must be cold, and even more uneasy than Tamar was herself.

She approached Jane again, laid a timid hand on her back. "Come with me into the kitchen. Let's fix you a cup of tea."

She made Jane sit at the table, then busied herself with a kettle. The old routine of preparing tea came back to Tamar as easily as if she'd never left England. She filled the copper kettle with water from a jug beside the pine cabinet and set it on the stovetop to heat. Then she peered into the various jars and tins in the small pantry until she found a good-sized vessel stoppered by a cork. Inside was a medley of fragrant leaves and the dried petals of flowers—an herbal tisane. Most Mormons considered real tea too strong for the righteous to drink, but brewing anything and sipping it slowly was an act of meditation. The tisane would be a far cry from a proper cup, but in a pinch, it would suffice.

Tamar took a pair of heavy clay cups from the cabinet and dropped a heaping spoonful of the herbs into each. Jane went on crying in her quiet, hopeless misery until the water was steaming and Tamar had set the cup on the table before her.

Jane looked up, tilting her head in that funny way she had, looking sidelong at the tea. After a moment, she wiped her eyes on her wet sleeve and sipped carefully. Tamar took the chair opposite, cradling her own cup in her hands, waiting for the girl to speak.

At length, Jane said, "The worst of it is that I've always respected Tabitha so. There was no one I liked more in all the valley—not that I'd met many people. But I'd always thought Tabitha such a wise, patient, kindly woman."

"She is all those things," Tamar said softly.

And I've cut her to the quick. Stabbed her to her heart.

"How can I ever look her in the eye again?" Jane said. "Tom has made me into Tabitha's enemy when I would have loved nothing more than to be her friend."

Tamar had no answer. The same sickening realization was swimming in her stomach.

A tap sounded at the door. They both rose at once.

It wasn't Thomas, however, but Charles Kimball, the young boy who ran errands at Tabitha's behest. Tamar had often seen him coming and going from the Ricks home, carrying Tabitha's instructions or packets of herbs to the sick and injured.

"Good day, Sisters," Charles said, raising his cap. "Brother Ricks sends his word. The young lady is recovering. Her breathing is easy now, and Sister Ricks has the illness well in hand."

"Thank God," Tamar said.

"Sister Ricks says the girl is to stay at her house till she's satisfied her health is restored. Says this rainy weather might set off another spell, and she must find the right medicines to keep her breathing easy no matter what may come."

Jane made no reply. She only watched Charles with dull acceptance—yet a little of the strain had vanished from her face, her mouth relaxing into a neutral line rather than a scowl.

"Thank you, Charles," Tamar said. "Please tell Brother and Sister Ricks we're grateful for the news and will pray for everyone concerned."

After the boy had gone, Tamar and Jane returned to the table. Jane sighed heavily, rolling the cup between her hands, watching the leaves rotate slowly on the water.

"Now he has Sarah Ann," she said, "and he has me exactly where he wants me—parted from my sister."

"Not forever, and only for your sister's good."

"I hate him," Jane muttered. "He's a dreadful, wicked, sinful, loathsome man, and I hate him with all my heart."

"He is none of those things. Thomas is brave and good. I've seen how he has risked his life to help others—to save others from death, and from fates worse than death. I know him, Jane, and I swear to you, he is a righteous man. It's only the strain of the day that has you feeling so grim." She attempted an encouraging smile. "It has been a dreadful one, after all."

Jane only scowled back at her.

"The world won't seem so gray," Tamar went on, "once you've warmed up and dried off. Thomas brought your bundle inside. Do you have a change of clothing?"

"Only a nightdress."

"I'll lay it over the stove to warm, and then you must remove these wet things. It won't do to take a cold."

Tamar pushed back her chair and made to rise, but Jane's bitter laugh stopped her.

"Why are you being so kind to me?"

Tamar asked herself, *Why, indeed?*

She cast the unworthy thought away, remembering what her father had told her on the trail when Tamar had still believed they would both reach Zion together. *The harder a sacrifice comes, the greater its weight in Heaven. This is part of my sacrifice—to hold us all together. To suffer what I must, in service to God.*

She fetched the bundle and unfolded it, pulling a flannel nightdress from among the few scraps Jane had brought—a pair of woolen stockings, some threadbare linen drawers.

"It's only natural that you would feel suspicious," Tamar said, more cheerfully than she felt. She draped the nightdress across the stove. "It isn't easy being separated from one's family. I know that all too well. I came to the valley with my family, you know—just as you came with Sarah Ann. But they aren't here in Centerville. They're in the city, and I've been unable to visit them all winter long."

"Why are they in the city, and you here?"

Tamar paused. She had never asked herself that question—at least, not so directly. In the first weeks after her arrival, she had found the Relief Society's explanation sufficient reason: room for the handcart refugees had been limited. Now, under Jane's scrutiny, Tamar saw her circumstances in a different light. After those first weeks of scramble and scurry to find housing for every refugee, the Loaders' benefactors might have found some opportunity to bring the family together again.

Would I have gone to them if the chance had arisen? Or would I have insisted that I must remain with Thomas?

"We've corresponded by letter," she said, "but it isn't the same as seeing your family in person and holding them close. I do miss my sister Patience especially. I never thought I could; she's all prickles and spines. But I'd give anything to see her now. I wish . . . I wish I could have had her at my wedding. *Our* wedding. But Thomas said we mustn't tell a soul about our arrangement—not yet. He said there will soon come a time when all of Deseret knows about the Principle, and nothing is hidden, but until God decrees, we must keep a sacred silence."

"Your family is still living? They're all well and whole, down in the city?"

Tamar hadn't planned to tell of her father's death—not yet. She wasn't certain she could speak of him at all without her heart crumbling to dust.

"They're in the city," she said. "But—"

"Then how dare you." Jane lurched to her feet, snatching her night-dress from the stove. "Your family still lives. You've lost nothing. And yet you think you've suffered as I have?"

She stormed toward the only room that contained a bed.

"Please," Tamar said, "allow me to explain."

The girl turned in the doorway. "No, Tamar; let me explain this all to you, since it seems you're too foolish to grasp what has happened to us. A madman has deceived us and outraged us, and now we're stuck in the thick of his sin. Yet there you sit, defending him, calling him a good and honest man. He has trapped you. The sooner you wake up and face the dawn, the better off you'll be. And I'll never be your friend—not as long as you go on defending Tom Ricks and his vile ways."

She disappeared into the room and slammed the door.

Tears filled Tamar's eyes, not for the first time that day. Her wedding day. What a tangle all her bright dreams had become—what a scattered, broken mess. She sank down on the horsehair sofa, which would be her bed that night, it seemed.

She breathed deeply, steadying her nerves, and the tears dried unshed. A malicious thought crept in, burrowing into her heart.

What would Papa think of me now? What would he say, to find his daughter in such an arrangement as this?

The silence of the house gave Tamar no answer. The rooms were empty, a void stretching cold and dark all around her—a great, hollow hunger.

17

JANE

Centerville
March 1857

Jane woke late the following morning. After the initial disorientation of finding herself in a strange room, the great, crushing weight of the previous day's humiliation descended so abruptly that for a moment she couldn't breathe. She could feel Sarah Ann's absence like a black void inside—a cold, yawning place, as if some seam of her heart had been torn open and left unmended.

She slid from the bed and stood hesitating in her nightdress. The room still smelled of wet wool from her rain-soaked wrapper, which she'd hung on a peg beside the window. Jane stared dully at the faded pink dress that had been her wedding finery, draped over the back of a chair with petticoat, shift, stockings, and drawers heaped upon the seat. The dress looked as if it had dried thoroughly overnight, but she recoiled at the thought of wearing it again. Her mother would be horrified if she could see how Jane had donned that sentimental frock only to mire herself in sin. Yet what other choice did she have? She couldn't present herself at Tabitha's door clad in a night shift.

She gritted her teeth and put on her old things, then paused before exiting the room. She had left Tamar to sleep on the sofa, without any blanket or cushion for her head. A new kind of shame overwhelmed her, cold as a flood and rising just as fast. Tamar had done her best to offer kindness, and Jane had responded heartlessly.

I mustn't treat Tamar as if she were my enemy. She's also deceived by Tom. But why can't she see it? What sort of fool makes excuses for a man who has trapped her like this?

She decided that Tamar must lack either wits or a spine. Either way, Jane felt disgusted by the woman, despite her resolve to pity a fellow victim of Tom's lechery. The Englishwoman was obviously pampered and silly, without the sense to realize she was being outraged by a cad.

I needn't be cruel to her, but neither will I waste my efforts on a woman of her sort. Let her moon about the valley, goggle-eyed over her Principle, her Zion. It's nothing to me.

She swung the door open, firmly resolved to breeze past Tamar, but the house was empty, save for a few small chests and carpetbags left in a tidy collection on the parlor floor. Tamar's belongings, Jane supposed—brought over by Tom in the earliest hours while Jane had still been sleeping. She skirted the goods as if making her way around a pit of rattlesnakes and slipped from the house.

Forceful sunshine had replaced the previous day's grayness. The lake glared with such fury that Jane had to squint as she walked from the log house to Tabitha's whitewashed clapboard. By now, Jane reckoned that Tabitha had had ample time to treat Sarah Ann's malady. Much as Jane respected the healer's expertise, she could no longer tolerate the separation. She must know how her sister was faring—must see Sarah Ann for herself, and do whatever she could to explain these miserable circumstances to Tabitha.

By the time she was standing at Tabitha's door, one fist raised to knock, Jane still hadn't the least idea what she ought to say or how she must comport herself. She was furious, outraged, sick at heart, and saw no reason to hide it. No recited speech would help her now, but neither would she grovel—not in her mother's dress.

The door swung open before Jane had touched it. Tabitha was pale and silent. A definite redness tinged her eyes, as if she, too, had been crying. For a long moment, she stared at Jane with the stillness of a cat watching a sparrow.

"Tom isn't here," Tabitha finally said.

"Good. I don't want to see that man—not ever again, if I can help it. I've come to see my sister."

That seemed to thaw Tabitha a little. She lifted one brow, and her eyes traveled from Jane's face to her boots and back again, assessing the whole of her—unkempt hair, burning cheeks, wrinkled dress, same as she'd worn the day before.

She stepped back. "Come in."

Jane had to steady her nerves as she crossed the threshold. Yesterday's scene at the meetinghouse had erased months of trust in the healer. She'd never imagined a woman so sensible and calm could fly into a fit of violence. Yet why shouldn't Tabitha have raged at her husband—at all of them, Jane included?

She followed timidly to the parlor. The workbench was still piled with the herbs and implements that had captured Jane's interest on her visit last fall. A surge of longing rose in her chest.

"Sit," Tabitha said.

Jane sank down onto one of the parlor chairs. It seemed much too large for her body. In her mother's best dress, she felt as if she were a child pretending to be grown.

"Before you may see your sister," Tabitha said coolly, "you and I must have words."

"I agree. We must."

"Mother," a small voice called from another room, "I'm hungry, and Baby waked up."

Tabitha sighed and lifted her face toward Heaven. Jane thought if she could have seen Tabitha's expression clearly, she would find the woman's eyes rolling in exasperation.

"Everything was easier to manage with Tamar's help," Tabitha muttered. Louder, she said, "Wait a spell, Catherine. I'll fix you a bite soon. As long as Junior isn't fussing, he may stay in his crib awhile longer. Play with him, if you like, but keep quiet, dear. You know we mustn't wake the sick girl."

Mention of the sick girl restored Jane to her purpose. "My sister—" she began.

"In due time. First, explain how you came to be in this situation."

Jane clasped her hands in her lap, trying to order her thoughts. "Our stepfather died this past autumn—Sarah Ann's and mine."

"Did he? Why did you never tell me, Jane?"

"I suppose I didn't think to tell you. I didn't have much time for thinking about anything, except how to get a little money now and then, and survive one week to the next. Sarah Ann has been a little better on the medicine you gave me, but she never perked up enough for my liking. I took a job for the winter at Smoot's store so I could keep her warm and fed."

"You should have come to me. I could have changed the dose, added another remedy. It would have been a good education for you, as a healer's apprentice."

Jane hesitated. She kept her gaze fixed on the braided rug, a swirl of bright colors that coiled and furred into one another. She was too ashamed to look at Tabitha directly, even if she couldn't see the woman's face clearly.

"I was going to refuse your offer," Jane finally said. "With Elijah gone, I could tell already that I must work every minute to keep us both clothed and fed. And then after I began working for Smoot, I suppose I never had the time to send you a proper message. Or maybe

I never thought of it. I couldn't really muster enough perk to plan for anything."

Tabitha said nothing. Jane tilted her face surreptitiously, peering through her lashes, trying to read the woman's silence. Tabitha wore a mask of perfect neutrality. There was no sympathy in her expression, but neither was there anger.

"After a few weeks," Jane said, "I lost my place at Smoot's. I suppose, in the end, it was for the best. I couldn't have gone on working so far away from Sarah Ann. But I guess when Smoot let me go, I finally saw the truth of things. I knew I couldn't do it on my own. I decided I needed a husband, and to tell you the honest truth, Tom was the only man who ever had any interest in me, so I figured he would have to do."

Jane expected an outburst from Tabitha—a scornful laugh. The silence continued, however. She swallowed hard, and even that small sound filled the parlor.

"This was almost a year ago, mind—when Tom said he'd like to marry me. I thought him absurd. I told him right off, said I never would be his wife, not if he were the last man alive. But once I got to be so desperate, I figured I'd better find a husband if I hoped to save my sister's life. I told Tom he must marry me after all. It was my idea, you see—but only because I never knew he had a wife."

At last, Tabitha spoke. Her tone was measured and even. "I suppose you couldn't be expected to know. You aren't entangled in the church, and you came only rarely into town."

"I knew you were a Mrs., and I knew your last name was Ricks, but you never mentioned your husband's name—not where I could hear. And I surely had no cause to think any man would say he'd marry me if he already had a wife."

"No," Tabitha said, "I suppose you had no reason to suspect. Even within our church, there are few who know about the Principle."

Jane tilted her head again. She wanted to read the woman's expression now, and make no mistake about her feelings. "You told me once—that day when you said I might become your apprentice—that certain practices among the Mormons had angered folks back East. You said some men in the government thought Mormons committed the same sin as folks did in the Southern states. Slavery."

Dread filled her stomach like a great, cold stone. Was that the sort of life she would have now? Was she nothing more than a slave to Tom?

Jane forced herself to speak on. "This was what you meant, wasn't it? You were talking about the Principle."

"Yes. Would to God you'd never learned about the practice at all, Jane. But if you had to know it, this is an especially hard way to find out. Tricked into a plural marriage in a moment of desperation, and you little more than a child. It's a good thing for Tom's sake that he's gone to the city today—always to the city, always back to Brigham Young. If he were here now, I'd spatchcock that man on your behalf."

"You aren't angry with me?" Jane tried to temper her surging hope. Tabitha might be a sensible woman, but the sharpest mind and the stoutest heart must surely boil at this outrage.

"I'm furious," Tabitha answered. "I won't pretend I'm taking this all in my stride. But it isn't you who's angered me. I can see that plainly, now that I've heard your side of things. You're a victim of Tom's callous stupidity, as much as I am. Tamar, though—" A hard edge came into her voice. "She's a different kettle of fish. She knew full well that she had no right. More to the point, there was no greater need between herself and Tom. Not like your need, I mean—this difficulty with your sister. There's nothing but lust between Tamar and my husband. I would much rather they'd lain together in my own bed than this. I could have forgiven that trespass more easily."

Jane couldn't help raising her brows. "I would find either sin unforgivable."

Tabitha's sardonic tone vanished, replaced by an air of mysterious pain. "It seems a far greater sin to deceive one's wife than to lust," she said. "Or to love. I'm a member of the church, as you know, Jane, though I must confess, I'm not an especially conventional member. I've seen other ways of living. Here in Deseret, we're all so certain we have the right of things. We suppose any fool idea that comes into a man's head must be divinely inspired. But living by the Bible—even a restored Bible—isn't the only way."

Jane edged forward on her seat. She could sense a proper story behind Tabitha's wistful words, and curiosity overtook her anger and shame.

"When I was about your age," Tabitha said, "I lived among the Ponca Indians for a few years. This was before I came to the valley, of course. That's where I found my training in the healing arts: A Ponca wisewoman took me in, just as if I were her own daughter, and taught me everything she could. In exchange, I taught her and her people the English language so they could fare better in trading with Mormon pioneers—and, I hoped, so they might have some means of avoiding the fate so many other tribes have faced."

Tabitha was sober now, her eyes distant. "I think about my Ponca family all the time. I hope they've survived. The white men certainly haven't slowed in their march west. Not even a disaster like we saw last winter can dissuade the converts from coming—that business with the Martin company. I fear there's little hope left for the Ponca, or for any other tribe."

"I had no idea," Jane said, "that you'd learned among the Indians."

Tabitha gave a gentle laugh. The sweet pain of nostalgia seemed to hang about her like a rose's perfume. "I lived so differently in those days. Among the Ponca, it was no sin to love freely. There were marriages, but there were other arrangements, too. The heart of mankind yearns toward its own. We need one another, and there are many different kinds of need, different kinds of togetherness.

"If the men of this valley hadn't thought lust a sin," Tabitha went on, "if they'd been sensible like my Ponca family instead of blundering through this world like a lot of ham-headed louts, they would have no need for this practice. The Principle, as they call it. The same goes for the women; they're every bit as much to blame. But rather than accept mankind's nature for what it is, this church has decided that all human urges are the work of Satan."

Jane glanced around the parlor—the dark plank walls, the woven carpet of rags, the botanical clippings in their rustic frames. She couldn't seem to look at Tabitha directly. Not while discussing such things—the urges of the flesh, the acts that occurred between women and men.

"Where do such feelings come from," Jane asked carefully, "if not from the Devil?"

"It was God the Creator who made our bodies. Therefore, all the many things our bodies do and feel—all things our bodies create—are part of His great design. But because so many in Deseret have decided to accuse their own bodies of sin, we're left with our bitter entanglement—you and I, and Tamar, I suppose."

"But I don't understand. How does one follow from the other?"

"You've always asked good questions," Tabitha mused. "Still as sharp as ever, even when you're in distress. Let me put it plainly. There's no point in mincing the truth. Men who fear the wages of sin have convinced themselves that if they marry the women after whom they've been lusting, then they've committed no trespass against God. As the Bible says, if a man looks on a woman with lust in his heart, then he has already committed adultery, even before he touches her. Yet if he marries that woman—" Tabitha shrugged. "One can't commit adultery with one's own wife."

Jane couldn't keep a laugh at bay. "What kind of fool thinks he can outwit God? And with a trick as simple as that?"

"What kind of fool, indeed."

"But Tom never lusted after me. No man would look on me the way he might look on . . . well, Tamar, for example. She's so delicate and pretty—"

Tabitha broke in. "You must think poorly of yourself, but you're far more appealing than you suppose. You're young and fresh . . . and there's something inspiring about you. Don't frown at me that way; it's true. You aren't a girl who can be beaten down by life's hardship. Just look at you now. Here you are, confronting me the day after you've stolen my husband."

Tabitha hadn't spoken harshly, but neither had she made her words gentle. The tears came so quickly to Jane's eyes that she was humiliated all over again. She wanted to hide her face behind her hands. Instead, she forced herself to face Tabitha squarely.

"I don't want any of this," Jane wept. "I never suspected Tom would do such a thing. And the worst part is . . . I like you so well. Like you and respect you. When I most needed a friend, you were there to help me. Oh, I don't suppose you can ever forgive me. I feel as if I'll never forgive myself. There must be some way for you to have this all undone. I won't try to prevent you, even if it means Sarah Ann and I will be on our own again. If you told a sheriff or a judge in the city—"

Tabitha cut her off with an impatient gesture. "Put it out of your head. I might have it undone, if I wanted to take the trouble. I won't, however. My mind is made up, and believe me, I was awake all night, fretting over the question, asking myself what was best. Morning brought clarity, as it so often does. You may do as you please, Jane— leave Tom and curse him soundly on your way out the door. But I must make do with Tamar—and, I suppose, any other women he might pick up like so many dropped pennies. The men of this valley are enamored of their Principle. They defend it fiercely—those few who know about it—and if I tried to undo this marriage, or interfere too much with my husband's whims, I would only find myself scorned by the whole valley. The men would never allow me to live it down. And if I meet with scorn, my practice as an herb-woman is over. I'll lose the trust of the people. Without their trust, I have no livelihood—and nothing of my own. I would become Thomas's wife, and nothing more."

"Can't you go to Brigham Young?" Jane asked. "He's the president of the church, is he not? Surely he wouldn't approve—"

"It's Brigham himself who told Thomas to get another wife or two. I've no doubt of that. Not every man is permitted to live the Principle. It's considered a great honor to be thought worthy of plural marriage, and the men who partake must be approved by the highest leaders of the church. Thomas has been much in Brigham's confidence since that business with the Martin company. And now that the Legion is reformed, Tom is needed again—training men, finding steel to forge into weapons. He's gone and set himself right in front of Brigham like a pudding, steaming hot from the pan. I half expected this might happen when I'd heard Tom had distinguished himself with the Martin rescue. I expected it—but I still hoped my heart would be spared, or that Tom would refuse, as some chosen men have done."

"Do you suppose he worked so hard for Brigham Young just so he could be called?" Jane asked carefully. "So he could have an excuse to take more wives?"

Tabitha shook her head. "I may be furious with him now, but even I must admit that Tom isn't that sort of man. But neither is he the sort who would refuse a command from the president and Prophet." She sighed, resting her head wearily against the back of her chair. Her eyes slid shut.

"If you told Brigham how you felt—"

"Then I would surely lose my reputation as a healer. I've told you, Jane." Tabitha hadn't raised her head. She was still sagging in the parlor chair, eyes closed as if she couldn't bear to see into the bleak future. "Brigham is much too powerful. He rules this valley like a king, and he's the staunchest defender of the Principle among all the men. I'm afraid my hands are tied. If I want to keep my practice, I mustn't upset the present order, nor draw any undue attention. And I can't give up my work. You know full well I can't save everyone whom I treat. But imperfect as I am, still I believe God has put me here to help those in need. I won't endanger my mission."

"Then I'll find some way out of my own marriage," Jane said, "for I won't be part of it—I won't hurt you, Tabitha. You're the closest thing I've had to a friend since I came to this valley."

"You might get out of it," she conceded, "after your sister is well. *If* I can heal her—which only time will tell."

Jane stilled herself, clenching her fists so hard the nails bit into her palms.

"Sarah Ann does need care," Tabitha went on, "and Tom is a man who can keep her safe. His success with the Martin company brought him a certain amount of security, and now that he's so much involved with training and equipping the Legion, he'll have greater means still. I'll speak bluntly: you need Tom's money. And even though you're a young, fresh girl, still I've no doubt that pity and charity were Tom's foremost reasons for taking you as a wife. He may be remarkably stupid at times, but he does have a tender heart. Tom intends to keep you safe and to save Sarah Ann's life—and those, I believe, are his only intentions where you are concerned. Tamar is another matter, but I've no objection to your making the most of a bad situation and remaining under this family's protection while we work to restore your sister's health. After we know for certain how she'll fare, you and I may sort out our differences, and then you can spit in Tom's eye, for all I care. Until that day comes, we both must make do with an uncomfortable arrangement, for Sarah Ann's sake."

Jane nodded. For a long moment, she could find no words to express the humility and gratitude that had settled into her soul. Her bones felt weak as water.

Finally, she managed, "Tamar said you're a good woman. She said you wouldn't turn Sarah Ann away, nor turn your back on anyone in need. I see that she was right. I see now that your goodness extends even to me—a girl who doesn't deserve your mercy." Apprehension swept over her. She drew a long, shaking breath. "Now tell me, if you can. What's wrong with my sister?"

Tabitha sat up straight once more. She folded her hands in her lap with an air of calm authority. "I can't be sure of anything yet. Perhaps I'll never find the answer. She has fits of bad breathing, as you already know. It's related to her heart—I feel sure of that, though I haven't discovered how, exactly. I won't coat the truth in honey, Jane. She's a very sick child. She may not survive much longer—though if there is any way to save her, I'll find it. I promise you that. She's a good girl, a sweet child. I've grown very fond of her, even in these few short hours. And I've always been fond of you, despite our present difficulty."

"May I see her now? Please, Tabitha."

"Of course you may."

The healer led the way down a short hall to a closed door. As Jane reached for the handle, Tabitha stopped her with a whisper. "She's sleeping, just now. You mustn't wake her."

"I'll be quiet as a mouse."

Trembling, Jane pushed the door open. Sarah Ann lay in a small bed, eyes closed, one hand resting on the pillow. A beam of late-morning light came in through the window, falling softly on her features. Her color was already better, and her chest rose and fell in a steady rhythm.

"May I come each day and help you care for her?" Jane asked quietly.

Tabitha smiled up at her sympathetically. "You may."

18

TAMAR

Centerville and Salt Lake City
May 1857

Tamar had finished her sewing by late morning. She slipped the needle back into its soft leather case, broke one final thread, and folded the fine cotton blouse carefully on her lap. The pin tucks and smocking were delicate enough to please the dressmaker for whom she'd worked in New York. She ran a hand over the garment, cherishing a fleeting moment of satisfaction. The feeling would be gone soon enough, replaced by the aching loneliness that had been her portion since the wedding.

If Jane had been about, Tamar might not have felt so isolated. But the girl had flitted off early that morning for Tabitha's house, eager for the time she would spend with Sarah Ann. Such was Jane's habit. Tamar couldn't blame her for the absence, given Sarah Ann's delicate health—and anyhow, the girl had vowed on their first day together that she would be no friend to Tamar. She had warmed a little over the intervening weeks, but Tamar had her suspicions that Jane's subtle thaw was entirely unconscious, an effect of their close proximity, a slow but steady progression from strangers to . . . not friends, exactly. But they were familiar now.

She sighed and wrapped the cotton blouse in a protective sheath of paper, setting it on the table where Mrs. Allred could find it easily when she came to pay Tamar her dressmaker's fee. Then she took herself outside to the long, straight lane. The day was sunny with a lively breeze. Tamar hoped the weather could lift her spirits.

She walked slowly along the twin ruts of the lane. In the tangled margin between her path and Jane's burgeoning garden, spring flowers bloomed in profusion. The verge seemed to clamor in a hundred colors, and bees hummed over the petals, their legs fat with pollen.

At the end of the lane, she stood leaning against the split-rail fence, gazing over the road to the salt flats and the lake beyond. The gentle weather had coaxed a deep-sapphire shade from the water, the most vibrant and alluring blue Tamar had ever seen in nature.

I wish Thomas were here to see it.

Tamar had scarcely laid eyes on her husband since the wedding, and the hours she'd spent alone in his company were rarer still. Thomas would have made more time for her—she felt certain of that—but as the season had unfolded, Brigham Young had called him ever more often to the city. An urgency had settled over the men of the valley; nearly every fellow of fighting age had volunteered with the Legion, and Thomas was often busy leading forays into the mountains, where the militia was trained and conditioned against the threat of Buchanan's army.

One day, all this mess with the army will be settled, she told herself, *and then Thomas will have plenty of time for . . .*

Even in the privacy of her thoughts, she couldn't continue. A telltale heat had risen to her cheeks. If there had been anyone on the road, she would have turned away in shame.

Instead, her eyes fixed upon the grove of willows at the edge of the salt flats, the last thicket of green before the earth gave way to the pale, cracked barrenness of the lakeshore.

The flats were hostile by day, but under the gentle hand of moonlight, they took on a new atmosphere. They revealed a secretive beauty, a pale delicacy, and a soft, mysterious glow.

Tamar knew. She had seen the flats a handful of times from the shelter of that willow grove. There she and Thomas had passed a few precious hours alone—stolen late-night walks along the edge of a moonglow plain. There they had expressed their love with more than mere words. No one could have seen, except the stars above and Heaven itself.

She had been unashamed on those rare, intoxicating nights. Thomas was her husband, after all. But when she was at home, with only Jane for distant company—or when she visited the shops in town, or sat in the back pew at the meetinghouse, surrounded by the other young women, the secret second and third wives, the fourths and fifths and fifteenths, a worm of discontent burrowed into her heart and gnawed at her spirit.

"Hello there, Sister Loader!"

She blinked her way out of her daze. Young Charles Kimball was jogging up the road, waving to Tamar.

She returned the gesture and considered going back to the house, for there was still a flush of heat on her cheeks. But the boy was headed in her direction now with the focused air of one who must see to some errand.

"Good day, Charles," Tamar said politely.

As he drew closer, the boy held up a few folded papers, each one sealed with beeswax. "Letters for you, Sister, from the city."

"Thank you, dear. How good of you to bring them by."

She slipped the letters into her pocket while Charles chattered happily about his success hunting rabbits, the wrestling match he'd won against his older brother, the grubs he'd found while digging in Tabitha's garden. Such was the boy's wont if he had no other pressing business. When at last the boy headed back to the Ricks home, Tamar hurried inside. She still hadn't told her family that she had moved out from under Tabitha's roof. She couldn't think of any way to explain the change without endangering her secret—for Patience and Mama would surely demand that she come and join them in the city, and how could she deny them?

I must thank God that Tabitha passes my letters along to me, rather than burning them up in her stove.

Tamar fixed herself a cup of the herbal tea she and Jane favored, and sat reading her letters in the stifling quiet of the log house. Zilpah's was short but welcome, full of updates about little Alpha, brimming with all the sweetness of motherhood. Zilpah's words kindled an anticipatory glow in Tamar's heart.

Mama's and Patience's letters were nearly identical—each imploring her to come for a lengthy stay in the city now that winter was long past and the roads had cleared.

Bishop Thorn is quite agreed that you must come visiting, Patience had written, *so let us have none of your excuses. Do come soon, Tamar. Mama and I miss you terribly.*

She wilted atop the stack of letters, resting her head on folded arms. As much as Tamar longed to see them, how could she answer when they asked how she fared and what new turns her life had taken?

Once my belly begins to grow, I shan't be able to visit them at all. And how will I keep them satisfied with my absence all through the summer and autumn?

The kitchen door squealed on its hinges. Tamar lurched up in her chair, wide-eyed with guilt. It was only Jane, whistling a cheerful tune as she hung her bonnet on a peg.

The song died when she noticed Tamar. "Whatever is the matter?" she asked.

Tamar gathered the letters hastily. "Nothing; not a thing in the world."

"Don't give me that nonsense," Jane said. "There's a full cup of tea beside you, and I'd bet a dollar it's gone cold, too. Bad news from the city?"

Jane moved aside the parcel containing Mrs. Allred's blouse, then sat opposite Tamar, waiting with her head tipped to one side.

Tamar could have spat. Of all the times for Jane to forget her prickly demeanor! With an effort, she tamped down her annoyance and asked, "How is your dear sister today?"

"Sarah Ann is fine," Jane said shortly. "As fine as she ever is. Come, now. I can tell something's eating at you. We shouldn't keep secrets from one another. We're stuck in this mire together."

The change in her sister-wife's demeanor was so unexpected that Tamar felt rather disoriented. She didn't quite believe she could trust Jane—as if this weren't the authentic girl at all but rather some changeling spirit. But Tamar did need advice just then, and no one understood her circumstances better than Jane.

She looked down at the tabletop while she spoke—at her cup of tea, which had gone quite cold indeed. "I've told you before that I exchange letters with my mother and sisters in the city. I've kept my promise to our husband all this time. I've told no one of our marriage, not even my family."

Jane waited, and Tamar couldn't find the courage to look up. At length, she went on.

"You've no idea how difficult it's been to tell them nothing, to make believe as if nothing in my life has changed. And how I've had to dodge around their questions, Jane! They ask me in every letter when I'll come to visit, or if they may come up to see me. I've told them there's no room to keep them in Thomas's house. They still believe I'm living with him and Tabitha. Now I think perhaps I must have a visit, after all. I might find some explanation for my living here, rather than with the Rickses, if you'll agree that they may stay with us for a few days."

"Of course I'll agree," Jane said. "It'll be a welcome distraction. Every day has been the same as the last, and I'd like to meet your family, Tamar. I'm sure I'll like them as well as I like you."

Tamar finally looked up. She had never expected awkward, silent Jane to like her. Gratitude welled up so suddenly that Tamar very nearly laughed at her own foolishness. "We'll have to tell them we've been keeping house together as two unmarried girls."

"I don't like the idea of misleading your family—nor anyone else who might ask. I've avoided talking about this mess by avoiding talking to anyone. But that will hardly serve for your family."

"Oh, you're right." Tamar sagged back in her chair. "It's no use. I can't ask you to prevaricate. I don't like the idea of misleading my mother or my sisters, either, Jane. But what else can I do?"

She squeezed her eyes shut. A small, insistent voice was scolding her from the inside. *Tell the truth, Tamar—once and for all.*

"Thomas has put us in a difficult place," she said.

Jane gave a humorless chuckle. "That's the plain fact."

"I must go to the city," Tamar said. "It's the only way to keep our secret. I can allow my family to go on believing I'm still a guest under Tabitha's roof. A lie by omission might be a lesser sin than a lie told outright. And I must go soon. Time is running out for me."

Jane stared at her—wide-eyed, forgetting to tilt her head in that curious way she had. Then she seemed to understand. The girl looked around the house with a cautious air as if she feared the whole town of Centerville might be crowded into the parlor, listening. "You're with child," Jane hissed.

Tamar nodded.

Jane had gone pale. "Thomas has put us in a difficult place, indeed."

Tamar watched from the window of a hired cab as the growing metropolis surrounded her. She had last seen Salt Lake City months ago, on that bewildering day when the wagons carrying the rescued handcart companies had rolled into Union Square. The streets had been still, the businesses closed, for almost every hand had turned to the work of aiding those in need. Now, however, the city fairly hummed with industry.

Great warehouses and factories, made of redbrick or pale sandstone, rose three and four stories high. The plank sidewalks were so crowded with people that they seemed almost like living things themselves—serpents shifting and breathing as they basked along the roads. Tamar noted the signs above doors and windows—mercantiles, dressmakers, carriage repair. There were barristers and cattlemen, makers of feather mattresses and fine carved furniture, even businesses offering instruction in dance, dramatics, and singing. A sign pointed the way to a sugar refinery. Above the flat roofs and the brick facades, a faint haze of smoke hung, dulling the brightness of the springtime sky.

The cab turned down a side street; the noise and bustle of the city's heart dwindled behind. Soon the carriage glided to an easy stop outside a fine brick home several blocks south of the business district.

Tamar drew a long breath. It did little to calm her nerves. All the long ride from Centerville, she had asked herself whether she was doing right or wrong. Thomas hadn't given his blessing on this foray into the city. But then, she'd scarcely seen her husband in weeks. His duties to Brigham Young and the Nauvoo Legion kept him so long away, Tamar's condition might be plain for all to see by the time he returned to Centerville. She had made the arrangements of her own accord—with Jane's help—and now she couldn't help feeling as if she were doing something dreadfully wicked.

Thomas only told me to keep our marriage secret, she reminded herself. *He never said I mustn't see my family.*

The driver appeared on the curb, offering his hand. Tamar took it and stepped down from the carriage.

"Here we are, Sister," the man said, lifting her carpetbag from the carriage. "Bishop Thorn's home—and a fine one it is."

She reached through her skirts to the inner pocket, withdrawing a handful of gold coins. Some of the money had come from Thomas—her monthly portion of the household income. By far the greater amount had come from her own work. Once word had made its way around Centerville that she'd been assistant to a real New York dressmaker, Tamar had found her services much in demand. With the weight of her own gold in hand, she felt a rush of pride and satisfaction. She had never realized how much she enjoyed having her own income until she'd finally made up her mind to spend it for her own enjoyment. And there was nothing she had longed for so much as the company of her family.

"Tamar!"

She looked around to find Patience hurrying down the walkway, her thin face flushed with excitement. Mama waited on the porch. Her silver hair was swept up in a becoming style, and though she wore mourning black for Papa's memory, she was beaming with both hands pressed against her heart.

Tamar thrust the fare into the driver's hand, picked up her bag, and rushed for the wrought-iron gate. She reached it before her sister did and fumbled with the catch.

"Oh, bother the gate!" Patience pulled her into an embrace over the waist-high bars.

Tamar never knew whether she was laughing or crying. She pulled back and helped Patience open the gate, then hurried up the walk, reaching out for her mother. She kissed Mama's dear weathered cheeks.

"I'd begun to think I would never hold you again, my sweet girl," Mama said. "This is a blessed day."

Sister Thorn, the mistress of the house, had laid out a fine luncheon. Four children were crowded together at the end of the table—two girls, neither of them quite ten years of age, and two small boys. The children's attention flitted between Tamar and the platters of food, especially an apple pie that was still hot from the oven.

"These are Sister Thorn's children," Mama said.

One of the girls spoke up. "Is she your sister, Auntie Pay?"

"Yes, dear," Patience said. "This is Tamar. You remember: she helped me make the calf's head soup on the trail." She turned to Tamar with an expression somewhere between chagrin and amusement. "The children have decided I'm their auntie. I've tried to convince them I've only one nephew—Zilpah's little boy—but they will have none of it."

Tamar clasped her hands behind her back to keep herself from touching her stomach. It seemed a great injustice that she couldn't break the news to Patience that she would soon be an aunt again. *I can't tell her now . . . I can't tell her ever. Shall I hide my own child from my family? He deserves to know his aunts and his grandmother. He must know them, one way or another.*

Tamar swallowed her sudden discontent. Patience had too keen an eye. If she saw the least unhappiness in Tamar's expression, she would hound her until the truth came out.

To the children, she said, "I'm pleased to meet you. I hope we'll be good friends."

"How long will you stay?" the eldest girl asked.

"For a week. I shall go back home to Centerville next Monday morning."

Sister Thorn came sweeping in from the kitchen, wrapped in a cheerful red apron and carrying a board of sliced bread. She was a plump and pretty woman, brimming with welcome.

"We'll be glad to have your company for the week," she said. "I'm sorry you must share a bed with Patience, for, with so many children about, there's little room to spare."

"I won't mind a bit." Tamar took her sister's hand. "Patience kicks in her sleep and she snores, of course, but I've missed her all the same."

Sister Thorn gathered her little ones under her arms and herded them out of the dining room. "I've set the children's lunch in the kitchen, and after they've eaten, we'll all take a walk up to the temple to see how it's coming along. You'll have all the time you'd like for talking over family matters."

After the Thorns had gone, Tamar sank gratefully into a chair while Mama began filling the plates. The growing baby had made her ravenous; she never could eat enough for her satisfaction, and the relentless hunger brought dark memories of the trail. She knew some women were sick in the early months of pregnancy. Tamar would rather have suffered nausea than the constant reminder of the deprivation she'd endured. The trail was still too close, a specter that haunted her days and her nights.

She groped for a diversion as she took her plate from Mama. "How *is* the temple coming along?"

"It hasn't changed one whit since you saw it last," Patience said. "Still a great black hole in the ground with cut blocks lying everywhere. But it is jolly to walk past the square and watch the builders at their work. I take the boys there whenever the weather is good. It gets them out from under their mother's foot, and they like to hear the hammers and chisels tapping away. Zilpah often comes out to meet me at the temple site; we have our constitutionals together, and Alpha likes to watch the builders, too."

"That temple will be a great sight one day," Mama said reverently. "We're blessed to watch its creation. I often think how dearly your father would have loved to see it."

Tamar set down her fork. She had wondered which of them would speak first of Papa. "I miss him every day," she said softly. "I wish I could tell him . . ."

She could say no more. The tightness in her throat constrained her as much as the weight of secrecy.

Mama reached out from where she sat and took Tamar's hand. A moment later, Patience took the other. They remained that way for a long while, silent in their shared grief.

The first days of Tamar's visit flew past in a joyful blur. By day, she talked with her family and basked in the glow of their company. She even played with the Thorn children, wondering all the while what her own baby would be—boy or girl, fair or dark headed, boisterous or shy. In the afternoons, she and Patience called on Zilpah, who had just moved with her husband to a small house not far from the temple square. John had found work on the temple site, mortaring stones—and though their home was old and cramped and would be drafty in the winter, he and Zilpah took great pride in their humble holdings.

One evening, Patience convinced Tamar to attend the ward dance, though Tamar hadn't brought a dress suitable for any such occasion. Patience would hear no excuse. She bundled Tamar into a new low-necked gown that she'd made herself—a stylish dove gray—and put on an old dancing dress, a castoff that one of Brigham Young's daughters had donated to the handcart refugees. Cast off it may have been, but the wine-colored silk was almost as fine and fetching as any London socialite could have wished for.

Patience pulled Tamar to her side. Shoulder to shoulder, they gazed at their reflections.

"We're perfectly killing," Patience said. "I won't be a bit surprised if we each land a beau tonight. We could be married by summer's end."

Tamar's answering smile was sickly and tremulous.

The dance proved a welcome distraction from her troubles. It was held in a new brick mansion called the Staines House—a French-styled marvel with mansard roofs of slate tiles and ornate balconies extending over a pillared porch. The city had turned out its finest entertainment for the night's celebration. A talented orchestra provided the music, and every hour, the guests assembled on the lawn to hear an aria or a duet performed by members of the recently formed opera company.

Tamar's dance card was much in demand, too. She reasoned it was no sin for a married woman to join in the dancing; a waltz or a reel was no declaration of intent. A few fine young men did ask whether they might call on her someday. Tamar accepted their compliments with a blush, then deflected by admitting she lived in Centerville and was only visiting in the city. She hadn't lied to anyone, for no one had asked whether she was anyone's wife.

The morning after the ball, Tamar woke alone in Patience's narrow bed. The light at the window was mellow and high. The morning had grown late, and Tamar's stomach ached with hunger.

She dressed quickly and slipped downstairs. The Thorn home seemed quite empty until she found Patience in the library. She was perched at a reading table, poring over a newspaper with curious intensity. A plate of toast and a half-empty cup of lemon-balm tea stood close to hand.

Patience glanced up from her paper almost dismissively. "Good morning."

"You must be reading an engrossing story," Tamar said, helping herself to Patience's untouched toast.

"Indeed, I am. Thursday is back-East paper day. The local papers printed by the church are all well and good, but I'm keen on the news from the States. Do you get any Eastern papers up in Centerville?"

"I don't know," Tamar admitted. "I've never thought to ask."

"You must inquire. Eastern papers make for the most fascinating reading. I've become quite enthralled by the goings-on in Washington. Americans have such complicated politics." She looked up with a sober expression. "It *was* interesting, I should say. Now I'm afraid I read them more out of fear than curiosity."

"Fear?" Tamar said.

"Surely, even up in Centerville, you've heard about Buchanan's threats."

"Of course. My hu—" Tamar caught herself just in time. She coughed, feigning that she'd choked on a bit of toast. She had very nearly said, *My husband is often away, training with the Legion.* Instead, she said, "My household often talks over the news about Buchanan."

"Sometimes I wonder." Patience was meditative now, almost conspiratorial. "Is there any truth to what President Buchanan has said about the church?"

Tamar's cheeks began to burn. "What has he said?"

"You know—all that talk about the sins of the Southern states, how Mormon women are used almost as shamefully as the Africans."

"I—I don't know what you mean," Tamar stammered.

"Listen to this." Patience bustled to a low shelf beside the parlor window. She located a folded newspaper and drew it out from between the spines of the books. "This is from the *Evening Star* in Washington, dated last March. We were still in New York then. But I found this issue here in the Thorns' library, and I saved it; I found it too intriguing to ignore."

She returned to the table and read from the old newspaper. "'Brigham Young continues to uphold polygamy for the purpose of raising up a royal priesthood. He said in a recent harangue: *Suppose that I had the privilege of having only one wife, I should have had only three sons, for those are all that my first wife bore, whereas now I have buried five sons and have thirteen living.*'"

Patience looked up with a wide-eyed expression, half scandalized, half thrilled. "Have you ever heard of such a thing in all your life?"

Tamar could think of no safe answer. She stared back at her sister.

"I'm confident it can't be true, after all," Patience said, returning the old paper to the shelf. "Men taking any number of wives. Imagine it! The Americans will tout any salacious story that comes into their heads, and all in the name of discrediting our church. They're only making fools of themselves."

Tamar managed to speak at last. "Surely rumors are nothing to fret over. Why trouble yourself over gossip?"

"Buchanan has made so much of these rumors that he's tied the fate of his presidency to Deseret. He seems to think if he can force Brigham Young to kiss his ring, the Southern states will fall in line, too, and all talk of rebellion will cease."

Tamar nodded. She understood the situation between North and South as well as any Englishwoman could. The escalating tensions had been the most popular subject for discussion in the dressmaker's shop in New York where Tamar had worked. Americans had been frantic that year with talk of the Jayhawkers, Bleeding Kansas, the Topeka Constitution. Tamar had understood little of the gossip, but she had gleaned this much: Americans seemed convinced that the South was ready to attempt secession.

"This president must be desperate to hold the nation together," Tamar said. "Why else would he believe such . . . strange stories?"

"Desperate, indeed. I've been keeping a close eye on the news out of Washington, and I tell you, the United States is frantic to avert a civil war. One would think we're well beyond such troubles in Salt Lake Valley. Yet the States seem bent on drawing our church into the fray. See here—this is the *Orleans Independent Standard*. It's the freshest news I've had in weeks; this issue is dated the first of May. It says the chief justice of Utah Territory has resigned his post in protest."

"In protest of what, exactly?"

Patience read again. "'Judge Drummond's letter sets forth so plainly and directly the whole enormity of the outrages and crimes of Brigham Young and his satellites, that we copy the principle portion of it.' There's some preamble, and then: 'Brigham Young, the governor of Utah Territory, is the acknowledge head of the Church of Jesus Christ of Latter-day Saints, commonly called Mormons, and as such head, the Mormons look to him—and to him alone—for the law by which they are to be governed. Therefore no law of Congress is by them considered binding in any manner. Secondly, I know that there is a secret oath-bound organization among all the male members of the church, to acknowledge no law save the law of the Holy Priesthood, which comes to the people through Brigham Young, direct from God, he—Brigham—being vicegerent of God and prophetic successor of Joseph Smith, who was the founder of this blind and treasonable organization.'"

"It isn't untrue," Tamar said carefully. "Brigham did choose this valley because it was so far beyond the reach of the American government. The church has intended all along to create a state ruled by God's law."

"Yes, but we aren't committing *treason*. Deseret has ordered itself in accordance with popular sovereignty."

"I . . . I don't follow, I'm afraid."

Patience gave a toss of her head. "The governors of Deseret— Brigham especially—have done everything in accordance with established American precedent. This is how all the states have come about, and we've every right to order our lives and our land as we see fit. And yet the Americans have worked themselves into a frenzy over the fact of our sovereignty. They're inventing falsehoods—dangerous lies. This very article goes on to claim that Brigham burned a set of American lawbooks as an act of deliberate rebellion. I've never heard such nonsense in all my days. And these foul tales of polygamy. Did you ever!"

"I know Brigham has called up the Legion," Tamar said. "Thomas . . . that is to say, Mr. Ricks—the man who has . . . taken me in . . ." She trailed off and gulped down the last of the tea, unable to meet her sister's eye. "Mr. Ricks has been often away, working for Brigham Young, preparing the Legion. He has said there's little danger in it—that Brigham is only taking precautions. You don't really think this business with Buchanan is so very dangerous. Do you?"

Patience sighed, folding the newspaper. "If you'd asked me that question a few weeks ago, I would have chucked you under the chin. Now, though . . . They're calling us traitors, Tamar. They're claiming we're in rebellion against the United States. I pray we'll be spared any real strife, but a wise woman is prepared for anything."

Below the line of the table, Tamar let her hand rest against her stomach. Had she only imagined the fluttering inside, or was her child quailing in fear?

Later that morning, Tamar and Patience walked through the bustling city to the site of the temple's foundation. Zilpah was waiting on the corner where she most often met Patience. She was bent forward, holding Alpha by the hands as he attempted to pull himself up to his feet. When the baby recognized Patience, he gave a happy squeal.

Zilpah looked up, beaming. She swept Alpha into her arms and kissed Tamar's cheek. "What a joy it's been to have you here in the city. It feels almost as if we'd never been parted."

They remained on the corner for some time, talking easily of years gone by while the builders climbed in and out of the dark foundation and the music of chisels filled the air. Alpha was transfixed by the sound and commotion. He stared at the building site, dark eyes wide, sweet mouth hanging open in wonder. Tamar watched the baby with almost as much fascination. She longed to take him from Zilpah and press him against her heart. Never had she felt such a longing before—a desperation to hold and protect and kiss that soft, precious creature.

"Don't you agree, Tamar?" Patience said.

She blinked, turning away from her nephew with monumental effort. "I'm sorry. My thoughts drifted."

"I said, by the time the temple actually starts to rise up out of that hole, Alpha will be old enough to go courting—and what a handsome young man he'll be."

"Oh," Tamar said. "Yes, of course. He's a beautiful lad."

"He'll be begging me to let him join his dad on the building crews the moment he learns to talk," Zilpah said. "Sometimes he fusses so, and nothing will calm him, except to come out and watch the builders. There are some small boys who work on the site—clearing away chips of stone and fetching water. But I shan't allow my son to work until he's a proper age."

"There's amusement enough in watching," Patience said. "Sometimes one does witness extraordinary feats. I saw the men lower one of the cornerstones into the foundation a few days back."

"Look," Zilpah said, "they're bringing out the tackle now. We'll see them drop another stone into the foundation. What luck!"

Tamar turned back to the building site, where some of the men had begun fixing ropes around a great block of limestone. Something pulled her gaze away from the builders, however. A large, broad man was standing at the edge of the lot across the road from Tamar and her sisters. The brim of his hat was pulled low across his face, but the sight of his heavy black beard sent a jolt of anxiety down her spine.

It's Thomas. And he's looking right at me. Whatever shall I do?

At that moment, Alpha began to whine and fuss. Zilpah spoke to him softly, but the boy wouldn't be soothed. The sound of his distress only heightened Tamar's dreadful anxiety—until, finally, Alpha spit up across the front of his mother's blouse.

Patience gave a wordless cry of disgust, but Zilpah bore the indignity with a saintly, resigned air.

"Happily," she said, "home is only a short walk away. I'll go back and find something clean to wear. I won't be gone five minutes."

"We'll come along," Patience said. "We can mind Alpha while you're changing."

Tamar cut another frantic glance across the street. Thomas hadn't moved. He was tipping up the brim of his hat with one finger as if trying to get a clearer view of the women on the corner—trying to decide whether he was truly looking at Tamar.

"I'll stay here, if it's all one to you," Tamar said. "I'd like to . . . contemplate the temple. Goodness knows when I'll visit the city again. I haven't the privilege of watching the construction every day, like you do."

Patience took Zilpah by the arm, gingerly avoiding the mess on her blouse. "Suit yourself. We won't be long."

As soon as they'd rounded the corner, Thomas hurried across the road. Tamar watched him come, clenching her fists behind her skirt, willing herself to coolness.

Thomas pulled his hat from his head, glancing up and down the street. A wagon trundled past. Other groups of women and children had assembled farther down the way, the little ones cheering as the builders hauled on their pulley lines and the great block of limestone crept toward the edge of the pit. No one stood near enough to overhear the conversation.

"Tamar—it is you."

"Of course, darling."

He shook his head in astonishment. "You've caught me off guard. I never expected to find you in the city. After all, I never heard you'd made plans to travel. I never gave my blessing."

Tamar scowled at him. She couldn't seem to stop herself. She knew that women in her condition were subject to changes of mood, but this sudden bleakness had gripped her so strongly that she could have shouted at him, or cried. Thomas didn't seem happy to see her. He seemed rather annoyed by her presence.

"Is there some law that a woman mustn't enter the city without her husband's permission? One could wonder why you're so unhappy at finding me here, Thomas. Perhaps you're courting another woman." She never knew where the accusation came from, yet now that it had entered her head, it seemed the most obvious explanation for his chagrin. "Is that why you're so often away? You foisted Jane upon me without any warning, and now you'll trot out some other girl—"

"Hush!" He stepped closer, reaching for her arm but stopping short of touching her. If he placed his hands upon her where anyone might see, there would be little hope left of keeping their secret. "What's all this wild talk about other girls? It's duty to the church that's kept me away. You know that."

He softened with a short exhalation. His broad shoulders dropped. "I know I haven't seen you as often as you'd like—nor as often as I'd like. If I had my way, you and I would be together every second night. We'd go walking beside the lake, as we did that night . . . you remember. The night with all the stars shining, when we found that spot under the willows—"

"I remember," she said quietly.

"Soon I'll have more time to spend back home, or so I pray. Affairs between Brigham and Buchanan are tense, but the whole mess can't drag on into eternity. Something will give—and once I'm no longer needed to drill the Legion, our lives will be sweet again."

She felt the small life stir inside and crossed her hands protectively over her stomach. "Is the Buchanan affair really so dangerous?"

"The Legion will keep everything in hand," he said at once. "I'm confident of that."

His haste told another story, however.

Thomas seemed to read her misgiving in her stiff posture and wide eyes. "I'm sorry," he said, "for upsetting you. I don't want you to be frightened. But to find you here in the city, where I never expected to see you . . . You've rattled me some. I've had so many surprises of late. So many things I never expected. Not all of them have been as pleasant as seeing my dear wife. But no one must know—"

"This business with Washington, with Buchanan. It's because of the Principle, isn't it? This is why you're so jealous of our secret. The politicians back East—they know about the Principle. They've called us all traitors because of it."

"It's more complicated, I fear—bigger, more tangled. But, yes, the Principle is part of the Buchanan affair. If you knew the half of what I knew . . . but I can't speak of it. I've sworn silence to President Young himself. Suffice to say, we can't be too careful—you and I, and Jane. Too much could be on the line if . . ."

He trailed off into silence.

Tamar drew a shuddering breath, then finished the thought for him. "If the army comes to Deseret after all. If Brigham falls, and Buchanan wins. We're facing a war, aren't we, Thomas? A proper war, with bloodshed and cannons and—"

"Hush, now—hush. There's no cause for so much fear. You forget: God is on our side. But we can't be too cautious till the matter is settled and there's no more threat from Washington. And the more time you spend with your family, the likelier they'll guess about our marriage."

A peculiar hardness stiffened her spine. Perhaps that, too, was an effect of her condition. Never before had she felt such offense at Thomas's authority and guidance. She stared up at her husband, bold and assured. "I agreed to keep our secret—not to turn my back on those I love. I crossed the plains with my mother and sisters. There are bonds between us that you can't begin to understand. I'll submit to your authority, but only so far as it's just and wise. Try to keep me from my family, and learn how far a husband's authority reaches."

Thomas relented at once. "I'm sorry. You're right, of course. You must have the company of your family; I can't expect anything else. As long as you guard what must be guarded . . . but I know I can trust you, Tamar. The Lord wouldn't have brought us together if you weren't a trustworthy woman."

Satisfied, she lowered her eyes.

"You mustn't mind my dark mood," Thomas said. "I'm on edge from . . . well, everything I've learned, everything I've done for Brigham and the Legion."

"I've been on a knife's edge, myself," she admitted, "wondering what kind of world we're making here in Deseret. What kind of world our child will inherit, when he is born."

She glanced up at Thomas, shyly, and found him watching her with an expression of awe and delight.

"Do you mean . . . ?"

She nodded.

He stepped a little closer, then reached out tentatively and took her hand. The touch lasted only a moment. Then he'd moved away again.

"I wish I could kiss you now," he said softly.

Tamar kept her eyes on the dusty red ground. She would have kissed him, too, with all the fullness of her love, all the desperation of her fear. But there were eyes all around them, and rumors did fly.

"My sisters will return soon," she said. "We must part now, for our secret's sake."

He nodded and replaced his hat. Tamar watched him cross the road, dodging easily between carriages. But when he reached the edge of the temple lot, he turned once more to look at her. He watched her for a long while, so long that her cheeks burned.

19

Jane

Centerville
Summer 1857

Jane and Tamar pulled the fresh linen sheet taut between them, then lowered it to the feather-stuffed mattress. Tamar tucked her edges of the sheet quickly, but Jane took her time, smoothing every ripple away, shaping the folds at the corners of the bed. There was no sense in hurrying. She wanted everything to be perfect for Sarah Ann.

Once the sheet lay to her satisfaction, Jane wrestled a quilt out of a pinewood chest and spread it over the mattress. The pattern of four-pointed stars, set against a field of pale-blue octagons, brought cheer to the little room, as did the pitcher of flowers on the small table below the window. The hopeful light of a summer day glowed amid yellow balsamroot, spires of mountain bluebell, and the flat white parasols of wild carrot flower. Jane had gathered the bouquet amid the sweet, cool wind and the dew of early morning. She'd been too excited to sleep late, for Tabitha had told her the evening before that Sarah Ann could finally come home.

"The room looks lovely," Tamar said. "I know your sister will adore it, Jane. And how glad she'll be to live with you after all these weeks."

"I'm only thankful we found a bed," Jane replied. "It's a lucky thing Mrs. Shelby's boy had outgrown it and she had one to spare."

"Lucky Sarah Ann is such a small girl. Otherwise, this old child's bed would have done us no good."

Tamar seemed to realize she had chosen her words poorly, but it was too late now to call them back. Jane turned away. She lifted her boot and nudged shut the lid of the chest. It closed with a bang like a rifle's report.

"I'm sorry," Tamar said. "I didn't mean—"

Jane forced herself to smile. "You've nothing to apologize for. Sarah Ann *is* small; there's no use in running from the truth."

She understood the truth all too well. Her sister was little better than she'd been in March. Tabitha had found no cure for the strange illness that afflicted Sarah Ann. But neither had her condition declined, and so Tabitha had agreed that the sisters should be reunited.

Jane wasn't without reason for happiness. She had worked three months now as Tabitha's apprentice—first learning the properties and uses of local plants, then accompanying the healer as she treated the simplest cases. The work was so engrossing that Jane often forgot her troubles for hours at a time. There was a peaceful rhythm, a meditative ritual, to the healer's arts. She took comfort in the grinding of herbs, the precise measurement of doses, the sweet-sharp, dusty scent of roots and remedies that filled Tabitha's parlor. And when Jane could see a treatment working—dulling the pain of an injury or bringing restful sleep—a warmth of accomplishment filled her till her bones seemed to hum with satisfaction.

But what good will an apprenticeship do me if I can't cure Sarah Ann?

She left the bedroom and wandered to the kitchen. Tamar had baked hand pies to celebrate Sarah Ann's arrival; the scent of honey and warm, buttery pastry filled the house. Jane took one of the pies and broke it open. It was filled with strawberry jam—usually one of Jane's favorites, but now she found she had little appetite. She put the hand pie on a tin plate and sat at the table, watching the hot jam spill from the crust in a slow ruby flood.

"What is it, Jane?" Tamar joined her at the table. "I'd thought you would be glad today."

"I am glad. Mostly. You can't imagine how hard it was to be parted from Sarah Ann while she was living with Tabitha. But she's not much better, and I'm afraid that if Tabitha couldn't cure her, there's no hope at all."

"You mustn't give up. God can bring about any miracle. We both must pray—"

Jane tossed her head, an impatient dismissal. "Anyhow, I'll be run ragged caring for Sarah Ann. Hot weather has always been hard on her, ever since we left Winter Quarters. I don't know if it was the dust of the trail or the heat, but she never seemed to recover from that journey. It's almost as if her body remembers the trail itself—like the trail never left her. And the garden will soon reach its peak. Between Sarah Ann and the garden and my work with Tabitha, how am I to keep up?"

"I shall mind Sarah Ann during the day," Tamar said. "I can look in on her and see that she takes her medicine, for I'll only be sewing. You shall tend the garden and help Tabitha while Sarah Ann and I—"

"I don't need your help."

Jane had snapped out those words before she'd thought better. Her face burned with shame, for she certainly would have to rely on Tamar—and her sister-wife deserved none of her wounded scorn.

Sister-wife, Jane mused. She'd heard Tamar refer to their relationship that way now and again. Jane didn't think she would ever come to see Tamar as any sort of sister. She was no replacement for Sarah Ann; that was certain.

But she did need Tamar. She needed all the help she could find. Tom was always diligent about sending money to the log house, but his duties to Brigham Young had kept him so occupied that he was rarely in Centerville himself. He sent letters along with the banknotes—sickly-sweet love notes to Tamar, which she insisted on reading aloud to Jane. For her part, Jane was pleased that the letters Tom wrote to her were straightforward and plain, with no pretenses at romance.

You must tell me at once if you or Sarah Ann want for anything, Tom's notes most often read. *I'm most anxious that you and your sister should be cared for properly.*

Jane had no doubt that Tom would have seen to it if she'd requested any particulars. He would have sent Charles Kimball over to do whatever work Jane couldn't manage herself, or some fully grown man if Charles couldn't manage it. But what use was there in asking? Sometimes she felt as if she needed more help than the whole town could have given. The memory of her mother's grave was very near—Elijah's, too, hastily dug at the edge of the garden while the sun had beaten down on her weary back. Would she soon dig another grave? Must she lay her dear sister under the earth—lay the last of her family to rest in the cold and the dark?

She wrestled her fear and anger back into a dim corner of her heart. In a measured tone, she said, "You've got your hands plenty full with your sewing, Tamar. I can't ask you to care for my sister, too."

"Nonsense; I'll welcome the company."

"This is likely more than you can handle, anyhow."

Across the table, Tamar had gone very still. Jane peered at her from the corner of her good eye.

Stiffly, Tamar drew herself up. "What exactly do you mean by that?"

"Never you mind. Forget I said it."

"I'll do no such thing. I can tell you think me frail and stupid; don't try to deny it. I've lived alongside you all these months—long enough to know you aren't subtle in your opinions."

Jane's face burned hotter still.

"I'm stronger than you think," Tamar insisted.

Jane gave a quiet laugh. She couldn't seem to stop herself, though she knew in that instant it had been a mistake. Tamar was a pampered English rose, higher born and better off than Jane had ever been. What could she understand of suffering and loss? What did she know of grief?

Tamar had blazed up in response to her sniggering. "You spoke of the trail, how one's body remembers. Let me tell you what my bones remember. We'll see how weak you think me, then."

Jane folded her arms on the tabletop and scowled off into the kitchen, but Tamar was undeterred.

"I *will* be heard, Jane, whether you like it or not. I've done my best to make peace with everyone in this mad entanglement. I've tolerated Tabitha's endless hatred and your cold disregard. Thomas's absence, too. All this time, I've tried to remain obedient to God's will. I've no more stomach left for the effort."

Jane could only stare at Tamar's doubled image. When had this delicate lady ever lashed out with such force? Tamar's sudden assertiveness stole away Jane's protestations and left her starkly ashamed of her sarcasm and temper. She could only sit, transfixed by remorse, while Tamar recounted her experience of the trail in unforgiving detail.

She spared nothing in the harrowing account, speaking with such grim precision that Jane could feel the ache in her own back, the shivering in her own limbs—all the long pain and weariness of hauling a handcart over rough terrain, the humiliation, the hunger. She told of her beloved father's illness, his body flagging even though his spirit never did. Jane burned from the mountain fever when Tamar described how she'd lain useless in the invalids' camp. She quailed with terror at falling behind the company, at knowing her sister must give birth in the howling wilderness. When Tamar spoke of the long struggle to regain their party—stumbling through the night, never knowing whether they still had the trail while brush fires encircled the family like some inevitable snare—Jane's eyes began to sting from unshed tears. And when Tamar's father succumbed at last—so far from the valley he'd longed to see, farther still from the homeland he had loved—Jane could almost feel his frail hand clutched in her own.

She hoped Tamar would relent once she'd spilled out every heart-rending detail of her father's death. But the story grew darker still.

Next came the deprivation, the cold, the hunger that turned to starvation. She told of the man whose mind had broken under the strain, who'd turned savage as a wolf and had tried to eat a child's hands while the girl was yet living.

"And when the men carried the bodies of those who'd died to the wagons," Tamar said, "I saw butcher marks in the flesh—"

"Stop," Jane finally said. "I can't bear this story." Tears ran down her face. She wiped them away with the back of her hand, but still, they came.

At length, Tamar said, "Now I feel rather wicked for having pushed you so far."

"Is it all true?"

When Jane looked up, Tamar nodded.

"How did you ever survive?"

Tamar gave a small sigh. "Even now, I can't say. By God's grace, I suppose—yet it seems the wrong answer. Or an incomplete answer."

Jane tipped her face so she could see her sister-wife clearly. "I'm sorry. I thought you couldn't possibly understand what I'd lost to the trail—my father, my mother. And now . . . now I may lose Sarah Ann, too."

Tamar opened her mouth to speak, but Jane lifted a hand. "Please don't try to tell me otherwise. I know you'd say it out of kindness, but I must face the truth. Sarah Ann could die yet. Perhaps it's even likely. I'd thought myself the greatest wretch in the valley, and I'd considered you nothing more than some dainty lady from England who couldn't feel what I'd felt, who couldn't have survived what I had. How wrong I was. I'll be glad for your help, if you're willing. And I hope you'll forgive me for being a fool."

Tamar and Jane stood in the same moment; they stepped around the table, and Jane reached out a hand as if to shake—for it seemed a right and proper gesture in that moment, an offer of good will. Instead of shaking, Tamar pulled her into a tight embrace.

"It's I who should apologize," Tamar said. "I wanted to hurt you with my story—make you feel what I'd felt."

"You did just that."

"But it was cruel. No one deserves to know such pain, not even by proxy. None but God can say what will become of Sarah Ann, and I can never take her place in your heart—nor can you take the place of my own sisters. But we are sisters of a kind. This marriage hasn't been what either of us had wished for. Still, I hope we can make the best of it together."

Jane said nothing for a long moment, but in Tamar's arms, she felt some of her habitual stiffness fall away. "I've never held anyone but Sarah Ann. And my mother, God rest her spirit."

Tamar hugged her all the tighter.

Jane gave a self-conscious chuckle, then gently backed away. "You're right; we should make the best of things, together. I've had to rely on myself for so long that I'm not good at asking for what I need . . . nor accepting help when it's offered. But if you'll forgive my bad manners, I'll do my best to behave."

"There's nothing to forgive. Let us both think of Sarah Ann now. Whatever she needs, we'll provide—together."

Jane sank into her chair again. She took one half of the broken pie and pushed the plate across the table to Tamar.

"If I could only learn what exactly she needs, I wouldn't be so frightened."

Tamar gave Jane a sober look while she tasted her half of the pie. "I meant what I said before. You should pray for guidance and intercession."

"I'm no Mormon. When have you ever seen me at the meeting-house? I'm sure if Tom were in Centerville more often, he would expect me to attend Sunday services, but I've been perfectly content to keep to myself and talk to God in my own way. Though I'm not convinced He has ever listened."

"You might be more a Mormon than you've ever suspected." There was a distinct note of amusement in Tamar's voice. "Here you are, in a plural marriage—the most Mormon of all circumstances."

Jane laughed as she picked at the hand pie.

"God never fails to hear earnest prayer from the heart of a true believer," Tamar went on. "I learned that on the trail. It was faith that delivered me from my suffering, and the apostles' prayer lifted my fever. Surely you and Sarah Ann can both be delivered, if your faith is strong enough."

That dry, cynical voice in Jane's heart whispered, *And what of your father, Tamar? Wasn't his faith sincere? Didn't he pray for his life to be spared, even as he lay dying?*

But she had promised to treat her sister-wife with greater kindness. She wouldn't speak the bitter thought aloud.

"Perhaps I'll try it," Jane said, "one day."

Summer ripened, the days growing longer, the light hanging lazy and golden over the great expanse of the lake. June gave way to July, and even the early mornings felt thick and monotonous with heat, with the drone of insects in the tall grass. Jane and Tamar were forced to do the better part of their daily work in the open air on the northern side of the house, where the shade was forgiving and a cool breeze stirred. There Jane would sort through the harvest from her garden—shelling peas, snapping the strings off bean pods, cutting potato sets for the fall planting. Tamar would spread a blanket in the grass and put the finest, sweetest tucks and ruffles into the petticoats and blouses she made while Sarah Ann sprawled on the quilt beside her.

The girl's hands still trembled too much for sewing, but she loved to lounge beside Tamar and watch her tidy needlework. Sarah Ann exclaimed over yards of linen lace or sorted through Tamar's basket of notions. Sometimes she merely lay with one hand bunched in a soft cotton voile, staring up dreamily at a perfect blue sky.

Now and then, Jane would round the corner of the house with a bushel of beans on her hip and overhear Tamar answering the girl's countless questions about life in England, or demonstrating how to fell a seam just so. Sometimes Tamar recounted the fairy stories she had loved when she'd been a child, and then Sarah Ann would doze with a contented smile. Tamar was an endless source of delight to Sarah Ann. Sometimes, Jane felt rather jealous, and wondered if Sarah Ann were coming to love Tamar more than she loved her. More often, she was grateful to the point of tears, for comfort and affection had never been her strength, and Sarah Ann deserved every softness, every care.

July passed slowly, its final days blazing with the white torridity of the salt pans. By night, the valley was cooled by merciful breezes that smelled of brine and white clay, but the close, stifling heat of day affected Sarah Ann poorly.

She was limp and sleepy when the sun was high, resting on a bed of cushions in the northern yard. When the girl felt energetic, Tamar allowed her to pull lengths of linen thread through a knob of beeswax, and then Sarah Ann would watch while Tamar demonstrated the right way to fold a French seam, or how to stitch two lengths of lace together so that they seemed tatted of a single piece. Sarah Ann had less pluck, however, as the season advanced. There were days when she scarcely sat up at all, and Jane was obliged to pull her to her feet when lunchtime came.

On the afternoon of the first of August, Jane and Tamar left the girl sleeping on her cushions in the shady lee of the house. They took their lunch together on the flat-topped stones that overlooked their lane and the road beyond.

"Is that Mary Smithies coming up the road?" Jane set aside her plate of cold bean stew.

"Yes," Tamar said. "She told me she would visit today. I've finished her new green dress; no doubt she intends to wear it at tonight's dance. I never thought to look for her until the afternoon."

When Mary caught sight of them on the stone bench, she picked up her pace despite the heat. Jane could already sense that the woman was bubbling over with a need to talk.

"Oh, girls, I'm so glad to find you both," Mary said. "Have you heard what happened at Big Cottonwood Canyon?"

Jane and Tamar glanced at one another. Tamar said, "We've had little time of late for listening to news. You'd better tell us all about it."

They made room on the stones, and Mary sat, though her feet fidgeted in the dust. "Half of Salt Lake City went up into the canyon on the twenty-fourth of July—a big picnic, a proper celebration."

Jane knew already that the date was almost sacred in Deseret—the anniversary of Brigham Young's discovery of the valley.

"President Young got up in front of the whole crowd," Mary went on, "and made a proclamation. He said he'd just learned that the army was already on the move. He told all the people to make ready for evacuation."

"Evacuation?" Tamar exclaimed. "Surely it can't be true!"

"Who can be certain of anything?" Mary said. "It could be wild rumor. I haven't found anyone yet in Centerville who was actually at Big Cottonwood. Goodness knows what President Young really said. He might not have been there at all; you know how tales spread."

Despite the heat, a chill ran through Jane. She felt suddenly much too far away from Sarah Ann. She needed to stand over her sleeping sister, brandishing any weapon that might come to hand—a rake from her garden, even one of Tamar's sewing needles. It would be better than meeting this threat empty-handed.

"I wish we could know," Jane said. "Even if there were an army headed for Deseret, it would put my mind at ease to really *know* it, rather than suppose. At least then we could prepare."

After Mary had gone away with her new dress, Jane found she had no more appetite. She flung the beans and bread out into the grass for the birds to peck.

"I'm sure there's no cause for alarm," Tamar said. "Thomas told me once that the valley is easy to defend. If an army wishes to invade, they must get through the mountain passes—and they're narrow enough that the Legion can hold the passes against thousands of men."

"Still, I don't like it," Jane declared, "and curse my luck for stranding me here with Sarah Ann to care for. If Elijah had lived, we might be in California by now, and out of harm's way."

Tamar gave her a level, chiding look.

Ever since the day Sarah Ann had come home, Jane had felt the weight of her promise to pray for intercession. Tamar had never mentioned prayer again, yet whenever Jane had expressed doubt or frustration, Tamar had cast eloquent eyes in her direction, and her expectant silence had spoken volumes.

And Jane knew she had much to be grateful for. She no longer fretted about food or shelter. She had all the clothing she and her sister needed; a fine, comfortable home; and even the joyful opportunity of her apprenticeship. Since she'd made up her mind to like Tamar, she'd found the liking easy. She was no longer a lonesome soul, even if she had no desire for the dances and parties Tamar loved to attend. And if she had to be snared in a shameful arrangement, at least the man who'd trapped her was a gentleman. On the rare occasions when Tom had found himself in Centerville and had visited Jane and Tamar, he'd treated Jane more like a sister than a wife, making no attempt to touch her, for it went without saying that she would have none of it. Tom seemed content to leave it at that.

Strange as this marriage was, it had brought Jane many blessings. Perhaps it was finally time to throw her pride and stubbornness to the wind and bow her neck before the Lord.

Anyhow, if God could heal Sarah Ann, then Jane might contrive to vacate Deseret before the army reached the Rocky Mountains. She knew Tom would let her go without complaint if she insisted on setting out for California.

Jane cleared her throat. "I thought I might go out alone this evening. To be with my thoughts. To . . . to pray."

Tamar took her hand so suddenly that Jane started.

"Oh, I'm so glad. I know prayer will be such a comfort to you."

"I must ask you to look after Sarah Ann while I'm away."

"Of course, I shall—gladly. Take all the time you need, Jane dear. It's no trouble to me."

Late that afternoon, as the worst of the day's heat began to dissipate, Jane rode her old black mule slowly through town. A long golden flare of light lay along the earth, casting dark shadows from the houses and shops of Centerville. She felt shy and clumsy, uncertain where she ought to go; how did one pray effectively, anyhow? She felt instinctively that some ceremony and ritual were required. Muttering a Psalm under her breath wouldn't do—not if she hoped to get the Almighty's attention. Nor could she direct a few earnest thoughts toward an unseen, distant God. If she hoped to produce the miracle Sarah Ann needed, she must imbue her prayer with import, with an air of the sacred.

When she came to the old road that led up the foothills to the abandoned cabin, she hesitated only a moment. The canyon would suit perfectly; there was no place in all the world as sacred as her mother's grave.

She ascended the rutted road toward Parrish Canyon unconscious of everything save her thoughts. When the mule stopped of its own accord, she looked up and found the cabin before her, dark and still under the Wasatch slope. The garden and the wheat field had gone to weeds. She could just make out, near the roots of the big willow, the wooden marker on Elijah's grave.

Jane kicked her mule and pressed on, past the cabin that had held so much of her desperation and misery. The creek was running low in the summer heat. The water scarcely whispered over pale mountain stones.

As the walls of Parrish Canyon closed around her and the old, familiar coolness set in, her thoughts cleared a little. She still knew the way to the trail and the bristlecone pine, and as she turned up that path, an unexpected peace came down like a fall of light. She had come to the right place; Jane was sure of that now. A wind hushed through the canyon, stirring the dark branches of the pine tree ahead, scattering dried leaves across the trail.

When she reached the grave site, Jane slid from the mule's back and ground-tied the animal, then moved toward the earthen mound with reverent purpose. Twigs and cones had fallen from the tree. Jane cleared them away and righted the cross at the head of her mother's grave, propping it in place with a few loose stones.

Then she sat on the earth beside the grave, wrapped in silence.

The wind stirred again from higher up in the canyon. Jane could hear it moving toward her, breathing through the scrub willows and the stunted oaks. When it reached the grave and touched her back, she felt as if a great, unseen hand had cupped protectively around her. A sudden clamor of emotion rose in her chest—awe and wonder, longing and fear. All the love she had for her sister and for her lost mother burned inside her like a fire. She was weeping now, tears streaming from her eyes while sobs racked her body.

She was in the presence of God. Jane knew that at once, for the first time in all her young life.

Please, her heart whispered.

She didn't know what else to say, what words to use, so she gave up all the emotion inside, confident her feelings were sufficient, that God would understand. She sent it all out into the wind—her need for Sarah Ann, her desperation to keep her sister safe, her willingness to do whatever the Almighty required if only He would do this one small thing, if only He would spare this one small life.

The wind moved on down the canyon. The air grew still around her. Jane climbed slowly to her feet, comforted and reassured—feelings so foreign in her experience that it seemed as if she moved through a world made new.

She mounted the mule and headed back toward the canyon's mouth. All would be well; she knew that much, and never knew how she knew it. The how didn't matter. It was a fact, and Jane breathed in the cool, shadowy, dust-scented air as if it could carry away the darkness that had festered so long inside her.

The canyon had slid into twilight while she'd prayed. The stone walls yielded their color; the shapes of thicket and scrub merged into masses of blue. As she rode out from the canyon's mouth, she saw that the evening was soft and gentle, and the stars were coming to life in a deep velvet sky. A trace of rosy light still hung behind the western mountains, casting a faint blush on the surface of the lake.

Jane rode home with a light heart. The houses of Centerville glowed with candlelight, and bats darted around her, sudden blurs of a deeper blackness against the dusky night. She was smiling by the time she passed Tabitha's house.

A light glowed in the parlor window, and Jane saw the figure of a woman move across the pane. She couldn't discern the woman's features, of course, but she knew the figure was too tall for the healer. Whoever was in Tabitha's parlor was holding one of the children in her arms, pacing as if trying to coax the little one into sleep.

Idly, Jane wondered where Tabitha had gone. No doubt the healer had been called away to tend to some illness. Jane wished her well.

A few minutes later, she reached the lane that led to her home. Some instinct flashed through her blood, causing her to sit up so abruptly that the mule grunted and stopped in the lane.

Something was wrong. A dreadful stillness hung in the air, a tension of sorrow. The front door was hanging askew, a bar of sallow lamplight spilling out into the grass.

Jane turned the mule loose in the corral and hurried toward the house. Before she'd even crossed the garden, a cry had torn from her throat as if wrenched from her soul by God's own hand.

The kitchen door swung open. Jane could hear the hinge squealing, the footfalls coming toward her through the tangled rows of her plants, but she saw nothing. Her eyes were shut tight against a terrible knowledge. The light in Tabitha's parlor, the woman watching her children. The door left hanging open in haste to save a life.

"Jane!"

Arms wrapped around her. It was Tabitha; Jane could tell by her stature and the smell of dried herbs that clung to her dress.

Then she heard Tamar, weeping as she spoke. "Sarah Ann took a turn, Jane. I ran to fetch Tabitha, and she came with all speed, but—"

"No," Jane cried.

"We did all we could for her," Tabitha said. "Come, Jane. Open your eyes. Look at me."

Jane obeyed. She saw nothing but a dim, featureless blur.

"I held her hand," Tamar said. "Until the last moment, I held her hand and told her how you love her—how we all love her."

Tabitha was stroking Jane's hair now, brushing it back from her face. "She went peacefully into God's keeping. I don't believe she was ever aware of any suffering."

"I wasn't with her." Jane could scarcely choke out those bitter words.

"You were," Tabitha said. "She said your name once—not in fear, but in love. I told her you were there beside her, and she smiled. You've always been beside her, Jane. That was all that mattered to her."

Jane rounded on Tamar. "You said if I prayed, God would hear me!"

Tamar flinched back into the shadows of the garden.

"God is nothing!" Jane shouted. "There's no power in your God, nor in any other! He's a cruel, uncaring thing."

"Jane, please—"

Shock and pain choked Tamar's voice. Jane didn't care; she lashed out with the sharp edge of her grief.

"Why do you worship this brute of a god? We're trapped here, in this miserable marriage, because of Him. Why would anyone come to Deseret, this vile place, this valley of hypocrites and swindlers? Everyone who's come all this way is a fool!"

"I told you," Tamar said, trembling, "of everything I suffered on the trail. If this faith is false, then what was my pain for?"

"Your pain? What of mine? And what sort of God would make a woman as good and kindly and loyal as you suffer to prove her faith? Why do you allow it, Tamar? And you, Tabitha. What sort of God would give you such wisdom and skill only to yoke you to a man like Thomas who takes any wife he pleases right under your nose? Why do either of you believe in this madness?"

Tabitha laid a hand on her shoulder. "Enough, Jane. Enough."

She spoke gently, yet Jane recognized the authority in those simple words. She had heard that tone often enough while working at Tabitha's side. She swallowed the anger that still raged inside and turned away from them both.

"I'm alone now," she said, calm with a terrible knowledge. "I've no one in this world. No one at all."

Tabitha's arms encircled her again. A moment later, Tamar embraced her, too. They stood that way for a long time in the deepness of the night while the stars moved unconcerned overhead.

PART III

SISTERS IN ZION

1858

20

JANE

Centerville
Winter 1858

The wildflowers beside the long dirt road faded to brown, then dried and broke and crumbled among the sere, exhausted grass. Across the dun valley, heat yielded to the cooling winds that swept up from the lake, smelling of dry earth and the bitterness of salt. Jane's birthday had come and gone in the dull, dark weeks after Sarah Ann's death. She was sixteen now. Sixteen, and alone in the world, except for Tamar and Tabitha.

Each woman had been a balm and a comfort, though for different reasons and with disparate styles. Tamar always seemed to know when Jane needed a friendly embrace or a kind word—or a good feeding up, her favorite way to lavish care. Tabitha's steady mind and resolute sensibility had provided Jane with some reassurance that the world wasn't such a place of voids and omissions as her darker musings sometimes led her to believe. Life went on because Tabitha went on, and Jane had little choice but to keep up.

She applied herself to her work as the healer's apprentice with the same focus and intensity she'd had before her sister's death. But now the work felt rote rather than joyful, even as Tabitha expanded Jane's education, bringing her along when she was called out as midwife to guide new babies into the world.

When her work was finished, Jane would walk back to her own small house like a spirit among the living, struggling to remember what had passed that day—what she'd seen and done, and whether she'd learned anything from her efforts. Sometimes she couldn't be sure her feet were actually treading the ground. Jane was as gray in her heart as the salt-blasted valley. She was waiting, like the vast, indifferent world, for winter.

She woke one morning startled by the darkness, by morning's reluctant half-light. She slid from her bed and found her room cold, her night shift inadequate against a deep blue chill. A letter lay open on the small table in the corner of her room. She picked it up and read it. A note from Tom, explaining that Tabitha had written and told him of Sarah Ann's death. *I'm so sorry, Jane,* Tom had written. *If I could have done more to save that dear girl's life, I would have done it, and gladly. Write to me. Tell me how you're holding up.* She blinked at the letter, uncomprehending. She must have read it a dozen times, for the paper was worn and soft from long handling. But she couldn't remember reading the note, and she was certain she'd never sent any reply. She stared out the window to her garden. The rows were covered and rounded with snow.

When had the season changed? Jane couldn't recall the colors of autumn, the first October storms, the frost, the snowfall. She had a vague recollection that she'd attended her twelfth labor sometime the week before. She knew she'd been focused and reliable whenever Tabitha had called on her to lend a hand. Yet how could it be true? How had she managed to do her work as Tabitha's apprentice when she couldn't even take note of the snow falling or the shortening of the days—when she couldn't pick up a pen and write to Tom in answer?

It's December, she recalled. *Tamar's baby is due the first week of February.*

She could recall the announcement of Tamar's pregnancy clearly enough, if she remembered little else. It had fallen on Jane to pass the news to Tabitha. Although Tamar had run to the healer when Sarah Ann had taken her turn, the two women still held themselves fastidiously apart. Tabitha's grudge against the second wife endured, and Tamar was as frightened of the first wife as she had ever been.

Yet when she'd informed Tabitha that Tamar was expecting, the healer had only raised a brow.

"You aren't angry?" Jane had asked.

Tabitha had answered, "What good will anger do me now?"

Jane wrapped herself in her warmest shawl, pulled on an extra pair of stockings, and went out into the kitchen to see about breakfast. She wasn't hungry, exactly—she couldn't recall feeling anything as simple as hunger since Sarah Ann had died. But she did know that a body must have its sustenance if it was to remain upright through the long hours of work, and Jane intended to remain upright even if she accomplished nothing else.

She found Tamar stirring a pot of oat porridge on the stove, one hand straying dreamily over the swell of her belly.

"Good morning," Jane said.

"How do I look?" Tamar asked, patting her hair—which, Jane now noticed, she had rolled and pinned carefully around her head. "I do hope I'm presentable. Thomas is coming to breakfast, though we've got nothing better than porridge and bacon. Oh, if only there were a few eggs this time of year!"

"Thomas?" Jane said vaguely.

Tamar laughed. "Surely you remember our husband."

"I'm sure he'll be content with porridge and bacon," Jane said.

"It's been so long since we've had a proper sit-down with him. I do wish we could lavish something good upon him. He deserves some fine treatment, don't you think?"

291

Jane shrugged. Tom had proved himself a charitable man. She could say little else in his favor, for she knew him no better than she knew Mr. Smoot at the mercantile.

"I don't know when he plans to arrive," Tamar said, stirring with vigor. "I got up early to make myself presentable, for I wouldn't like him to catch me in my night shift with my hair undone. I suppose if he saw me that way, he'd—"

A knock sounded at the front door.

"Mercy." Tamar lifted the kettle from the stove. "That must be him."

When Jane opened the door, however, she found Charles Kimball on the step, touching the brim of his cap, proffering a folded slip of paper.

"Brother Ricks asked me to bring this note to you ladies," Charles said. "I must be off now. Tabitha has more work for me at the house."

Jane surrendered the note to Tamar, who read it aloud by the light of the parlor lamp. "'Can't come today. Legion called up suddenly. Riding for Echo Canyon with Brigham Young. Blessings to you both, till we meet again. Tom.'"

Tamar lowered the letter to her side. Jane heard a whisper as the paper fell to the floor. She tipped her face, struggling to read Tamar's expression clearly—and when she saw the horror on her sister-wife's face, a dreadful sharpness came to her mind, the dull vacancy of the past months peeling away like the skin of an onion.

"What's the matter?" Jane demanded. She was prickling with fear, beset by a terrible certainty that something was amiss—something she would have seen coming, if she hadn't been sleepwalking through life.

"The Legion called up now, in December," Tamar said quietly. "It's dreadful, Jane—it must be. What Mary told us last summer about the army—it was no rumor, after all."

"How can you tell?"

"Brigham wouldn't move the Legion in the dead of winter unless the situation were dire. This must be a response to Mountain Meadows.

Thomas told me once that it would take something far more serious than Brigham's rebellion to bring an army all the way across the plains, but the moment I first heard the tale of Mountain Meadows, I knew it would mean the worst sort of trouble."

"What are you talking about?" Jane demanded.

Tamar blinked at her in surprise. "Surely you know. Everyone in the valley has heard. Even in your state, you must have heard about the slaughter."

Slaughter?

Jane sank down at the kitchen table, dazed and queasy. "I can't . . . can't recall now. Anyhow, whenever I've gone out, I've been working with Tabitha. We never talk about anything but herbs and illnesses and birthing. You'd better tell me everything. It seems I've missed something important."

"I should say so." Tamar spooned up a bowlful of porridge. "It happened in September. With all the talk of an army coming—you *do* remember those stories, I trust—it seems the men down in Iron County got rather frightened, and . . . well . . . they reacted out of all proportion."

"What do you mean, exactly?"

"There was a party of wagons passing through Deseret, on their way to California. No Mormons, of course. More than a hundred people from Arkansas—women, children."

Tamar set the bowl before Jane, who found she could only stare at the steaming porridge while Tamar spoke on.

"The company meant to camp for a night at a place called Mountain Meadows, but our men had seen them coming and mistook them for the United States Army. Or so they later claimed. The Iron County branch of the Legion surrounded the camp and—"

"My God," Jane swore. "You don't mean to say the Mormons killed innocent people."

Tamar shifted uncomfortably on her feet. "I didn't realize it had passed you by. I've scarcely heard anyone speak of anything else since autumn. Even in letters to my family, this is practically all we've discussed. My sister Patience said that word of the killings would make its way back to Buchanan, and then there would be no hope of avoiding battle. I suppose she was right. Buchanan might reasonably turn a blind eye to most of Brigham's behavior, but he can't ignore an outright massacre of American citizens."

Tamar fell heavily into her chair. She covered her eyes with both hands. "Oh, Jane, what are we to do? I've heard such terrible stories. Once, the governor of Missouri commanded that all Mormons should be exterminated—did you know that? Exterminated! And he was only a governor of one state. Buchanan is the president of the whole nation!"

Jane had gone numb, mind and body, but somehow, she managed to stand. She went to Tamar and pulled her sister-wife into an embrace, struggling to find words of comfort. "The danger isn't immediate. The mountains are impassable with snow. Even if there's an army on the move—and we don't know that for certain, Tamar—they can't possibly reach us till spring. We've time to prepare, and Brigham Young has time to negotiate. He'll find some way to avert a war. You know he's a clever man."

But even as she spoke, Jane was chilled to her heart. Tamar was right to be afraid. If the Mormons truly had slaughtered a company of travelers, there was no hope for the valley. Buchanan would have no choice but to respond with a great show of force—and Jane would be caught in the middle.

She could have gotten out in the autumn, if she'd been in her right mind—for Sarah Ann's delicate health no longer held her to Deseret, or to Tom Ricks. She was free to go, whether Tom willed it or not. And if she'd been a sensible girl, she would have left while the leaving was good.

I can't go anywhere till the spring thaw, Jane realized. *I must sit tight and hope for the best till the snows have melted.*

When the seasons turned again, they wouldn't do so unnoticed. Jane would be watching the skies and the land, ready to make her escape the moment the roads were passable. She would set her feet to the trail and put Deseret behind her forever. There was nothing for her here—no reason to remain.

~

The new year turned, and hour by hour, the days began to lengthen. Jane plotted her escape from Salt Lake Valley with meticulous care, for she meant to be well on her way to California by the time the mountain passes had melted to bare stone. Scrap by scrap and crumb by crumb, she gathered everything she would need on the trail west— sturdy clothes, a better pair of boots, portions of grain and preserved meat, which she skimmed carefully from the larder, never in such an amount that Tamar might notice. Each night, after Tamar had gone to bed, Jane rummaged in her pine chest, looking over the items she'd assembled, trying to imagine every possible contingency along the trail.

By the middle of January, she still hadn't puzzled out exactly how she might escape the valley. If she'd made her departure the previous September, she could have hoped to join a wagon train, but in the wake of the shocking attack at Mountain Meadows, a wagon seemed too much to hope for. No wagon parties would dare to pass through Deseret now. She had traded away the old black mule months ago, for he'd served no purpose at the log house. Jane supposed she might find where the mule had gone and see if she couldn't get him back. Better still, she might find a proper riding horse with a sturdy saddle—but a saddle and horse would be costly, and Jane had only a few dollars to her name.

One evening, after she'd cleared away the supper dishes, Jane sat musing at the kitchen table, eyeing the parlor, wondering what sticks of furniture or braided rugs she might sell—and whether she could spirit them away without alerting Tamar to her purpose.

Tamar was leaning easily in her ladderback chair opposite Jane. She sipped from a cup of her favorite herbal tea with one hand while the other rubbed absentmindedly at her great, rounded stomach.

"I do hope Thomas is warm and dry," Tamar was saying. "I worry over him so, up there in the mountains with the rest of the Legion. Of course, I'm glad the Legion is there to protect us all, but still, I would rather have our husband home, safe and sound. Wouldn't you?"

Jane had only been half listening. She grunted in reply. That embroidered footstool beside the parlor stove might fetch a few dollars at Smoot's store. And, of course, there were the old lap quilts Sarah Ann had made. If Smoot would take the quilts, Jane just might have enough money for a saddle horse.

Not a very good one, she thought. *It would be old or ill-tempered. How long is the trail to California, anyhow?*

She gave a little start. Tamar had asked her a question, yet she hadn't heard.

"Pardon?" She blinked hard, forcing herself to focus on the second wife.

"I said," Tamar repeated, "I suppose Tabitha has had word from Thomas sometime this winter, since he left with the Legion. I know she and Thomas exchange letters all the time. More often than Thomas writes to me, I'd wager. I try not to be envious, for I'm sure they have ever so much more to say to one another, between the children and Tabitha's doings all across the valley. But I do wish Tabitha would tell us what she knows. Perhaps one of us ought to go over tomorrow and ask for word of Thomas."

"Tabitha is away just now," Jane said. "Gone up to Farmington. Old Mr. Kellogg has been fearfully sick for some days. He isn't expected to survive. With the roads as they are, Tabitha will probably stay at the

Kellogg place till tomorrow afternoon, at least. Mrs. Shelby's two eldest girls have gone over to tend the children."

Tamar smiled a little sadly. "Catherine will like that. She's very fond of the Shelby girls; they always let her play as long as she likes before they put her to bed."

Tamar levered her bulk up from the chair, ready for another cup of tea. Then she paused. Jane tilted her head, and Tamar slid into clear view. Her face had gone still with a distant, half-panicked expression—a look that seemed almost animal.

"Are you well?" Jane hurried around the table. "Can you hear me? Speak to me!"

Tamar gave no answer, except to lift her skirts slightly. Jane could see the fluid soaking her wool stockings. A few drops of it spattered onto the floor between her boots.

"Mother of mercy," Jane breathed. "Your waters have broken already."

This was early—weeks too soon. Jane felt as if she were clawing and kicking at some vast, suffocating blanket, struggling to push back the gray fog that had followed her since Sarah Ann's death. She needed her wits now, and she needed them sharp. How many weeks remained in Tamar's pregnancy—three? Four?

"What has happened?" Tamar whispered. "Is it time already? But I haven't felt any—"

She clutched suddenly at her belly. The first contraction wrung a cry of pain from her throat.

"Breathe," Jane ordered, taking her hand. "That's it . . . deep breaths."

"It's too soon." Tamar swayed on her feet. Her voice was faint and frightened. "This is much too soon, Jane, I—"

"No need to worry. The dates are always imprecise—Tabitha told me so. You could have counted the weeks wrongly. Sometimes it's hard to be sure."

"But Tabitha is away! What shall I do?"

"Go and lie down on your bed. Rest. Breathe easily. I've helped Tabitha deliver a dozen babies by now. I can bring you through this as easily as she can." Jane wasn't at all certain that was true, but she wouldn't let Tamar see her fears—not now. "I'll run down to Tabitha's place for her midwife kit while you get into bed. I'll be back before you know it."

Once she'd seen to it that Tamar was lying down, Jane hurried to the kitchen door and snatched her warmest shawl from its peg. Her head was reeling as she crossed the garden in the biting cold. A pale half-moon cast ragged shadows over the yard; they seemed to reach with greedy hands.

Marching double time through the snow, she tried to call up every lesson Tabitha had taught her over the preceding months, all the routines and protocols of labor and birth. But she had blundered through each of those deliveries in a haze, and now she could summon only the barest facts to her mind. She bit her fear back ruthlessly and pressed on into the night.

At Tabitha's house, Jane slipped and skidded up the icy walk to the front door. She didn't pause to knock but barged inside—which made the Shelby girls squeal in alarm.

"Beg your pardon," Jane called, thrusting past them toward the parlor-turned-apothecary. "Emergency birth. It can't wait."

There was Tabitha's large leather bag, exactly where she always kept it, on the leftmost end of the workbench. Jane seized it and spun on her heel, dodging around the Shelby sisters and their questions.

"No time," she called as she flew back out the door.

The midwife's kit was heavier than Jane had remembered. She kept having to shift it from one hand to the other as she scurried toward home. Jane could only pray that Tabitha kept it fully supplied, for she hadn't thought to check its contents while she'd still been in the healer's parlor.

When she reached the log house, Jane could see Tamar up and out of bed, pacing restlessly from window to window. She cursed under her breath and hurried up the lane.

"What are you doing out of bed?" Jane scolded. "I told you to stay put."

Tamar paused, holding her belly with both hands. She turned a baffled, vacant stare on Jane. Then her eyes went wide. She tensed as if she'd been slapped—and gave a hideous, ripping scream.

Jane gasped as the sound cut through her—pain and terror in a single cry. Something wasn't right; Jane was certain. This wasn't the way babies typically came, in her limited experience. The birth was progressing too fast, too painfully. And it was weeks too soon.

It'll be a miracle if Tamar survives, let alone the child.

That thought froze Jane in place. The leather bag fell from her grip, thudding on the floor.

She hadn't been able to save her mother or her sister, despite her best efforts. She had dedicated every waking moment to sparing both their lives, but in the end, death had staked its cruel, irresistible claim.

What makes you think you can save Tamar? That voice seemed to come from outside her head—a sly, amused whisper. *Death follows everywhere you go. You can't save Tamar. You never could save anyone.*

Tamar cried out again. Jane shook her head, trying to drive away the terrible voice. She went to her sister-wife, took hold of one arm, tried to push or pull her toward the bed.

"Please, you must lie down. Rest while I find more women to help."

Tamar seemed not to hear. She was panting and moaning—then she began to gag and heave from the pain.

I can't leave her, Jane realized. *Not till she's calmer. She'll go mad with fear if I leave her alone, and then there's no telling what she might do.*

"I'm here." She brushed the sweat-soaked hair from Tamar's brow, willing her hands to move slowly, as one soothes a frightened animal. "I'm here, Tamar. I won't leave you."

It cost Jane the better part of an hour to coax her into walking a few steps, and even then, she wouldn't go near the bedroom. Tamar seemed to have an instinctive terror of lying down. The fog of confusion parted for a moment, and Jane could hear Tabitha's words—recalling the advice as sharply as if the healer were standing at her elbow, speaking confidently into the trembling, constricting room.

Let the laboring woman choose what she must do. If she wants to walk, let her walk. If she wants to stand or squat or crawl on all fours like a dog, let her do it. Very often, her own body knows best.

"Come, I'll walk with you." Jane pulled Tamar's arm across her shoulders, taking as much of the woman's weight as she could bear. "I'll hold you up. Walk with me."

They paced around the parlor for what seemed an eternity, Tamar pausing every few minutes to pant and groan and holler in Jane's ear. The pains were coming closer together all the time—too close for Jane's liking.

The front door swung open, admitting a gust of snowflakes that curled on the air. Mrs. Shelby was there, with Mrs. Sanders just behind.

"Heaven above," Mrs. Shelby said. "My girl Emma came running; told me you'd said there was some emergency. I figured it must be Tamar."

"She's weeks early," Jane said, "and the pains are coming fast."

Mrs. Shelby shook her head ruefully, positioning herself under Tamar's other arm. "A fine time for Tabitha to be away."

"She'll be home tomorrow afternoon," Jane said. "But it hardly matters now. This baby won't wait."

As if responding to a cue, Tamar planted her feet on the parlor floor and wailed. "I can't go on! God preserve me, I'll surely die!"

The very blood in Jane's heart turned to ice. One part of her mind—that part that still belonged to the quick-thinking healer's apprentice—knew full well that women often made such declarations when the baby's arrival was imminent. The rest of Jane—a far greater part—heard only Tamar's certainty of death and knew she could never bear it. She couldn't lose another beloved soul. She couldn't dig another grave.

"Now, now," Mrs. Sanders said, rubbing Tamar's back, "you certainly can go on."

Tamar buckled with another hoarse cry and sagged to her knees.

"Bend her forward," Jane said. "Help me with her skirts."

With Tamar on hands and knees, legs spread wide apart, Jane pushed the skirts up over her back and parted the sides of her linen drawers. She could see the baby's head already. *Thank God it isn't coming feetfirst.* That was one small mercy.

Tamar began to push while Jane and the other women urged her on. The baby's head was out into the open air more quickly than Jane could credit. She touched the wet, warm face with reverent awe, cradling the head in her palms. Tamar gave a guttural bellow, then another push—then a high, piercing scream. The baby's shoulders were in Jane's hands. A moment later, the rest of the small red body slid out in a rush of fluid. The baby opened its mouth, sucked in a ragged breath, and cried with an angry rasp.

"Mercy!" Jane said, laughing and crying at once. "Go fetch some towels from the kitchen, Mrs. Sanders, and a blanket from my bed. I didn't even have time to prepare that much."

Jane wiped the tiny girl clean and bundled her in a blanket while the other women maneuvered Tamar onto her bottom.

"You must pass the afterbirth," Mrs. Sanders told her, "and we will cut the cord. Then you can hold your baby."

"Let me hold her now."

Tamar's voice was weak, trembling. The sound of it roused the same cold fear in Jane. She tilted her face to look at Tamar more sharply. Her skin was pale with a sickly cast. She'd gone grayish-blue around the mouth. Tamar's head lolled on her neck as if she hadn't the strength to keep it upright.

Something is still amiss, Jane thought.

In the same instant, she heard Tabitha's words again, insistent this time. *Let the laboring woman choose. She knows best.*

"You can hold your baby as soon as the afterbirth has passed," Mrs. Sanders said patiently. "First things first."

"No," Jane said, scooting on her bottom across the floor, stretching the swaddled infant out to its mother. "Let her have the baby now."

Mrs. Shelby began to argue. Jane ignored her, pressing the newborn into Tamar's arms. "Here she is, Tamar. Your daughter. What do you want to do? Tell me and I'll help."

Tamar clawed weakly at the bodice of her dress.

"She wants to nurse the baby," Jane said.

Mrs. Shelby glanced up from between Tamar's wide-spread knees. "Time enough for that in a few minutes."

"Now." Panic rose in Jane's chest, ringing in her ears. "Let her do it now."

"Jane, really—"

She never knew what possessed her, where she found the strength. She took hold of Tamar's bodice and ripped with a wild fury. The hooks and eyes parted, tearing the fabric, exposing the shift underneath. Jane tore the shift, too, clawing at the insertion lace and the ruffled collar till she'd made a rent large enough to work her fingers inside. She wrenched her hands apart, and the linen parted with a loud hiss.

"For goodness' sake, Jane!" Mrs. Sanders was trying to restrain her now, but Jane shook off her grip. She found Tamar's breast, exposed it, and guided the baby's mouth to the nipple.

Tamar made a weak but grateful sound as the baby began to suck.

"I've never seen such goings-on," Mrs. Shelby muttered. Then: "Ah, here comes the afterbirth."

Tamar had to be coaxed to push out the afterbirth, for she was dazed and still distressingly pale. But she held her baby doggedly to her breast, and the infant went on suckling. The other women examined the red mass and pronounced it whole, then severed and tied the cord with Tamar's sewing kit, which they'd found in a corner of the parlor.

"All's well that ends well," Mrs. Sanders said warmly. "I don't believe I've ever seen a first baby come so quickly, but I guess this little one didn't want to wait any longer to meet her mother. What a fine, strong girl—even if she is a bit small. You did well, Tamar."

"Let's get her to her feet," Mrs. Shelby said. "She needs her bed."

Jane, still crouched at Tamar's back, gripped her shoulders protectively. "Not yet. Don't move her."

"There's no danger, Jane. You're fretting over nothing. I declare—"

Mrs. Shelby stopped abruptly, staring down at the rug below her feet. Her eyes widened; her mouth fell open in silent horror.

Jane craned her neck to see what had gone wrong. Something dark and wet was spreading out from Tamar's thighs—a stain that soaked rapidly into the rag carpet and crept across the floor.

Jane's heart seized in her chest. Tabitha had told her what such bleeding meant. This was the danger she had sensed all along. This was what she had feared.

"No!" Jane shook Tamar by her shoulders, shouting into her ear. "Don't die! You can't! I need you, Tamar. I need my sister!"

Jane had never seen the dreadful rush of blood that sometimes follows a birth. All the births she'd attended with Tabitha had gone smoothly enough. But though this particular danger was new to Jane, every word of Tabitha's instruction on the subject came back with a blaring insistence. She had only minutes to spare—perhaps not even that long.

Jane scrambled across the floor, grabbed Mrs. Sanders by the wrist, and forced her to push down hard on Tamar's body, squarely over the womb.

"You," she snapped at Mrs. Shelby, "push here, on the other side. Hard! Don't let up, either one of you!"

Jane stumbled to her feet, snatching the midwife's bag from where she'd dropped it. In the kitchen, she knocked the lid from a crock of honey and poured a great amber gob into a bowl, then rummaged through the bag till she found what she needed: the black powder of ergot and the dried inner bark of fir balsam. There was no time to weigh and measure. Jane could only hope for the best. She poured equal parts of the two remedies into the honey and stirred it with her fingers, hoping she'd prepared a sufficient quantity. Then she ran across the house to where Tamar lay.

Jane dropped to her knees in the pool of blood and pushed her hand up into the terrible red heat of Tamar's body. She packed the honey and powders against the mouth of the womb.

They stayed that way for more than an hour—the two neighbor women bearing down with all their weight to stanch the bleeding while Jane applied and reapplied the fir-and-ergot dressing. When Tamar was breathing easier and some of the color had returned to her cheeks, Jane swallowed hard, then nodded to the others. It was time to let up a little of the pressure and learn what had come of their desperate effort.

Jane held her breath as the other women eased off slightly. Tamar moaned, but no more blood gushed forth. The women withdrew a little more, then finally removed their hands from her body. Tamar sighed, exhausted but alive, and the baby made a contented sound, still suckling away at the breast.

"I think the worst is behind us," Jane whispered.

She rose, shaking, to her feet. Tamar's blood had begun to congeal on her skirt; she was stiff and light-headed, sickened by the gore soaking into the rug, and grateful—more grateful than she had ever been.

The others helped her bathe Tamar with cool water. She applied one more honey pack, and then they dressed her in a clean shift and lifted her and the baby together, carrying them to Tamar's bed for a hard-earned rest.

After Tamar had slept peacefully for several hours, Jane felt confident enough to let the neighbor women return to their homes. She stumbled to the door with the women at her side.

Mrs. Sanders wrapped her in a long embrace. "You're a marvel, Jane. I declare."

"I don't think Tabitha herself could have done better," Mrs. Shelby added.

She watched them walk home through the deep snow and the blowing wind as the first flush of dawn tinted the horizon. The sky was pink as a rose petal, pink as the newborn baby nestled in her sister-wife's arms. The spreading light pushed back the gray remains of winter.

21

TAMAR

Centerville
Winter 1858

What sort of world have I brought you into, little one?

There was no need to speak her thoughts aloud. Somehow Tamar knew, with a visceral instinct, that the tiny, exquisite thing sleeping beside her had heard and understood. The baby's delicate hands lay curled below her chin, and her sweet lips moved as if she might answer.

Tamar didn't want to know what her daughter might say, if she had the power of speech—if she could understand the tangle and mire of this life. A stab of guilt racked her, almost as sharp as the pains that still coursed now and then through her torn and weary body. Yet she was glad to bear it all for the sake of her baby—the agony, the remorse, the staggering weight of this love.

I was promised a love greater than any I'd known, if only I came to Zion.

She had found it at last. What a fool she'd been to think it was Thomas who would fulfill the Lord's promise. The man was no reward; Tamar understood that now. There was nothing malicious in her husband's nature—she would still vow to that—yet he was a blundering, careless soul. He had spared no thought for how this precarious arrangement would affect his wives—or their children. Tamar had found herself unable to think of anything else while she was awake. She gazed at her baby by the hour, and all the while, she pleaded silently for the child to forgive her, to understand the entanglement Tamar could scarcely comprehend herself.

When she slept, Tamar dreamed of her baby—sometimes as a warm weight in her arms, sometimes as a grown woman with Patience's face and her mother's voice, calling across the sunlit rows of Papa's garden, far off in another land. In those dreams, Tamar had already begun to think of her daughter as Amy—her mother's name. She supposed it must be the baby's name, too.

And yet how can I tell my mother I've named this child in her honor? How can I tell my mother that I am a mother now, too?

It was a mercy Thomas was away with the Legion, for Tamar would have been unable to restrain herself from raging at him, from saying things she could never take back. She had made no mention of her condition to her family. She had fended off, with crushing regret, their requests for her to visit again, insisting they must not come to visit her, for there was no room to house them, or because invented illnesses were raging through Centerville—any excuse she could find to keep them at bay. And as she'd clung feebly to life, bleeding on the floor of her own house while Jane had worked to save her life, her foremost thought had been, *I shall die now, and neither my mother nor my sisters will be given the truth for comfort.*

"I'll go and see who's at the door."

Jane put aside her knitting and rose from her chair at Tamar's bedside.

"I never heard the knock," Tamar said. She'd been too lost in her grim thoughts, the worry and betrayal.

Yet if she had no family left to speak of—if Thomas had cut her off from the ones she loved most, intentionally or not—at least Tamar had Jane. The girl had scarcely left her alone since little Amy had come, unless it was to boil a kettle of broth for Tamar to drink or to fetch more blankets to keep off winter's chill.

Tamar heard a murmur of voices from the parlor. Then the bedroom door creaked on its hinges. She struggled to push herself up against the headboard without waking Amy.

"Please, lie back. Don't get up on my account."

Tamar drew a sharp breath. She had expected to find Jane coming in to resume her knitting and her companionable silence. Instead, it was Tabitha who stood on the threshold. She was looking at Tamar with a hesitant expression that was almost apologetic. The first wife's eyes were brimming; her face was pale.

Save for that terrible night when Tamar had run for help—*Poor, dear Sarah Ann,* she thought—she hadn't been so near the first wife since the wedding day. Sometimes Tamar believed she could still feel the sting of Tabitha's slap.

Jane slipped into the room and took up her accustomed perch. "I tried to convince her you're doing well enough, but she wants to examine you herself. You should allow it, Tamar. Tabitha knows far more than I."

Tamar hesitated, but only for a moment. There was no anger in Tabitha now. "Very well. You may do as you think best."

"I won't hurt you," Tabitha said as she approached. "I give you my word on that. You needn't fear me anymore."

Tamar's heart began to pound, but she made herself smile in welcome. "Of course I don't fear you."

Tabitha took the baby first, unwrapping the swaddling to assess Amy's color and the soft, floundering movements of her limbs. A wild terror gripped Tamar, to see her baby in any other woman's arms— Tabitha especially, who had good reason to hate the child. Yet the healer went about her examination with an air of detachment and handled

Amy gently. When she was satisfied, she swaddled the baby again with a few expert tucks and pronounced her small but healthy.

Next, she turned her attention to Tamar, questioning her closely, inquiring after every sensation that had afflicted her before and after the birth. Did she still have pain, and what movements caused it? How much blood was she passing? How were her appetite, her sleep, her elimination?

Finally, Tabitha nodded in satisfaction and stood, hands clasped at the waist, looking at Tamar and yet seeming to stare through her to a distant vista, the landscape of which Tamar could only imagine. The first wife was drawn, more sober than Tamar had ever known her to be. She opened her mouth as if to speak, closed it again, then met Tamar's eye with a deliberate air.

"I truly didn't think you would give birth so soon. The baby came at least two weeks early, by my estimation—perhaps more than that. Even so, I ought to have remained in Centerville."

"You had business in Farmington," Tamar said. "Brother Kellogg—"

"I do take such work seriously—caring for those who've reached the end. But I'm a midwife, first and foremost. My greatest duty should have been to you . . . no matter my personal grievances. I knew your baby was coming. If I'd done my work as I ought, I would have examined you before I left town. I might have noticed some sign that birth was imminent. Instead, I neglected you inexcusably. It was my own anger that made me do it. I've never before turned my back on a woman in need. I'm ashamed that I did it now. Whatever my feelings on this . . . situation . . . however justified those feelings may be, I did wrongly, and I hope you will forgive me."

Tamar felt dizzy. She prayed it was only from amazement and not from her condition.

"You needn't ask my forgiveness," she finally said. "I can well imagine your feelings just now. And I had Jane with me, so all was well."

Jane and Tabitha shared a solemn look.

"Thank God you did have Jane," Tabitha said. "Sister Sanders came running to my house the moment I returned this afternoon. She told me everything. You saved Tamar's life, Jane; I've no doubt about that. By allowing the baby to suckle straightaway, you may have reduced the severity of the bleeding. I've heard stories—and my Ponca teacher certainly believed—that suckling helps the womb recover more swiftly. Your quick action with the honey poultice did the rest. What did you use?"

"Ergot and fir balsam," Jane said.

Tabitha put a hand on her shoulder. "Good girl. That was exactly the right combination. Will you excuse us? I would speak with Tamar alone."

Jane took her knitting and slipped from the bedroom.

Tamar almost called her back, for she was gripped by a sudden chill. She was weak from her ordeal, helpless in the bed. Tabitha may have asked forgiveness, but she bore Tamar no love; that was plain to be seen in the woman's eyes as they flicked over her face, her body, the baby clutched protectively in her arms.

"I'm relieved that you've survived," Tabitha finally said, choosing her words with obvious care. "And your baby, of course. I would never wish ill on a child, no matter what sort of sin engendered it."

"I had hoped," Tamar said with equal care, "you and I might see each other differently now."

"Why now?"

She pressed her lips together, studying the footboard of her bed, searching for words that wouldn't turn Tabitha sour. "We have something in common now. Something precious. Our children share a father. Surely that ties us together in a special way. I had wished—"

"Why wish for anything?" Tabitha broke in. "We find ourselves where we presently stand. There's no use wishing our circumstances were different. Not even prayer can change this; goodness knows, I've tried. I've prayed and hoped and wished for months that my heart might soften, that I might be made to see what purpose this madness serves. That I might come to understand why my heart had to be broken and my trust destroyed. There has been no answer from God."

"I know. I've done my best to abide by faith and trust all things to the Lord. When Thomas first taught me the Principle, I convinced myself it was righteous and just. But how can this be righteousness?" She looked at the baby. Tears blurred her vision, then broke to run down her cheeks. "Why must I choose between my family and my child? If I go to visit them again, I must leave Amy behind—or else I must confess what I've done and face their scorn. My daughter must grow up never knowing her grandmother and her aunts. Or she must grow up under the shadow of my shame. How many men in Zion practice the Principle? How many women?"

"Only a small part," Tabitha said. "The rest think it an eccentricity at best, and an outrage at worst."

"The rest think women like me harlots. You've said as much, yourself."

Tabitha lowered her eyes.

"What sort of life will my daughter have? She will suffer, no matter what I do. And you have suffered, Tabitha. You, who never deserved this pain."

Much to Tamar's surprise, Tabitha took her hand. The small fingers tightened briefly.

"And yet—" Tamar forced herself to look up at the first wife, to hold her eye. "I cannot regret what I've done. Not entirely."

Tabitha freed her hand. Gently, she traced the outline of the baby's cheek. "No. I suppose you can't, at that."

"I don't believe Thomas thought any of this through. He never considered what might come. How we might suffer—his wives and his children. I don't believe he foresaw how the burden of this secret would weigh on us all. And we haven't even his presence for comfort. With our husband so often away, I sometimes find myself thinking I've no family left at all."

"You certainly have a family still."

Tabitha held her gaze for a long moment. The baby stirred, uttering a small, sleepy sound.

Tamar wanted to ask whether Tabitha meant herself and Jane—or whether she referred to Mama and Patience and Zilpah, down in the city. She never had the chance. Tabitha stood without another word and left the room.

Only the stillness remained, and the ache in Tamar's body, the sharp pain deep in her heart.

~

Later that day, she dreamed.

Tamar knew it was a dream straightaway, for the light had that old familiar quality, a golden glow, and the edges of the world were softened—the trail, her dust-covered boots, her hands on the crossbar of the handcart all blended into one another and lost themselves in a confusion of fire and light.

She knew she was dreaming, and yet she knew her body and spirit were out there in the wilderness, dragging the weight of her faith along a hard, narrow path.

It's another vision, she realized, and trembled in her heart.

God had sent another sign of His everlasting command. She hunched her shoulders and threw all her strength against the crossbar, trudging down an endless, empty trail.

Tamar didn't want to know what the Lord was demanding of her now. And yet she knew. The question was answered even before she'd asked it.

She looked back over her shoulder. The handcart was empty, save for the small, swaddled form of her daughter.

She stared forward again. *No,* she thought. She wanted to shout the word. But her tongue remained silent, and her feet kept moving, one in front of the other.

The trail sloped upward. The shifting, brilliant light was too intense for her to see exactly what lay ahead, yet she knew she was moving toward a grim destination. She choked out a few sobs as the trail led her on. Her hands were blistered and raw, her body too weary for life, but still, she did not stop.

The slope leveled out. Tamar discerned among the golden flare a pile of stones and debris. At first, she thought it was a grave. Goodness knew, she had passed enough graves along the trail. But the construction was waist high and flat at its top. And the trail ended there.

She stood staring at the heap of rubble while the weight of the crossbar dragged at her arms and shoulders.

It's an altar. A place for sacrifice.

A frantic fear rose in her chest, beating at her insides like the wings of a trapped bird. She shook her head, denying the command, and yet she could not deny it. Slowly, she lowered the crossbar and let her handcart rest against the earth.

Tamar took her baby from the bed of the cart and stepped toward the altar.

What are you doing? she wailed at herself, she screamed in the confines of her mind. *You cannot—you must not! No!*

But it seemed nothing would deter her. She reached out through the light and the fire. She placed her infant daughter on the stones.

Tamar woke with a hoarse cry.

Jane's knitting needles clattered to the floor; she was on her feet, laying a palm against Tamar's sweat-damp brow. "What is it? Are you in pain? By God, Tamar, you're soaking."

"I'm all right," she answered shakily.

"You are not. Hold still and let me check you for fever."

"Where is Amy? Where is my child?"

"She's right there beside you, and she's perfectly well. I'm not so certain about you, though."

Jane was right. Amy was bundled securely beside Tamar's pillow, snuffling in her sleep. The dream hadn't come to pass—not yet. She sank back into the mattress, shuddering with relief.

"You aren't hot to the touch," Jane said. "That's something. And your color is good, your pulse is strong—though it's fast."

"A dream. It was only a terrible dream."

It was a vision, a command from God. And He expects me to obey.

Amy woke and began to fuss. Tamar reached for her, but Jane stayed her with a hand on her wrist. "She'll be wanting a change about now. I'll give her a clean cloth. You stay here and rest. I'll brew more nettle tea for you while I'm up. It helps heal the womb after birth, and it takes away fever. You're cool to the touch, but I won't take any chances."

Tamar let Jane carry the baby away without complaint. It was almost a relief to have her daughter beyond her reach just then—for there was no doubt in Tamar's mind about what that vision had signified.

I placed her on the altar. Just like Abraham, ready to sacrifice his beloved son.

Tamar had always harbored a secret disgust at that particular tale. She knew it was wicked to think poorly of any story in the Bible, and especially any story of the great patriarch, the chosen father of God's people. But she'd never been able to help her feelings. Whenever Abraham's sacrifice had been discussed in church, she had thought, *He failed the test. Wouldn't God have blessed him all the more if he had refused? If he had stood fast and defended his child, even against an attack from the Almighty?*

By and by, her panic receded, and her breathing slowed. But the shame and disgust never left her. In her dream, she'd been all too ready to obey without restraint. She had never asked herself how the innocent might suffer for her faith.

Jane returned and tucked the baby in Tamar's arms, but as she made to fetch the nettle tea, Tamar said, "I want to get up, Jane. I want to walk in the fresh air."

"I don't know if that's wise."

"Tabitha said I might, if I were feeling strong enough. I need to move. I must get out of this bed."

Jane chewed her lip, considering. Finally, she nodded. "If you'll allow me to wrap you up as warmly as I see fit. And you must leave Amy with me. And you may only have a quarter of an hour at most. I won't have you breathing in the cold air any longer than that—not in your weakened state. You lost a lot of blood, Tamar. It'll be some days before your strength is restored."

When Tamar rose from the bed, her legs did not shake. She submitted to Jane's ministrations with patient amusement, and when she was swaddled almost as thickly as the baby was, Jane walked with her to the kitchen door.

"I'll be watching from the window," Jane said, with the baby propped against her shoulder. "If there's any trouble, I'll come running."

Tamar nodded and stepped out into the winter twilight. Jane's comings and goings had beaten a flat track through the knee-high snow, across the sleeping garden to the road. Tamar took careful steps, for the way was slick, but her body bore her up and the fresh air was bracing.

Far across the settlement, the muted, muffled sound of a violin came threading through the deep-blue night.

Blue. Everything was blue and sharply defined, not flaring and softened as in her dream.

The Lord had all but commanded Tamar to sacrifice her child—not to take that precious life but to deny Amy her heritage and her due. Tamar wanted her daughter to love and be loved by her whole family—those from England as well as those from Deseret.

If I go on protecting Thomas's secret, I must do it at my daughter's expense.

She blinked and realized she was no longer walking. She'd halted among the snow-covered rows of the garden, more or less in the same place where she'd caught Jane in her arms on that terrible night when Sarah Ann had died.

What had Jane said that night?

What sort of God would make a loyal woman suffer to prove her faith? Why do you allow it, Tamar?

She turned and gazed back across the blue snow. The log house was sharply defined against the dusk, all its edges and angles precise, its walls as solid as the earth itself. Lamplight glowed in the kitchen window, and there was Jane in silhouette, looking back at Tamar.

I will not place my daughter's happiness on the altar. Any God or man who expects me to do so is one I shall never obey.

She walked back to the kitchen, peeling away the wool wrappers as she went.

Jane hurried to meet her at the door with Amy clutched in her arms. "Are you well?"

"I've never been stronger in my life," Tamar said.

She went to the table and sat, upright and expectant.

"Can I bring you anything?" Jane asked.

"Yes. Paper, ink, and a pen. I've a letter to write. It can't wait any longer."

～

When a brisk knock sounded three days later, Tamar knew her sister had come.

She'd been sitting on the overstuffed sofa beside the parlor stove, feeding Amy in perfect contentment. The rap of Patience's knuckles sent a jolt of alarm through Tamar, then an absurd wash of guilt. Her first instinct was to scurry to her bedroom and hide away, make believe she wasn't there, and pray the baby would stay quiet.

The next moment, her better senses caught up with her. Despite her burning cheeks, she remained seated, determination written in the line of her hard-pressed mouth.

Jane gave her a wary glance. She knew, of course, that Tamar had summoned her sister to Centerville. Jane had even listened while Tamar had read the note aloud.

I've something important I must share with you. I should have told you long ago. It can't be committed to a letter; you must come to see me if you wish to know the truth. Take a sleigh, if you dare to travel in the snow. I know the roads are dangerous, but do come, Patience, if you think you can.

Tamar nodded. "Open the door, Jane."

The hinges squealed, and the snow-bright light of midday poured into the parlor, along with the biting, smoky smell of winter. Patience stood on the threshold, wrapped in layers of wool, her narrow cheeks pink from the cold or from her worries.

"Good day. I've come to see Tamar Loader. Do you know where—"

Patience glanced past Jane's shoulder. Her eyes met Tamar's and widened in surprise. Then she looked down to the bundle in Tamar's arms, the open bodice of her dress. Her mouth fell open.

"For once you've no words," Tamar said to her sister. "Come in. It will do neither of us any good for you to stand there gawping."

Jane stepped back, and Patience crept warily into the house. She seemed to move as if in a dream, mistrusting her feet or the solidity of the floor.

She stopped halfway across the parlor as if she could force herself to go no farther. "Tamar. What is the meaning of this?"

"You can guess the meaning well enough for yourself."

"But I . . . you aren't . . . you have no husband."

Jane pulled a chair away from the kitchen table. She set it firmly behind Patience. "You'd best sit down, Miss Loader."

Tamar drew a long breath. She spoke before she could convince herself to hold her tongue. "I do have a husband. I am the second wife of Thomas Ricks. Jane here is his third. We've been living the Principle since last March. I know you've heard of it; I needn't explain what this means."

"Merciful Heaven." Patience sank slowly onto the chair without looking around.

"This is my daughter, Amy. She was born five days ago."

"Little wonder you've been rebuffing our invitations all these months. No doubt, you hoped to hide your shame—"

Jane crossed her arms, casting a hard look at Patience. "I don't see where shame comes in. Tamar and I were both tricked, in a way— Tabitha, too."

Patience gave a small, bitter laugh. "Aha. Is she the first wife?"

"Yes," Tamar said.

Patience rolled her eyes toward the ceiling as if entreating the angels to grant her forbearance.

"Each of us came into this marriage for reasons of our own," Tamar went on. "We have our separate feelings about our circumstances, but we find ourselves standing where we stand. None of us can change what has transpired. We are in this together, by God's will, for better or for worse."

"For pity's sake, of course you can change it. You can have a divorce, Tamar."

The thought had occurred to Tamar now and then, during her moments of greatest loneliness and despair. Yet she had shrunk from the idea. She would find just as much difficulty holding her head up high whether she was known to be a plural wife or whether she was known to be a cast-off woman.

"I don't want a divorce," she said. "Not at this time. I made my vows to Thomas before the eyes of God. That meant something to me. It still means something, however complicated our situation has become."

"Complicated," Patience said wryly. "Indeed. I must say, this is an outrage."

"It's no outrage; this is my life." She held her baby more tightly. "Whatever your opinions on the Principle—however justified those feelings may be—I have my daughter now, because of Thomas. I wouldn't wish her away."

Jane added quietly, "Tamar fought hard to bring that baby into the world. She very nearly died in the struggle."

Patience turned to Jane with an astonished look. The color drained from her face. When she looked at Tamar again, all her scorn vanished. "You might have died? And we never knew."

"She bled terribly," Jane said. "It's only by grace that Tamar is still with us."

Tamar smiled affectionately at her sister-wife. "If there was any grace, it was all in Jane's quick wits. If not for her, I would have lost my life."

Patience made a strangled sound, somewhere between a sob and a moan. She rose stiffly, closed the distance between them, and fell to her knees, pressing her face against Tamar's shoulder.

"My dear sister. What should I have done if you'd been lost? Oh, this is all madness, I'm sure of it. It's not the life I would have chosen for you. But if you can honestly swear that you are content—"

"I am," Tamar said.

She wasn't happy. Perhaps she never would work out just how to navigate this strange current. But as she gazed over Patience's dark head at sturdy, sensible Jane, she knew she was content. Admitting the truth had done much to ease her heart—as had choosing of her own accord whether to share the secret or keep it.

By and by, I'll build my happiness. But no happiness can stand without a foundation of contentment.

Patience sniffed. "Then I shall be content, too, for as long as you are."

"Thank you, Patience dear."

Patience pulled back and looked at the baby. Tears beaded her lashes. "She's beautiful. Our little Amy. Mama will be delighted when she hears."

"She won't," Tamar said. "Hear, I mean. Not yet. This will require a great deal of explanation. I'm not sure how to manage it without our mother fainting dead away."

"If Mama had ever been the fainting sort, the trail surely beat that tendency right out of her."

"You're right. All the same, please don't tell her, Patience. Not until I've worked out the right way to do it."

"As you like. May Zilpah know?"

"Yes—so long as she also swears to keep the secret for now. I *will* tell Mama, in due time. I promise you that."

"Try not to drag it out too long. She'll be so happy, with another grandchild to love."

$$\sim$$

That evening, after Patience had gone, young Charles Kimball came tramping through the snow to summon Jane to the Ricks home. A child on the southern edge of town was suffering from the croup, and Tabitha wanted Jane to learn the remedy firsthand.

Alone in the log house with only her daughter for company, Tamar brewed the sweet herbal tea she favored and fixed herself a simple supper of soft goat's cheese spread over toast. Amy was nestled in a sturdy linen sling, sleeping contentedly against her heart.

The visit with Patience—and the confession of her secret—had fortified her spirit. The emptiness of her home didn't feel lonely that night. The stillness was sacred, a peace more complete than Tamar had felt in any church or prayer. Armored by tranquility, she cupped her palm around the curve of her baby's back. She said to the God whose command she had ignored, *You cannot have this child. If she comes to You one day, it will be by her own choosing. But I will never sacrifice her happiness—not even to You.*

She was no Father Abraham. She was glad to know her faith wasn't as perfect as his. Idly, she wondered what Sarah would have done—Abraham's wife—if God had commanded that woman to place her child on the altar.

Several hours after the winter's dark had fallen, she heard boots stamping on the packed snow of the lane. Jane was returning from the croup case, it seemed. Then she heard a low murmur of voices. Just before the front door opened, Tamar realized who'd been speaking to Jane.

Tabitha.

She rose quickly from the parlor chair. Amy gave a cry of protest at the sudden movement.

Jane already looked anxious and half ashamed as she led the first wife in from the cold. "I had to tell her about your sister, Tamar. It was only right; she needs to know."

Of course. Tamar couldn't have expected her visit with Patience to remain a private affair. She cast her fears aside. "Welcome, Tabitha."

The first wife stood with her fists on her hips. She said more calmly than Tamar had expected, "Why did you do it? Tell me that."

The answer was ready on her tongue. "My daughter will know her family. My mother and my sisters are the greatest joy in my life—the very light of my days. I won't keep them under a bushel in service to some man's devices."

For one heartbeat, no one spoke or moved. Then Tabitha's expression shifted subtly, the stern detachment giving way to a small, almost mischievous smile. "Some man?"

"As I've told you before," Tamar said, "our husband scarcely thought before he pulled us into this mess. Why should I hold myself prisoner to his demands when he never considered how those demands would affect the innocent? I was once a silly, lovestruck girl, but now I'm something entirely different."

"A mother." Tabitha's voice carried a note of appreciation. Then she went on more cautiously. "But you know, Tamar—the situation with the Legion, with Washington. It isn't only about Brigham Young disregarding federal laws or the attack at Mountain Meadows. It all goes back to the Principle. If the Legion should fail and the army should invade—"

Jane pressed a hand to her stomach as if the very idea made her sick.

"Buchanan will make a spectacle," Tabitha went on. "He'll be looking for men to punish. I've no doubt that any man who's been living the Principle will face the worst consequences. The heads of plural households might be imprisoned. They could be hanged, for all we can say."

Tamar's head swam. She hadn't considered what exposure might mean for Thomas. "Surely it won't come to hanging."

"None of us can know. We can only pray for deliverance. And if we aren't delivered, then we must pray for mercy—for ourselves, and those we love." Tabitha nodded once, satisfied that she'd made her point. She headed for the door.

"You aren't angry with me?" Tamar called after her.

The first wife stopped on the front step and looked back. Those sharp blue eyes softened. "You made your own choice, Tamar. I respect that. I do."

~

As winter melted away and a new season swept the valley with gentle shades of green, Patience came to visit more frequently. Sometimes she stayed overnight, sleeping in the third room that had once belonged to Sarah Ann. Now and then, she brought Zilpah and little Alpha, who was fascinated by his small, mewling cousin.

At first, Zilpah was shy, and every bit as scandalized as Patience had been on her initial visit. Eventually, however, she warmed and blossomed out into her usual affection. On a rainy April afternoon, she watched the other children frolic around the parlor—Alpha and Tabitha's little ones, who were overjoyed to have a new playmate.

"I haven't told John," Zilpah swore, cuddling Amy against her cheek.

The baby was dressed in a pretty new frock that Tamar had made from a bright calico fabric. Thomas had sent the flower-printed calico along with a yard of machine-made lace, and a note that read, *These poor gifts are the best I can do to welcome my beloved daughter to the world. Would that I could welcome Amy properly, with a loving father's affection. And would that I could give my tenderest love to you, dear Tamar, face to face as you deserve. Until I'm released from my duty to the Legion, these letters and presents must suffice.*

Tamar still wondered where Thomas had found the cloth and lace, so far up in the mountain passes. She supposed he must have written to some woman in the city and asked her to choose the gifts for him, and send them along to Centerville. She was grateful, in any case. Thomas *could* be a thoughtful man, when he tried. And such affection for little Amy boded well for Tamar. He'd be more likely to forgive her once he learned how she'd disregarded his commands and spilled out the secret to her family. Everything she'd done had been for their daughter's sake. Surely Thomas would understand.

"It's none of John's concern, anyhow," Zilpah was saying, "not unless you want him to know. Nor have I told Mama the news. But you must tell her someday. It's nearly a crime to keep this sweet baby from her grandmother."

"Amy will be almost five months old in June," Tamar said. "She'll be sturdy and fat by then. I haven't wanted to travel with her—not even those few miles to the city—for she was born so small and early. I've always feared that any stress might sicken her."

Tabitha called from the kitchen, where she was helping Jane salt down a few cuts of lamb. "I've told you already, Tamar—that baby is strong as an ox. You needn't fear for her health. But a mother must always do as she thinks best."

Patience let herself in by the front door, lowering her umbrella and shaking it hard on the step. She picked her way through the pack of tumbling, squalling children.

"Auntie Pay!" Catherine shouted. "Did you bring us candy from the store?"

Patience cast a long-suffering look at Tamar. "I'm Auntie Pay everywhere I go. But yes, I've brought you each a peppermint stick. You must ask your mothers before you eat them!"

The children cheered as Patience fished a parcel of candy from her coat pocket and passed the sticks around.

She drew out a folded newspaper, too. "Here's the real reason why I walked all the way to that shabby little mercantile in the rain. Look, Tamar—a real back-East newspaper!" She spread the paper across the table, humming and narrowing her eyes as she pored over the columns. "This one is a month old, but there's always something about Brigham and his kerfuffle with Buchanan."

Tamar peered over her sister's shoulder. The head of the paper read, *Port Tobacco Times and Charles County Advertiser.* She hadn't the least idea which state it might be from.

"Ah!" Patience stabbed a forefinger at the paper, pinning down a small, seemingly insignificant column near its foot.

She read aloud. "'We have accounts from the Utah expedition to the ninth of January, at which time the troops under Colonel Johnston were in excellent condition, in good health, and blessed with favorable weather.' No mention of where those troops were, however. 'The extemporaneous court organized by Judge Eckels, in Greene County, has found . . .'"

Patience trailed off into silence.

"Has found what?" Zilpah prompted.

Patience swallowed hard, then continued. "'Has found bills of indictment for high treason against the following Mormon leaders.' It lists Brigham Young and some twenty other men."

"Let me see that list." Tamar held out her hand, and Patience passed her the paper. Tamar's pulse felt thick and wild in her throat as she scanned the men's names. Thank God, Thomas was not among them.

She returned the paper to Patience and shared a sober look with both of her sisters. In the kitchen, Tabitha and Jane had fallen silent.

"Deseret is headed for a terrible disaster," Patience said. "This could mean open war."

22

JANE

Centerville
June 1858

Jane paused at the edge of her garden, leaning on the handle of her hoe, surveying the blurred and blended world with a strange tickle in her stomach. She couldn't decide whether she was giddy over the warmth of the day, the mad singing of the sparrows, the honey scent of flowers on the air . . . or whether some instinctive caution had coiled like a snake inside her. There was a thrumming below her heart, and it made her uneasy.

You've been so long under the shadow of sadness, you've forgotten what it feels like to be happy, she told herself.

That sounded sensible enough. And yet Jane couldn't entirely believe it.

The spring thaw had long since passed. May had swept bright and sunny across the valley, the foothills flushing with color under carpets of wildflowers. The garden was rich with greenery; bees dipped and circled around the blossoms of beans and peas. And yet the subtle anxiety persisted. Jane felt distinctly that something was coming—as if a great beast had risen from slumber, somewhere just beyond the indistinct horizon, and was treading inexorably toward the valley.

She dropped her hoe in the grass and circled the house, staring all the while at the still road, the passive town. Tamar was seated on the flat stones in the front yard with her sewing in her lap and the baby giggling and waving her fists in a wicker basket at her feet.

"Hello, Jane," she called cheerfully. "My, but it's a lovely day. I couldn't resist taking my work outside."

Jane held up a hand, and Tamar fell silent. She'd felt something—truly felt it. It hadn't been her imagination; she was certain. A low rumble tingled through the soles of her boots. For a moment, she thought it must be distant thunder, but the sky was an unbroken blue from one end of the immense lake to the other.

"What is it, Jane?" Tamar asked.

The rumble grew louder. Jane gazed north along the road, toward the village of Farmington. She could just make out a large, dark mass in the distance—a commingling of color as if some great crowd of people and animals were advancing on Centerville.

Buchanan. Her mouth filled with the copper taste of fear.

Then she remembered that Echo Canyon—the army's only real passage into Salt Lake Valley—lay somewhere to the south. This couldn't be Buchanan's army on the march. Not yet—not coming from Farmington.

"Look north, Tamar. Tell me what you see."

Cautiously, Tamar laid her sewing aside and stood. She held up a hand to shade her eyes. "I see people. Scores of them, and stock, too."

"That's what I suspected."

"It almost looks as if the whole town of Farmington is on the move. But why?"

They shared a long look, both frozen and stunned. Then something kicked inside Jane's ribs, and a desperate, hot energy roared like a brush fire into her body. She grabbed Tamar by the wrist and hauled her toward the house.

Tamar twisted away, snatched up the basket where Amy lay.

"What are you doing?" Tamar cried. "What's happening, Jane?"

"We need to pack our things. Whatever you can think to take; whatever we might need."

"Need—for what?"

Jane hustled Tamar inside and slammed the door. The baby began to cry.

"All of Farmington is out there," Jane said, "marching south. Don't you understand what it means?"

Tamar's eyes were distant with fear. When she spoke, Jane could scarcely hear the words, for she whispered as if the enemy were already close by, and hunting for her. "Brigham Young has ordered the evacuation. When Mary Smithies said he might do it, I never believed it could truly happen. But it has. The army is coming."

Jane hurried to her room. The old supplies were still cached below her bed—the sacks of dried beans and grain she'd hidden away in the days when she'd still dreamed of California. She began dragging them into the open light, calling over her shoulder, "Gather what you think we'll need. God alone can say how long we'll be hiding, so bring clothing warm enough for autumn and winter along with the rest."

A faint clangor made its way in through the log walls. Near the center of town, people were beating pots and kettles, raising an alarm. Jane sorted quickly through the contents of her trunk, pulling out the warmest and most serviceable garments she owned. She could hear Tamar muttering in her own room.

"There's a good leather bag in the pantry," Jane shouted. "We can stuff it with everything we'll need for Amy. We have no bedrolls, but if you get the old wool blankets from the third room, they might do for sleeping mats."

While Tamar hunted for the blankets, Jane raided the larder, tossing every crust and crumb of trail-worthy food into an empty flour sack. There was a small wheel of cheese with a sturdy rind, a few smoked ham hocks, several strings of dried apple slices, and the two loaves of bread Tamar had baked that morning. Nothing else was fit to take on the trail, for the weight of crocks and jars would only impede their flight. She wrapped one of the kitchen knives in a length of towel and dropped it into the bag, then seized a ball of twine from the pantry shelf.

By the time she returned to the parlor with her sack of provisions, Tamar had already strapped Amy to her chest with a sling. Tamar had filled the leather bag with necessities, too, and a stack of wool blankets waited on the parlor floor.

Jane dropped the twine atop the blankets. "Roll those tightly and tie them well, then come and help me pack my own bag."

It took perhaps a quarter of an hour to assemble the most basic necessities. Jane and Tamar worked in grim silence, tying their bundles and fashioning straps from the bracers Jane had found at the bottom of her chest—the same straps she and Sarah Ann had used to carry their goods down from the foothills on the day of the wedding. Then Jane pried up a loose floorboard in the third bedroom and hid their trinkets of modest value—Tamar's sewing kit with its fine needles and silk threads, an agate necklace Tom had given her, a few yards of well-made lace. She stamped the plank back into place and hefted her bundle to her back.

Jane took a few experimental steps across the parlor. The makeshift pack was heavy and poorly balanced, and the straps of Elijah's old bracers bit into her shoulders. But the bundle seemed likely to hold. She helped Tamar position a pack on her shoulders, then scooped the bags of provisions into her arms.

"Right," Tamar said stoically. "We're off, then."

When they stepped outside their door, the crowd from Farmington had arrived. The road was overwhelmed by jostling, shouting people. Women with drawn faces clung to their children's hands. Babies screamed, and young boys shouted commands to the flocks and herds they drove. Some families had managed to flee in wagons, and these made their way steadily down the center of the road, the drivers calling out to warn the women and herdboys who stumbled wide-eyed through the dust.

"Where are all the men?" Tamar asked.

Jane tilted her head, struggling to see the crowd more clearly. Tamar was right. There were women and children everywhere she looked, and a few old grandfathers with white beards. But Jane could find almost no grown men in the crowd—nor any youths older than thirteen or so.

There was no time to ponder the mystery. "Who can say? Let's get on the road. The longer we wait, the more danger, for all we can guess."

"I can't take Amy out into that crowd. See how they're shoving; what if she's crushed?"

"We haven't got a choice. The army is coming, Tamar."

Jane led the way from the log house, into the press of the crowd. Tamar stumbled along behind, so close she often bumped into Jane's pack. Several times, Jane nearly went sprawling or lost her hold on the precious bags of provisions. The burden was already desperately heavy; her arms ached and trembled, but she was determined not to abandon the food. Without a rifle for hunting, those oats and beans were all that stood between survival and starvation.

The road was so congested that after several minutes, they hadn't even passed the Shelby house.

"It's no use," Tamar said. "We're taking a step back for every two we take forward."

A greater commotion stirred just ahead.

"Here now," someone shouted. "What do you think you're doing?"

Another woman called, "You're headed the wrong way! We're to go south, not north! Brigham's orders."

Then a familiar voice cracked above the crowd. "Get out of my way or, so help me God, I'll run you down!"

"Tabitha," Jane said.

The crowd parted—foot travelers jostling to make way, wagons swinging aside. A buggy was driving straight toward Jane and Tamar, against the tide of bodies. There was no mistaking the spotted pony in the traces—nor the hard, determined face of the woman who held the reins.

Tabitha halted her buggy a few paces ahead. Now Jane could see the two children perched on the driver's seat. Catherine held tightly to her little brother, Thomas Junior, who was wedged between his sister and his mother's hip. The boy's pink face was pinched with fear.

"Get in, both of you," Tabitha said.

Jane deposited her bags on the floor of the buggy, then slung her pack onto the seat. She climbed in after, wedging the pack atop the provisions, fitting her feet in around the supplies as best she could. Tamar's pack was crammed onto the seat to Jane's left.

"Give Junior to me," Jane said. "He can ride on my lap. Tamar, you take the front seat."

The buggy turned slowly amid the crush and noise of the crowd, but once they were headed south, Tabitha maneuvered her way to the edge of the road where the grasses and wildflowers grew in a thick fringe. There she urged her pony to a brisk trot, and the buggy skimmed into the heart of Centerville.

"What have you heard?" Jane asked. "Is there news of the army?"

"The Legion sent word from Echo Canyon this morning," Tabitha said. "Buchanan's force has come, all right—marched out of Kansas some weeks ago. Buchanan must have sent the whole lot to Kansas after he got the news in September."

There was no need to ask what news Buchanan had received. Jane hadn't stopped fretting over the terrible violence at Mountain Meadows since she'd heard the tale herself.

There was never any chance the Mormons would get away with it, she thought. *More than a hundred Americans murdered in cold blood.*

Buchanan had evidently waited long enough for the weather to turn and the mountain passes to clear. Now the reckoning was at hand.

"Brigham has ordered every city and settlement to evacuate," Tabitha went on. "Thomas has been keeping me apprised of the plan since last autumn. Neither he nor I believed it would truly come to this, but here we are. At least Brigham made thorough preparations. We're to head south as quickly as possible—all women and children, and everyone over the age of forty. Men and boys old enough to hold the priesthood will stay behind."

Jane asked, "Why shouldn't the men and boys evacuate with the rest of us?"

Tabitha took her eyes off the road just long enough to pass a cool glance over her shoulder. "Someone must remain to burn everything to the ground."

"Burn it?" Tamar cried. "We can't allow them to burn our homes!"

"Talk sense, for goodness' sake," Tabitha said. "You know what they'll do to us if they fall on us—the women and the children. You know what mobs have done before to Mormons when they found us at their mercy."

Jane swallowed hard. She didn't know the history of the church as intimately as Tamar and Tabitha knew it. Even so, she'd heard enough stories of persecution to make her blood run cold. She knew the church had been driven from one place to another in the years before they'd settled in the valley—from New York to Ohio, from Ohio to Missouri, Missouri to Illinois. And even those assailments hadn't satisfied the men who hated or feared the Mormons. It seemed every member of the church carried a litany of horrors in their heads, a remembrance of the massacres that had propelled them from one place to the next, and finally across the plains to this valley. Jane had heard of every tragedy: the burning of the temple in Illinois; the destruction of the settlements in Missouri; the bloody slaughter at Haun's Mill; the siege of Far West, where women and even young girls were tied to schoolhouse benches and used in the cruelest manner. She'd heard of the ruin of Nauvoo, the Illinois haven that was supposed to be a new Eden for the church. Their prophet had been murdered in the Nauvoo days—an insult it seemed no Mormon would ever forget.

"The army won't treat us kindly if they find us here," Tabitha said. "Thomas wrote that Brigham feared it might come to this. He's told the men to prepare to set fire to every building if the army can't be held off at Echo Canyon. He won't see the United States capture Deseret—not after the work we've done to tame this place and make it flower. I can't say I entirely disagree with him. Why should we give Buchanan a fine city like Salt Lake, and all the towns and farms around it?"

"I do pray that Brigham will find some way to spare our homes," Tamar said meekly. "And the city—oh, if only I could know my mother and sisters are safe! They must be so frightened."

Tamar sounded on the verge of hysteria herself.

"At least Brigham has prepared a way for all of us to save our hides," Tabitha said. "Apparently, he spent the last year cutting new roads from the city down into the Sanpete wilderness. Thomas said in his letters that he thought the evacuation roads were an excess, but now I'm sure he's glad Brigham took no chances. I know I'm grateful. It gives us some hope of escape, but once we're in the wilderness, we must find our own shelter—mountains, canyons, ravines. Brigham has moved provisions into place—Thomas said there are secret storehouses hidden in the Sanpete wilderness, full of grain and tents and other necessities, enough to see the whole population of the valley through a year of exile—so we won't be living on weeds and dust. Even so, we may be in hiding for months, and we must find a good location near the storehouses if we're to make the most of Brigham's plans."

Centerville had erupted into activity. Carts and wagons stood in every yard; even the smallest children rushed from houses to the waiting vehicles, toting bags and blankets, chickens in wicker cages. The buggy soon left the small town behind. Farmland opened around them—and there, too, Jane could make out the bustle of frantic preparation. On distant farms, she could just discern the motion of women loading wagons, boys on horseback merging their herds together, driving them toward the crowded road.

Tabitha's pony was a competent trotter, even with a loaded buggy to pull. Once the road broadened beyond Centerville, Tabitha deftly wove among slower vehicles and passed them all—the drays and harvesting wagons, the dogcarts pulled by old or lazy animals.

They came within sight of Salt Lake City less than two hours after fleeing Centerville. Jane had never visited the city, and even through a fog of anxiety, she couldn't help but marvel at the stately buildings and the orderly grid of its wide streets. New houses and stores were evident by their pale wood and the clean white of freshly cut limestone.

As they rolled along the central street, headed due south for the new evacuation road, countless other carts and wagons merged into the flow. Tabitha was forced to rein her pony in, slowing to a walk, for even the broad, flat streets of the city couldn't accommodate this hasty exodus without gridlock.

They passed a large green park, a clamor of people and carts rolling and running through the grass. Women shouted to one another, carrying ragged bundles above their heads. Across the street from the chaotic park, Jane found a vast, empty lot, entirely bare, the red-brown soil freshly turned.

"The temple," Tamar exclaimed. "Where has it gone?"

"There was a temple here?" Jane asked.

"A foundation, anyhow. And great white blocks of stone everywhere. I saw it on my first day in the city and, later, when I visited my sisters. I know it was here. How is it possible that the temple has vanished?"

Jane could hear Tamar sniffling on the seat in front of her. *She's just learned her house may be burned to ashes, yet she's weeping over a temple?*

"They've buried all the stones in the foundation pit, I suppose," Tabitha said. "Won't allow Buchanan's men to touch any part of the temple."

"It seems a terrible omen," Tamar said quietly. "What's to become of us all? And where are my sisters, my mother?"

"Hush," Tabitha said gently. "We'll find them, Tamar. By and by, you'll see them again."

Jane turned away from the empty lot. She watched the road ahead—the flood of refugees fleeing their homes, joining the frightened masses of women and children who were already moving south. Her heart began to pound as the buggy made its way toward the southern fringe of the city.

Jane couldn't help remembering the bleak story Tamar had recounted of her journey with the handcarts. Would this be another march of deprivation and despair? The Mormons were plunging into the wilderness again—the hungry, gaping mouth of an untamed land— and Jane had no choice but to go down with them. She could only pray she was strong enough to survive.

23

TAMAR

Salt Lake Valley
June 1858

By sunset, they reached the open fields where Parley's Creek merged with the sluggish Jordan River.

"We must stop and rest for the night," Tamar said—the first word any of them had spoken since leaving the city. "The pony needs feeding and watering, and so do we all."

More than a hundred families had gathered near the creek, on open grassland beyond a plowed field. Tabitha allowed the pony to walk the distance between the road and the growing encampment. The low red sun threw shadows over the grass, and a damp chill was rising. It would be a cold, wet night, and they had no tent—only the blankets Tamar had salvaged from the house.

At least there were plenty of fires to drive back the chill. As the buggy delved into the mass of refugees, sparks snapped to every side and flames licked up against cook pots; already the aroma of onions and beef wafted across the encampment. Her stomach cramped with hunger—that old, accustomed enemy, the nightmare beast that had haunted her down the length of the handcart trail.

She turned compulsively toward an especially rich-smelling cook fire—and froze. Bishop Thorn and his family were gathered beside a fine, large carriage, shaking out a few quilts and making their preparations for the night. Patience and Mama were with them, too busy with their work to notice Tamar as the buggy passed. Despite a great flood of relief, she jerked away by instinct, shielding her face behind the brim of her bonnet and hugging Amy more tightly against her chest.

Tabitha found a clear space apart from the other vehicles. "I'll take the pony to the creek," she said. "Jane, you gather branches for a fire. Tamar, find something to feed the little ones. I know I packed a tin of biscuits, but I'll be blessed if I can say where they are now."

"There's a smoked ham hock somewhere in this mess," Jane said, "and a big sack of dried beans. That will do for our supper."

They set about making camp and caring for the children with quiet efficiency, moving easily around one another, each woman anticipating the others' needs and offering help without being asked. Tamar found a long-handled wooden spoon in the bottom of the cart so Jane could stir the soup; Jane located the biscuits and doled out one apiece to Junior and Catherine, which kept the children occupied and out from underfoot. Meanwhile, Tabitha moved about the camp, speaking to the other refugees, gathering information, locating as many neighbors from Centerville as she could find.

Just before dusk, the bulk of the camp assembled in a great mass at the edge of the plowed field.

"What's going on there, do you suppose?" Jane asked, picking at her bowl of soup with little appetite.

"No doubt Tabitha will tell us when she returns," Tamar answered. "She must be among that crowd."

Tamar and Jane went on minding the children in tense silence. Now and then, they could hear murmurs swelling from the gathering. The crowd was discussing something—or debating. Tamar was half tempted to take Amy and cross the distance, learn for herself what had stirred up the refugees. But if she met with her mother along the way, she would have to explain the baby in her arms, and she didn't yet know how to raise the subject. Not with Mama.

You're fretting needlessly, she told herself. *You would have broken the news to Mama this very month—told her all about your marriage and your daughter. If Buchanan hadn't intervened.*

Yet everything was different now. The news of the army's advance had turned the whole world on its ear.

Shortly after twilight, the crowd dispersed, and Tabitha returned through the dim blue night. Tamar ladled a portion of soup into Tabitha's bowl and sat on the quilt beside her while she ate.

"I suppose everyone has come to a decision about the best way forward," the first wife said. "Three older men have set themselves apart as leaders—Bishop Thorn, as well as Second Counselor Wells and Apostle Richards."

"I remember Franklin Richards," Tamar said. "He blessed me on the trail. I had no idea that men so esteemed were among us."

"At dawn, this whole encampment is to be divided up into three smaller groups," Tabitha said. "We'll go out into the wilderness with these men as our leaders, and we're to hide as best we can for the duration of the conflict."

"How long do the men expect this to last?" Jane said.

Tabitha shook her head wearily. "No one has the least idea. They tossed out some guesses—three weeks, or six—but there was no real certainty. Richards gave some useful information about those secret storehouses, though. Apparently, Brigham has designated a whole troop of men to make deliveries into certain areas once every week. It will be up to the refugees to meet with the suppliers and retrieve their rations. Richards suggested that each group should prepare a special wagon and team for that task, so plenty of food may be hauled back to our bolt-holes to keep our bellies filled until the next distribution of supplies."

She sighed heavily. "For all Brigham's careful plans, this seems rather disorganized."

Tamar's heart had begun to pound while Tabitha spoke. For a long moment, she couldn't understand why. Then she narrowed her eyes, watching more intently as the nearest families scraped and scrabbled for enough food to satisfy their hungry children. A new clarity shone through her fear, illuminating their precarious situation with a stark, unforgiving light.

"I don't like this," she said. "Not one bit."

Jane and Tabitha both stared, waiting for her to go on.

Tamar took a deep breath. Apostle Richards had made the decision, along with Brother Wells—the right hand of Brigham Young. *To turn one's back on the authority of the apostles is almost as terrible as turning one's back on God.* Then another thought occurred to her, with a sickening dread. *Didn't you already turn your back on the Lord when you spilled out your husband's secret? What's done is done, Tamar.*

She swallowed hard and went on. "If we divide into three companies, there will never be enough food to go round."

"Brigham's caches—" Tabitha began.

Tamar cut her off. Rising fear had made her impatient. "Look around, Tabitha. These families left home so quickly that most of them couldn't supply themselves as well as we did. And the three of us are scarcely prepared. People are already scraping the bottoms of their barrels, and goodness knows how far we must travel into the wilderness—how many days we must survive before we can find Brigham's supply points. Even then, what if we end up too far away? What if we can't reach the caches every week? We might only manage one visit a month, at best."

Her voice had risen; it was shaking. Tamar knew it, and yet she couldn't calm herself. She had eaten her fill of the bean soup, yet suddenly she could feel the unending hunger once more, the persistent, haunting pain of the trail.

She pressed on frantically. "My father intended to make the journey to Zion in a wagon, not by handcart. If he'd been left to do as he'd thought best, I believe he would still be alive today. Instead, he gave in to the demands of the church, and we all suffered for his choice. He suffered worst of all. I tell you, Tabitha—we've enough already to keep us well fed for weeks at a time—but only our small number. If we join one of those companies, we'll be made to consecrate our goods to the whole."

"As well we should," Tabitha said slowly. "I won't allow any woman or child to suffer when I've food to spare—or any other charity to give."

"Just so," Tamar agreed, "but if we're in a smaller group, we'll be able to care for our whole far better. We won't suffer in such dreadful extremity. We mustn't extend ourselves beyond our means, though— only the three of us, and our children. Perhaps just a few more families, if they've supplies to add to our cache or other useful things like rifles for hunting. But if we join a vast company, then I tell you now, we will surely starve."

"It can't be so bad as you're fearing." Tabitha spoke as if to a small child, trying to soothe away an irrational fear.

Tamar would not be comforted. "I lived on the trail, Tabitha—in the wilderness, with only the small rations allotted to us by the leaders of this church. I watched people sicken and die with nothing but faith to sustain them. My sister Zilpah . . . her milk nearly dried . . . I won't do the same to Amy; I won't!"

Jane wrapped an arm around Tamar's shoulders. "Listen to her; you must. Tamar knows what she's talking about. I've heard her stories from the trail. If she says it's folly to join a large company, then I believe her. You'd be wise to do the same."

"As I stood there," Tabitha said thoughtfully, "listening to those fellows make their plans, I suspected there was something amiss. I couldn't understand my own misgivings, but now I believe you're right, Tamar. Large companies will be harder to feed and nearly impossible to hide. If the army breaks through . . ." She shook her head. "I hear your warning. I promise you that. But I can't countenance leaving anyone behind. Not if they ask for my help."

"Most won't break from these men," Tamar said. "The greater number will trust to Richards and Ward and Bishop Thorn. We might have a few families join us, but no more than a handful. We can manage with a dozen or so women and their children, but no more than that."

"I'll need your help," Tabitha said. "I don't know much about living in the wild. Even when I was with the Ponca, I stayed in a fine village with gardens and hunting parties; we never wanted for anything. I can forage for helpful plants, but that will be the extent of my use in open country. I know your memories of the trail are still very close. We'll rely on you to help us make the best decisions."

"We won't follow any of the men, then?"

Tabitha shook her head.

Relief rolled through Tamar. A heartbeat later, guilt followed. Those two springs of disparate emotion welled up, and she overflowed with tears.

"Why, Tamar," Jane said, "you're crying as if your heart will break."

"It's my family," she choked out between sobs. "They're here; I've seen them. I would ask them to come with us, but I'm sure they've brought nothing to add to our supplies—nothing! They've lived in style all these months with Bishop Thorn; they can't be prepared for life outside the city. I must allow them to go with a larger company, and yet how can I do it, knowing they'll suffer in the wilderness as they suffered before?"

Tabitha and Jane were both silent. Tamar couldn't look at either of her sister-wives. She pressed her hands to her eyes as if she could hold back the torrent of her tears.

At length, Tabitha said, "Go and ask your family to join us."

"They haven't anything to add to our cache," Tamar said. "I know it's true."

"All the same. We'll sacrifice some of our food to keep them safe, won't we, Jane?"

The girl rested her head on Tamar's shoulder. "Gladly, Tamar. For you."

~

When she'd dried her tears and calmed herself, Tamar set off across the encampment in search of her family. Countless small fires threw back the darkness, casting all the world in a harsh light—the crying children, the drawn faces of the women, the stoic anger of the few men who moved among them. She walked through that strange red glow with an eerie coolness, for all her fear and misgiving had drifted away as if caught up and carried off by some merciful angel. If she still felt any shame, then shame was a distant thing. It was hung far above, among the stars, and Tamar had no use for it now.

Amy wriggled in her sling. Tamar patted her baby's back and whispered, "Now is the time, my darling, my love. You shall meet your grandmother at last."

She found them halfway across the trampled ground, gathered with Sister Thorn and her children on a thin blanket, sitting with their backs against a wheel of their carriage. Zilpah was there, her son curled on her lap, but John was nowhere to be seen. No doubt, he'd stayed behind to help burn Salt Lake City to the ground. The bishop, too, was missing. Tamar supposed he'd gone off with the other leaders to make arrangements for the morning.

Patience was first to see Tamar as she stepped into the ring of their firelight. She drew a startled breath, then climbed to her feet—but Mama was only a heartbeat behind.

"Tamar! Thank God you're here. I've worried for you so. I—"

As Mama approached, her eyes fell to the bundle tied against Tamar's chest. She stopped in her tracks.

Tamar watched in determined silence as her mother's bafflement gave way to grim understanding. Then a pain furrowed her mother's brow, so deep and poignant that Tamar nearly cried aloud.

She knows I either conceived this child out of wedlock . . . or that I've been hiding my marriage from her—from everyone.

And there was only one reason why a woman of Deseret would keep her marriage secret.

Tamar decided in that moment that she would neither explain nor excuse her decision. The road she had traveled, the trail she had walked, had made her a mother and given her this child, this small girl whom she loved beyond all reason. Let all the world judge the path she'd taken. Let them call it crooked or cursed. Tamar would find no fault in that road, for her daughter's sake.

"Yes," she said with quiet dignity. "Whatever you're thinking, whatever you assume, it's true. We shall leave it at that."

Mama's eyes lifted to meet Tamar's. She looked wounded and pale—yet also grateful and full of wondering joy.

Tamar pulled back the side of the sling to show the baby's face. Mama reached out a trembling hand.

"Her name is Amy," Tamar said.

When Mama looked up again, the firelight glinted on her tears.

"I've come to ask you," Tamar said, "to come with me and my sister-wives. You and Patience and Zilpah. We're going out into the wilderness together—a small group, with plenty of food. We shall find it easier to hide that way. Easier to survive."

"But the bishop—" Mama said.

Patience laid a hand on her shoulder. "Tamar might have the right of it. Smaller parties will be harder for the army to track down, if they break through Echo Canyon."

"But with more hands to help," Zilpah argued, "we shall all manage better. Brigham Young has planned everything with care. I say we disregard the Prophet's design at our peril."

Tamar wanted to lash out with a sting of sarcasm. *And the peril we endured on the trail? Was that not by the Prophet's design?*

Wisely, she held her tongue.

"We've met Tamar's sister-wives before," Patience admitted, casting a guilty look at her mother. "They're both good women."

"But to go out into the wilderness without any men to protect us," Zilpah said. "It's madness, Tamar. Why don't you join us instead? We'll be so glad, and I know Sister Thorn won't mind."

"You must make the choice," Tamar said to her mother. "Shall the three of you stay with the bishop's company? Or will you join me?"

Mama took her hands, clinging to Tamar in the tight, expectant silence. A branch in the fire broke, sending a column of sparks high into the air, but Tamar never flinched. All her attention, all her hope, was trained on her mother.

Finally, Mama answered. "Bishop Thorn holds the priesthood. God will not turn his back on the bishop, nor anyone under his care."

Tamar let out a long breath she didn't remember holding. "And I will not turn my back on my sister-wives. They are my family, as surely as you are. I can't abandon them now."

"Wait, Tamar," Patience said.

"Look after Mama, both of you. Protect her with your lives, if it should come to that."

Zilpah could make no reply. She kissed Tamar's cheek and left the dampness of her tears behind.

"Before we part ways," Tamar said, "I would pray with you all. Please."

They walked some distance apart from the Thorn family, then joined hands. Mama led them in prayer.

"Are you sure you won't come with us?" Zilpah asked when the prayer was finished.

Tamar only kissed her cheek. "Hug your sweet little boy for me."

She made her way back across the field, alone but for the baby murmuring against her breast.

~

The three wives of Thomas Ricks had their buggy packed and the spotted pony harnessed by dawn's first light. More carts stood ready, too: six mothers from Centerville—fifteen children among them all, none old enough to have stayed behind for the burning—and Brother and Sister Finch, a white-haired couple who'd insisted they would go wherever Tabitha led.

Tamar swept the small company with an assessing gaze. "It's the right number, I believe. Many more, and we'll find it difficult to hide out there."

"Let's be on our way, then," Tabitha said.

Her buggy led the way through the heart of the great encampment toward the road beyond. The others from Centerville fell into line. Curious women looked up from their preparations as the file rolled past, but Tamar paid them no mind. She prayed for her family's safety—for the protection of everyone present, for all those who'd fled their homes at Brigham's behest. Their fates were in other hands now. *God's will be done.*

As they neared the edge of the campsite, a man held up his hands, commanding a halt. He had a sharp nose, deep-set eyes, and a thick graying beard. Tamar had never seen him before—yet she recognized the air of authority that hung about him like a stately mantle.

This must be Brother Wells, she thought. *Brigham Young's right hand.*

"Whose party do you belong to, Sisters?" Wells asked. "None have set out just yet."

There was a pause—only a fraction of a second, yet in that flash of silence, Tamar felt her own fears reflected from Tabitha on the seat beside her.

Tabitha said, "We belong to our own party, Brother Wells."

"Your own . . . ? Now see here, Sister. There's no sense in traipsing off into the wilderness without protection."

"Protection?" Jane asked slyly from the back seat.

"We've organized everyone into companies. We must have order, if we all hope to get through this trial in one piece. And you must be under the leadership of a man—"

"That's where you're wrong, Brother," Tabitha broke in. "My sisters and I have done quite well for ourselves these past many months without a man to guide us. We'll do just as well in the wilderness."

She flicked the reins, and the buggy lurched forward a few steps, but Wells stepped into the pony's path.

"Sister," he said, astounded, "you're disobeying the direct instructions of a priesthood holder. Of the second counselor himself!"

Tamar slipped her hand into the first wife's and squeezed.

"Go and tell it to the Angel Moroni," Tabitha said dryly.

She slapped the pony's rump with her reins. Wells jumped back as the buggy rolled on. They left the camp and the second counselor behind, towing the ragtag company in their wake.

Tamar looked back over her shoulder. Brother Wells was staring after them. She fancied that she could still see the dismay on his face.

"Whatever possessed you to say such a thing?" she asked with a chuckle.

The first wife lifted her shoulders. "If you could find the strength to defy Thomas and do what you thought best, I figured I could defy the whole priesthood. We don't need the menfolk to survive. We only need each other."

24

TAMAR

The Sanpete Wilderness
June 1858

The small company traveled south for hours that morning. Tamar never knew whether the larger parties, led by the apostles and Bishop Thorn, had taken the same route—or whether they'd chosen another road entirely. Whenever she looked back, she found no signs of the other refugees. No signs of her family.

We're moving faster than they can, she told herself. *A small group is much more nimble. There's no need to worry; they will find a suitable place to hide.*

By midday, with the help of one of Thomas's old letters to guide her, Tabitha located the new evacuation roads that Brigham's men had prepared. The road was little more than a rough track hastily beaten over difficult terrain, but it led deep into the foothills, and soon the road to Provo was lost behind undulations of sage land.

Tabitha's party made slow but steady progress throughout the punishing heat of afternoon. Tamar could scarcely believe that a city and its surrounding villages, home to tens of thousands, lay anywhere close by—for no mark of man's influence could be found, other than the trail itself. No smoke of industry grayed the horizon at her back, and beyond the forlorn rattle of the refugees' carts, the hills were silent. Even the wild creatures were pressed down in the shade, waiting out the heat of the day.

Shortly before sunset, the trail dipped into a bottomland, a long cove running from the broader valley to the east into a green depression between two neighboring lines of mountains. The grass was cool and inviting at the base of those hills, and ample broadleaf trees spoke of reliable water just below the ground, though no river ran on the surface.

"Brother Richards told us to look for a dry green valley," Tabitha called to their party. "It's close to one of the caches and will be a location for the distribution of supplies. I believe this must be the place. We'll follow our track down to those bottomlands, let the horses feed, and camp for the night. At sunrise, we'll find a hiding place where we may dig in for weeks."

Tabitha led them down into the cove, then a few miles farther along that cool sanctuary. She didn't want one of the apostles' companies to overtake them and—if luck turned against them—draw the army's eye. As the sky reddened and shadows deepened, the ground became boggy and the sharp, metallic trill of red-winged blackbirds filled the air. Blue water pooled in the depressions between cottonwoods. Another quarter mile up the draw, Tamar could see that the shallow marsh condensed itself into a proper stream.

"Salt Creek," Tabitha said. "It has to be Salt Creek; Richards described the place. How many other bogs can there be in these hills? We'll camp here where the ground is driest. But I want to explore that creek. Do you see how it flows out between two steep hills? I'd bet all of Thomas's money there's a canyon up there."

The company unhitched their horses and made camp with admirable speed. Tabitha's long service as healer of Centerville had given her an air of authority; the members of the small party trusted her good sense without hesitation. When Tabitha asked them all to lay out the supplies they'd brought from home, they were quick to comply, and shortly, she and Tamar had taken stock of what resources the company had.

Eliza Whitney had packed a small can of lamp oil. "I don't know what I was thinking," she said, "for I didn't bring a lamp. I was so harried, getting my five little ones into the cart with everything they might need. I simply grabbed whatever came to hand without considering whether it would be of any use."

"I believe that oil will be useful after all," Tabitha said. "It's fortunate you've brought it."

Tabitha shouted for two of the boys who'd been splashing in a warm, boggy puddle. "Nephi! Samuel!"

The boys came running. They were eleven or twelve years old, all elbows and knees, bounding through the grass like colts.

"Can you fellows make a pair of torches?" Tabitha asked them. "Find some good, sturdy branches under those cottonwoods—not too long or heavy, for I must carry one. You can tear this sacking into strips and wrap it around one end. Then we'll douse the sacking in lamp oil. Jane, you'll come with me once the torches are ready. We'll make our way up Salt Creek, and with any luck, we'll find a good place to hide."

"Why not wait till tomorrow?" Jane said.

"The other companies could overtake us by then. If we're drawn back into their ranks, we'll have done ourselves no good. We can make a thorough exploration tonight if we've torches to light the way."

The other Centerville refugees smoothly took charge of Tabitha's children, feeding and distracting them while their mother trudged away through the meadow with her torch in hand and Jane at her heels. Brother Finch, the kindly old grandfather, tucked Junior under his arm and told him stories to keep him from wailing in distress.

Some two hours later, the torches reappeared along the distant line of the creek, glowing through a deep-blue twilight.

Eliza ladled up two dishes of bean soup to feed the hungry explorers. Tabitha told them all what she'd found as she settled beside the fire to eat her supper and kiss her children.

"There is a canyon, just as I'd hoped. It's narrow for most of the way—we'll need to drive our carts right up the middle of the creek in some places—but a mile or so in, the walls open out into a wide, sandy draw. There's even a fine meadow of grass for our horses. We'll be safe and comfortable there for as long as we must stay. Or we'll be as comfortable as anyone might hope to be in the wilderness."

The matter was settled. In the morning, they would proceed up the canyon to the site Tabitha and Jane had found. The torches were extinguished, the bedrolls laid out, and the company settled in for a night under the stars.

"I'll stay up for a few hours," Jane said. "With our numbers so few, someone might as well keep watch. We don't know whether Buchanan has scouts in these hills, and Indians may pass through the meadow."

"You'll make a poor sentry with your eyes," Tabitha said.

Tamar glanced at Jane, but the latter only nodded. Under usual circumstances, Jane would have lashed back, for she was always sensitive about her eyes. These were no ordinary times, however. There was no room for tender feelings in a small camp of women and children, with the wilderness looming all around. Jane seemed to understand that.

"Nephi and me can stand watch," Samuel said. "We got lots of energy, Sister Ricks."

Tabitha hesitated, eyeing the two gangly boys. In the firelight, they looked younger than ever, too soft and breakable for the demands of an untamed world. Finally, she nodded. "I daresay you do have plenty of vim. You must take turns, however. One of you may sleep while the other keeps watch for a few hours; then you can trade. Wake me at once if you see or hear anything unusual. At once, do you understand?"

The boys nodded, and after a whispered negotiation, Nephi climbed up into the driver's seat of the tallest cart while Samuel took to his bed.

Tamar remained sitting on her blankets, feeding Amy while the camp settled into sleep. The boys had stoked the central fire with plenty of fallen branches, and it blazed with dancing cheer, yet her worries had gathered in the darkness behind her. She could feel them waiting, as vast and consuming as the night. That feeble ring of firelight couldn't keep her thoughts at bay for long.

She watched the faces of those who slept around her—the frail elderly couple, the women without husbands or fathers to guard them. The children who must rely on this small, ill-equipped band to preserve them, somehow, against all the dangers of the world and the army bearing down.

They were all so far from home now. Only the Lord could say how far, exactly. Fifty miles? A hundred? Tamar had no sense of the distance, except to know straight through to her soul that the separation was too much to bear. She loved her little home. She had never realized until that moment how much peace and comfort that small log house had given her.

The men will burn our home to ashes if the army breaks through.

Tears filled her eyes at the thought. It was a grief heavier than one little house should warrant. She was weeping not for that home, but for everything she'd lost—all the homes she'd never had, not since her family's exile from Aston Rowant.

Tamar chided herself for crying uselessly, and once Amy was fast asleep in her swaddling, she decided the only sensible thing to do was to get some sleep. She settled back on the hard bedroll, tucking the quilts around herself and the baby. But sleep evaded her, and memories of Aston Rowant seemed to move like a blowing fog against the firelight—visions of the cottage and her father's garden sliding in vivid color across the dim vista of the campsite, the black hills beyond.

She turned restlessly for hours, cramped and miserable, but sleep continued to evade her, and her memories brought no peace.

Tamar shifted yet again, struggling to find a comfortable position without waking her daughter. As she turned her back to the fire, a sudden, sharper dread took hold, stopping the breath in her throat. The echo of the flames was still blaring in her eyes. She lay still, cold and acutely frightened, while the violet glow dimmed and faded and her eyes adjusted once more to the dark.

Then she understood the source of her fear, for now she could see two yellow points of light shining in the tall grass—the eyes of a predator staring straight back at her.

Tamar couldn't have guessed how far away the creature was, for night had flattened and distorted the world. Nor could she have said what animal it might be—bear or coyote, or some terrible chimera of God's invention, striding through the veils of grass to proclaim destruction.

She heard a howl in the foothills.

Wolves.

Tamar glanced at the cart where Nephi had been perched. The boy was lying along the bench seat now, chest rising and falling in a steady rhythm. Her first instinct was anger, but she checked herself. Nephi was only a child. They were all vulnerable—everyone in the company.

Tamar drew a deep breath. She tried to shout, but her voice wouldn't come. It had vanished, or fled; some unseen force had torn it away.

The yellow eyes blinked. Then they shifted—coming closer, one hungry step at a time.

Tamar rose smoothly from her bed, fixing the animal with a stare. Dimly, she was aware of more flickering pinpoints of gold—a pack circling the meadow, drawing in around the refugees.

Amy lay small and helpless among the rumpled quilts. Again, Tamar tried to shout, to wake Tabitha and the rest, but it was no use. Her voice was gone.

She could feel the fire's heat against her back. She remembered the torches lying nearby. The fire was only a few paces behind her, but she would have to turn away from the wolves if she hoped to reach it, How quickly could those creatures move? Could she move faster?

Tamar scrambled among her frantic thoughts, trying to assemble a hasty prayer. But that, too, was a fruitless effort. No petition or supplication came to her mind—and with a sickening chill, she recalled that she had angered God. She had refused to give Him what He'd demanded, and now He'd taken away her voice and turned His back on her suffering.

A jealous God will have His due. I wouldn't sacrifice my daughter's happiness, and now, to punish me, He will take Amy's life instead.

But even as she thought it, Tamar knew that nothing would take her child—no wolf, no army, no god. Not without a fight. That sharp certainty severed whatever invisible bonds had transfixed her. She spun away, darted to the fire, and snatched both torches, then thrust them into the flames. The torches blazed to life with a reek of burning oil.

Tamar ran back to her bedroll, the fire streaming from her outstretched hands. She stepped over Amy's tiny body and thrust the torches into the darkness. A surge of heat ran through her; the sparks seemed to crackle in her throat. She faced the creature in the meadow, beating those fiery brands against the night, against all the great black cruelty of God's creation.

The wolves fled. She could see their pelts vanishing between clumps of grass. And now she could hear startled cries from the camp, the sound of blankets being kicked away, mothers calling to their children, the horses whinnying in alarm.

There was another sound, too. *"You won't have her! You won't!"* Only very slowly did Tamar realize it was her own voice, returned to her—reclaimed—crying her defiance to the world.

Someone seized one of the torches, prying it from her hand. Tamar never looked around. She went on shouting and flailing with her brand until the eyes in the grass had blinked out and the night was quiet once more.

She turned, panting, and looked back at the camp. Jane was cradling Amy against her chest, Tabitha's little ones holding tight to her skirt. And on the far side of the fire, Tabitha held the other brand aloft, watching the night with cool composure.

The first wife lowered her arm a little, looked back over her shoulder. Tamar met her eye. In a sidelong blaze of torchlight, Tabitha smiled.

25

JANE

On the day they'd left the marshland, following Salt Creek up into the high hills, Jane promised herself she would part with her sister-wives as soon as she'd seen them properly hidden beyond the reach of the army. She was no Mormon, after all, however much she may care for Tabitha and Tamar. Why ought she to remain cowering in the canyons in fear of a punishment meant for Mormons alone?

One day, Jane had told herself, she would slip away unnoticed. She would ride south through the dry wasteland till she found the place called Mountain Meadows, the site of the terrible massacre against the Arkansas company. From there, surely she could find the trail. California lay some seven hundred miles to the west. She could make it on her own—or join a wagon party, if she chanced to find one.

She'd repeated to herself that very same tale as the pale stone of the valley had given way to formations of startling red, sculpted by wind and water into pillars that brought to mind a legion of angels watching over the company. The creek had cut a hard vertical cleft into the flank of the mountain. The mouth of the canyon had beckoned with purple shadows, promising coolness and security within its twisting passage.

The company had proceeded into that fissure of stone. The way had bent like a hairpin, and the walls of the canyon had seemed to lean overhead, blocking out the sky. Now and then, the cold convolutions of stone had drawn in so tightly that there was no sandy bed left for walking, and the party had been forced to drive and wade up the center of the creek, as Tabitha had predicted. But at last, after more than an hour of travel, the walls had pulled back to reveal a broad, sandy wash dotted with willows and flush with green grass, entirely enclosed by a fortress of steep red stone.

Jane had stepped down from the cart, allowing the world to double and blur as she turned slowly in the rustling shade. The canyon stronghold had looked quite different by torchlight, when she and Tabitha had found it. By day, the walls of the canyon slid into an indistinct haze of rusty red, touched here and there by the green of willow and cottonwood. A jagged track of blue had snaked above where the canyon walls gave way to sky. The creek, far across the meadow, had flashed in fragments of violet and turquoise-blue.

That had been weeks ago. Yet Jane was still with the company.

It's because this place is so peaceful and pretty that I haven't gone yet, she told herself as she squatted beside the creek, cleaning and skinning a jackrabbit the boys had snared.

Surely her sister-wives had nothing to do with her stagnation. She may be fond of them, but it wasn't reluctance to leave Tabitha and Tamar that had stranded Jane in the canyon. A land of golden opportunity was waiting for her. She might reach some settlement in the distant hills of California and set herself up as a healer, a woman of independent means, as Tabitha was. What was she waiting for now?

Dear Tabitha. I'll miss her when I go. And Tamar—so sweet, so generous, so gentle at heart.

Jane had told herself the same story every day as June warmed and the sky deepened into summer's fierce azure. She'd told herself the same story—*when I go, when I go*—as the Centerville women made their weekly treks to the marsh valley to retrieve Brigham's supplies and the hidden camp blossomed into a proper rustic settlement.

Now, in the tail end of July, no one slept beneath the stars any longer. The supply men had given them proper canvas tents, sturdy shoes for the children, rifles and bullets for the boys so they could hunt and mount a proper watch against Buchanan's invaders.

Jane staked out the rabbit skin to cure in the sun. She tied the carcass to a good willow stick for roasting, then rinsed her hands in the creek. She could hear the easy, contented conversation of women in the camp behind her—Eliza Whitney sitting with Sister Finch in the door of her tent, helping the old woman weave baskets out of reeds while a pack of children played in the grazing meadow.

Their sanctuary was one of perfect peace, now that they'd all grown used to their predicament. The threat of invaders felt very far away, as inconsequential as rumor. The weekly trips Lanora Christiansen made to fetch their allotment of supplies were the only times of real worry, for Lanora always brought back news along with the sacks of grain and other necessities. The woman always pressed the supply men for the latest from Echo Canyon and Salt Lake City. She'd told Jane that she never knew where the supply men got their information. *Must be some messenger rides back and forth between Brigham and the storehouses,* she'd said. But however word traveled from Echo Canyon to the Sanpete wilderness, Lanora was always diligent in fetching the news along with sacks of grain and crates of clothing.

When Lanora's cart would return at dusk, filled with necessities from the secret cache, everyone would gather at the cook fire to discuss the latest information—how far into Echo Canyon the army had pressed, how the Legion fared in holding them back, whether Brigham

Young was likely to issue his fateful order to burn every home to the ground.

Now, for the first time since they'd found their canyon stronghold, the serenity darkened Jane's heart. The peace of this place had become a trap, and she'd allowed herself to get stuck in it, right up to her neck.

She stood and dried her hands briskly on her apron. She had dawdled too long; no more of the summer could be wasted. She hated the thought of leaving without explaining herself to Tabitha and Tamar. And yet her heart would surely break if she bade them farewell. Very likely, if Jane admitted she intended to leave them for good, their hurt would show on their faces. Jane couldn't bear the sight. Her resolve would crumble if tears came to Tamar's eyes, if Tabitha's brows drew together in disappointment.

I must slip away on my own, if I hope to cut ties at all, Jane decided.

She could use the canyon maze to her advantage, be gone before anyone would notice. She must do it now, while Deseret was quiet. If she waited till Lanora brought grim news from the rendezvous, it might be too late; the whole valley might be overrun by Buchanan's army. And Jane wouldn't pass another winter in Deseret. She was determined to reach California by autumn's end.

She carried the spitted rabbit to the cook fire, struggling to put a neutral expression on her face. She knew she was frowning in deep thought, and if Sister Finch caught the sour look, she would intervene with her usual grandmotherly compassion.

"We'll have a good supper tonight," Eliza called from the mouth of the tent. "Thank you, Jane. What would we do without you?"

Jane mumbled a reply. She refused to look at the two women as she propped the spit above the coals. The cook fire was still smoldering from the morning meal. The jackrabbit would roast slowly, but it would be all the more delicious for that.

I'll be long gone before it's cooked. See if I'm not, this time.

Jane made her way to the tent she and her sister-wives shared. In one corner, her makeshift pack was unrolled but still in its usual order. She knelt and began bundling her belongings, tightening the lot with the old leather bracers. Bitterly, she regretted all the goods she'd cached in her pine trunk back home—the extra boots, the woolen shawls, and most of all, the money. Those gold coins would have been a welcome advantage on the trail, for surely there were forts and trading posts along the route. She could have purchased anything she was wanting. As the matter stood, she would have to make out as best she could with the few items she possessed—a change of clothing, one warm wrapper, her tired old boots, and a paltry few blankets. At least she still had the kitchen knife she'd brought from Centerville and a box of matches for making fires. She found an empty flour sack in the corner of the tent and stretched it between her hands, wondering how she might fill it with grain and beans without drawing any attention.

But as she left the tent, Jane heard a thin, panicked voice calling from down the canyon. "Help! Come quick! Nephi's hurt!"

She dropped the flour sack in the sandy wash. Tabitha was already striding from the willow thicket where she'd been gathering bark for her medicinal supplies. Jane dodged back into the tent, snatched the healer's leather bag, and ran to meet her.

They converged at the edge of the creek, just as the boy Samuel came pelting along its shore. He was red-faced, gasping for breath.

"Sister Ricks!" he panted. "Nephi fell off a pillar! I think his leg is broke!"

Jane swung the bag toward Tabitha, who caught its handle deftly and passed the strap over her shoulder. The boys of the camp spent their days keeping watch over the canyon from a high vantage—the red stone pillars that had, at first sight, reminded Jane of angels. Tabitha had grumbled about the dangers of a fall, but in the end, even she had agreed that someone must act as sentinel from some high place if they hoped to spot Buchanan's men in time to flee farther up the canyon.

"Catch my horse and bridle her," Tabitha said to Jane. "Samuel, you'll stay here and drink water, but slowly. I don't like the look of you; you're already overheated. Now tell me what you know about Nephi—"

Jane had no time to hear more. She returned to the tent and fetched Tabitha's bridle, then ran to the meadow where the company's horses grazed. The spotted pony came eagerly when Jane mimicked Tabitha's whistle. She had the mare bridled in moments, and led her back to Tabitha as quickly as she could induce the animal to move.

Jane gave Tabitha a leg up onto the pony's bare back. "Do you want me to come with you?"

"No. Samuel has given me good directions to the place, and it doesn't sound as if Nephi is in serious danger—though I'm sure he's in a great deal of pain. I'll splint his leg and get him up on my pony, then bring him back to camp. You and I will give him a more thorough treatment once he's here. Tamar is watching my children; tell her I'll be longer than I'd expected."

Tabitha kicked her mare and wheeled about, cantering around the bend of the canyon.

Jane stared after her, listening to the pony's hoofbeats echoing from the stone. Soon the sound had faded to nothing. She turned slowly to Samuel, who was still panting at the water's edge.

"Drink," she said, "but not too much, and not too fast."

I must go now, or not at all.

The chance might never come again. If she hoped to slip away without notice—without making that agonizing farewell—she couldn't ask for a better distraction.

Jane darted once more to the tent, slung her pack onto her shoulders, and found the flour sack among a tangle of sagebrush. She hustled to the cart that had become the company's larder and storehouse, grabbed a bridle from among a tangle of tack, then filled her bag with as many dried beans and measures of barley as she could carry. She knotted the bag closed. It swung heavily around her knees as she pressed on toward the meadow.

Tamar was lounging with the children in the shade of the willows. She called out with obvious concern. "Jane? Is something amiss?"

"Tabitha will be back later." It was the only answer she could think to give.

In the meadow, the horses tossed their heads and evaded Jane; she growled in frustration, trying to catch their manes, but her cursed eyes played tricks on her, and the horses' necks were never as near as she expected them to be.

She'd begun to sweat from the strain. Finally, she thought to untie her grain sack and offer a handful of barley. At once, the horses crowded around, whickering, shoving each other aside, lipping at her fingers. She managed to slip the headstall onto a big dark-bay gelding, the farm horse that pulled Lanora's cart for the weekly supply. He was a tall, rangy beast, and his goose rump and ewe neck made him look ill-suited for long riding. But he would have to do.

Cursing and hopping, Jane managed to pull herself up to the bay gelding's back. Her hasty pack nearly slipped from her shoulders, and the sack of provisions balanced awkwardly on the gelding's withers, but she was mounted and ready to ride. The whole camp would turn its attention to the injured boy; no one would spare a thought for Jane till late in the evening. By then, she would be miles away to the south.

She kicked the gelding in his ribs, and he sprang forward with an indignant grunt.

"Jane!" Tamar cried.

She didn't stop, didn't look back. She trotted through the camp to the water's edge, then rounded the curve of red stone and pressed on doggedly toward the canyon's mouth. She would ride for an hour at least before she reached the marsh, and then the valley beyond, but soon enough, Deseret and all its troubles would be behind her.

She'd gone no more than half a mile when she heard a frantic splashing ahead. Jane slowed the bay, then stopped on a scant margin of shore. The canyon narrowed ahead—one of the places where one must ride or walk through the creek itself—and someone or something was charging through the water, directly toward Jane.

There was no time to hide. All Jane could do was clutch her reins and hope it wasn't some dangerous beast—or the army. A copper-and-white blur burst from the curve of the canyon. Jane gave a startled cry—then realized it was only Tabitha's pony, running back toward the encampment.

But as the pony galloped past, its rider was nowhere to be seen.

Jane gasped. "Tabitha!"

She kicked her horse into motion, thundering down the narrow passage. Its hooves churned up water and soaked her skirt, but she pressed on with her heart thudding painfully in her chest. Where had Tabitha fallen? Jane prayed she hadn't landed in the water, for in her headlong rush, she might not see Tabitha before it was too late to stop her mount.

In a few moments more, she reached the base of the pillars where the boys liked to keep their watch. Jane exhaled with relief, for Tabitha was plain to be seen, sprawled on the ground just below the nearest pillar. Then relief turned to terror, for the healer wasn't moving. Jane shouted her name, but Tabitha never stirred.

The bay slid to a stop near Tabitha's body. Jane let the sack of provisions drop. She followed it to the ground and ran to Tabitha's side, where she fell to her knees, schooling herself to calm thought, running through every word of the healer's lectures on blows to the head and how to treat them.

Jane could see Tabitha's chest rising and falling, though the breaths were shallow. Her eyelids fluttered, and she gave a faint groan.

"Tabitha," Jane said, firm yet urgent, "you've fallen. You've struck your head. Listen to me carefully, now. You mustn't move unless I tell you to."

Gingerly, frightened her hands might slip and do more harm than good, Jane eased her fingers below Tabitha's head and palpated the back of her skull. Thank goodness, there was no sign of broken bone, though Tabitha whimpered unconsciously at the pain.

Next, she prodded carefully at the vertebrae of Tabitha's neck. Those, too, seemed intact—as far as Jane could tell.

I must wake her up, Jane realized. *Sleep is the worst enemy of a blow to the head until the medicine has taken down any swelling of the brain.*

She tapped Tabitha's cheeks, one and then the other, with increasing vigor.

Finally, Tabitha's eyes opened. "Where—?" she croaked.

Jane knew she must assess her mental acuity. It was often the best indicator of how far damage had spread within the skull.

"What's your name?" she asked with authority.

"Tab-Tabitha Ricks."

"And who is in your family?"

Tabitha murmured the names of her children, and Thomas. That satisfied Jane well enough. Then Tabitha added, "Jane Shupe. Tamar Loader."

Startled, Jane rocked back on her heels. She allowed her eyes to lose their laborious focus, just for the moment. She hadn't known, had never suspected that Tabitha considered her family.

She heard more hooves churning through water, turned to find three horses coming down the creek. One certainly carried Samuel, for his youthful form was unmistakable. Another white-haired rider must have been Brother Finch.

"My boy!" the third rider cried. Eliza Whitney, then, coming to find Nephi.

Jane stood. "Quickly! I need your help."

In moments, they'd gathered beside her, and Tabitha was moving feebly on the sand, pressing a hand to her aching head.

"Eliza, Brother Finch, help her sit up—and don't let her fall asleep, whatever you do! Sleep could be deadly just now. Keep her talking and keep her wide awake. Samuel, come with me. Show me where to find Nephi."

Jane scooped up the healer's bag and followed the boy as he scrambled up and over a red foot of stone. The lookout pillar rose steeply above, but happily, Nephi was close at hand. He'd fallen from a ledge some fifteen feet up the pillar. The boy lay curled on his side, teeth clenched as he gripped his ankle with both hands.

Jane spoke softly to Nephi as she coaxed his hands away and probed the ankle with her fingers. When she turned the foot in her hands, he cried out in pain, but she felt no friction of broken bones.

"Thank your lucky stars: I don't believe it's broken. But it is badly sprained. Samuel, go down to the creek bed and find as many good, sturdy sticks as you can. We'll need to splint you, Nephi, and once Tabitha is recovered, she may decide you've broken it after all. But you'll mend; I'm sure of that."

Jane ripped the hem from her skirt while Samuel foraged along the creek. When he returned, she chose the best pieces of willow wood and tied them securely in place with the strips of linen. Then she and Samuel helped Nephi to his feet and guided him carefully down the slick stone to the creek bed.

Tabitha was sitting up by then, clear-eyed but wincing from pain.

"I need . . . ," Tabitha began.

"Goldenrod leaf," Jane said briskly. "The smoked preparation, not a tea. That'll clear the fog from your head. When we get back to camp, it'll be yarrow leaf in cold water and plenty of willow bark till the pain is gone."

She rummaged through the leather bag till she'd found the folded leather packet of goldenrod leaves and the medicinal pipe Tabitha used for inhaled medicines. She had to reach into her own pack—the one she'd assembled for her escape—to find the matches.

Tabitha looked at Jane's pack with unconcealed surprise, but she said nothing, and drew obediently on the pipe when Jane held it to her lips. When she coughed, Jane pressed a hand against the back of her head to help ease the pain. A knot the size of a goose egg was forming there.

"Let's get everyone back to camp," Jane said to the others. "Brother Finch, Samuel—help Nephi onto his mother's horse. She can ride behind him. Tabitha will ride with me."

~

Late that night, the stars had gathered in a strip of velvet sky above the canyon walls. Jane sat in the mouth of the tent with Tabitha at her side, soothed by the cool evening breeze and the gentle music of water over stone.

All the day's excitement had died away. The company was satisfied that both Tabitha and Nephi were well—all save Jane, who still wouldn't allow Tabitha to sleep, not until she'd taken one last dose of yarrow and willow bark. Tabitha tolerated her ministrations with an affectionate smile.

Jane swirled a small clay cup, peering into it doubtfully, for little starlight reached into the canyon, and even in the brightest light, she would have found it difficult to gauge whether the cold extraction was ready.

"Smell it," Tabitha suggested. "If you can easily recognize the scent of yarrow at six inches' distance, it's strong enough."

Jane held the cup near her face and sniffed. "Not yet."

Silence returned, but Jane could sense an uneasy expectation. Tabitha wanted to say something more. Jane resisted the urge to glance over her shoulder at the pack, which lay discarded beside Tamar, who was sleeping in her bedroll with the children snuggled around her. Instead, she amused herself by trying to track the darting black shapes of bats as they flitted and swung above the creek.

Finally, Tabitha said, "If you want to leave, Jane, you may do it with my blessing."

Jane swallowed hard. She didn't answer.

"Perhaps it's wise to get away while you still can. We can't know what will become of Deseret—of the valley, our homes. Not even our lives. If I were you, I would leave this mess to the Mormons. You aren't one of us, after all."

"I might not be a Mormon," Jane said softly, "but I am a part of this family. When I saw you lying there, helpless on the ground, I thought . . ." Her breath caught in her throat. She blinked back tears, and pressed on. "I realized how much I still have to learn from you, Tabitha. And how little I'd like to be parted from you, in any case. There may be no future for Deseret—who can say? But I have to believe there's a future for me. And I know it lies with you. With you and Tamar."

Carefully, Tabitha scooted closer. She wrapped an arm around Jane's shoulders. "We make a peculiar family indeed, but thank God we have each other."

26

TAMAR

The Sanpete Wilderness
July 1858

Late in the morning after Tabitha was returned to camp, Tamar looked up from her work to find Jane exiting the tent. She laid aside the trousers she'd been darning. Quickly, she rose from the willow log where she'd sat with two other women, working their way through a pile of children's clothes in need of mending.

"Are you well?" Sister Wyles asked.

"Quite. I only need to speak with Tabitha." Anxiety twisted inside her like a knife. "You don't mind watching Amy, do you? I shan't be long."

Tamar hurried across the sandy wash. Jane had spent all morning stuck like a burr to Tabitha's side, monitoring the lump on the back of her head and preparing various concoctions for Tabitha to swallow. Now Jane was making her way upstream, casually swinging a small basket by its handle. She looked unconcerned—that boded well for Tabitha's recovery—and if she'd gone out to forage for more healing plants, she might be absent long enough that Tamar could speak to the first wife alone.

She didn't look forward to the task. Yet it couldn't wait an hour longer. The day before, she'd seen Tabitha blinking and dazed, held pillion on the horse with Jane's arm wrapped tightly around her, and a terrible wave of guilt had almost drowned Tamar. Tabitha could have died in that fall. And Tamar had realized in a lightning flash of illumination that there were words she needed to say to the first wife. There were words Tabitha needed to hear. They must be spoken now, in this life. Atonement couldn't wait for eternity.

Outside the tent, she breathed slowly and deeply, trying to steady her nerves, or at least to set her clamoring thoughts in order. It was useless, however. Tamar could think of no delicate way to broach the subject, to admit her guilt and make amends. There was nothing for it but to face Tabitha squarely and put in an earnest effort.

She lifted the flap and stepped inside.

Tabitha was lying on her side, head pillowed on a folded quilt. She looked up expectantly but said nothing.

"How are you feeling?" Tamar asked.

"As well as can be expected, considering I fell from my horse and cracked my head on a rock. Or so Jane tells me. I don't remember any of it. But the pain isn't too severe. It's getting better."

"Can I . . . bring you anything?"

Tabitha made a small huffing sound—a careful laugh. "Heaven preserve me. Jane has been begging to bring me this and that all day long. No—I'm quite content. I only need rest. I'll be on my feet before you know it."

It was a clear dismissal. Tamar almost left the tent, and even half turned toward the door. But she caught herself and faced the first wife once more.

"In truth, Tabitha, I . . . hoped I might speak to you. Alone."

Tabitha arched her brows. "Now is the time to do it, I suppose. Sit, if you like, and unburden your soul."

Tamar sank down on her own bedroll. Her fingers twisted in her lap as she searched for the right way to proceed.

"I know you've had small affection for me, all this time since . . . since I agreed to marry Thomas. I only wanted to tell you that I understand."

Tabitha considered her for a long moment. There was no malice in her eyes, but neither was there any warmth. She said quietly, "Do you understand? I'm not sure you can, Tamar."

"I suppose I can't, after all. I won't ask your forgiveness. I know that's too much to hope for. I only wanted to—"

Tabitha lifted a hand from beneath her blanket, a small but commanding gesture.

Tamar fell silent.

"Let me tell you," the first wife said, "how I came to marry Thomas. I was thirteen years old when my family came to Nauvoo. We took a riverboat up from Louisiana, hopeful to join the Mormon faith. But we arrived only two days after the Prophet's murder, and Nauvoo was in chaos—fighting in the streets by day, the Legion against the Illinois militia. By night, no one could sleep for the gunfire and the flash of powder. So after only a few days, we left again. We took to the trail, headed west for Zion. Before we could reach Winter Quarters, a terrible snowstorm overtook us."

Tamar flinched, recalling the agony of cold, the weight of a collapsed tent pressing down, the eyes of the feral man as he'd loped away across the camp, mouth stretched in a hungry grin.

"We were saved," Tabitha said, "by friendly Indians—the Ponca tribe. They found us along the trail and took us to their village. They housed us and fed us, and one of them—their healer—treated my sister, who'd fallen ill as the snow set in. If not for that wisewoman, I know my sister would have lost her life. And I knew in that moment that I was called to be a healer, too.

"I managed to convince the Ponca and my family that I should stay in the village. I offered to teach them how to speak our language so they could trade to better advantage with the trappers and pioneers. And, I hoped, so they might avoid some of the nastier tricks the Bureau of Indian Affairs likes to use. In return, their healer took me into her own home. I worked as one of her apprentices till I was sixteen, learning my trade from a master of the healing arts. Now and then, I would ride to Winter Quarters to visit my family. They'd decided not to continue on to Zion, you see; my brother-in-law Neriah had seen the opportunity in supplying the pioneer companies, and over the years, he'd become quite wealthy. By then, he was one of the richest men in the area."

Tabitha sighed. Her eyes went distant, and for a moment, Tamar thought she would speak no more. Just as Tamar was about to ask what happened next, Tabitha went on in a stiff, matter-of-fact tone.

"Neriah decided I was of marriageable age, and in any case, my continued association with the Ponca was a sore point with him. He wanted me back in the white man's world for good. There was nothing I wanted less, for, by then, I thought white ways backward and confining compared to the natural freedoms of my Ponca friends. But I wasn't Ponca, after all. I knew I couldn't stay with them forever. When Neriah threatened to marry me off to a man I despised, I joined one of the largest pioneer companies headed for Zion. I had no affinity for the church by then, but I knew my skills as a healer would be appreciated along the trail. And Deseret was far away from Neriah and his plans for my future.

"That was where I met Thomas. He was nineteen years old and handsome as the Devil. We got along well that first day—a good thing, for we were soon to be much in each other's company. Our very first night of travel, some Omaha boys stole a few of our horses. I tried to convince the leaders of our company it wasn't worth pursuing them— I'd made plenty of acquaintance with the Omaha while I lived among the Ponca, and I knew these were only spirited boys trying to prove their manhood. They were inexperienced, and if we went after them, far worse trouble might follow.

"If only Thomas and his friends had listened to me. He and some other boys rode off in pursuit—never knowing that one of the Omaha had a rifle. Thomas was shot. He fell from his horse and was left for dead."

Tamar gasped. "Thomas never said a word to me about any of this. How terrible!"

"We managed to find him, and thank God, he was still alive. It was a bad wound, though. I stayed with him in a wagon for almost the whole journey, tending to him day and night, using every scrap of knowledge I'd gained from the Ponca to save his life. At one point, it seemed hopeless. I knew Thomas would die. I prayed that night more earnestly than I ever had in all my life. I begged God to save him—and swore that if He would let Thomas live, I would rejoin the church, be baptized a Mormon, and always trust to His design. I would question nothing, obey every divine command, and gratefully take up any burden the Lord set before me."

Tabitha fell silent. She gave Tamar that expectant look again, prying, waiting.

"And," Tamar said reluctantly, "the Lord set me before you. This marriage, this . . . Principle."

"With all my heart, with all my soul, I believed it was my prayers that had saved Thomas's life, in the end. Not my medicine but my God. And yet ever since . . ."

She trailed off, blinking. Tamar's face burned with shame.

"I've struggled," Tabitha said, "since all this came to pass. I've struggled to hold on to any faith. There've been days when I've known, down to the very blood in my veins, that God Himself betrayed me. I feel that way still. And I've never known what to make of it—this certainty that my faith meant nothing to Him, that my loyalty never mattered, that He would take from me the man I loved even after a lifetime of dedication and service to His will."

A sudden memory overtook Tamar—the feel of her father's hand in her own as she'd bent over the handcart. The sound of his final breath had filled her head and all the world.

She said, "I can't undo the damage I've done to your life or your faith."

Tabitha looked at her again, dry amusement in her eyes. "But?"

Tamar shook her head. "There is nothing more to say. I'm bitter with regret, for I have hurt you—the one person in all the world who least deserved to suffer. If he comes back from the Legion, I will divorce Thomas. I'll move in with my mother, and whatever scorn may fall on me, I'll accept it as my due portion—my penance for what I've done to you. I broke your faith, Tabitha. Faith is a fragile thing. It can never be made quite whole again once it's broken."

"I don't know if faith is fragile, exactly," Tabitha said. "But it is deceptive. It changes its form just when you think you've worked out all its dimensions."

Tamar hugged her knees to her chest, waiting for the first wife to say more.

"I no longer have Thomas," Tabitha said, "not in the way I'd expected to have him. Perhaps none of us shall have him anymore; the army is still out there, as far as we know, and Buchanan is thirsty for Mormon blood. But my life is bigger now than one man. My world is bigger. I've found a treasure buried under the red earth of Zion. Perhaps that was God's true will all along—His real promise to me, the reward He gave me for my faith."

Tamar smiled. She remembered a snowy day near Christmas, the crowded meeting hall, the bishop reciting his sermon. "'For behold,'" she said, "'I have refined thee. I have chosen thee in the furnace of affliction.'"

Tabitha smiled up at her, then reached out and took Tamar's hand. "I don't want you to divorce Thomas—not unless you truly want it, unless you think it's best. We've gone through too much together. You're a part of this family, Tamar. That can never be undone. You're my sister now. Stay with me, if it suits you."

Tamar remained by the first wife's side until late in the afternoon, until the mourning doves began to call from the cool purple depths of the canyon.

~

The next day, Tabitha felt well enough to resume some of the lighter tasks of the campsite, tending the coals of the cook fire and making flour cakes to feed the hungry children. And on the next appointed day for retrieving their supplies, she was hale enough to attempt making the trip with Sister Christiansen. Jane caught her trying to climb into the cart and scolded her into staying behind.

Tabitha was annoyed but conceded that it was in her best interest to remain close to help, in case any lingering effects of her fall should creep up on her.

"I'm only itching for a change," she admitted. "We've been camped here for weeks. Thank God we've gone unnoticed, but what a long summer this has been. If only we had some reliable word from Echo Canyon. I'd give almost anything to know for certain how the Legion is faring. One can only subsist on rumor for so long."

Lanora Christiansen returned that evening with a rumor at least as substantial as her bags of grain. She was already calling out to the women of the camp as she drove the supply cart around the canyon's final bend. "News! News from the Legion and Echo Canyon!"

Tamar bundled Amy into her sling and hurried to meet the cart. Nearly the whole camp had left off their work and emerged from their tents.

"I can't say for certain it's true," Lanora said as she climbed down from the driver's seat, "but President Young's supply men told me a truce has been made."

"A truce?" Eliza sounded as if she were caught somewhere between disbelief and wild jubilation.

"So the story goes. Buchanan has agreed to call off the army, they say—but there are two conditions. First, a regiment of soldiers must remain in Deseret to be sure no one starts thinking of rebellion. And all men who've taken more than one wife must renounce all wives but the first. Or else they'll be imprisoned."

Tamar glanced across the small crowd. Tabitha was looking back at her, with Jane at her side. The first wife made a small motion, a sideways nod, and began strolling away toward the creek. Tamar followed with Jane dogging her heels.

"So it's come to this," Tamar said when they were alone. "Thomas will be made to set us both aside—Jane and me—or face imprisonment. I suppose that settles a few matters."

"It settles nothing," Tabitha said wryly. "I've no doubt Brigham Young will swear to Buchanan that every man in Deseret will give up polygamy, but he'll do whatever he pleases the moment Buchanan looks the other way. I shouldn't expect that Thomas will feel compelled to turn either one of you loose. Nor would I expect him to land in the jailhouse. Thomas has been one of Brigham's most reliable men these past two years. Brigham has plenty of failings, but at least one can say that he appreciates loyalty and rewards it duly. Thomas will be sheltered from the truce; you may count on that. Though if you decide to remain as his wives—and it will be your choice to make—you may expect a greater demand for secrecy."

"I suppose it'll be all the more important to hide the marriage," Jane said thoughtfully. "There will be soldiers stationed here, if Lanora has the right of it. The soldiers will be watching for transgressors. I'm not sure I'll like bearing that burden. This has all been heavy enough."

Torn by her own misgivings, Tamar took Jane's hand. "Are you going to divorce him, then? Tell me, Jane. I don't know what's best to be done."

"I don't know," Jane said slowly. "I do intend to remain in Centerville for a few more years—that is, supposing the truce is real, and not just a rumor. Supposing the whole valley isn't burned before we can get back home. I want to go on learning from you, Tabitha. But whether I'll do it as one of Tom's wives . . . well, I just haven't made up my mind. Not yet."

"I can't decide, myself," Tamar said faintly. "I don't wish to condemn Thomas to prison, whatever I choose—"

Tabitha broke in sharply. "It's long past time for all of us to put our interests before Tom's. Your happiness and your future matter, Tamar, regardless of what any man—or any god—tries to tell you."

Tamar looked down at the baby sleeping in her sling. God had brought her to Zion with the promise of a precious gift, a love greater than any she'd known. She had found it, and she didn't intend to squander her riches now.

"You're right," she said. "I once thought I was in love with Thomas—that no love could be stronger. Oh, perhaps I do love him still; perhaps when this is settled and he has come home for good, we'll find the kind of love you and he have shared, Tabitha. But I've greater concerns now, and more important duties than what a wife owes her husband."

Tabitha made no answer, and Tamar looked up, startled by the silence. She found the first wife watching her with an air of warm regard.

"You've been refined indeed," Tabitha said, "both of you, from rough ore into gold. You're a treasure in my hands—the two of you together. I won't like to let either one of you go. I hope we shan't have to say goodbye. But we'll make our own choices when the time comes for choosing. I pray that God will guide each of us to our happiest endings."

27

JANE

The Sanpete Wilderness
July 1858

One week passed, then another, the days merging easily together, the hours all the same—a quiet, cooperative industry of looking after the camp's flock of children, preparing food, tending to the horses, while the gentle susurrus of flowing water and the merciful shade of the canyon cast a mantle of peace over all. If any member of Tabitha's company had forgotten they were in hiding from an army bent on the destruction of the Mormon church, they might have been forgiven. Even rumor of a truce—however unlikely—had brought a certain satisfaction to the camp, for if the men who'd stayed behind were talking of truce and an end to the conflict, then surely they'd had good reason to believe Deseret would go on. Nothing remained now but to wait for Brigham's order to return to the valley. The small company dug in and went doggedly forward, treading through each day with the inexhaustible faith that had carried them all the long way to Zion.

Tamar declared her intent to remain as Thomas's second wife only a few days after she'd spoken with Tabitha. Only Jane was left with her future undecided. She would continue learning at Tabitha's side—on that matter, there was no question. But would she carry on as Tom's third wife?

Uncertainty haunted her as the days rolled on in drowsy placidity. She worked alongside the others, pulling her weight without complaint, but all the while she wandered a maze of thought, turning this way and that along those tight, confining corridors.

If she left Tom Ricks, would she stand before God as a fallen woman, a breaker of vows? Jane had lost the greatest portion of her regard for that capricious deity when He'd taken Sarah Ann away. But He was still the Almighty, and she couldn't help feeling as if her eternal fate were in His hands.

And a more persistent fear gnawed at her heart. If she divorced Tom, would he allow her to go on with the apprenticeship? Or would he turn his back on her for good, casting her out of his household?

He might turn me out anyhow, she thought, moving mechanically through her work, through the unchanging hours of the day. *Tabitha might be wrong; Tom may very well decide he can't risk prison. When we see him next, he might declare that Tamar and I are no wives of his, and never were.*

And what would she do if Tom said such a thing? Would she weep or rejoice to hear it?

The question was no closer to being settled when Lanora returned to camp with the weekly supply. Her face was shining as she came around the canyon's bend. Even Jane could read her excitement in a starched-upright posture, in the bright sound of her voice.

"More news! News from the valley!"

Jane met the cart and caught the horse's bridle.

"Where's Tabitha?" Lanora was almost laughing with joy as she lighted on the sand. "I've got such thrilling news for her."

The camp assembled, eager for the report, but Tabitha was last to arrive. Jane watched her emerge from the thicket of willows and cross the wash with a slow, deliberate pace.

"It's no rumor this time," Lanora said. "The men were sure of it; they swore it's true. Brigham has made peace with Buchanan. The army has already pulled back, and all our homes have been spared. What's better, not one of our men has been lost. Our husbands, our brothers, our sons—all safe and whole. Most of them have already returned to the city and the settlements. They'll be waiting for us when we come home."

Jane smiled down at the red sand while the camp cheered around her. Women wept in gratitude; children whooped with happiness.

Brother Finch burst out in song. His voice was surprisingly deep. "Morning breaks, the shadows flee; lo, Zion's standard is unfurled—"

"And, Tabitha," Lanora called over the din, "wouldn't you know it, your Thomas is on his way here, right now, to this very canyon!"

Tabitha's air of thoughtful detachment fell away. "He is?"

"Once those fellows with the supply wagons knew for certain that the battle was over and the army had withdrawn, they began passing word back to the city, telling all the men where their wives and children were hidden . . . if they'd known at all. And they got word this very morning that Tom Ricks is headed here to find his family and take them home. I guess he'll be down in the marsh soon enough. They thought he might arrive by evening's fall."

The celebration went on, but Tabitha drifted away again, back to the green seclusion of the willows. Jane and Tamar shared a glance, then followed her across the camp.

Under the dappled leaves, the first wife turned to them in expectant silence.

Tamar patted Amy's back, for the baby had begun to fuss in her sling, but she said nothing—only looked in her turn at Jane.

"Well?" Jane said at length. "What are we to do?"

"The time has come for you to make your choice, Jane," Tabitha said.

Jane tipped her head, and Tabitha's image clarified before her. There was no mistaking the tension around her sharp blue eyes.

She's been fretting over this moment, Jane realized, *almost as much as I have.*

"We don't need that man," Jane burst out. "We're halfway to the trail now. We can make it to Mountain Meadows in a few days, then go west together. We could be in California by—"

Tamar chuckled. "Jane, talk sense."

"Yes," Tabitha added, not unkindly. "It will cost each of us dearly to leave the valley now. I would have to give up my practice, for certain. Even if I made it to California, I can't be sure any other town would allow me to do my work—not without a husband to make me proper and trustworthy." The sudden grit in her voice was proof of how little she cared for that idea. "And if Tamar leaves, she'll be cut off from the rest of her family. That's too great a heartbreak to bear, after so long a journey from England."

Jane swallowed hard. "If I go to California, there'll be no apprenticeship for me—no future."

"Not as a healer," Tabitha agreed.

"It might not be our decision to make," Tamar said. "Thomas might cast us aside, after all."

Tabitha answered without hesitation. "If he does, I'll divorce him on the spot."

Jane stared at the first wife in open disbelief. Tamar, too, was goggling.

"He promised to care for you both," Tabitha said. "He vowed to be your husband. I'll hold him to that promise. I won't see either of you turned out into a cold world without recourse. You're my sisters now. I'll uphold you, whatever you choose . . . but if Tom casts you out, he'll cast me out. We'll go into the wilderness together."

Jane pulled the first wife into a rough embrace. A moment later, she felt Tamar's arms encircle them both.

"I've already made my choice," Tamar said. "My daughter will know her whole family—her father included. I've no doubt we'll face scorn. Perhaps we'll even face the threat of Thomas's imprisonment. But I won't deny what my family is, nor the choices I have made."

"And you?" Tabitha said.

Jane shook her head helplessly. She still didn't know what to choose, couldn't see where her best future lay.

Together, they harnessed Tabitha's pony to the old buggy. They snared Catherine and Junior from among the pack of tumbling, shouting children. And as the sky reddened overhead with a late-summer sunset, they drove along the secret passage of the canyon to meet their husband in the marsh.

Jane kept her thoughts to herself all the long drive. California still beckoned, but she also remembered the soft brown shadows of Tabitha's parlor, the dusty scent of drying herbs, the spots of colored light dancing on the walls. And she still had a home standing far to the north in Centerville.

By the time the buggy reached the canyon's mouth, the sun had vanished behind the western horizon, a long, unbroken band of deepest blue. The marsh swept out from their vantage point on the hillside. Cool shadows lay between the cottonwoods, and the frogs that had held on through the summer's heat called now and then from pools of dark water.

Jane could just make out a blocky shape moving through the marsh, picking its way among clumps of reeds, drifting this way and that along the crooked course of dry land. It was a single rider on a tall red horse.

For a moment, none of them moved. They watched their husband weave his way closer, closer, while the stars showed themselves in a dusky pink sky. Then Tabitha stepped down suddenly from the buggy, walked out to the open flank of the hillside, and waited.

Tamar was quick to follow, wrapping both arms around her child—the daughter who had yet to meet her father.

A quiver ran through Jane's chest. She said to Catherine, "Stay here with your brother. Don't leave the cart, no matter what."

Then she set the brake and scrambled down into the rustling grass, but she didn't go forward to join her sister-wives—not yet. She still hadn't made her decision. She could feel it hanging in the air all around her, a question pressing in, waiting for its answer.

She tilted her head to see the world more truly. Perhaps because of the fading light, the marshland and the far horizon and the man riding steadily in her direction remained an indistinct blur. But the two women on the hillside resolved into perfect clarity. She could see now that Tabitha and Tamar had linked their arms together. They faced Thomas side by side, calm and assured in one another's company.

Jane knew then what she would do. She strode forward, scarcely glancing at the rider, and took the first wife's hand.

Tabitha's fingers laced tightly with her own. Tamar looked across at Jane and smiled.

The three wives stood together under a banner of stars. The night was gentle around them.

AUTHOR'S NOTE

Tamar Loader, Jane Shupe, Tabitha Ricks, and Thomas Ricks were all real people—actual pioneers who made the journey from their places of origin to Salt Lake Valley in Utah Territory during the great Mormon migration of the mid-nineteenth century.

I know some readers may be clamoring right now to know how the story ends—what Jane decided, and whether Thomas went on "living the Principle."

Not only did Thomas continue his marriage with all three women who appeared in this novel—he went on to marry two more several years later: Ruth Dille and Ellen Yallop. As Tabitha predicted in chapter 26, Brigham Young swore to President Buchanan that all men in Utah Territory would renounce polygamy and dissolve their plural marriages or face imprisonment . . . and then, once the army had withdrawn and the so-called Utah War was over, Brigham did exactly as he pleased, carrying on with his own plural marriage—he had forty-nine wives at the time, with six more to follow in later years—and mandating certain favored men to continue engaging in the practice, as well. Polygamy wasn't ended—formally and doctrinally—until 1890. Wilford Woodruff, fourth president of the church, ended polygamy for good in response to the Edmunds-Tucker Act of 1887, which barred polygamous men from voting in federal elections.

Mormon history is complex and fascinating. No doubt, that's why I'm so drawn to write about my culture of origin, even though I'm no longer a member of the church.

Readers who enjoyed my 2021 novel, *The Rise of Light*, already know that I was born in Rexburg, Idaho, to a traditional Mormon family. I grew up hearing stories about Thomas Edwin Ricks, who founded my hometown (the name Rexburg derives from the surname Ricks—Ricks being an Anglicization of the Latin Rex, for "king").

Rexburg has always made much of its founder—Thomas certainly lived his fair share of adventure, including the crucial role he played in the rescue of the Martin handcart company. I knew I was a descendant of his from my earliest childhood, but until my thirties, when I began delving deep into genealogy, I never knew which of Thomas's five wives was my foremother. In 2015, I set out to discover exactly who my third great-grandmother was and how she came to live the polygamous lifestyle.

Polygamy is so closely associated with Mormonism in the popular imagination that most people who've had no direct experience of the culture believe that *all* Mormons practiced polygamy in the nineteenth century—and many believe that all Mormons practice it still. However, the celebrated historian Laurel Thatcher Ulrich—certainly the foremost expert on nineteenth-century Mormon culture, especially women's experiences—has estimated that at the height of its practice, polygamy touched only about 30 percent of the church's population. That figure includes the many children born to large polygamous families, so the actual number of adults who entered into plural marriage was perhaps 20 percent of all members, if even that.

Understanding how rare polygamy actually was, I felt compelled to find out what had drawn my foremother into her unusual marriage, and how she felt about it. When I finally verified which of Thomas's wives was my direct ancestor—Elizabeth Jane Shupe—it was an emotional moment. I was still more deeply moved when I discovered the single extant photograph of Jane as a young child, at about five or six years. I realized that I looked exactly like Jane when I was the same age. The resemblance is so uncanny that I sent the black-and-white photo to my mother without explanation. Mom said, "I don't remember dressing you up in pioneer clothes and taking this picture . . ."

It was a delight to find that photograph, but it was almost all I found regarding Elizabeth Jane Shupe. Only a few scraps of information were recorded about her life and personality. I learned that she preferred the name Jane or Janey. I discovered she'd found herself living with her stepfather by the age of fourteen—no mention anywhere of whether her mother still lived, or whether she'd been orphaned and left in Elijah Shaw's care. I knew she had a younger sister called Sarah Ann (who actually survived to adulthood, unlike her sad fate in this novel). I knew that Jane and Tamar married Thomas Ricks on the same day—and I imagined that could have caused some sore feelings. And I knew that Jane had strabismus—a crossed eye—about which she was very sensitive.

Jane died at age forty-eight due to "the hardships of pioneer life," according to the lone and very spare life sketch her descendants preserved. But all her sister-wives survived well into their eighties and nineties; Tamar was ninety-one and Tabitha ninety-four when they passed away. Many of Jane's descendants also died between their forties and sixties, including my own father. I suspect Jane might be the source of my family's genetic tendency toward heart disease, which I have also inherited. Thank goodness for modern medications and treatments, and let's hope I don't expire anytime soon. I'll be forty-two by the time this book is published, and I like to think I'll write many more books before my time is up.

Though little information could be found regarding Jane, I stumbled into a glut of records detailing the lives of Thomas's first and second wives, Tabitha Hendricks Ricks and Tamar Loader. Each of their life stories was so fascinating and ripe with adventure that I originally set out to include all three of their perspectives in this novel. The book became much too long, however, even for my liking (and I do tend to write doorstoppers). I've saved all my notes on Tabitha's fascinating life for a possible future novel, but I finally decided that Tamar and Jane together made plenty of interest for one book.

I pored over the records, trying to determine what to include in a novel about this unusual family and what to leave out. More critically, I debated with myself for months about *how* I ought to portray a polygamous marriage.

I've been keen on early Mormon history for many years, so I knew already that no two women felt the same way about the practice. Every woman involved in polygamy seemed to have her own opinions on its benefits and challenges, and on the origin and righteousness of the doctrine.

Some were coerced into plural marriages, threatened by their spiritual leaders with a promise of damnation if they rejected a proposal. Some seemed to earnestly welcome the opportunity, defying societal norms as a demonstration of their faith. Others seemed to have little opinion about polygamy, one way or another; it was simply a fact for them—the way they lived their lives, the shape their families took. Some viewed polygamy as a form of slavery and took to the national stage to speak out against its evils. Others used polygamous culture to their advantage, for it provided a way for some queer women to live their fullest lives. Sarah Louisa Bouton Felt, for example, was known openly as a lesbian. She convinced her husband, Joseph Felt, to marry the women she'd fallen in love with so that she and her partners could enjoy their own romantic relationships without fear of persecution, under the protection and legitimization of an apparently heterosexual marriage.

It was safe to say that if I were to represent Mormon polygamy as an exclusively and universally negative experience, I would be doing a disservice to the lived experiences of real people—as I would if I'd represented it as a universally positive experience. The truth lay somewhere in the middle and was nuanced with many shades of gray. That's usually the way history pans out.

The more closely I looked at the Ricks family in particular, the more I saw these shades of gray. For example, it was clear to me that all five women in Thomas's household felt themselves bound together in an unusually tight and cooperative family—for though I could discover almost nothing about Ruth Dille, his fourth wife, I did learn that she and Thomas had divorced a few years after their marriage, yet Ruth continued having children with Thomas. Their marriage was no longer considered valid by the church, for reasons I've never uncovered, but they went on raising children together, and Ruth is even buried beside Jane in the Rexburg cemetery. This seems to indicate that, despite the divorce, Ruth still thought of Thomas's other wives as her family, and apparently didn't wish to be parted from them, even in death.

I understood that the bond these five women shared had a deep significance to each of them. That significance seemed to reach far beyond the bond of matrimony.

If I had little information to help reconstruct Jane's life, at least I had plenty where Tamar was concerned. The Loader family is well known among fans of Mormon history, for Patience was a gifted and remarkably open memoirist, writing about the difficulties of the Mormon trail—and the horrors of the Willie and Martin handcart disasters—with an emotional intensity seldom found among nineteenth-century diarists. Patience's memoir has been a treasured document within the culture since its publication; her frank account of life and death as a handcart pioneer has colored the cultural imagination for generations.

Any LDS readers have no doubt felt confused by the paucity of Loaders in this novel. They were a large family—Tamar was seventh of thirteen children—and Tamar traveled with all her younger siblings on the trail, as well as her parents, Patience, and Zilpah—who was, in reality, two years older than Tamar. A novel is a work of fiction, however, so I was not obligated to paint an accurate picture of the Loader family. Still, I regretted cutting most of them out. They all shared this struggle together.

We know that the Loaders met the Martin company at Florence, Nebraska (called Winter Quarters in this book—an older name), but it's unclear to which company they'd initially belonged. There were several handcart companies traveling west that summer, and many left Iowa City between July 25 and 30. We know the Loaders left on July 28, but Patience didn't record which company she traveled with. I depicted them as leaving Iowa City earlier in July, merely for the sake of not cramming too much narrative into what would feel to the reader like an improbably short period of time. I wanted to give a sense of long, weary travel while still maintaining some semblance of pace—and I didn't think a trudging, footsore journey would feel believable or high stakes enough if I zoomed right from a farewell at Iowa City to Zilpah giving birth in mid-August. Such is the privilege of the historical novelist. We get to tweak history here and there in service to story (so long as we confess our sins in a good author's note).

Virtually all of Tamar's story depicted in this novel, right up until she is sent to the Ricks home in Centerville, was taken directly from Patience's memoir. Some of it actually happened to Patience herself— the curtain on the ship's bunk catching fire, for example, and the vision of the face in the flames. I assigned this action to Tamar for obvious reasons, and again I will play the fiction card as my excuse. However, Tamar was afflicted by "mountain fever"—which most historians now agree was most likely Rocky Mountain spotted fever, a tick-borne illness—and did receive a blessing from the apostles that she would recover and "walk into Zion."

If not for the memoir Patience so carefully wrote, we might know very little about the stranding of the Willie and Martin handcart companies—the deadliest event ever to befall a group of American pioneers, Mormon or otherwise. The story of the Donner Party looms larger in the imagination, but the Martin disaster ended more than 250 lives—five times greater than the Donner Party's casualties.

The fact that the Donner Party was forced to eat their own dead has given it a historical cachet that resonates through the ages and still sends a shiver down anyone's spine. If any members of the Martin and Willie companies actually resorted to cannibalism, no historical record has preserved that fact. However, it seems inevitable that those desperate people must have done whatever was necessary to preserve their lives. Of course, the handcart companies kept pressing westward; they left a trail of dead loved ones in their wake, with no time to pause and contemplate that most dreadful question, so it may be true after all that none of the Mormon pioneers resorted to cannibalism. At least one tried, however. The account of the man who attempted to eat the fingers of a sleeping child comes directly from Patience's memoir.

Even without the specter of cannibalism, the Martin and Willie disaster left scars on the Mormon community. Many people were permanently disabled due to loss of limbs and other physical damage caused by frostbite, and many children were orphaned during that treacherous October. It was without any doubt a horrific tragedy, and it could have been prevented if church leadership had opened their coffers wide enough to provide real wagons and teams for the pioneers.

It's easy to feel scorn for these people—to think of them as fools or zealots so blinded by faith that they would risk their own lives and the lives of their children for their church. You must view the Mormon migration in its proper context if you hope to understand why these people risked so much.

Yes, they were making a faith-based pilgrimage . . . but these were also refugees. Some were fleeing violence in America—Mormons had been persecuted and even massacred several times before—while others fled the untenable living conditions among the working class in Europe, especially in England. The Loaders were upper class and made the journey purely for their faith, but the vast majority of Mormons who immigrated to America came from factory-working families. Factory workers led incredibly dangerous, deprived lives due to the rapid expansion of the industrial revolution. It was common for people to suffer terrible, maiming injuries as well as gruesome deaths in accidents. Most factory workers were so impoverished that they had to send their children to work at very young ages, and children were among the most common fatalities in industrial accidents.

Mormonism offered these people hope—for, during that time, the church espoused its great dream of building Zion, a cooperative community where all who worked would have an equal share in production. Mormonism shone before these desperate families as a real hope for a good life. If they made it to Zion, they could live free from poverty and oppression, rather than sacrificing their health, their lives, and their children for the benefit of the men who owned the factories. Best of all, the church promised to pay for their passage across the Atlantic. It was an offer many couldn't refuse.

The decision to use handcarts rather than slower but safer team-drawn wagons was a financial consideration for the church, for by the 1850s, the Mormon promise of a life beyond the hellscape of the industrial revolution had inspired a boom in converts. So many converts were clamoring to come to Zion that the church had to cut costs, and they did so by doing away with wagon travel—a choice that would prove deadly for an astonishing number of desperate refugees.

The snows that trapped the Martin and Willie companies in the Rocky Mountains were not particularly unseasonable. The leaders of these companies should have foreseen the possibility of weather-related disaster; they should have passed the season at Florence (Winter Quarters), for safety's sake. We don't know for certain why the captains of these ill-fated companies chose not to shelter in Florence for the winter. Perhaps it was simply zeal, for the pioneers were constantly reminded by the highest leaders of the church that they were God's chosen people. They believed divine protection would see them all safely to Salt Lake Valley, and if their faith were strong enough, they would find the journey bearable.

Given how terribly the trek ended, it's a wonder any of the surviving handcart pioneers retained their faith and carried on as members of the church.

The conflict between Brigham Young and James Buchanan—usually called the Utah War—is one of those fascinating slices of American history that is little known by the population at large but deserves broader acknowledgment.

Most Americans today think of the Civil War as a rapid and largely self-contained eruption with clearly defined parameters—a definite beginning, a definite end. In reality, most politicians and a good many citizens could see the war coming from decades away. Buchanan wasn't alone in dedicating most of his administration to averting civil war. Previous presidents had done the same. Many in Washington had already drawn parallels between polygamy and slavery, and thus, the Mormons had been drawn into the conflict between abolitionists and slaveholders. No doubt Buchanan thought that if he could end the practice of polygamy in Utah Territory, it would settle some of the debate between those factions and prevent civil war altogether.

I still don't understand why Buchanan thought the wisest way to prevent a civil war was to send the United States military off to potentially massacre American citizens. In any case, the campaign was widely criticized at the time, and is still known today as Buchanan's Blunder.

The newspapers Patience quotes from in this novel were real; Brigham Young and his many scandals were an item of interest all across America, especially as Buchanan's presidential campaign gained steam, for he often referenced his distaste for the Mormons and framed many of their actions as treason, perhaps in an attempt to divert talk of treason in other spheres of American politics, such as the signs of impending rebellion among the Southern states. I found the archived copies of the *Evening Star* (Washington, DC, March 15, 1856), the *Orleans*

Independent Standard (Irasburgh, Vermont, May 1, 1857), and the *Port Tobacco Times and Charles County Advertiser* (Port Tobacco, Maryland, March 4, 1858) at ChroniclingAmerica.loc.gov.

I consulted carefully with my editor, Chris Werner, over the best ways to convey the complexity of the political entanglement between the Mormon church and the government of the United States—and how it led to the evacuation of Salt Lake Valley, which actually occurred between March and July of 1858. I compressed the timeline merely for the sake of pacing. I'm still not sure we nailed it; whole volumes of novels could be written to illustrate the lead-up to and the fallout from the Utah War.

Like the issue of Mormon polygamy and the reasons so many people had for taking to the long, dangerous trail, the full story of the Utah War is complicated, and nuanced, and it encompasses every shade of gray. The same can be said for all of history.

I relied on the following books in constructing this novel and am much indebted to their authors. *Recollections of Past Days: The Autobiography of Patience Loader Rosza Archer*; *A House Full of Females: Plural Marriage and Women's Rights in Early Mormonism, 1835–1870* by Laurel Thatcher Ulrich; *Rexburg, Idaho: The First One Hundred Years, 1883–1983* by David Lester Crowder; *The Polygamous Wives Writing Club: From the Diaries of Mormon Pioneer Women* by Paula Kelly Harline; *In Sacred Loneliness: The Plural Wives of Joseph Smith* by Todd Compton; *Kingdom of Nauvoo: The Rise and Fall of a Religious Empire on the American Frontier* by Benjamin E. Park; *Brigham Young and the Expansion of the Mormon Faith* by Thomas G. Alexander; *Brigham Young: Pioneer Prophet* by John G. Turner; *American Crucifixion: The Murder of Joseph Smith and the Fate of the Mormon Church* by Alex Beam; *The Mormon War: Zion and the Missouri Extermination Order of 1838* by Brandon G. Kinney. Additionally, I relied on the online resources of the Brigham Young Center for details on the Mormon War,

1857 to 1858, and the evacuation of Salt Lake Valley settlements to the Sanpete wilderness.

I am grateful to my family for being so supportive of my continued exploration of our particular history via the medium of fiction—especially my sister, Georgia Schelgel, and my husband, Paul Harnden. I thank my editor at Lake Union Publishing, Chris Werner, for his insightful commentary on this book and its characters. I am grateful to the whole crew at Lake Union for doing the best work in the publishing industry—and to my developmental editor, Jenna Free; my copyeditor, Michelle Hope; and my proofreader, Laura Whittemore.

Most of all, I'm grateful to my readers, who continue to ask for more of my books, and who continue to share my books with their friends.

Olivia Hawker
August 2021